Those Who Know

Cinematic Special Edition – The Chronological Telling of Someone Who Knows and The One Who Knew

J. Elle Ross

J.E.Ranch Publishing

The story, all names, characters, and incidents portrayed in this production are fictitious. No identification with actual persons (living or deceased), places, buildings, and products is intended or should be inferred.

Copyright © 2025 by J. Elle Ross

ISBN (PAPERBACK): 979-8-3115352-0-5 & 979-8-9914160-7-8 (HARDBACK): 979-8-3124821-3-3
ISBN (EBOOK): 979-8-9914160-6-1

Printed in the United States

JE Ranch Publishing

First edition March 2025

Dedication

For the readers who have brought books and reading back to life, the readers who believe in stories that cross genre lines and expectations, the readers who share their love of the written word to anyone and everyone who will listen. Thank you to the readers reading this story- you've made my wildest dream come true.

NOTE TO THE READER

Readers should be aware that this novel contains sensitive or difficult topics, especially for those who may have experienced similar trauma.

- Depictions of grief and loss

- Suggestions and scenes of child abuse and violence

- Scenes of self-harm and suicidal ideology

- Sexual violence and abuse

- Graphic violence and death

- Religious Trauma

A special message for those who have fought their way through their own trauma:

"Perhaps the butterfly is proof that you go through a great deal of darkness yet become something beautiful."   -Unknown

Muir Woods

SAN FRANCISCO

"Nathan!"

"Shit!" Nathan pulled the steering wheel hard left into the—thankfully—empty oncoming traffic lane to avoid the object on the road.

"What the hell *was* that?" He looked in the rearview mirror in time to see the small figure dart into the trees as he drove back to the right side of the road into his own lane.

"It looked like a young girl," his wife, Joanne, murmured, looking behind them.

"Dude, it was a ghost." Their son was already taking off his seatbelt, peering over the backseat, as their other son started to whimper in his booster.

"Stop that. You're scaring your brother. It is not a ghost. It's a little girl. Hand me one of those blankets. Here, take my cell and call 911 for help. She looks like she needs it." Joanne handed their son her cell phone as Nathan got out.

"Stay with your brother *in* the car. We're going to make sure she's okay," Nathan warned, closing the door behind him as he headed toward where the figure dashed off.

"But dad..."

"Stay with your brother," Joanne repeated, slipping out of the car after Nathan. "Nathan, is she...okay?" she whispered as she rushed to catch up, the blanket clutched to her chest.

"Jo, honey, go back and stay with the boys. I'll try and coax her out." The faint red glow of the emergency hazards illuminated a young face peering out from behind a bush.

Joanne followed the direction of his gaze. "She is terrified. You go back, I'll try."

"Seriously? I won't leave you out here alone. We don't know who she's running from." Nathan glanced around, looking for anything threatening.

Joanne nodded, taking a few steps forward.

"It's okay, sweetheart. You're safe now." The girl ducked down further. "It's so cold out here. I have a blanket for you. Would you like it?" Joanne took a few more steps.

"Mama?" a little voice called from behind them.

"Damn it," Nathan muttered as he looked back and saw both boys standing behind the car, watching them.

"Dad, they want to know where we are!" the older boy yelled, waving the phone.

"Please, get back in the car and wait for us," Nathan called out. Instead, the younger boy started running toward Joanne.

"Mama," he sniffled, clutching onto his mother's leg. The two children locked eyes. "We called the good guys," he told the girl, watching her curiously.

She stood, cautiously emerging from behind the bush, and began walking toward Joanne, her eyes never looking away from the small boy as Joanne held the blanket open.

"Good God in heaven," Joanne whispered as the girl approached them.

She was mostly naked, limping heavily on a large stick, dragging one misshapen leg, which was a deep shade of purple and grossly swollen, a blood-stained rope still tied to the other ankle trailing behind her, the flesh around her wrists and ankles torn and bloody. Dirt and dried blood caked her legs and hands. Large finger-shaped bruises covered her arms and thighs.

"It's okay, sweetie. You're safe now," Joanne repeated as she delicately wrapped the blanket around the broken child.

"Come on, you're okay now," the boy mimicked his mother's words. He took the girl's hand and held it tight as he tried to help her walk.

"That is very sweet of you, Davey. But she is having a hard time walking. Take Daddy's hand." Joanne guided him toward Nathan, then opened her arms to the girl. "Sweetie, I'm going to pick you up, okay?"

When the girl didn't resist, Joanne carefully picked her up and carried her back to the car, Nathan and Davey following closely behind.

PART ONE

INTERSECTING PATHS

Our connection is more than just coincidence; It's a sign that our paths were meant to intersect.

-Unknown

CHAPTER ONE

Ella Delaney

SAN FRANCISCO

Today was turning out to be the best day ever for Ella Delaney. Not only was it her birthday—she was six years old now—but she also got to go shopping with Nanny Marge.

Ella had begged Mother and Father for a Cabbage Patch doll for weeks. None of her friends in her first-grade class had one yet, and she really, really wanted one. Finally, Mother said she could get it today since it was her birthday. She gave Nanny Marge cash and instructions to take Ella for the afternoon so that Mother could get ready in peace.

Another fun thing Ella would get to do today was go to one of her parents' fancy parties—she never got to go—and that meant she could finally wear one of her fancy dresses, one that flared out when she spun and spun really fast.

Now, as Ella stood in the doll aisle of the toy department, she studied each of her options carefully. These were very important decisions. Boy or girl? Definitely girl. No hair, straight hair, curly hair? Curly, because it's fun. Brown hair, blonde hair, red hair? Red, like her own.

After the choices were complete and the purchase was made, Ella tore open the package in the backseat of the car.

"What does her birth certificate say? What's her name?"

"You can read it. Try sounding it out," Nanny Marge encouraged as she buckled Ella in.

"Sam, sam-an, Samantha. Roo, Roo-bee, Ruby. Samantha Ruby!" Ella's eyes shone proud, waving the paper back and forth in the air with a delighted squeal.

"Good job. Oh hey, it's our song!" Nanny Marge turned the radio way up so they could sing their favorite song, *Girls Just Wanna Have Fun,* as loudly as they could, which always made Ella laugh so hard she could never finish singing it.

When they finally pulled into their driveway, Ella was so excited to show Mother and Father she opened the car door and almost jumped out before they were completely stopped.

"Miss Ella shut your door," Nanny Marge called out, shaking her head in amusement.

"Sorry!" She ran back to the car, Samantha Ruby clutched tightly in the crook of her arm, pushed the car door shut, then ran full force back to the house, charging through the front door.

Father was first in her line of sight. He was on the phone, the long coiling cord stretching from the wall to the dining table where he sat with a newspaper open.

"Don't *'Oh, Declan'* me, Tom. I'm telling you, it will be a circus out there. The Queen coming to San Francisco will get all of the IRA sympathizers out in droves. Protests, riots, who knows what ruckus they will cause back home."

Father was excited about something, and not in a good way. Father called it, 'getting his Irish up'. He would talk fast, and the music in his voice would get stronger. Mother was the same. It always made Ella a little sad that she didn't have what Nanny Marge called an accent like they did.

Ella's parents moved from Ireland to San Francisco a few years before she was born. Even though they made sure to move into an Irish-prominent neighborhood and joined some fancy Irish society club as soon as they could, Ella went to school here all her life, so she didn't have the pretty music in her voice.

Since Father's Irish was up, Ella steered clear of the dining room. Instead, she ran up the stairs to find Mother. As she reached the top of the staircase, Mother came out of her room, her strawberry blonde hair in giant curlers, a green mask caked on her face like some monster coming up from the swamp.

Ella giggled and thrust Samantha Ruby out to show her. "Mother, look!"

"Ella, stop this pounding about. You're making far too much noise. You'll give me a migraine, child. Where is Nanny Marge? Marge? Marge!" Fiona called down from the top of the stair landing until Marge appeared.

"Yes, Mrs. Delaney?" she answered, looking up from the first floor.

"I need you to look for my grandmother's amethyst locket. I can't find it anywhere. And, please, start getting Ella ready. Quietly." She turned and started to stomp back into the bedroom.

Ella hung her head, all of the excitement evaporating from her. Without even trying, Ella could see it, lying in the rose bed. Now she would have to tell Mother where her locket was.

Ella hated telling Mother these things. She'd always look at her as if she were weird or, worse, scary. Not that it wasn't scary, or at least it used to be.

Since Ella could remember, sometimes she would know something she shouldn't know, could picture it so clearly as if she was looking straight at it. Mostly she saw things that were lost. Like Father's keys—he lost them all the time—or her toys after Nanny Marge would clean up, Ella could *see* which bin something was in. Other times, she would know something right before it happened. Like something said on TV or the phone about to ring. But sometimes, she would get feelings about people. Mostly good things, but bad things too. That was when it got scary.

Her parents never seemed too concerned about it. They never asked her about it, never took her to any doctors for it or anything like that. Sometimes they'd act weird around her, like something was wrong with her. But mostly, they ignored it, ignored her.

Nanny Marge never made Ella feel bad about her special power. She was the one who helped Ella try and make sense of it, especially when it scared her.

"When you see something bad or scary, pause for a moment. Remember that most of us are good and *bad inside. We conceal the parts we don't want to show. People*

don't think they have to hide their thoughts, so just because someone might think bad things doesn't always mean they'll act on them. You can't live your life that way, Miss Ella, in fear of the possibility of the bad. You have to live in spite of it."

She even helped Ella try to practice, but Ella still couldn't control it. She would either know right away or not at all.

Barely audible, Ella mumbled, "It's in your garden, Mother, by the yellow roses. It fell off when you went out to cut some for the table last week."

Mother looked at her for a long time, giving her the look she had given her many times before—eyes full of disbelief and a bit of fear. She nodded once to Ella, then closed the door firmly behind her.

Defeated, Ella's shoulder slumped, Samantha Ruby forgotten, hanging by a hand and dragging on the floor.

"Miss Ella, come on down here. I have a surprise for you." Even though Nanny Marge tried to hide it from her, frustration was etched in the lines of her face.

Ella dragged her feet down the stairs, her nose scrunched up, determined not to cry. Crying was for babies, like five-year-olds.

"Come on, now," Nanny Marge beckoned.

When Ella finally reached the bottom of the stairs, Nanny Marge led her through the swinging doors into the kitchen. "Close your eyes, now. Nice and tight. No peeking."

Ella could hear her rummaging through the kitchen. The sound of the refrigerator door opening and closing, a match striking, then the smell of sulfur filling the air. Finally, she said, "Open your eyes."

A beautifully pink cupcake sat on the counter in front of her, a purple candle lit in the middle of all that frosting. Mother forgotten, Ella jumped up and down, clapping her hands.

Nanny Marge gave her a warning look, putting a finger to her lips, then smiled and winked as she quietly sang Happy Birthday.

Ella closed her eyes tight, made the biggest wish, and blew out the candle.

The minute they walked in, Ella was entranced. It was like a castle in a fairytale. The room was dim, light cast from candles flickering in silver candlesticks reflected off chandeliers with hundreds of hanging crystals that sparkled like diamonds. A band was set up in the corner of the large room, playing some upbeat Irish folk music. Men and women in black uniforms circulated throughout the room with fancy-looking trays filled with fancy-looking food.

Mother took Ella's coat, handing it to one of the black uniform people. "Even though it is family night, that doesn't mean children will be running wild. You will mind your manners first and foremost. Stay quiet, no shouting, no running about, and do not, by any means, go into rooms you are not permitted to go into."

"Fiona? That *is* you! Darling, I desperately need your help. You just can't get good service these days—such a disaster. The caterer is phenomenal, or at least she could be. She runs that little shop that does all those authentic Irish dishes. Well, she calls and says she can't do the party because she would have no one to watch her child. I'm giving her this chance to make a name for herself, and she wants to cancel for childcare issues? So, I had to tell her to bring the child. Such a hassle. And then the candlesticks..." The woman who rushed to them took Mother's arm and led her out of the room.

Ella stood with Samantha Ruby in one arm and Father standing on the other, looking unsure of what to do with her.

"You run along and find someone to play nicely with," he said, leading her further into the room.

Ella looked around but didn't see anyone close to her age. A small group of teenage girls were sneaking sips by the champagne fountain. Outside, a few boys were throwing a ball around to each other, but they were also older than she was.

"Declan, fine sir. Finally, a reasonable man," a voice boomed from a tall man as he approached them. "Tell these, otherwise gentlemen, about the woes of having a woman mayor of our great city."

With that, Father was gone.

Standing in the middle of a room full of adults in poofy dresses and heavily teased hair, Ella was alone.

Staying close to the walls so as not to bother anyone, she made her way from room to room, looking for somewhere to play with Samantha Ruby. Soon, she discovered the food table and, next to that, the dessert table.

Looking around, making sure no one was watching her, Ella crept over to the desserts, her tummy already rumbling with anticipation.

"Hi."

Ella jumped at the unexpected voice. Across the desserts, a pair of big blue eyes looked at her through a tall cake arrangement.

Never one to be shy, Ella greeted the girl back with a boisterous, "hi!"

"I'm Erinne. My mom brought me. She made all these in her bakery. Want one?" Erinne, who looked about the same age as Ella, came around the table, her side ponytail bouncing with each step.

"Sure. I'm Ella, and this is Samantha Ruby." Ella held up the doll.

"This is Dream Date Barbie. She is in her party dress." Erinne smiled and held up a Barbie in a sparkling purple dress. "Ken has a party tux, too, but I couldn't find him."

Ella laughed. "That's because your dog Sadie ate his head. Your brother found him and didn't want you to be sad, so he hid him at the bottom of the trash bin." Ella could have smacked herself. She didn't want her new friend to look at her the way Mother did—like she was a freak. She hated when she forgot that other people couldn't see what she did, and that most of the time, it would scare them. But when she saw something so clearly, it was hard not to tell.

Erinne stared at Ella. "How do you know about Sadie? And my broth..."

"It's my birthday today! I'm six years old," Ella interrupted.

"Me too. It's not my birthday, but I'm six. I lost my front tooth." Erinne smiled a big, toothless grin to show the gap in front.

"Girls, have either of you eaten dinner yet? Save dessert until after." A pretty lady with dark hair and blue eyes like Erinne, wearing a black uniform and a white apron smudged with frosting, came out from the kitchen.

"But Mom, it's Ella's *birthday*," Erinne stated as if it were a fact her mother should have already known.

"Well, happy birthday Ella. And for that, you shall have a most special dessert. But for now, I'll make the two of you a plate of food first." The pretty lady led them back into the kitchen to a small table tucked in a breakfast nook. "Get on up there you two, your own special table."

Ella felt special indeed. It was her birthday, and she met a new girl who—she saw in her special way—would be her best friend, at least for as long as Ella lived. And they got to sit at a table all by themselves in the kitchen, where no one else was allowed. Laughing, both girls crawled onto the chairs, placing their dolls beside them.

Ella scanned Erinne's face, a slow smile spreading. "We will be best friends for the rest of my life."

Erinne looked at Ella curiously for a moment, smiled, and then shrugged. "Okay! I've always wanted a sister. I only have two older brothers. They smell weird and mostly ignore me."

For the rest of that evening, the two girls talked, giggled, and played as if they had always known each other.

CHAPTER TWO

Erinne Byrne

ALAMEDA ISLAND

The entire day was blurred behind veils of tears. The moment her eyes opened, the grief was too intense to fight, and she wept. It had taken all her energy to shower—more like a quick rinse—dress and pull her dark hair back out of her face. When *was* the last time she had brushed it? She couldn't remember.

Getting herself ready had been the easy part. Saying goodbye to the best friend she ever had—sister, really—would be brutal, devastating.

Sleep had been scarce, woken by either Sera's nightmares or her own, made apparent by the dark, puffy half-moons under her bloodshot eyes, the blue of them flat, faded. Erinne Byrne had been falling apart since the moment she'd received the news that broke her soul and changed her life. Being back in San Francisco only escalated her deterioration. But she couldn't think about that right now. She just needed to get through.

Don't think, don't feel, just get through.

With all of the anguish Erinne was going through, it was nothing compared to the young child she was now responsible for.

Sera, the little girl who'd started talking before she could even walk, still hadn't spoken. Not to the police or the doctors, not even to Erinne. Sera barely even made eye contact with her, let alone cry, or had much of any emotional response at all.

Wiping away another round of tears, Erinne entered Sera's room.

"Rise and shine." She lightly ran her finger down the center of Sera's forehead, tracing all the way to the tip of her nose, as she'd done when Sera was a newborn baby.

Sera blinked slowly. For a fleeting moment, a smile crept into those bottle-green eyes, the ones that had been identical to Ella's, but sadness quickly replaced it.

"I know," Erinne whispered as she kissed Sera's cheek. "We will get this day done with soon enough. Come on now, it's time for a bath. Crutches or chair?" Without a word, Sera reached for the crutches.

Erinne struggled to keep her face from showing the ferocious anger that swallowed her as she wrapped Sera's cast in plastic. Sera's tiny body still carried all of those vivid physical reminders, the cuts, the bruises. They would fade, eventually, and her broken leg would mend, but the internal scars would stay with Sera forever. Blinking back more tears, Erinne helped Sera wash her hair and soap her little broken body.

After Sera was washed and dressed, Erinne's next task was to feed the child. Trying to get Sera to eat anything had become a daily hardship. Erinne would cook what she hoped was a healthy meal, but Sera mostly pushed the food around for a while before taking her plate back to the sink.

She would eat when she was hungry, right?

Erinne added it to the list of questions to ask the therapist already tallied in her mind.

Finally, the most dreaded task of all, getting to the funeral director on time. Standing in front of that building caused an ache that tore through Erinne. Stepping through those heavy oak doors would make it real, final. So, she stood there, hand clenched with Sera's, procrastinating. The loud shutter clicks of cameras behind them reminded her that the moment was not their own. With a heavy sigh, Erinne pulled open the doors.

She led Sera to a bench up front, then knelt down to try to meet Sera's eyes. "I have to talk to that man for a few minutes. Will you be okay here? I'll be right there where you can see me the whole time."

Sera stared down at the floor. She didn't look up or say a word but let go of Erinne's hand. As Erinne kissed Sera's cheek and stood, her eyes filled with tears again, something that happened quite often these past weeks.

Soon, there was nothing else to do but wait. Wait for people to arrive. Wait for the service to start. But mostly, wait for the day just to be over.

As far as settings for funerals go, San Francisco could not have offered a more unsuitable day. The morning fog had already rolled out, the sky was blue and cloudless, as perfect as spring could be in the City by the Bay.

No matter how beautiful the weather, for Erinne, the sun had stopped shining. Every minute pulled at her, requiring a strength that she was running dangerously low on. She could barely focus, at least not on anything other than the picture of beautiful Ella and the urn sitting in front of it.

Endless strings of words were said by many, "Ella Delaney ... loving mother ... beautiful person ... unconditionally kind ... would have done greatness with medicine ... will always be fondly remembered."

Erinne hardly heard any of it.

She should say something, *anything*. She was the person who had known Ella best. They'd been best friends since they were six years old. But anything she thought of saying wouldn't be enough. Nothing would encompass the vivaciousness that had been Ella. Her zest for life, her love of love, the kindness of her heart, how Ella had never allowed a moment to pass without living it to the fullest.

Instead, Erinne quietly let herself mourn her lifelong friend, the best person she had ever known. Until that grief began to simmer into anger. Anger at Ella for being right all along. She almost hated her for it.

Ella'd had a way of knowing things. Even when they'd first met as children, Ella had said something strange about being—not best friends forever as other children vowed—but to be best friends *her* whole life, as though Ella had already known she would die young. The same way she'd told Erinne about her dog eating her missing Ken doll and how her brother tried hiding it from her so that she wouldn't be sad.

If only Erinne had taken Ella's superpower—something they'd affectionately called *The Knowing*—more seriously. If she had, would things be different now? Would she have been more vigilant in getting Ella to take her safety more seriously? Could her murder have, somehow, been avoided?

Maybe Ella had been right in keeping all her boyfriends, even Chris, distant from her, never fully committing to any of them, knowing that she would leave this world too soon and break everyone's hearts, including Erinne's.

The flash of anger that ignited in Erinne quickly fizzled away. Erinne knew, better than anyone, that Ella hadn't been built that way. Ella could never have lived afraid, alone, unloved, just waiting for some phantom guillotine to fall. Instead, Ella had dared to live far better than anyone else.

Erinne slowly blew out a deep breath as tears threatened again.

Don't think, don't feel, just get through.

At least this would be the only funeral they had to attend. Chris's family had been like Ella's, denying Sera's existence. They had taken his remains back to wherever they were from, Erinne couldn't remember, refusing a public service in fear of a media spectacle, the same way they refused Sera as their grandchild.

Well, good riddance. Their loss.

Sera didn't need that negativity in her already difficult life anyway. Erinne wasn't expecting to lose her best friend and become an instant mother to a traumatized child either, but here she was, doing her damn best, even though she had no idea what the hell she was doing.

Thankfully, the drive home was mostly uneventful. For the first time in weeks, the vultures that were the media didn't follow them. Though there had been a horde of them in front of the funeral home, and there were still plenty of them camped out in front of Ella's house when they returned. Reports of such a cruel crime, especially one that involved a promising young medical student and her child, had been sensationalized, spreading fast through the community, social media, and news channels nationwide, exposing the six days of horror Ella and Sera went through.

Erinne got Sera into the house, locked the deadbolt, tested the door, and then repeated this new ritual, moving from room to room, checking each door and window, with Sera following closely behind. She'd found out the hard way that Sera refused to go to bed until she was sure everything was secure, ensuring that evil would not return for her.

Even then, it took longer each night to get Sera to sleep. Erinne would hold Sera close, stroking her long red hair—so much like Ella's—and hum as many songs as she could think of to lull her to sleep, hoping that maybe this time, Sera wouldn't be awakened by the nightmares that hadn't stopped plaguing her.

Once she was sure Sera was asleep, Erinne crept out of the room, closed the door quietly, and leaned against it. She let out the shaky breath she'd been holding for what seemed like hours.

She started back toward the guest room where she'd been sleeping but stopped in front of Ella and Chris's bedroom door.

Erinne was unprepared for Ella's scent wafting through the air when she pushed the door open, bringing the flash of a memory of them playing in Erinne's mother's room, spraying each other with perfume, laughing hysterically.

From Barbie's to boyfriends, they'd been inseparable.

Hesitating only for a moment, Erinne took a deep breath, walked into the room, and lay on Ella's side of the bed. She pushed her face into one of the pillows, taking in the smell of Ella as she curled up under the covers. Another fist of grief sucker-punched Erinne.

It wasn't long before she noticed Sera standing at the door. Erinne smiled at her through her tears, reaching her arms out. Sera made her way over, dropping the crutches to crawl onto the bed, then curled her little body into the curve of Erinne's. Erinne wrapped her arms around the last piece of Ella Delaney in the world.

Anger tangled into her grief again. She wanted to scream at the unfairness of it all, hit something, throw things against a wall. Instead, she kissed the back of

Sera's head, determined to dig deep and find the capability to care for this child who had already endured too much.

At twenty-six, Erinne was barely a few months older than Ella, but she hadn't even started thinking about having kids of her own. Besides, she needed to find the guy first. Erinne had never even trusted herself with a pet, dared not torture the poor thing with her inept abilities. Yet, Erinne now had the enormous responsibility of keeping a *human* child alive.

When it came to children, she had no idea what was normal or what to expect. But Erinne knew Sera, and Sera was not the child she once was. How much was it her age, and how much was it the trauma?

The fear that her lack of experience and complete incompetence would only further screw up Sera's life all the way into adulthood never left her thoughts.

Was this what parenting was? Constant worry and anxiety?

Chapter Three

I went to my secret hiding place. Again. There are so many trees here that it would be easy to get lost, but I don't. Even though I wish I did so I wouldn't have to go back there.

I have a special tree with a big hole in it, big enough for me to sit in. I snuck a towel out of the house to put in the tree so I could sit in there for as long as I could until it got too cold or I got really hungry. I even peed outside instead of going back so they won't find me.

I can stay in my special tree for hours until the lightning bugs come out. The only good thing about this horrible place is the lightning bugs. Their blinking lights make everything magical, especially when you catch them and put them in jars.

I like bees, too. If I could catch them, I could make my own honey. But they sting you before you can catch them. Maybe I should be like the bees—sting first before getting hurt by everyone else.

My brother had already taken off on his bike with his friends. Since I don't have any friends, I'm always all alone. I hate being here alone. He's lucky. He's ten, a whole five years older than me, and he gets to escape whenever he wants. Our grandmother gets mad at Mom when he goes off like that.

Grandmother yells at Mom, even hits her, screaming that her evil spawn will end up godless demons like our father if she lets us run unattended through the streets. I guess Grandmother used to hit Mom all the time when she was a little girl. But Mom says nothing to Grandmother to defend Daddy or us. She never fights her off, either. She just lets Grandmother hit her over and over, just like she lets Grandmother hit us all the time.

And Grandmother is wrong. Daddy is *not* a demon.

He used to yell at Mom a lot. Sometimes, he even pushed her around. But he had always been nice to me. At least before he left us to live in this horrible place with our scary grandmother and a mom who never helps us. I don't think Mom even loves us.

Mom didn't like it when Daddy was nice to me. That was scary, too. She would look at me with suspicious, sad eyes that told me I did something bad. Then, she would make me kneel with the book I can't read yet and tell me to be sorry for whatever I did to make Daddy say nice things to me. She would kneel, too, praying for my soul.

Grandmother always stares at us with her mean face, waiting to punish us. All I did was run in from outside to get a jar for the lightning bugs I wanted to keep, and she looked at me like she wanted to kill me.

"Be still, and lead a tranquil and quiet life in all godliness and dignity. Don't forget you come from a long line of deviants and criminals. I refuse to have you turn into one in *my* house," she hissed at me with her mean-looking eyes, the eyes that told me she was going to hit me with the book again.

The book hurt a lot. It's heavy, and the edges of the pages cut me sometimes. Or she'll make me kneel for a long time with the book and tell me that I will burn forever because I'm so horrible. I hate when she makes me do that. It hurts my knees really bad. Sometimes, they even bleed. Mom never helps me when Grandmother is hurting me. She just sits there, looking sad.

The baby is screaming again. She does that all the time. It makes my head hurt when she cries and cries. Mom acts like she is going to cry right along with her. Instead, she stares at that big book, completely ignoring the baby, just like she ignores us.

It makes me miss Daddy so much. I thought maybe he went to prison like his daddy. Why else would he go away and not take us with him? But then Mom said

Daddy left us for another woman, that he didn't want us anymore, he wanted a new life and new children. He hasn't come back, so I guess Mom isn't lying. Lying is really, really bad, and you get hit with a belt when you lie.

Sometimes, a lot of times, I get mad at Daddy for leaving us here alone. I wonder all the time what I did to make him leave, to want other, better kids. Maybe, if I could be better, Daddy would come back. Maybe when I get bigger, I'll be able to go off on my bike like my brother does, and I could go look for Daddy. Maybe he would let me stay with him and his new family, since he had always been nice to me.

CHAPTER FOUR

Sera Delaney

ALAMEDA ISLAND

Her heartbeat pounded in her ears, increasing faster and faster. It was dark—so dark. She couldn't see in front of her, only heard the roaring of her heart.

Sera was standing, looking down at herself, unconscious, sprawled out on the front seat, her head on the lap of a man who was not Daddy, a knife to her throat.

"Don't even think about screaming, or she's dead."

"You." The word came out of her, but it was Mommy's voice. Angry. Scared.

"You remember me. I knew you would. Get in."

She slowly got into the passenger seat, scooping her other self into her arms.

Sera's hands were not her own either, they were bigger than her six-year-old-sized hands. Mommy's hands. She could hear Mommy's thoughts, see like Mommy could see, feel the terror Mommy felt, and her fury.

She was Mommy.

"You will not touch my daughter. I will kill you first."

The man reached over, grabbed a handful of the other Sera's hair, and yanked her out of her arms, putting the knife back to the other Sera's throat.

"No!" She grabbed for her, trying to pull her back. A bead of blood appeared as the knife pierced the other Sera's skin and slowly rolled down her throat.

"See what you made me do?"

She let go. "Don't hurt my baby. Please."

"What did I just get finished telling you?" The knife cut deeper, another bead of blood.

"I'll follow your rules. I will, I promise. Please stop. You're cutting her."

Sera's body jumped awake, her hands frantically searching for the blood dripping down her neck, but her hands were only wet with sweat. The scabs from those wounds had long healed over.

Her breathing was too fast. It was too dark. Her heart raced until she recognized her bedroom. Home. She was home now. Safe. It was just another nightmare about *that* time.

Sera started to turn in her bed when another darkness took over, and the sounds of her room disappeared.

Slowly, dim light faded back in. Sera was not in her bedroom anymore. She was somewhere else.

She was in a place with a lot of trees. So many trees that there were no roads, no paths. One of the trees had a big hole in it. Sera started crawling into the tree, holding a jar of lightning bugs. But her hands weren't hers.

Sera wasn't Sera, but she wasn't Mommy either. She was someone else.

Darkness slammed back into her, pulling her under, blacking out the trees, blacking out everything around her. Sera wasn't there anymore. She was nowhere. Strange feelings overwhelmed her, and her breathing quickened, desperate for air.

The darkness slowly faded away as the room around her came back into focus. Sera was back in her room, in her bed.

She started to call out for Mommy, but then she remembered that Mommy wasn't there anymore. Daddy was gone, too.

She stuck a thumb in her mouth and curled up under the blanket. She wanted to cry every time she woke up and remembered, but the tears didn't come back anymore—not since she had cried so much *that* night.

It was strange that she couldn't cry. Not since Mommy took her last raspy breath in her lap. Sera thought she would never stop crying. She cried until all the tears dried up inside, and then she never cried again.

The memories hurt. They made her tummy tumble and ache. The way Mommy smiled, and then the way Mommy's face was all smashed up. The way Daddy always did funny things to make her laugh, and then the way his throat bled all over before he fell on her in the backseat of the car.

The worst was when she first woke up in the mornings. For a few seconds, she forgot that they were gone, but then she always remembered. That hurt worst of all.

"Sera, are you alright?" Sera heard Erinne whisper at her door.

She closed her eyes tight before Erinne came in and could see she was awake. She wanted Mommy and Daddy, not Erinne. Erinne meant no one else was coming. But Sera was also terrified that Erinne would leave her too.

CHAPTER FIVE

Jeffrey Mason

ARKANSAS

Jeffrey Mason was collecting his uncle's beer cans to recycle for pennies again. His uncle never left him any money for groceries or anything else they might need in the god-forsaken trailer. At least he could make a few bucks with the damn cans.

He got creative finding ways to make some money, be it recycling or pawning some of the stuff he lifted from the rich dick-head kids at his school. They never noticed anything missing from their precious, privileged lives. He even sold those spoiled idiots some pot here and there. Whatever it took to eat.

His uncle worked most of the time, though there wasn't much to show for it. The lights stayed on and the trailer was their own, no one could kick them out on the streets, so at least that was something. The rest of his uncle's hard-earned cash was drunk away, hence the small income Jeffrey made recycling.

Not that Jeffrey needed his uncle much anyway. He didn't need anyone. Not since Pop landed himself a life sentence for beating the shit out of his mother, almost killing her, along with all the other stupid shit he'd done. And not when his mother dumped him on her brother's doorstep at eight years old to go off who knew where. Jeffrey has basically been fending for himself ever since, especially now that he got his driver's license this past year. He was able to get himself wherever he needed to go to do whatever he wanted to do.

As luck would have it, while he was bagging the numerous cans left scattered around the trailer, he found one of his uncle's porn magazines. Dropping the bag, Jeffrey plopped down on the ratty couch, opened the magazine, and thumbed through the waxy pages. It was a good one, where the women were tied up in interesting positions, dressed in leather and chains. His arousal was almost immediate.

A quiet knock on the screen ripped him out of his fantasy.

"Go the fuck away."

"Jeffrey? It's me," the whisper of mousey Ingrid, who lived a few trailers down, drifted through the door.

Maybe it wasn't such a disturbance after all. Trying to get Ingrid to do all sorts of dirty things was a source of entertainment Jeffrey hadn't tired of yet.

He hid the magazine, straightened his pants to disguise his obvious excitement, and opened the door.

Ingrid quickly looked around the trailer park, making sure no one had seen her. Jeffrey knew she'd sneak out of the small window in her bathroom when she could, which was usually during their bizarre afternoon prayer ritual when her parents locked Ingrid and her siblings in their rooms for the hour. He'd asked her once why they did that, and she'd told him it was to contemplate their wickedness and ask for forgiveness for their sinful ways.

As far as he was concerned, Ingrid's parents were part of some religious cult, homeschooling all of their kids for fear the ways of the wicked world would ruin their precious spawn. That family was fucking loony tunes.

Jeffrey gave Ingrid a sideways smile and pulled her into the trailer, letting the screen slam behind her.

"*Shh!* They'll hear," Ingrid startled nervously.

"So what? What will they do, beat me?"

"They'll beat *me*."

Jeffrey quieted her by crushing his mouth on hers, pushing his body against her, and letting her feel his hardness against her thigh.

She pretended to be shocked and tried to pull away, but Jeffrey held fast. "Uh-uh. Stay here. Feel this. You like it. This is why you keep coming back." He pulled her dress up and yanked her panties down, shoving his fingers against her, rubbing with a heat he could barely control.

"Jeffrey, I can't," Ingrid huffed, the breath sucked out of her. "It feels too good. I'll surely have to pray for hours for forgiveness."

"Shut. Up." Jeffrey inserted his fingers inside of her, rubbing her at the same time.

"Oh my god." Ingrid's body wracked with a violent shutter.

"My turn." Jeffrey turned Ingrid away from him, pressing her face against the wall.

"No. Jeffrey, I can't," Ingrid half protested, starting to move away from him. He pushed her up against the wall harder, holding her in place.

"Relax. I won't take your precious flower. Yet." But he wanted to. He might, anyway. A quick slip, and it would be done. She might be upset afterward, but she'd get over it. Then come back for more.

Maybe he would just put it in her ass. Yeah, maybe that would do for now. He held her against the wall, rubbed himself against the crack of her, rubbed hard, back and forth. He wasn't going to do it. He was just going to rub himself off on her, but at the last minute, when he was close to peaking, he grabbed himself and, with a quick thrust, shoved it inside of her ass.

"Stop! It hurts!" Ingrid cried, her tears and snot sliming the wall where he pressed her face.

When Ingrid screamed out, the explosion of pure bliss engulfed Jeffrey as he spilled his climax into her. Her cries only made his orgasm stronger, lasting longer than any time he had ever jerked himself off.

"It feels divine," Jeffrey moaned, his eyes rolling back in his head as he savored the pleasure of each stroke. When he was finished, he let Ingrid go.

She wiped her face, quickly pulled her half-torn panties back up, straightened her dress, and rushed to the door.

"Hey, it wasn't bad. You're still a virgin." Jeffrey fastened his pants, then went back and sat on the couch, watching as Ingrid straightened herself out. "And you got off too."

"I told you *no*. And that hurt," Ingrid sniffled as she walked out of the trailer, quietly closing the screen.

She'll be back for more. Jeffrey shrugged, pulling the magazine from the cushions where he had hidden it. It didn't take long to become aroused again.

Chapter Six

Erinne

Alameda Island

From the doorway, Erinne watched Sera sucking her thumb—something that she had stopped doing by age two. It killed her to see her regressing. She walked over to Sera's bed, knelt beside her little body, and stroked her hair off her forehead.

"Alright. If you need me, I'll be in my room, right next to yours." She bent over, kissed her cheek, and started to rise.

Sera grabbed Erinne's hand before it left her shoulder.

"It's okay. I'll stay." She crawled into the bed, curling herself around Sera.

When Sera had fallen back asleep, Erinne quietly snuck away and went downstairs to make herself some tea.

As Erinne waited at the stove for the tea kettle to heat, she looked around at the emptiness of the kitchen. In the stillness of the night, the house felt soulless.

When Erinne would visit from Ireland, usually in the winter after the busy season quieted at the Inn, Ella's home had always been warm and cozy, full of joy and life. If she closed her eyes, she could still hear Chris and Ella's laughter and Sera's giggles. It had been a happy house.

Now, it echoed with deafening silence, something it never had before. The air was still, and the warmth was gone. There was no life here anymore. It was just a place now, an empty frame.

San Francisco used to be home. It was where she and Ella met and grew up, all the way from first grade through high school. Erinne would never have left San Francisco—she'd definitely never have left Ella's side—until her grandparents' accident took Erinne and her family back to Ireland to run Lantern Light Inn, the inn that had been in their family for generations. The piece of her heart that stayed in San Francisco died with Ella.

Before she let sorrow overtake her again, Erinne called her mother, as she had done almost daily since leaving Ireland. She missed her parents terribly. She even missed bantering with her brothers, which she would never admit to them.

"Hey, kiddo. Isn't it really late for you over there in good ol' Cali?" The deep voice of her brother answered her mother's cell phone.

"Hey Bri. Where's Mom?"

"She's got her hands full of flour."

"You mean you conveniently 'stopped by' in time for...breakfast service." Tears broke her last words, visualizing her mother in the kitchen where her talents shined so brilliantly. Or maybe it was just hearing her brother's voice that made the damn break.

"Aw man." Brian, the eldest of the Byrne children, always the first to harass and tease his baby sister, dropped the lightness of his tone at once.

"Bri, I don't know if I'm equipped for this. I mean, you know me, I can't keep a houseplant alive. I'm not exactly qualified. I've never even changed a diaper, except that disastrous attempt when Sera was first born."

"Erinne, she's six. Safe to say she's past the diaper stage."

"Why haven't you had kids yet? I should have had lots of practice by now."

"Shelly isn't ready, which is fine by me. And how is this *my* fault?"

Erinne sighed. "It's not. I just...I don't know how to do this. Ella was the first person I'd call about something like this. She was the first person I'd call about everything. It kills me that I can't call my best friend anymore. Ever."

"I know. It bites. Chris was *my* friend, too."

"I know he was. I know..." her words drifted away.

Erinne could hear Brian fumbling with the phone, putting her on speaker, most likely so their mother could listen to the conversation.

"Erinne, I'm here, Love," her mother's voice sang through. Erinne could hear the peck on her brother's cheek and her mother whispering something about taking a plate of food with him.

"Hey, Ma. I'm sorry to call you. Again."

"Now, there's no need to ever be sorry for calling. Especially now. This is the worst of times. I wish I could be there next to you, giving you the shoulder you'll be needing right now."

"You guys have done more than enough, maxing out your credit card on my airline tickets. I am so grateful for it. I promise I will pay you and Dad back."

"Stop this talk about payback. Ella and Sera are family. I wish we could've done more. What's going on with you?"

"What if I'm doing everything all wrong? What if I'm making things worse, and she never recovers?"

"My sweet daughter. Let me tell you a secret. No new parent knows what to do at first. We all stumble along and hope for the best. And we always worry. About everything. That's just parenthood. And that's what you are now, a new mama."

"Ella never worried about anything."

"No, she really didn't. That girl was so full of light. She was just what you needed growing up. You were always one to worry a little more than you should and the first to get angry. Always the protector. And there she was, pulling you along in her happy radiance. The two of you were just a joy together." Erinne heard her mother try to conceal a sniffle. "Erinne, it's midnight there. You, of all people, need your rest."

"Sleep is hard to come by these days. I miss you. So much. And Dad. Even Brian and Erick. I want to bring Sera home to Ireland. The media...It's awful for Sera here, and I'm not enjoying them either. I'm starting to feel the urge to commit assault, and that is never a good thing. Especially when trying to prove that I'm a fit guardian."

"I know it. Those bastards boil my blood. Even here, that terrible story is on the news every day. They have no souls, pestering the poor child. Bring her home. Away from all that madness."

"I think I will, if that's okay. Sera's therapist gave me the name of a trauma specialist out there. We can meet with him as soon as next week. I'm not too proud to admit that I need *my* mom."

"And I'm not too proud to admit that it warms my heart to be needed. I would love to wrap my arms around Sera. I've missed her so much. The last time I got to hold that little girl, she would have been just about a year old when Ella and Chris moved back to the U.S. I'll get Ella's old room ready for Sera. It'll be perfect since it adjoins with yours."

"Thank you, Mom. Really. I have no idea what I would do without you."

"Now don't go sayin' things like that, Love. You'll make your mother cry in the dough."

"We can't have extra salty dough. I love you. Talk to you soon."

A soft beep ended their conversation.

Knowing that sleep was not to be had, it was time to begin. It would tear her heart into pieces, but there were a few of Ella's things she desperately wanted to keep for Sera.

Armed with a small packing box, Erinne's heart pounded hard in her throat as she walked over to the closet. Another wave of grief drowned her like a tsunami as she slid open the door to reveal Ella and Chris's clothing, still hanging neatly, all waiting to be worn.

Erinne saw what she was looking for, the shimmering red material, in the back of the closet. The dress Ella wore the night, only months before, Chris proposed—once again. Though he'd proposed to Ella playfully every six months or so, this time he got down on one knee, and he had a ring. And Ella had finally said yes.

Erinne put the red dress into a garment bag, carefully folding it and placing it in the box. Next, she found the old picture album and placed it in the box as well. When a young, pregnant Ella had been cast out of her parent's house, she'd taken the family album with her, along with the pay-off check her father had written for her to stay out of their lives.

Last, Erinne pulled the wooden box that held the letters that had become their lifeline to each other after Erinne moved to Ireland. Every thought, every dream, every crush, happy times, sad times, and every moment in between was written in those letters. Ella would sign hers, ***Someone Who Knows***.

She did always know.

Erinne would keep both of their letters together and give them to Sera when she was older. Maybe she'd even read them to Sera, sharing all of their stories with her.

When Erinne was finished, she stood in the middle of the room, looking around once more. With a mournful sigh, she picked up the packing box, stepped out into the hallway, and closed the door, the finality of the soft click echoing like a shot to her heart.

Just before getting Sera into the taxi, Erinne watched the little girl look back at the house.

"Don't worry, it'll be here, waiting for you to be ready to come back. Maybe when you're all grown up."

The white porch swing swayed gently in the breeze. What seemed like thousands of daisies, Ella's favorite, were beginning to bloom. Erinne remembered Ella and Sera on that swing, spending hours reading and swinging, Chris happily tinkering with something in the background.

Silently, Erinne said her own final goodbye, then turned and got them both into the taxi.

It might be over for now, but it will never be forgotten.

CHAPTER SEVEN

Erinne

SAN FRANCISCO

Erinne tried her hardest not to let her hands shake on the indicator as they waited for it to move across the Ouija board. It was bad enough that Ella had already teased her earlier for the hitch in her voice when she'd asked why they had to do this in the dark. Ella never answered. She only looked at her with a sneaky smile as she lit the candles she'd placed around the room, really setting the creepy atmosphere.

Ella's superpower, *The Knowing,* has never weirded Erinne out. Not when Ella would know who was on the phone before it rang, or when she would know where something lost was, or how she would know what was hurt on a wounded animal they'd happen across. Which is why Ella swore she was going to become the best doctor, like, ever.

Never once did any of that scare Erinne. But *this* did.

"*Why* do we have to do this?"

"*Shh!* Concentrate."

Erinne quieted, peeking out of one eye. Ella was still as could be, eyes closed, breathing steadily in total concentration. Erinne closed her eyes again, gulping down the lump of fear stuck in her throat.

Then she heard it, a faint tapping, slowly getting louder. Nothing on the board moved, the indicator still painfully frozen. Still, the tapping got closer. Erinne's eyes popped open.

"Ella..."

"Shh!"

The door burst open behind them so hard that it rebounded off the wall behind it. Both Erinne and Ella jumped up screaming. Erinne's dog, Sadie, started barking in response.

"Sadie!" Erinne yelled as her heart hammered against her chest.

Both girls looked at each other and then started laughing hysterically.

"Jesus, you two. Why do you have to be so obnoxious?" Erick, the middle Byrne child, stomped down the hall from his room to Erinne's, slamming her door shut behind him, which made the girls laugh even harder.

"Oh, he's so funny when he's mad," Ella said, wiping laughing tears from her face.

"He acts all big and bad, but he's just a softie underneath all that pretending." Erinne got up and turned on the lights, petting the dog that almost gave her a heart attack.

"When do you think he'll tell your parents?" Ella asked, a woeful look passing over her face.

Last year, Ella told Erinne that Erick liked boys instead of girls. She'd said it made him anxious and sometimes confused, but what caused him pain was keeping it from their parents.

"Who knows? He still pretends to have crushes on girls that he never calls or goes out with," Erinne said, shrugging. "I don't know why he is so scared. It's the 90's. People aren't as mean as they used to be."

"Um, yeah, they are. Maybe even worse than before. But *your* parents are amazing. He needs them in his corner. Once he tells them, he'll feel so much better about everything. He'll be much more confident. Besides, Erick will eventually get his Happily Ever After."

Erinne looked back at Ella. Her voice had hushed and she had that far-away look on her face she got when *The Knowing* came to her.

"Well, that's good to know. I only want Erick to be happy. He deserves it," Erinne said, taking Ella's hand. Erinne smiled at her when the look faded away and was quickly replaced by embarrassment.

Ella's first reflex was always to try and hide *The Knowing*, to be ashamed of it. Her parents were the least understanding people Erinne had ever met. They made Ella think she was a freak when she had her moments of *Knowing*.

Erinne didn't care for Ella's parents. They made her so mad that she'd fantasized about putting them in their place on numerous occasions.

Like, when they were eight years old, Ella had woken up screaming from the nightmare she had a lot, the one about dying. Terrified, Ella went to her parent's bedroom, sure she was about to die. Instead of comforting her and reassuring her that everything was okay, her mother yelled at her for waking them, for talking nonsense, and for telling lies. After that, Ella never bothered her parents when she had those nightmares again. Between sobs, she'd told Erinne the next day. From that day on, Erinne couldn't stand Ella's parents.

Then again this year, on Ella's twelfth birthday, her parents said she was too old for Nanny Marge and told her they'd already let her go. They didn't even let Ella say goodbye. Nanny Marge had basically been Ella's mom in that house. Ella had come over to Erinne's house and cried and cried. Erinne's mom, Annabelle, felt so awful for Ella that she called Nanny Marge and had her come to their house so they could say their goodbyes.

Since then, Nanny Marge—just Marge now—and Annabelle became good friends and Ella got to see her all the time, so the joke was on Ella's parents.

"Anyway, my experiment failed," Ella sighed as she blew out all the candles.

"Okay, *now* will you tell me why we did this?" Erinne asked, reaching for the box to put the scary-as-hell Ouija board away. She fully intended to throw it in the trash as soon as possible. If she were brave enough, she'd burn it. But she'd seen too many horror movies and knew trying that was a very bad idea.

"I've never been able to control *The Knowing*. I thought if I opened myself up somehow, I'd finally be able to. Guess not."

"Bummer. Hey, maybe your powers will come full force when you go through puberty, like Teen Witch."

"I'm not a *witch*. I wish I was. Then I could do a lovespell on my parents, get them to like me. And then I would get all pretty and get the cute boy."

"Ella, you *are* pretty. Too pretty," Erinne scoffed and threw a pillow at Ella's head.

"Ow. Brat." Ella threw it back at her. "Besides, I have gone through puberty, thank you very much."

"What? When? Why didn't you tell me?" If Ella started her period and didn't tell Erinne, she would be *so* mad at her. They were supposed to be best friends, and best friends told each other *everything*. Besides, Erinne was eager to start hers, and she was older than Ella by four whole months.

"I'm telling you now. I started my period last night. My mom got so mad at me. I'm not even sure why. I never know why." The green of Ella's eyes brightened and teared up like they usually did when talking about her mother.

"E," Erinne scooted over to Ella and put her arms around her, "we can share my mom. She loves you as if you were one of us anyway."

"Okay. Can I move in, too?"

"Yes. We can share my room. Wouldn't that be the bomb? We would be like real sisters. You already have an "E" name and everything."

"Speaking of puberty, when my daughter has kids, I want them to call me G-ma, Gigi, or Gammy. Something fun, not boring, old Grandma."

Erinne shot a look at Ella. She swore that one day she'd get whiplash trying to keep up in their conversations. "You're twelve. You just got your *first* period. Why are you already thinking about grandkids? You're crazy." She nudged Ella.

"It's just something I wish I had time for."

"Oh my god, you're *not* going to die. You don't know everything, you know." The only time Erinne actually got angry with Ella was when she said that she was going to die young.

It was a knee-jerk reaction, shooting Ella down when she said that. Erinne definitely didn't want to be like Ella's parents, but it was the one thing that did scare her, besides Ouija boards. Erinne couldn't imagine losing her best friend, didn't even want to think about it because it hurt too much.

"Okay fine, enough of that. What is *our* fabulous mother making for dinner?"

CHAPTER EIGHT

Erinne

IRELAND

D id you brush your teeth?" Sera jumped onto her bed where Erinne waited for her, crawled over to Erinne, opened her mouth, and huffed out a breath in Erinne's face.

Exaggerating a cough, Erinne laughed as she said, "Mmm. Minty fresh."

In the months since coming to Ireland, Sera had slowly started to show signs of the child she used to be.

They had found their routine, which seemed to ground Sera. Sera was eager to help Erinne's mother, Annabelle—Nan to her grandchildren, which Sera was considered—in the kitchen in the mornings. She followed each of Nan's directions happily and with careful precision. Folding and kneading dough became her favorite thing to do. In the afternoons, Erinne and Sera helped fix up guest rooms. Then, it was pajamas, teeth, and letters before bedtime.

Over time, Sera had even begun to venture outside on her own. She'd go out to the small stable that housed their single horse. Old Gypsy, the black and white paint, was gentle and slow in her old age, but she loved the child's attention and didn't mind the treats Sera brought to her either. She'd pet and nuzzle the white star on Gypsy's nose, and then she'd sit next to her stall for long periods of time.

But bedtime became their most cherished ritual of the day when Erinne would read Ella's letters to Sera. Sera would grow more excited as that time drew near, rushing to brush her teeth and put on her pajamas.

"Okay, where did we leave off?" Erinne kissed Sera's cheek as she snuggled into her.

"Tell me about when Mommy met Daddy again."

So simply, Sera spoke as if she had been speaking the entire time. Not silent for almost a year.

Possible or not, Erinne thought she felt her heart actually stop for a beat or two. She took a quick breath, trying her hardest not to overreact and dampen the moment.

"Okay. Alright. As I've told you before, their love story is one of the best I know. When your mom met your dad..." Erinne couldn't stop the tears that welled up and tipped over the edge. She kissed Sera's head, hugged her tight, and told her about the first time Ella had told Erinne about Chris.

When her breathing became rhythmic, Erinne carefully pulled her arm free from under Sera, tucking the covers in around her.

As Erinne replaced the letters in the box, she rifled through the assortment of envelopes, trying to depict which would be next to read to Sera. They were in no particular order. The extent of the organizing she'd done so far was combining hers and Ella's.

Erinne began looking through and making piles of letters by dates and years. They really did write a lot of letters. Even after cell phones came into the picture, they kept writing.

At the bottom of the box, under all of Ella's letters, was a folded manilla envelope that she didn't recognize. Erinne's name donned the front in Ella's handwriting. No address, no stamp, and it was still sealed.

Of course, Ella knew Erinne would keep the letters, just as she knew she'd find this one.

Erinne took a few deep breaths before opening the letter to clear the tears that came to her eyes and settle the thumping of her heart. When she was ready, she slowly ripped open the envelope.

Dear My Bestest, My Soul Sister, Erinne,

I hate to say I told you so…but…if you're reading this, well, you know.

I am so sorry I've left you. It might be really hard right now for you to understand everything, but I have left you with my heart, my soul. You are the only one who can raise her to be the woman she is supposed to be.

Please, will you do this for me? I know it is a lot to ask, everything to ask, but you are the only one I trust and love enough to have her. I know you'll be the best of both me and you for her.

Push her to fall in love, all of the time, and as many times as possible. Then, hold her close when she has her first heartbreak. Push her out of her comfort zone to do crazy fun things. Push her to let people in, to make friends. Push her to laugh, to cry, and to feel everything in between. Guide her through life like you would, like I would.

I thought Chris would be the one to mold Sera, raise her, but I feel it creeping in, the dark, the cold. I think I may have led Chris to his demise as well. I hate myself for it.

I've been getting things ready for a while now. I had my will written up and put the rest of my parents' money into an account for you, for Lantern Light.

Before you get all defensive, it's already done, so stop arguing with me. I'm dead, so I get the last word. Don't make me 'haunt' you down and make you use it.

Seriously, though, you have been so supportive of me, accepting all of my weird quirks, encouraging all of my hopes and dreams, and being there for me when I became a mommy. Lantern Light will be your legacy. It is going to be absolutely amazing, I know it. I am so proud of you.

The other account is for all things Sera-related. I hope she'll want to go to college, so there is plenty for that. If she doesn't, she can have it for whatever she likes after she turns 21.

When she's old enough, give her my great-grandmother's amethyst locket. She'll cherish it as much as I have. Which reminds me...I'll apologize now for her teen years. I hear those are quite challenging. I'm sorry it will be you instead of me battling the attitude and sass.

Thank you for everything you have given to me in my life. You were my family when I had none. You kept me grounded when I would float away in the clouds. You have been the best friend and sister any gal could ever hope for.

Even though I won't be physically there to watch you fall in love for the first time (please let it be soon), to help you get ready for your wedding, to hold your hand (or a leg) when you have your babies, I will be there in spirit. Because you know I'll do everything I can to watch from afar, I promise.

Forever, With All My Heart,
Someone Who Knows
P.S.
Don't forget, when Sera has her babies, don't let them call me anything boring. I want a good name, like 'Oma' or 'Gammy'. Gammy was always a fun Grandma n ame.

Erinne read the last words in a whisper, wiping a tear from her face. She fingered the diamond lightning bolt that hung at her neck, the last thing Ella had given her, as the grief simmered up again. Hearing Ella's voice one last time was a gift, and it broke her heart all over again.

She dumped out the rest of the contents of the manilla envelope. The amethyst locket engraved with Celtic knots surrounding a purple stone in the center fell out, along with two bank account books and two bank cards, one with Erinne's name on it and the other with Sera's.

Erinne reread the letter a couple more times through a free flow of tears.

CHAPTER NINE

Sera

IRELAND

It was dark. So dark she couldn't see in front of her, only heard the pounding of her heart. Mommy's thoughts were in her head, her voice.

She was too late.

She had to stop him from hurting her baby again.

She was sure she had died, at least for a minute or two, and that cost her baby girl everything.

It was hard to think, a splitting pain in her head, her chest heavy, broken, blood bubbling up with each shaky breath she took. But she had to keep breathing. She couldn't hesitate any longer, or it would be too late.

Get her baby out.

With all she had left, all of her stubbornness, and all of her rage, she pulled herself up with Mommy's hands that were now her hands, torn and bloody.

There was a screwdriver.

Lungs, heart, brain.

Take him down, quick, silent.

Jugular, carotid, trachea.

The fury tore through her with an urgency and terror that Sera didn't understand. Sera heard her own voice humming, humming, somewhere behind her. But it was Mommy's voice that came out of her.

Mommy was fighting back. The cold metal gripped in Mommy's good hand. She lunged, penetrating the metal into his neck.

Sera startled awake. Her heart didn't slow until her surroundings reminded her that she was in Mommy and Daddy's old bed in Ireland. The bed they used to sleep in when they lived here a long time ago.

She hated it when she had these scary nightmares. They always made her really thirsty. Sera started to get out of bed for a drink of water when all the sounds around her stopped, everything fading into complete blackness. The blood pulsing through her veins began to thump loudly in her ears.

Then Sera was somewhere else.

She was in the woods, in the hole of a tree. Her hands looked strange to her. They were different, like when she dreamed of Mommy, and she had Mommy's hands.

But these weren't Mommy's hands, and they weren't her own hands. They were someone else's, and her eyes weren't hers, either. She was watching through someone else's eyes.

These hands were catching fireflies—or lightning bugs, her mind corrected. The hands grabbed one and then another from the air, putting them in a jar. The hands that were someone else's picked up the jar and ran into a house, where an old woman stood staring down with the meanest, most terrifying look Sera had ever seen anyone have. And it really scared her.

All the sounds of the night from Sera's room came crashing back.

She began to shake uncontrollably. Her breathing gasped out of her as she quickly looked at her hands. They were her own again. Her eyes shot up and scanned the room. No one else was there, and she was in the same position on her bed, her legs draped over the side.

She thought she had wet the bed again but realized it was only soaked with sweat, as was the rest of her body, clothes, and hair as if she had just emerged from a pool of water.

Her dinner rose from her belly and spilled onto the floor.

CHAPTER TEN

Erinne

IRELAND

Erinne was pulled up out of sleep by a strange sound. As her eyes fluttered open, she recognized the sound of retching coming from Sera's room, making her jump out of bed.

"Oh no, are you sick?" Erinne pulled Sera's hair out of the way of the vomit that kept coming.

Sera shook her head. When she seemed to have nothing left in her and her little body stopped heaving, Sera looked up at Erinne, her eyes full of worry.

"I dreamed without sleeping again."

"Another nightmare? I'm so sorry." Erinne pulled Sera into her arms and held her close, stroking her hair down her back. "You're safe now. It's all over."

She felt so damn helpless. All she wanted to do was take the pain from Sera, take away all the horrible memories that continued to haunt her.

"But it was now. Just somewhere else."

Erinne pulled away to look at her. "Do you want to tell me?"

Sera nodded.

"Okay, let's talk about it. But first, do you want me to clean you up a bit? Then we can go to my bed and sleep together there tonight. Does that sound like a plan?"

Sera nodded again.

The poor girl had vomit stuck in her hair, and her body and bed sheets were soaked through. Erinne would worry about cleaning up the other mess from the floor after she got Sera cleaned up and back to sleep.

Sitting on Erinne's bed, Erinne ran a comb through Sera's freshly washed hair.

"Okay, tell me about it."

"Sometimes I sleep and dream of Mommy and *that* night. But in those nightmares, I *am* Mommy. This time, it was when she stopped the bad-man. Then I wake up. But then I have another dream after I'm awake. I'm somebody else, I don't know who. They like to catch fireflies. But they are so sad and so lonely and really scared."

"Do you think maybe you just dreamt that you woke up, but you were still asleep? I've had dreams like that before."

Sera shook her head fiercely. "I was awake!"

"Okay. Well, that sounds really scary. Who do you think it is? Do you have a guess?"

Sera shook her head again. "No. I don't know who it is."

"Does that scare you?"

"Not as much as the bad-man ones."

"Yeah, those are the worst. Do you want me to ask Dr. John if there is a way to help with these nightmares at our appointment next week?"

Sera sat quietly in thought for a moment. "Okay. We can tell him. All of it." Then Sera smirked at Erinne. "He likes you."

"I like Dr. John, too. He seems to be a good doctor for you."

"No, Aunt Erinne, he *likes* you. I think he's funny. He is a good guy, not a bad guy. You should love each other."

Erinne wanted to ask where she got such an idea but left it alone.

"Don't be silly. Alright, hair is all combed. Are you ready to try and go back to sleep? I'll be right here with you."

If Erinne hadn't grown up with Ella, hadn't watched in awe all of Ella's unusual gifts emerge and get stronger as they got older, if she hadn't experienced the sheer magic *The Knowing* was, she might have explained away Sera's nightmares as manifestations of the trauma she had experienced, as Dr. John had been teaching her to recognize and do.

Just John, as he kept insisting, not *Doctor* John.

Doctor John Kleinhaus—German name, Irish roots, as he'd explained on their first visit—had a calm, natural ease about him. He wasn't as old as Erinne had expected, either. Quite young, actually. He looked maybe to be in his early to mid-thirties. He had proven to be very good at his job because Erinne instantly felt she could tell this man anything, and apparently, so had Sera. She took to him by their third visit, which she hadn't done with anyone, including Erinne, since everything had happened.

He'd worked wonders with Sera, earning her trust, helping her through the bed-wetting and age regression, and being patient with her until she finally began to speak again. Though she still refused to talk about the nights she'd been taken, Dr. John—*just* John—assured Erinne that Sera would find her own time to go back.

But this was different. Erinne knew in her gut that these weren't *just* nightmares because she *had* seen Ella's magic.

As time continued at Lantern Light, Sera had started to exhibit other similar abilities. Like, when she first set Sera up in her parents' old room, Sera knocked on the adjoining door with a special knock, the secret knock Erinne and Ella came up with as a joke after Chris came to Ireland. Instead of a sock on the door, they had a special all-knowing knock, asking if it was safe to enter.

On another occasion, Erinne and Sera were sitting in the main den. Sera wandered over to a corner of the room, stood quietly for a moment, then started laughing.

"What's so funny?" The rare sound of Sera's laughter was so welcome that Erinne laughed along with her.

"Daddy is so funny."

"Yes, your daddy sure had his funny moments." It was an unexpected comment, but she wasn't wrong. Chris *had* been genuinely funny. It was really hard not to like him. It was no wonder Ella had fallen so completely.

"How come he gave you one sock and a door knocker for Christmas? Those are silly gifts." Sera looked at Erinne with the first real joy in her eyes since before *everything*.

Erinne's mind raced. Then she realized Sera was standing where they set up the Christmas tree each year. Sera had only been a baby at the time. And *that* Christmas story had never been mentioned in any of the letters they'd written.

"Well, the sock and the knocker were a grown-up joke between me, your mommy, and your daddy. I'll tell you that story when you're a bit older," Erinne said, heat rushing to her face. She wasn't ready to have the birds-and-the-bees talk with a seven-year-old.

"What about the violin he gave you? What did that one mean?"

It was unmistakable. Sera was *Special,* just like Ella.

"I always wanted to learn how to play when I was growing up, but we couldn't afford a violin or music lessons," Erinne remembered. "The Christmas you all were here when you were just a tiny baby, he gave me the violin and said that I had no excuse not to learn anymore. Your daddy was funny, but he also had a sweet side."

"Did you ever learn how to play?"

"No, I never did. I got busy, I guess."

"Can I see your violin?"

As soon as Erinne placed the instrument in Sera's hands, the child fell in love with it.

Erinne made sure she found a tutor willing to come to Lantern Light once a week to give Sera the lessons she'd always wished for as a kid.

CHAPTER ELEVEN

Sera

IRELAND

I call this person Bee." Sera was trying the new set of paints on the art table. Dr. John always had really fun things to draw and paint with.

"Bee? Why is that?" Dr. John looked directly at her when they spoke, not like all those other doctors she had to see before at her old house. They'd always stare down at their notebooks, scribbling a bunch of things instead of looking at her.

Sure, Dr. John had scared her at first, like everyone else did. But something told her that he was good, not bad, that she could tell him scary things. Like now, as she was telling Dr. John about the Mommy nightmares and the Bee dreams, he kept looking directly at her, and he never looked at her like she was weird.

"Because bees sting others before they get hurt themselves. Bee wants to do the hurting instead of always being the one who is hurt."

"Bee doesn't frighten you?"

"Not really. I think hurting other things is bad. But Bee is sad and hurting, too."

"How is Bee hurting?"

"Bee has a bad house. The old grandma has a big bible book that she hits Bee with a lot. Bee has to kneel on the floor all the time. Sometimes, Bee's knees bleed, too. And Bee's mommy doesn't do anything to help. I don't stay with Bee very long. When Bee gets really upset, I get pushed away, and then I'm awake-awake again."

"I know a little exercise that might help with your nightmares. For some kids, it helps them take control or stops the nightmares completely. Would you like to learn?"

Sera eagerly nodded.

"Okay. Watch what I do and then copy me." Dr. John sat cross-legged on the floor, closed his eyes, took a long, deep breath in through his nose, and let it out in a long exhale through his mouth. Sera copied.

"And then, with your eyes still closed and still taking deep breaths, do this with your fingers and count out loud. Ready?" Dr. John sat with his palms face up on his knees and started to touch each fingertip with his thumb, counting each finger as they touched. He then counted backward, going back the other way. "Do that as often as you need until you feel like yourself. Once you're there, think of a door. Any door. It can be a fancy door, a pink door, a fuzzy door."

Sera giggled. "Doors aren't fuzzy."

"Why not? This is *your* door, in *your* dream. It can be whatever you want it to be. Think of this door really hard. Can you see it? Your special door?"

Sera nodded.

"When you see your very special door, open it and walk through. Your special door will take you anywhere you want to go. Into a nice dream or into your room where you can wake up. Wherever you want the door to go, it will lead you through. Want to try it again?"

Sera nodded again. After the second time, Sera stood up and walked over to Erinne.

"Aunt Erinne, you can tell him about everything now. I can go play with Ms. Lady in front for a while."

"Ms. Lavry," Erinne corrected. "Okay, only if you're sure?"

"I'm sure." Sera smiled and let Dr. John lead her to the front play area where the receptionist, Ms. Lavry, could watch her.

Before Dr. John turned to go back to Erinne, Sera took his hand. "I think you'll love Aunt Erinne really good. Like how my daddy loved my mommy." Then, she turned to pick one of the coloring books and some crayons, making herself comfortable at the table and started coloring.

CHAPTER TWELVE

Erinne

IRELAND

"The easy way Sera leaves my side when we are here still shocks me," Erinne said when John returned.

"This is a good thing. Sera is regaining some of her self-identity. It also shows that she feels safe enough to be in the next room, knowing you won't disappear."

"If you say so, Dr. John."

"Please, *just* John. It always feels strange when adults call me *Doctor* John." He sat in the chair across from her.

"I'm sorry, habit." Erinne wiped her palms on her jeans, trying to gather the courage to start. "Sera and I talked about it, and she is okay with me filling you in on some *other* things..." Why was she so nervous?

Her family had never questioned Ella or *The Knowing*. Chris never acted as if it was anything out of the ordinary. Everyone who knew Ella accepted and loved everything about her. Except for Ella's own parents, maybe. Erinne never had to explain anything to anyone. They knew, or they didn't.

Maybe that was why Erinne felt the words stick in her throat as she tried to figure out where to begin. Because John hadn't known Ella. But if this doctor, *just John*, was going to fully understand Sera and where she came from, then he needed to know everything.

"What kind of other things, Erinne? What is making you feel anxious?" John sat back, watching her.

"Are you trying to shrink me, *John*?"

"I'm sorry, habit." He put his hands up and smiled as he mirrored her own words. The smile that put her at ease.

"Ella was special."

"I understand that."

"No, she was *special*." When she said nothing further, he waited quietly. "You, being a doctor of science and all, might think what I am about to say is hogwash. Which must be why this is really hard to get out."

"I'm all ears."

"Okay, here it goes. Ella, my best friend, Sera's mother, was special as in she had this gift of knowing things. Since we were kids, she knew things like where lost keys were or little things that would happen the next day. We called it *The Knowing*, her superpower. Nothing giant, like knowing winning lottery numbers or anything like that. These nightmares Sera has been having, they're getting worse. And these awake-dreams, they seem to be *more*, they seem to be Ella-esque. I think Sera has a form of what Ella did." After she spit it all out in one long breath, she waited for his reaction.

And again, she was surprised by him.

"There's actually a significant amount of research about abilities of premonition. It's quite fascinating. Some studies have discovered that a specific density of the myelination of the neurons in the brain differs in people with premonition abilities. They seem to have this unique capacity to fire messages..." he stopped and scoffed. "Sorry, that nerdy doctor of science in me tends to get carried away with research and whatnot."

Erinne just grinned at him. "Please, don't apologize. I would really like to know about those studies. I've lived most of my life wondering how it was possible, how *she* was possible. So, I am completely intrigued."

"Don't threaten me with a good time," John said and chuckled. "I have my own superpower, one that could bore a person faster than a speeding bullet."

"I'm serious," she said as she continued to smile and laugh. It felt good to laugh, like a bit of the weight she hadn't known she was carrying lifted from her shoulders.

He wouldn't judge, wouldn't cast them out. Not only would he listen, he might be able to shed some light on how it all worked and where to go from this point forward.

"I think, if it is alright with both of you, I'd like Sera to be in here. We can all discuss this and get everyone's unique viewpoints and experiences."

"Yes, that would be perfect."

PART TWO

COURAGE TO ENDURE

"The courage to endure is more difficult to find than the courage required for a one-time act of heroism. This everyday courage to drive on day in, day out requires more than overcoming fear."

-CPT George Tyler

Chapter Thirteen

I thought I'd feel something the moment after she'd taken her last breath. I thought I'd be sad, upset, feel some kind of emotion. I thought I'd cry, that I would yearn to have her back.

I felt less than nothing. I was empty.

She had never wanted us, hadn't wanted the life she had. Grandmother said it was her punishment for giving into mortal sin, a sentence to a life of hell on earth, and we were her consequence.

My brother wasn't here when she slipped away in that back room. He didn't get to experience the constant smell of human rot and urine, or watch her hospice nurse sit by her side day after day, giving her high doses of pain medication, or hear her moaning day and night.

If my brother had known about the pain meds, the high-quality type that he paid top dollar for on the street, he might have made it a point to come back and visit us once or twice at the end.

Most likely, he was blacked out in some dirty alley, high off whatever he got his hands on. His easy escape from what had been our reality.

Since I had no way of knowing how to get a hold of him, he probably had no idea that we had moved back into our childhood home so that Mom could be close to her oncology doctors.

Surely, he didn't know that our mother was dead.

My brother got kicked out years ago after things around the house kept coming up missing. He would steal or pawn anything he could get his hands on for drug money. It was the perfect excuse for Grandmother to finally be rid of him.

I shouldn't be here anymore, either. Already twenty-one years old, I could have left years ago. But I have nowhere else to go, no one to go to.

And then, Mom had been diagnosed with stage four breast cancer.

I was the one who'd had to drive her back and forth to her plethora of appointments. Grandmother certainly had no sympathy for Mom. She turned up her shriveled face, as she always did when she was about to preach one of her high and mighty speeches, and told Mom it was her ultimate retribution, being struck down by the sinful womanly parts that led her away from God and tempted her into spawning with the Devil himself.

If all we were to my mother were her consequential punishments, then of course that is why she had never shown any love or affection toward us, why she had basically ignored us completely, why she had never come to our aid when Grandmother beat us for whatever sin she felt we'd committed.

Our father didn't love us enough to stay, and our mother hated us.

I felt nothing as she died in that back room, alone.

Not that feeling nothing is anything new to me. I feel nothing most of the time.

Sometimes, when I cut into my skin, that temporary, beautiful pain is what lets me know I am still here, alive. It even takes away some of my emotional pain, turning it into something physical, something I can control.

There is no reason to feel anything. I have no one, only the constant whispering in my head, reminding me that I am insignificant, unimportant.

If I bleed, no one cares. If I disappeared, no one would cry, no one would miss me, no one would give a shit. They had forgotten about me long ago because I am no one.

The whispers remind me that it is up to me to find my own way out so that I might finally be rid of this darkness, this pain of nothingness.

As I lay in a pool of crimson relief, it is the first time I've ever felt real happiness wash over me, knowing that I have taken complete control of my own life, and soon, the bottomless emptiness will be over. For once, I bleed because of me, not them.

No one will touch me again.

Until my sister barged in and ruined this moment for me.

"What have you done? Suicide is a sin. You'll burn in hell for all eternity. Grandmother!" she screamed out, her skinny, plain face all crunched up.

"I'm already in hell. Get out." I heaved my already weakening body at the bathroom door to close it on her face and barricade it with my weight as I began to pass out.

Grandmother forced the door open, slamming it into my head. She grabbed me by the shoulders, shaking me violently, her wretched face screaming into mine, slapping me over and over again. Not screams of fear for my life, but of rage at my audacity, inviting the Devil into her house, screaming at me to pray to God for forgiveness.

I finally yelled back at her for the first time in my whole miserable life. "I won't pray to your God. I won't pray to something that doesn't exist." Then, there was beautiful darkness.

But the dark didn't last.

There were flashes of bright white light, as bright as the sun, masked faces rushing around me, poking, prodding.

Then silence again.

When I woke up, I was in a room that was a little too cold and a little too sterile. I couldn't reach my face as my hands were strapped to the steel bars of the gurney I lay on. My wrists bandaged and sore.

It didn't work.

I was still trapped in this dejected world.

CHAPTER FOURTEEN

Sera

STANFORD

She held her hands tight to her ears, just like she promised Mommy, humming the only song she could think of. Whenever it came on the radio Mommy would laugh and turn it way up so they could sing along as loud as they could. It was Mommy's favorite song when she was a little girl, so it was Sera's favorite song, too.

Sera hummed Girls Just Wanna Have Fun, her body rocking back and forth, tears running down her face, dribbling into her mouth. But she didn't stop humming. She had promised.

She could still hear things, like the sound of Mommy's body hitting the floor when the bad-man hit her, over and over. She hummed louder, wishing so badly to go home.

Sera woke with a jump, adrenaline tingling down to her toes. Sweat moistened her brow and dampened her hair, plastering it to her forehead.

She closed her eyes, took a few deep breaths, and got ready to start counting her fingertips, just as John had shown her all those years ago.

And then, sound stopped. The room around her darkened to blackness.

There was blood. So much blood. Her head felt woozy like she was going to pass out.

Then sudden light burst in her eyes, bright fluorescents glaring, masked faces staring at her.

An overwhelming sadness blanketed her, a disappointment like she'd never experienced before in her lifetime.

The room fluttered under heavy eyelids. Then, mercifully, it went black.

Sounds came crashing back to Sera's ears. She bolted upright in her bed, chest heaving as she fought to pull enough air into her lungs. She was soaked through with sweat, a wave of nausea threatening. She quickly looked at her wrists, her arms, her body. No blood. It wasn't hers.

The awake-dreams.

It had been years since she'd had any as a kid. Not since John helped her learn to take control. She'd almost completely forgotten about them.

Almost.

She had worked so hard to forget all of it. If she'd had the ability, she might have given in to the urge to weep. Since she wasn't able to physically cry anymore, she forced the nightmare away. She wouldn't think about it, wouldn't let herself remember.

Sera got up and pulled off her sweat-soaked sheets. If she changed them quickly enough, she might be able to get a few more hours of sleep before the long day of moving out of her dorm room and heading back home to Ireland, as she did each summer.

For everyone else, the end of spring brought on the promise and excitement of new possibilities as graduation season usually did. But for Sera, completing her bachelor's degree in biology only brought exhaustion, confusion, and guilt. Always guilt.

Sera's confusion wasn't about her future. Since she could remember, she had been working toward medical school—not just any medical school, but Stanford Med like her mother—to become the doctor her mother was supposed to have been. The confusion lurked in her lack of contentment with getting one step closer to what she'd been working so hard for.

Instead, she was more lost than ever. Getting into Stanford Med should have been exhilarating. Yet, for Sera, it was just another box checked off. It was like she didn't even *want* the medical degree anymore.

She pushed the seeping doubt back down, deep. It wasn't about what she *wanted*, it was what she was *supposed* to do.

Seeing as there was really no one to say goodbye to—Sera kept painfully private, never befriending those in her classes or her neighbors in the dorms, not even her dormmates—it wouldn't take long to pack up her things, giving her plenty of time before her flight to call Erinne.

Personal relationships required sharing personal information, something Sera found tedious and uncomfortable. It wasn't that Sera *never* tried. She did until she just couldn't anymore. People always had questions, too many questions. Enough years had passed that she wasn't recognized often, and she wanted to keep it that way for as long as possible.

At least until later in the summer, that is.

"Why you didn't want us there still baffles me. We are your biggest fans, you know. Graduating with your bachelor's degree is a big deal. Why do you act like it's just another day, just another semester?" Erinne asked, voice thin over the phone.

Sera knew that tone, the one Erinne was trying to hold back. Not only was Erinne upset, but hurt. The nag of guilt tugged at Sera.

"Because it *is* just another semester. I didn't even walk. This is not the one I want to celebrate. I promise you that when I get my medical degree, my cheering section all better be here. You, John, and the rest of the clan, front and center. This degree is just a stepping stone." Sera shouldered her cell phone to pack up the last of her things. Another year, another dorm room to move out of.

"Fine, it's a stepping stone. But what about celebrating that you got into Stanford Med? That is definitely something. You worked so hard for this, and we are so proud of you. Like it or not, we want to celebrate you, so John and I upgraded your ticket back home for the summer."

"You didn't have to do that. I know how busy you guys are."

"It was a few clicks online, big deal. The surprise is that you'll not board another plane when you get to New York. Did you know you can take a passenger ship from New York to Ireland, not just a cruise, but as transportation? We found that out and thought it was the perfect graduation gift. You'll have ten glorious days to just rest and relax before getting here and being bombarded by this crazy, loud family."

"I love my crazy, loud family. It helps me feel somewhat sane," Sera joked. Taking a ship did sound mildly enjoyable and also downright terrifying. "It sounds interesting, Aunt E, but with that Docu-Series about Jeffrey Mason coming out soon, and all those people. I don't know. Ten days is a long time..."

"What is even more *interesting*," Erinne cut her off, "is that all the food, drinks, and *booze* are included. Have a damn drink or two. You're twenty-two for Christ's sake! Lounge by the damn pool, read a damn fiction novel. Just relax a little. You've earned it."

"Well, damn it, maybe I will," Sera said, chuckling at Erinne's constant insistence that she be a 'regular' person. Sera loved her to the bottom of her heart, but Erinne would never truly understand. There is no way she ever would. No one could. Not that Sera ever let anyone get close enough to try.

"That's the damn spirit. And don't start worrying about that documentary. It hasn't even been aired yet. Do me a favor and please *try* to relax and have some fun. I can't wait to see your face."

"See you in a couple of weeks. Thank you, Erinne. Thank John for me, too. It does sound pretty amazing."

She wouldn't tell Erinne about the night terror, wouldn't add it to the long list of things Erinne worried about. Besides, she wasn't even sure if it was one. From what she could remember, this one was different from any of the ones she had as a kid.

She was probably just stressed out about that damn documentary.

CHAPTER FIFTEEN

Jeffrey Mason

ARKANSAS

Life was not turning out how Jeffrey Mason had wanted or expected it to. At seventeen, he had been discarded and trapped all in one swoop. This time, he had only himself to blame, he supposed. His uncle had been all too eager to rid himself of the burden of Jeffrey once everyone found out that he had knocked up Ingrid.

Ingrid's parents had stormed their trailer, dragging along a sixteen-year-old, sniveling Ingrid, refusing to leave before confronting Jeffrey and his uncle. They demanded Jeffrey do right by their daughter and marry her before she gave birth to the bastard child since he had already damned her, and she would be forever denied life everlasting, doomed to burn in the fires of hell and all that crazy crap.

To Jeffrey's amazement, his uncle only laughed—at Jeffrey.

"You're some kind of dumb ass, kid."

He then signed permission for his minor nephew's marriage.

Jeffrey's first impulse was to take off to some far-off place without Ingrid, parents, or uncles. But he had zero money to go farther than the liquor store on the corner.

Instead, he accepted Ingrid's father's firm suggestion of taking a job at the factory where he worked, and married the plain, feeble Ingrid in a conference room at the county clerk's office.

He thought his luck was taking a turn when she miscarried. It could have had something to do with him knocking her around, might not have. But he was already stuck. It took money to get divorced, money he still didn't have.

Now, at twenty-two, he found a dull but consistent rhythm to his life. He would go to work—which he was actually pretty good at. So much so that after Ingrid's father died, the good ol' boys brought him into their group to be groomed and taught the ways of the older, wiser men.

In the evenings, he would go home, and on an adventurous night, he would test how far he could make Ingrid go. She'd occasionally let him do certain, more adventurous things to her. *Let him* might be a stretch, but she had been willing enough.

Darker urges had begun to take up larger residence in Jeffrey's mind, his fetishes amping up, the need to act them out intensifying. There was a line he couldn't cross with Ingrid unless he wanted his secret out of the bag. It wasn't long before Jeffrey had the first affair, or the second, and the third.

Fucking random women he had no obligation to helped keep those needs under control. Though, it was only a matter of time before it would get old, and his desires would grow to the point when he couldn't wrangle them in any longer.

CHAPTER SIXTEEN

Ella

SAN FRANCISCO

This sucks so bad." Erinne couldn't stop crying.

"We will write to each other, and we can call every day," Ella sniffled, hugging Erinne close.

She was losing a piece of herself. This was worse than any breakup she ever had, and there had been a few. But those boys never had her heart like Erinne did. Erinne was her best friend, her sister, her soulmate.

But she had to act brave, if only for Erinne's sake.

Ella had been helping Erinne pack the last of her things in her room all afternoon. Her parents had already sold, thrown away, or packed up the rest of the house, but Erinne had been dragging her feet.

"The school year will be busy, but I can come visit you every summer."

Erinne wiped the tears that kept streaking down her cheeks. "You promise?"

Ella nodded.

"Even all the way from Stanford?"

"Cross my heart." Ella gestured an X across her chest.

"It's going to feel like I'm missing one of my limbs without you."

"You've definitely become my right-hand woman," Ella said and chuckled.

"This is so unfair. This summer was going to be the best one ever. We just graduated from high school, and you got accepted to Stanford. We are supposed to be celebrating." Erinne started crying again, wrapping Ella back in her arms.

"I know. But it's not like your grandparents intentionally got into that accident." Ella stroked Erinne's long, dark hair down her back.

"God, you're right. What an asshole I'm being." Erinne straightened up, wiped her face again, and blew her nose in the wad of tissues she was holding. "Okay. Okay. I'm pulling myself together now. Let's get these last boxes down to the truck."

For the next hour, the whole family finished loading up in silence. No one wanted to leave, but they had responsibilities to take care of.

The week before, they'd received a call from a hospital in Ireland notifying them that Erinne's grandparents had been in a serious automobile accident. Her grandfather hadn't made it, and they didn't think her grandmother would pull through, which she didn't.

Lantern Light Inn was the legacy of the Byrne family. It had been in their family for generations, and Erinne's grandparents had been running it for decades. With her grandparents gone, the doors had been closed for the first time since it had opened centuries before. It was an emotional choice, but ultimately, Erinne's parents decided to go home to Ireland to run Lantern Light.

Ella would have gone with them without hesitation. But Stanford, her dream college since she could remember, had just accepted her college application. She *had* to be a doctor so that she could use the *Knowing* for the greater good. And she would be good at it—no, one of the best. It was her calling. She knew it in her soul.

But at this moment, with every fiber of her being, Ella wanted to chuck the Stanford dream and crawl into the truck with the Byrne family. *Her* family, the family that mattered, the family that took her in and treated her like one of theirs, who loved her unconditionally the way her own family could not. Instead, she fought the urge and held firm.

"Ach. I'll miss you something fierce, Love." Annabelle said, kissing both cheeks and bringing Ella into a fierce hug.

"I'll miss you more than you know," Ella whispered back.

"Well, you'll come whenever you can, for as long as you can."

"I will."

"My turn. I am so proud of you, girl. Give 'em hell over there." Erinne's father, Brian Senior, took Ella into a bear hug, the kind that sent her into hysterical giggles when she was young, the kind that let her know she was loved and cared for. This was the father who actually raised her alongside Erinne, and Ella's heart was breaking piece by piece.

Ella nodded again, stifling the lump in her throat, holding back the sobs that wanted to tear out of her.

"Take it easy on those Ivy League boys. Have a little sympathy for their poor, preppy hearts." Brian Junior, Erinne's oldest brother, stepped over to her, ruffling her hair as he always did. As a girl of the '90s, this usually made her squeal and twist away before Brian could mess up the carefully over-teased and sprayed hair—which was his whole purpose. But now, it only made the loss of a brother that much harder.

Ella kissed Brian's cheek. "I will."

Then there was Erick, the sweetest heart of them all. He was already bawling when he hugged Ella. "Thank you. For being there for me when I wouldn't let anyone else in. You've always loved and supported me." Erick kissed Ella's cheek and held her close.

Ella lost it. The sobs she fought so hard to hold back won out, bursting from her as she and Erick held each other tight, rocking back and forth.

When she felt like she could form a sentence again, Ella pulled back from Erick. "Hey, don't be afraid when *the guy* wants to whisk you away." She winked and kissed Erick's cheek again.

The family piled into the truck, everyone but Erinne.

"This is it, then." Erinne shrugged and dropped her arms to her sides, her cheeks wet from the tears flowing down her face.

"This isn't *it*. This is only the beginning." Ella grabbed Erinne one last time, one last hug. "I love you. With all my heart. You are and always will be my soulmate."

"And you're mine."

Both girls stood in each other's arms, crying openly on the curb of the street. No one rushed them, no one made any remarks. The world stopped for their long goodbye.

"Lantern Light Inn," Erinne's voice carried through the thousands of miles of distance as though she were just in the next room.

"Hey there, stranger," Ella said, smiling into the phone. She called way too often, she knew. Even though they wrote letter after letter to each other, sometimes she just needed to hear Erinne's voice. Six months apart already felt like a lifetime.

"Ella, your phone bill is going to be astronomical."

"Meh, that's my parents' problem. They don't care as long as it keeps me out of their hair. Besides, I didn't want to wait to tell you my exciting news through a letter."

"Hold on, let me get Brian to man the front desk and go to my parent's office. One sec." Erinne put Ella on hold. Some fun Irish music played softly in the background.

"I'm back. Spill it."

"I'm moving into an apartment right off campus with two other students, Matt and Ruby. I have to get out of this house. It's like a freaking tomb." Ella looked around her bedroom. It was as it had always been. And yet, it was never hers. It had been whatever her mother's interior decorator made it. Her true room was Erinne's. She'd spent more time in that one than her own.

The first semester at Stanford was finished, and she was more than ready to move out, start her own adventures, and get out from under her parents' privileged superior thumbs. "I can't stand the coldness here. Since they've all but worn out their bragging rights about me going to Stanford, advancing themselves in their social circle as far as it's going to take them, they've barely spoken more than a few words to me."

"Yeah, well, screw them. But your own apartment? That's rad! You'll get, like, the real college experience. I'm kind of jealous."

"What are you talking about? You're about to get your own college experience. I'm so excited you took the plunge and signed up for business classes," Ella teased. It was always fun to slightly shock Erinne.

"Of course you know about that," Erinne chuckled on the other end.

"Of course I do. It's great, Erinne. Those business classes are going to be perfect for you. Lantern Light is going to be fantastic. You're going to transform it into this wonderful place. I know it."

"Because of your superpower."

"No, because I know *you*."

There was a pause in the line, then a hurried rush of words.

"Why do you have to stay there to become a fabulous doctor? Ireland is stunning. This peacefulness washed over me as soon as we got off the plane. And this place, Lantern Light, it's like it has a soul. It's pretty small now, but people love coming here. Lantern Light could be a big destination spot. It's surrounded by woods on one side and cliffs on the other. You can see for miles out on the ocean. If you were here with me, we could make it into the greatest hotel in the world. Mom would do all the cooking, of course. I would do the design and our business plans. Dad and the brothers would do the build. Well, one brother, anyway. I have news, too, but we'll get back to that. You could be the guest relations guru because you can charm a snake, and everyone loves you. It would be perfect."

"It will be all of that and more, I promise you. What's your news?" Ella fluffed up her pillows and laid back on her bed, looking at the picture on the nightstand of her and Erinne taken when they were ten.

She wanted to run off to Ireland almost as badly as she wanted that medical degree. It was harder and harder not to every time she spoke to Erinne. The only thing holding her back in San Francisco was knowing she was *supposed* to be there. She wasn't sure why so much as felt it deep inside.

Ella never did figure out a way to control *The Knowing*, no matter how many crazy experiments she tried since she was a kid. When she saw something, had that picture so clear in her mind, or felt it deep within, she knew it was inevitable to try and fight it. No matter what she did to change it, the circumstances might alter, but the same outcome would come to fruition.

Besides, how could she abandon the ability to come up to someone sick or hurt and just *know* what was wrong? With schooling, she'd finally learn how to fix the hurt and heal the sick. She may have never learned to control her abilities, but she was learning how to hone them into a specialty. It was the least she could do with this superpower that had been more of a burden than a blessing.

She had long since stopped telling Erinne about the heavier stuff. As tough as Erinne was—the first one to stand up to bullies and the first to fight, always the protector—when Ella told her the harder things, Erinne would shut down and deny its existence, especially Ella's doomed timeline. She wasn't about to tell Erinne that the feeling was getting stronger by the month. Ella was only eighteen years old and could already hear the clock start the countdown to her end. The ticks were soft, but they were there.

"My news is about Erick. He met a dashing Englishman. His name is Rich, and the guy is hot. Whew. And that accent? My god, I almost wish he were straight so that I could steal him from Erick. Anyway, Rich is already trying to tempt him into moving away to London."

"Erick bagged himself an Englishman straight out the gate. That's awesome. When he moves to London, I am totally going with you to visit."

"Won't that be fun? Speaking of love. Are you still seeing Mr. Bartender?"

"Johnny? Nope. He ruined it by falling too much in love."

"Geez, Ella. Are you ever going to give any of them a chance? Poor guys. I wish I could be there to watch all the drama unfold. It would be like watching The Real World in person. You wait, one day, one of them is going to get into that heart of yours, and it's going to knock you on your ass. And I am going to love every second of it," Erinne challenged.

"I've loved them all in my own way. Love is anything you want it to be. Life is too short, especially mine. So, I want to fall in and out of love whenever I can. I want to live each moment. Truly taste things and savor them. I want to feel each feeling without holding back because tomorrow is never promised. You should try it, it's life changing."

"Shoot. With how often you're falling in and out of love, there won't be any men left for me. Even way over here. One sec," Erinne paused. Annabelle's voice was muffled in the background. "E, I gotta go. We'll talk soon?"

"Absolutely. I'll call you with the phone number of the new apartment when I get it."

"Love you. I miss you like a missing limb."

"An arm."

"Worse, a leg."

CHAPTER SEVENTEEN

Sera

ATLANTIC OCEAN

The chaos of JFK Airport always had Sera lost. Directionally challenged is what Erinne liked to call Sera. People were everywhere, all rushing in different directions. Loud voices carried through the labyrinth of hallways. Paths and luggage claims signs pointing out different directions seemed to have been made only for the airport staff to understand. No matter how often she navigated through these airports on her way back to Ireland, it never got any easier.

Minutes after finally finding her way out, she spotted the tall and shockingly thin man holding a sign with her name on it. Excitement started to tickle as she watched the passing of the New York City streets from the backseat of the black sedan.

It was rare that she got excited about much of anything. Sadness and guilt usually sucked it away, like a rip tide always threatening to pull her under. But the fleeting moment of excitement made her feel almost normal for once.

She sat back and watched the massive city pass by until the car turned into a parking lot facing the largest floating vessel Sera had ever seen. It was surreal, phantom-like. Surely, that massive building on water couldn't actually float.

After making her way onto the ship and navigating through the long, narrow corridors, she finally found her cabin suite.

She sat on the bed, looking around the room, when she caught her reflection in the freestanding mirror in the far corner. The immediate urge to look away took hold. Instead, she gazed at her face, a replica of her mother's, and felt that ever-present pang of guilt. She kneaded a fist into her stomach, trying to massage away the physical pain of it.

Maybe she had an ulcer. That would be just her luck. Or maybe it was the debt she owed having survived gnawing at her. She pulled an extra blanket from the small closet and draped it over the mirror.

It was the same when she looked at the family album, the instant slap of loss that burrowed deep when she saw her parents' happy faces. Nevertheless, Sera took the album everywhere she went.

On the nightstand was a printed agenda for each day of the cruise. Her assigned dinner hour was at six. It was already almost five o'clock. She had no desire to try and be social, dreaded it, actually. Room service, according to the printout, was always available.

Perfect, she thought as she picked up the telephone handset. She could hole up in her cabin, hang out on the balcony, and have her meals delivered with minimal socializing with other humans. *Maybe it would be a pleasant trip after all.*

Though she was curious to look around the massive ship, and it was still light enough for a quick walk before her dinner arrived.

Outside, she closed her eyes, inhaling the crisp, salty air that only the ocean could offer. Along the promenade deck, an elderly couple sat hand-in-hand on lounge chairs, taking in the view. At first, it made her smile, but she had to look away quickly.

It always hurt to see such intimacy between two people, knowing she would never trust anyone like that, enough to allow herself to be with someone so completely. Sadly, she knew in her darkest of hearts that she'd most likely never have that kind of love in her life.

She remembered few precious things about her childhood before *it* happened, but the way her dad looked at her mom, how his handsome face smiled as he leaned in to kiss her mom so sweetly, was something Sera would cherish forever.

They never got their Ever After. Why should she expect to?

He took that from her, took them from her. Even though Sera made sure she never thought about *Him*, or that awful time, sometimes she fell into that dark hole.

It had been happening more often the past year, ever since she'd first been contacted by a television producer asking her to interview for the documentary series they were filming about Jeffrey Mason. Sure, why not give him notoriety on top of everything?

Sera picked up speed as the pit of anxiety started to fester, nearly colliding with a woman as she rushed back to her room. She ran inside and slammed the door behind her, gasping, throat scratching as she tried to catch her breath, her eyes burning from tears unshed. She charged into the washroom, flung on the faucet, and splashed cool water on her face and neck.

She'd done it again, the thing she hated, getting worked up about *Him*, about her past. It was a personal failure every time she let those feelings in, worse, let them affect her.

She closed her eyes and took some deep, visceral breaths, as John had taught her to do when overwhelmed.

Finally calmer, she left the washroom, plopped down on the bed, and was suddenly more tired than hungry. She left the food covered and untouched on the table next to the couch, and before long, she fell under the curtain of sleep.

Sera looked at the bedside clock, almost midnight. She'd been asleep for six hours.

And that will be all the sleep I'll get for the rest of tonight.

Since staring at the ceiling was hardly an option, she dressed for a walk around the deck. The solitude would suit her as few would be out at that hour.

Trailing her hand along the railing as she strolled, she looked out at the vast sea of blackness. No lights from any direction were visible, only the moonlight reflecting over the ripples of water shining like thousands of black diamonds and more stars than she had ever seen sparkling above. Sera closed her eyes and let the sound of water lapping against the ship's hull calm the tension out of her.

Her mother's sweet face flashed in her mind. It wasn't the cool temperatures that caused the prickling of her skin, it was the distant sound of her mother's voice. Faint at first, yet so distinct.

Sera gripped the railing, listening to the words, words she couldn't understand. It was definitely her mother's voice whispering. Gradually, the voice got closer, louder. She kept her eyes closed, leaning further over the railing, trying to hear better.

The voice split into three voices, then five, above and around her, flying toward her, then past her, coming at her in an increasingly urgent manner from all directions, the whispers overlapping, echoing.

"Mom?" Sera choked out, her voice barely audible to her own ears.

The air was filled with voices flying all around her, screaming in her ear when they were close, fading as they flew away. Sera snatched her shaking hands off the railing and pressed them tightly over her ears as she slid down to the deck floor, curling her knees up to her chest.

She started to rock back and forth, humming the song that made her blood turn to ice any time she heard it, the one that she could never listen to again since. But nothing she did blocked out the screaming voices echoing around her.

The loudness overcame her sense of awareness, dizziness threatening to overtake her, breath quickening as she fought for air, nausea rising into the base of her throat. Black spots emerged behind her eyelids as her limbs turned to liquid.

The voices came to a sudden halt—the abrupt cessation of sound was deafening. Sera could hear nothing, not the boat mechanics, the lapping water, or the wind whipping at the flags.

No sound.

"This is *your* gift, Sera," her mother's whispers echoed in unison. "Don't think of it as anything other than that."

Sera's eyes flew open, darting around. Nobody was there. She was alone. Sera looked out onto the water between the rails. Standing on the water below, her mother stared up at her. Her face was detailed, but her figure transparent, the ocean water visible through her.

"MOM!" Sera jumped up from the floor, reaching an arm out over the railing. But as she did, the figure of her mother faded away. "No. Not yet."

A sudden throbbing in her head had her backing away from the railing, stumbling into a lounge chair, her shallow breathing increasing as hyperventilation gave way to an all-familiar panic. She stilled herself, forcing deep breaths in and out, palms up, fingers touching, counting.

One. Two. Three. Four. Five. Five. Four. Three. Two. One.

Her labored breathing began to slow, the spots in her vision cleared, and the nausea diminished. The door was there, ready for her to go through.

The sound of everything around her faded back in.

Not daring to move yet, she started massaging away the pain at her temples with one hand, the other gripping the amethyst locket that hung at her neck.

She looked back out to the ocean. No one was there.

Obviously, she was more exhausted than she thought. Picking at her food and the after-effects of finals week probably didn't help, taking a greater toll on her than she realized. Had she fallen asleep and not noticed? Was it another awake-dream?

This was twice now, and so different from anything she remembered experiencing in childhood. It *couldn't* be the awake-dreams.

"I thought *I* would be the only one crazy enough to take a walk out here at this hour."

Sera startled, screaming out, her head snapping toward the deep, unexpected voice coming from a silhouette of a tall man standing beside her. He stepped out of the shadows toward Sera.

His exceptionally striking deep blue eyes looked at her with concern, a slightly embarrassed grin stretching across his friendly face as he stuffed both hands in his pockets.

"I'm sorry. I didn't mean to scare you. I didn't expect to find anyone out here. I guess I wasn't prepared to be social. I'm Adam. Adam Wallace," he said, pulling a hand from a pocket and extending it to her.

Still reeling from what just happened, she shook the man's hand, drawing away quickly, figuring it was the easiest way to get rid of the stranger.

"I wasn't exactly prepared to be social either." She hoped he understood the not-so-subtle hint for him to leave her alone.

Instead, he sat on the chair beside hers, still looking at her.

"No problem. Midnight walks aren't really meant for sharing," he said with a half-smile and then looked away.

If he knew she didn't want company and said he didn't want any, then why did he stay? She didn't know what to say to this stranger, and she definitely wasn't in the mood to be friendly. Too much had just happened, too many things she was trying to figure out.

Was she losing it? Going crazy? And why was this man still sitting there? Not knowing what to do, she sat silently, looking at the water.

By this point, Sera would usually be terrified sitting this close to a man she didn't know. At first she was uncomfortable, but never threatened.

Then she could feel him, the pain he was in, the grief he emitted. It was raw and familiar. Since she wasn't brave enough to leave the chair, she did what she often did, remained still and silent. After a while, she even felt at ease next to this man, this stranger, though she had no idea why.

CHAPTER EIGHTEEN

Adam Wallace

ATLANTIC OCEAN

Adam had gone out to the deck to be alone, another lonely walk in the middle of the night to drown himself in self-pity.

Much of the past year he'd spent alone, usually in his room, in his bed, the curtains drawn and the door closed, unable to meet the day with much energy or desire.

But he'd been doing better. He made sure to prioritize spending more time with the people he still had in his life, those who mattered most. Still, he needed moments of absolute solitude to keep his frail sanity from breaking away completely.

His daughter had fallen asleep hours before, and his mother-in-law was now softly snoring in her room in their shared cabin suite. The walls were closing in on him, suffocating him. He had to get out, slip away into a blanket of isolation so that he could get lost in his dark thoughts.

But then he saw the girl backing away from the railing, falling into one of the lounge chairs, looking as though she was about to collapse. He couldn't just turn and go the other way in case she needed some help.

Yes, he could. Easily. It wasn't his business, and he didn't have the energy to make it so. He had enough problems of his own.

He started to turn on his heel to walk the other way. But the fear on her face was chilling. So, he'd gone over to her. Just for a minute. Just to make sure she was okay.

And now she was looking at him as if he had barged in on her.

Instead of leaving, he found himself sitting down next to her, fidgeting with his wedding ring as he did when he was anxious.

The silence lingering between them should have been awkward, but it wasn't. Even more strange was that the longer he sat next to this young woman, her sadness seeped into him, and somehow, he knew she was as lost as he was.

"I have just lost my wife," he said, his voice dropping deep, soft, in memory. "I guess *just* isn't exactly accurate. *Why* am I telling you this?" he scoffed at himself, shaking his head, something compelling him to continue, to talk to this girl he didn't know. "I haven't spoken to anyone about it. Unfortunately for my mother-in-law, who constantly insists that I see someone professionally. I did, once. But I guess you're expected to pour your wounded heart out to the therapist. They don't like it much when you sit there for an hour, not saying a word," he shrugged as he spoke, eyes transfixed at the black ocean. "I don't even know your name. Or maybe it's *because* I don't," he scoffed at himself in disbelief.

"She died a year ago this week," he continued, barely above a whisper. "Just an accident. A true, honest-to-god accident. She was driving home on the same road that she always did. It's a windy road, and it had been raining all day, so the roads were a little flooded..."

Grief was a bitch. It had been a year, and still, he felt the claws of it wrap around him, digging into him as if his wife had died yesterday. He paused for a long moment. This girl he didn't know kept silent beside him, her gaze steady on the water. He was quiet long enough that she looked up at him.

"She wasn't going too fast. No one was in front of her, and the person behind her was a distance back and barely made out what had happened. There was no evidence of any kind of animal on the road, no sudden swerving, nothing was wrong with the car. Nothing. She just lost control and went down the side of the hill," his voice wavered, sadness thickening it.

"Ava, our daughter, was supposed to be in the car with her. My wife picked her up from daycare every day. That was the deal. I'd drop her off in the morning, and she'd pick her up in the evenings. Alex hardly ever had to work late. I, however, sometimes pull all-nighters depending on the project or deadline. That night was the first time that my wife ever had to work late. So, I picked Ava up. We were at home waiting for Mom, but she never came home."

He felt the heat of tears welling in his eyes. He let them come. It didn't bother him anymore to be seen crying. There had been weeks when the tears wouldn't stop. Another thing he was working on, not letting the sadness cripple him to non-existence. "Her name was Alexandria. Alex."

The young woman's voice shook a little before she cleared her throat and asked, "How... old is your daughter?"

"She just turned two," he answered, smiling through his tears.

"So young..." she whispered. But then she gave him a hint of a smile. "Adam, Alex, and Ava? That's sweet."

"We thought so." Adam smiled, then went quiet.

"*I'm sorry* sounds weightless, doesn't it?" she said, as though she knew all too well how deep that kind of hurt ran. "Why did you tell me this? You don't even know me." She looked up at him with that brokenness he recognized in himself.

"Honestly, I have no idea. I don't do *this*. What's really odd is that the minute I sat down, I felt that you were like me. That particular type of sadness not many others understand." Adam held her gaze until she looked away from him.

Silence enveloped them, long minutes stretching out before she spoke again.

"My mother died when I was young, too. I was six," the words floated out in the air. "*Died* isn't exactly accurate, either. She was murdered, and so was my father. I haven't really spoken to anyone about it either. Little bits here and there to Erinne, my honorary aunt, the woman who raised me after my parents were killed, and my shrink, of course. My aunt actually married my shrink. Dr. John," she said with a chuckle, then her face went dark again.

"Not that it matters. The media did a thorough job telling everyone. And it's only going to get worse. They're doing a Docu-Series about the whole thing. Some big fifteenth anniversary special. Just when I thought I was done with it, the recognition, the pity. I've never told anyone everything that happened, not even Erinne or John. I've never been able to bring myself to relive it all. I've spent my life trying to forget. But it has its way of haunting me." Her eyes darted back to the railing. "Maybe I should just tell you. Like, get it out, just this once. Maybe if I tell *you*, it won't hurt as badly when the media tells the world." Her breath caught for an instant, going quiet again.

"Take all the time you need. I don't have anywhere to be." This young woman, so scared her body was visibly shaking, ebbed his own emotional turmoil. He'd needed a moment to purge his demons, the weight of that sadness and guilt. Though he wasn't miraculously better, he did feel like he'd made a positive step in the right direction. She had been patient enough—or maybe just too scared to leave—to let him have that moment. The least he could do was the same for her. He reached over and put his large hand over her shaking ones.

She startled at the touch, cringing away, drawing her hand back. But then she relaxed and left her hand under his. She took a deep breath and began to speak so softly that Adam had to lean in closer to hear her.

"His name was Jeffery Mason. He was a stalker, a rapist of the worst kind, brutal and sadistic. I don't think he meant to kill my mother when he had. He just... broke her," she paused, glancing up at him. She was searching him, watching his expression like a frightened bird, looking for any reason to flit away.

Adam made sure his face remained open and friendly. He was shocked at what she told him, the evil in this world always shocked him. But he wouldn't risk making this moment harder for her. Instead, he gave a slight nod, an invitation to continue, then looked back at the water again.

"From the moment that family found me in those woods, everyone started asking questions. Paramedics, police, doctors. So many questions. None that I could or wanted to answer. I couldn't find my voice anymore. It left me along with my tears. Everything dried up inside me and became this numbness that took up residence, a loneliness that at times was so deep it was hard to breathe, let alone speak. When people you love die, it feels like you should have died too. You don't want anyone to know that you survived. Grief can break you that way. My voice eventually found me, but I swore I'd never use it to speak of that night again. After so many years, I did forget. I remember pieces, mostly in night terrors. Jeffrey Mason became less of a monster figure and more human as I got older. He'd had a wife, kids—a *family*. What kind of person can completely switch between those two lives? I think maybe that's what's been scaring the hell out of me the most. You never know who people really are. He took everything from me, my father, my mother, my innocence. He destroyed me and broke me in a way that I'm not sure I can ever repair. Not just my body, but my heart," her words fell away.

"I've been letting him win."

The dramatic switch in her tone made Adam look back at her. Her face had changed, her brow furrowed, angry.

"I never let anyone get close to me. No friends, not even acquaintances. I've never let myself do anything that might be risky. No parties, no bars, nothing...fun. I've been so afraid that something bad will happen that I've stopped doing much of anything at all. I'm scared of *everything*, of loving, of living, of being hurt, scared of doing what *I* want. Coming on this trip alone is the bravest thing I have ever done, and I had to be forced into it. Pretty pathetic, right? I've been letting him win this whole time by not *living*. That's what I've been doing. I've been wasting minutes, hours, days that I can never get back. I've been wasting the life my mother sacrificed her own for. What a disappointment I must be to her."

Silence hung in the air.

This girl—well, more woman than girl—had seen the darkest part of humanity and was still fighting. Though she'd claimed to be scared, sitting there with him, so determined to get the venom out of her, was nothing short of courageous. Adam was in awe of her.

"From my perspective, you're already much braver than you think. You're out here crossing the Atlantic all on your own, and it sounds like you've made a huge leap just by speaking to me. I have never witnessed as much strength as I see in you. And let me assure you, as a parent, I can promise that your mother would not be disappointed in you." Adam squeezed her hand before he let it go.

"I can see that you're on the brink of a life-changing epiphany here, so before I leave you to your soul-searching, I have to say, your story is much better than the version that's going around the ship," Adam awkwardly laughed.

She stared at him with a look fixed somewhere between furious and amused. "I'm sorry?"

"You haven't heard? *Ah*, well, you see, this ship has two mysterious people. I am one of them, and you," he patted her hand as he had done before, "are the other. The story about me is that I am a dashing widower with diva-like qualities, which isn't too far of a stretch."

Adam had always had a problem with displaced humor, such as when it was or wasn't appropriate. But he was already in deep, so he continued.

"And you—the juice about you is that you have recently become filthy rich by some interesting fashion, a tech geek perhaps, a stock inheritance, or a lottery winner. However it came to be, you are now one of the most mystifying creatures to have ever stepped onto this ship," he emphasized with dramatic exaggeration. And then, she laughed. A rich sound.

"That can't be true."

"Sure it is. Gossip runs rampant on these things."

"Where would you ever hear anything like that?"

"It's everywhere." He widened his arms. "The cooks are saying it, the cabin attendants, everyone. Oh, I almost forgot." He leaned closer to her as if he was about to reveal highly confidential information. "*You* are also a close personal friend of the royal family, hence this trip." He grinned and squeezed her shoulder, giving her a reassuring nod as he rose from his chair.

"You have a beautiful smile and are most courageous to use it again. I wouldn't worry so much about this documentary. Your story, your courage and strength, will be an inspiration to so many people." He turned to walk away before she spoke.

"My name is Sera. Sera Delaney."

Adam looked back and gave her another brilliant smile. "It was nice to have met you, Sera. I've appreciated the quality of the time that we've spent together. I believe I have found a new confidant in you and a much-needed friend." He walked away, leaving her to stare at him.

CHAPTER NINETEEN

Ella

STANFORD

College was probably the best time of Ella's life, except for Erinne being thousands of miles away, which was the worst. Other than that, Ella was having fun.

She was surrounded by like-minded people in her classes and had more friends (except her best friend) than she ever thought possible. Best of all, she was free from her parent's disapproving stare.

Here, the boys were men, they were beautiful, and she had her pick of them. She tried each of them on, like new sweaters, just to see how they fit.

Parties were abundant, not that Ella went too crazy at them. She loved the music, the dancing, the laughing. Ruby, one of her roommates, had talked her into going to a homecoming baseball game and then to the celebratory after-party.

Ruby begged to go, stating that the whole team would be there, specifically the center-fielder Ruby had been crushing on the whole semester. So Ella went. Who was she to stop a budding love story?

Most of the team and half of the school were there celebrating their victory by the time they arrived. The music was loud, thumping through her body. Strobe lights flashed throughout the house, and already, some were stumbling about.

Ella grabbed a couple of drinks for her and Ruby, then found a few mutual friends. As they were all talking, the skin on Ella's arms dimpled, and the little hairs on the back of her neck stood. The urge to look behind her toward the back door overwhelmed her. The moment she did, the most beautiful man she'd ever seen stepped through. He was greeted by people as he walked in, and then he looked up, straight into Ella's eyes.

Shivers vibrated through her. Her heart rate kicked up a couple of notches, heat simmering along her skin, something she'd never experienced before.

"Oh, this is gonna be good," she said out loud.

Ruby looked up and followed Ella's gaze. "Chris Owens, shortstop. Careful, Ella. He's got a reputation."

"That makes it even better." Ella never looked away from him. Neither did he. Then he gave her a dazzling smile, half sweet, half sly. She could sense him, the way his lips would taste, how those capable hands would feel on her.

"Hey," his hazel eyes gleamed as he reached his hand out to her.

"Hello." When Ella shook his hand, he didn't let go. Instead, he led her out to the dance floor, pulled her close, and began to sway.

The boy could move, his hips expertly sweeping side to side. Never once did either of them break the eye contact.

She lost track of how many songs they danced to, body to body. Fast-paced, slow-paced, it didn't matter. Neither of them wanted to lose touch with the other. No words were needed. It was their bodies that spoke.

She shouldn't want him this much, this soon. But she did. And who was she to stop a budding love story?

"Let's go somewhere," Ella breathed in his ear.

"I'll follow you anywhere."

Ella laughed. "You don't even know my name."

"You don't know mine, either."

"Actually, I do. You're Chris, the shortstop."

Chris placed his hand over his heart. "I'm honored that you know who I am."

"My roommate told me as you walked over."

"Damn. Now I'm a little crushed. I hoped maybe you were a fan."

"I am now."

"It's a start. Where are we going, Miss...?"

"Ella."

"Never has there been a more beautiful name spoken."

Ella rolled her eyes. "No need to lay it on thick now. I already said I was a fan. Give me a second. I need to let my roommate know."

Chris held Ella's hand as they walked to her parked car down at the far end of the street. The glow of the few streetlamps accentuated the sandy color of his hair and the muscles that rippled underneath his fitted T-shirt. By the time they reached the car, Ella was breathless. Not from the distance but because of the need to put her hands on him. Just walking close to him teased every nerve throughout her entire body.

Unable to wait a moment longer, she turned to him, grabbed him by that wonderful shirt, and pulled his lips to hers, devouring his mouth. His hands wrapped up in her hair as he took the kiss deep. She let her hands explore his body as he did with hers. The ache for him was so intense she had a mind to push him into her backseat and take him then and there.

"I'm all for this, more than anything. But we're kind of still in the middle of the street here," Chris said, out of breath.

"I'm about to have you take me right here on the trunk of my car."

"Damn, girl. You're killing me." He took her mouth again, picking her up easily, wrapping her legs around his waist, carrying her over until she was backed onto the trunk.

She left her long legs wrapped around him, pulling his body into hers. Still, it wasn't close enough.

"Hold on. Hold on." Chris broke the kiss. "I need a breath."

Ella smiled at him. "What's the matter, can't keep up?"

"Beautiful Ella. I can keep up, I promise you. But I do have standards to keep. I like to woo, at least a little bit."

"You want to stop right *now* to woo me?" She couldn't help but laugh.

"Oh, I really don't want to stop. But I want you to respect me in the morning." That sly, sweet, dazzling smile was back, lighting up his entire face. "I do have more to offer than just hot, incredible sex."

"You can prove that after. Start wooing me in the morning. Right now, I need that hot, incredible sex." Ella pulled him back in. If they waited one more minute, her body might incinerate.

He didn't protest again.

Ella was always up for anything. Spontaneity was what she loved so much about life. Living moment to moment, seizing whatever came her way, living like nothing lasts because, for her, it wouldn't. Even so, this wasn't her usual way.

But the hunger for this man was like nothing and no one before. The only way to burn it out of her was to take him as soon as she could, wherever they were. Which happened to be on the back of her car at the end of a dark street.

It might have been the first time Chris and Ella made love, but it wasn't even close to the last. The moment they joined together, Ella knew she'd never again be with anyone else.

CHAPTER TWENTY

Sera

ATLANTIC OCEAN

Sera went out for breakfast, fully aware that it was the first time she had come out of her cabin during daylight hours. Though she felt the familiar nerves fray and tangle, it was tolerable. She assured herself that it was still early enough in the morning that the dining room should be mostly vacant, she'd basically be by herself.

For the first time since she could remember, she was almost hopeful. Erinne would often tell her that all she needed was a little curiosity about her future and that curiosity would eventually blossom into hope. And today, a glimmer of curiosity started to glow.

Though confusion still had its claws in her as well. The events before her confessional on the deck still clouded her mind. She *hadn't* fallen asleep on the lounge chair. She was sure of it. But then, what was the voice, the words that were said? What *gift*?

There was no way any of it was even real. It had to have been an awake-dream, like when she was little. Though, that didn't feel right either.

But *why* was it happening again? Why *now*? She'd made sure her life was calm, safe, boring even. She had no idea exactly what "it" was. A memory, a warning maybe. Definitely something familiar and just out of reach.

When she got home to Lantern Light, not only did she have so much to ask Erinne and John, but she also wanted to reread her mother's letters. Maybe there was something said in one of them that she needed to remember.

If it had really happened.

"Good morning. May I join you?"

A yelp escaped Sera as the jolt of surprise shot through her.

"Sorry. I keep doing that to you, don't I? I'll have to find a way to warn you when I approach. Maybe put bells on my shoes?" Adam grinned at her.

"No need to be sorry. I've always been a jumpy person. Comes with the territory," she said, smiling self-consciously as she motioned for him to sit. There would be a time when everything wouldn't scare her so much. *Wouldn't there?*

When Adam slid into the chair across from Sera, she noticed the servers staring over at them. She lowered her voice so that only Adam could hear as she nodded over his shoulder. "We're being watched."

Adam shrugged. "I'm sure this will be new delicious ammo for the gossip mill."

"No. You made that whole thing up. *Didn't* you?" Sera asked, laughing. There was something about his easy manner that Sera found comforting. His laid-back posture gave her the impression of a confident, easy-going guy with a sort of brotherly personality, one that evoked trust and safety. He reminded her a lot of how she remembered who her dad had been in life.

The night before, he had known exactly what she had needed. Maybe because it was the same thing that he needed as well. He'd called her a much-needed friend. Sera felt the same about him. Adam had expected nothing from her. He asked no questions, hadn't even asked what her name was. By doing so, Sera felt something she hadn't in a long time, maybe ever. A surprising inkling of trust.

"You never know." After the server brought their drinks, Adam leaned forward. "How are you this morning?" he asked in a gentle tone.

Sera searched his face for further meaning. "I'm doing fine, and you?" She couldn't tell if he was setting up for another sarcastic joke or if he genuinely wanted to know how she was.

"Just dandy. I feel much better after shelving it all out on you last night. I'm truly glad I ran into you. I saw you standing out there at the rail, looking so frightened. Then you sat down so quickly. I thought you might've been sick or about to pass out. The gentleman in me had to rescue the damsel in distress," he said, taking a sip of his water.

"How much did you see?" her words clipped out as anxiety crept in. Adam had seen her episode. Maybe he even saw something that would help her figure out what happened. Or maybe she looked like a raving lunatic.

"Hey, look, I'm sorry. I wasn't standing back, like, *watching* you or anything. I was already heading that way." A hint of embarrassment passed over his face.

Sera shook her head, annoyed with herself. "I didn't mean to imply anything. Wrong tone. Let me try again. Did you—I don't know—*see* anything out of the ordinary? Strange?" When he just looked at her, uncertainty heated her face. "Never mind, I'm sorry. I don't seem to know what's going on anymore or what's even real." The flush spread from her face to her neck. She tried to hide it by looking down at her juice.

"No need to get shy on me now. I understand. You have every reason to be cautious with your trust." He put his hand over hers. "The only strange thing I saw was the shade of white you turned when it looked like you were going down for the count."

"So, I *was* awake. I couldn't have imagined it," Sera whispered.

"You want to tell me what you think you imagined?" He kept his hand on hers after she only shook her head.

Their conversation lightened throughout breakfast and continued as they took their coffees to the deck together. He told her some of his fond memories of his wife, and she told him funny stories about her parents, those she could remember and some that Erinne had told her.

After more than an hour of talking, a tiny girl—not much more than a baby—appeared behind Adam. Her brown ringlets matched Adam's chestnut shade, as did her deep blue eyes. Sera watched her toddle up to him and place her small, chubby hands over his eyes, already giggling.

"Whose guess?" The little girl's lisp and giggles were the sounds of pure joy.

"Oh my, I wonder who it could be."

Adam took the girl's hands from his eyes, kissing them front and back. He turned and grabbed her, covering her neck with loud kisses. She squealed as she tried to wiggle free.

Sera couldn't help but laugh with them. Even though this child had suffered such a tragic loss, she had a father who would always be there for her. It was a privilege to witness their father-daughter exchange.

"This little monster is my Ava," he proudly introduced his daughter as she climbed onto his lap. Ava stared up at her father with adoring eyes.

"She's beautiful. She looks so much like you." Sera reached over to touch the girl's cheek. Ava gave a delighted squeal and threw her arms out to Sera.

"Whoa. How lucky you are, Sera. Ava is usually a bit shy with people she doesn't know," he said, laughing as his daughter reached for Sera.

"Well, I can't disappoint her then." She took Ava from Adam. The two girls stared at each other, both smiling. "You are just stunning," she said.

Ava giggled. "Stunning!" she repeated as she held one arm in Sera's face to show off a plastic beaded bracelet dangling from her tiny wrist.

"Wow. Yes, so is your bracelet." Sera laughed as Ava comfortably snuggled into her lap. Ava's attention averted to the bracelet, turning her wrist back and forth to make it sparkle in the sun. "Maybe it's because she feels that we have something in common," Sera said, smiling up at Adam. With the warmth of Ava in her arms, Sera felt her whole body relax.

"Do you have any other family besides your aunt in Ireland? I'm one of the fortunate ones. I have Ava. Who is it that you have? Grandparents? Extended family?" Adam leaned back in the lounge chair.

"No. Well, yes, I have grandparents—somewhere. They all have their own lives that never included us. Both my mom and dad were only children. But I have plenty of family in Erinne's family. They *are* my family. They are loud and feisty and very Irish. I grew up in Ireland with all of them, from age six until I went back to San Francisco for college. So, I have my aunt Erinne and her husband John. I also have two uncles, Brian and Erick, actually three. Erick is married to a man named Rich. They live in London. Another aunt, Shelly, Brian's wife, and their two boys. Then there are my grandparents, Nan—Annabelle, and Pops—Brian Senior," she explained and couldn't help but smile as she talked about her adopted family. Her love for them and theirs for her was her one constant in this life.

"My mom came from a well-to-do family, and so did my dad. They disapproved of, well, me, I guess. My parents met at Stanford. My mom, the beautiful medical student, and my dad, the gorgeous baseball jock. They had me a year later. The one thing I'll always remember is how much my dad loved my mom. He proposed to her *all* of the time. It took him six years to convince her to say yes." It was her favorite story, her parent's love story. She'd asked Erinne to tell it so many times through the years.

"My mom went to Ireland to stay with Aunt Erinne and her family when she found out she was pregnant with me. When my dad realized why she left, he immediately went after her. We lived there until I was about a year old. Mom decided she needed to go back to school to become the fabulous doctor she was meant to be," Sera said, nuzzling her cheek in Ava's hair. "My mom was this force of nature. If she wanted something, she found a way to do it. She put herself through college and then medical school. She was amazing."

"So, you've inherited her courage," Adam smiled. "Had she, or you, ever tried to contact your grandparents?"

"Mom tried to talk to her parents after I was born, but they kept true to their word and treated her like a stranger. They are mean people."

"*Means people,*" Ava mimicked, making Sera laugh, but also reminded her to be careful with her words.

Adam shook his head in disbelief. "Do they know about her death?"

"They saw the story on the news. They sent flowers, *'Our condolences.'* That was it."

"What jerks," Adam scoffed.

"Wat irks!" Ava exaggerated her father's shaking head, making the three of them laugh.

As the laughing subsided, Sera realized Ava had wandered up to them alone. Surely, Adam never left Ava alone, and she most likely didn't wander out on the deck alone, or Sera hoped she hadn't. However, he hadn't yet mentioned anyone else.

"You're not on this ship alone, right? I mean, who is with Ava when you go on your walks...or to breakfast?"

"We are traveling with my mother-in-law, Victoria. I saw her earlier, standing off in the distance. She gave me a wonderfully disapproving look before she walked away. Should be lots of fun seeing what I did now. It was her idea to go on this trip. Her family has a home in London, and she wanted to spend Alex's anniversary there. I thought it would be a good opportunity to spend some quality time with Ava before going back to work and life. And no, I would never leave my daughter unsupervised." He nudged Sera's leg with his knee as he chuckled. "Smooth way of asking."

"I was just...curious. She didn't stay? Maybe she left after she saw that Ava was safe with you?" Judging Adam's reaction, that was out of the question. "Or not."

"Hmm, well, I'll have to ask her about it later. So, Miss Ava, have you replaced me?" He stood, putting his hands on his hips.

Ava giggled and reached up for him. He took his daughter, kissed her forehead. "I should get back to the room and try to find said mother-in-law. Thanks for another comforting conversation."

"Comforting?" Every time she was in Adam's company, she was entertained by him, his comments so unexpected, if not amusing.

"Yes. Good stories are good memories. Every time we talk, I feel comforted. Maybe it's because *we* also have something in common." With that, he turned and walked away.

"Yes. Maybe we do," Sera sighed quietly.

Adam

ATLANTIC OCEAN

"Victoria?" Adam's voice echoed in the sitting room, followed by Ava's happy squeals and fast feet running into the room.

"Adam." Victoria walked past him to the bar cart and poured herself a brandy, not bothering to look at him.

"Gee, Victoria, is something bothering you?" he asked sarcastically as he watched her. Her usual refined stature was awry, tousled even. "What is it?" He took a few steps closer to her. She remained silent at the minibar, keeping her back to him.

"How could you?" she spat, anger shaking her voice. "It's barely been a year, and you're already parading around, looking to replace my daughter? Don't you have any decency?"

Adam felt a knot form in his stomach. When she finally turned, Adam saw her eyes were red, swollen, and tearing over.

"How could you *do* that to her?" she hissed.

Ava jumped up on the couch in the sitting room. "Daddy, play." She threw her arms out, waiting for him to pick her up.

"In a minute, sweetie. Why don't we go into the bedroom, and you can color a picture for Grandma?"

After Adam occupied Ava in the other room, he returned to find Victoria sitting on a chair, holding her face in her hands.

"Victoria..."

"What gives you the right? What kind of *man* are you?"

"Just hold on one minute. You are accusing me of something dangerously false. Will you stop insulting me and use your words like a grown-up?" Adam tried to keep his voice low but felt his composure diminishing.

He was usually an incredibly patient man. He'd learned that patience sprinkled with a bit of charm mostly got him what he wanted—having a legacy to run practically from childhood engraved that into him. The patience got him through, and the charm convinced others to trust him, maybe even like him.

However, patience in business was far easier than when it came to his mother-in-law.

Victoria had never been an easy person to get along with. She had been cold, even rude at times. Even after he married Alex, she'd hardly spoken to him. Not until Ava was born.

However, it was Victoria who never gave him anything but support throughout his disappearance in grief, though she, too, was grieving the loss of her own daughter.

After Alex died, it was Victoria who'd been the one taking care of Ava while Adam spiraled, when he became a ghost of a man, lost weight, lost touch with reality, when he didn't speak to anyone, and when the agony of absolute grief kept him in bed for days at a time.

He hadn't cared to shower, food had no appeal, raw anguish wracked him day and night. When Alex died, he wanted to die as well. He wanted to join the woman he had vowed himself to, the mother of his child, the woman he promised to love until death—which turned out to be way too short a time.

It was only when Ava crawled into bed with him, crying and scared, asking him for Mama, that he realized it was time to get up, get dressed, and keep living, if only for his daughter. She'd already lost her mother; she wouldn't lose her father as well.

"Are you going to tell me what is going on, or are you going to sit there and pout?" Adam toned his voice down to his usual playful manner. He sat on a chair across from her, fingering his wedding ring, waiting for a response.

"Last night, I went to check on Ava. Your bed was empty." Victoria finally faced him. "I saw you out there with *that girl* and again this morning. It's too soon. I will not allow you to taint my daughter's memory." When she rose from the chair, Adam caught her arm before she could walk away from him.

"Please. Sit down," he kept his voice tender. She sat hesitantly. It hurt more than angered him that she would think this of him. "Not that I have to explain myself to you, but I will. Last night, I couldn't sleep, as usual. I went for a walk, as I have done many times before. I saw this young woman standing at the railing, looking terrified and on the verge of passing out. I went over to see if she needed help. After I made sure she was alright, we got to talking for a little while, and she ended up trusting me with her story. She told me that, like Ava, she'd lost her mother when she was young in this horrible, brutal way. Both of her parents, actually. They were everything to her. I know a thing or two about that. *That girl*'s name is Sera Delaney."

Victoria looked down at the floor.

"I've never met her before last night. And this morning, I saw her sitting alone and just wanted to make sure she was okay. She had looked so scared," Adam repeated, remembering how Sera's face froze as she looked out at the water. "When Ava came out, she just took to her so openly. It was sweet. I think they both needed a little affection."

"Sera Delaney...*Delaney?* Why does that name sound familiar? Was her mother *murdered?*" Victoria's brows knit together.

"Yes, years ago, when she was just a child."

"I remember seeing that on the news. It's hard to forget such a terrible story. Her mother was raped by that maniac, and so was the little girl. He murdered both of her parents right in front of her. That poor dear," she whispered. "I feel like a fool." She hugged her shoulders, looking away from Adam.

"With the amount of sadness we've all been through, showing a little compassion just seems to be the right thing to do." Adam hugged his mother-in-law, a rarity in their relationship.

"Grandma, come see," Ava called from the other room.

Victoria awkwardly patted Adam's back before breaking the embrace. "Of course it is. Maybe you could introduce us if we should meet with her again."

"Sure." Adam grinned as he watched Victoria shuffle off. His daughter had impeccable timing.

CHAPTER TWENTY-TWO

Erinne

IRELAND

Erinne dove for the phone on the other side of the front desk, knocking over her textbook along with her ferociously scribbled notes. "Lantern Light Inn."

"I'm in love!"

"Again? With Mr. Frat Boy?" Erinne stretched the phone cord to reach the textbook and notepad that now lay upended on the floor.

"No. Not him, silly. He's still wonderful and all, but I wasn't the one for him," Ella's voice, light and happy as always, came through exceptionally clear, though they were thousands of miles apart.

"Okay. Makes sense. Though you say you're not the one for any of them."

"I'm not going to be around for too long, so I don't want to break these poor, beautiful boy's hearts."

"Ella, please, you're not going to die young. It breaks *my* heart every single time you say that."

"Which is why I'd never let you marry me, either. But it's too late. I already love you totally and completely. You're my soulmate, my soul sister."

"Yeah. Yeah. Such a sweet talker. So, who is the new beautiful boy?"

"He is, indeed, beautiful. But funny, like, really funny. My face hurts from smiling and laughing so much when I spend time with him. And he has such a lust for life, such a fun sense of adventure. He comes up with these crazy, spontaneous escapades. He's amazing. If anyone would be *the one*, it would have been him. He is... special."

"Does Mr. Special have a name?"

"Chris. His name is Chris," Ella sighed dreamily. "You have to meet him the next time you come out to visit. Hell, I should just surprise him for once with an adventure of my own and take him to Ireland."

Erinne could hear the smile in Ella's voice as she spoke about this guy. Ella sounded totally in love. Again. Who knows, maybe something *was* different this time.

"Speaking of visiting, I'm throwing in some design courses in addition to my business classes this semester. I don't think I'll be able to come out this winter."

"Boo. But I am so excited you're doing it. Erinne, your overhaul of Lantern Light will be more than amazing. It will change everything."

"I haven't even finished classes yet. Don't get too ahead of me. You know I don't deal with pressure very well."

"Well, it will. But okay. And speaking of class, I gotta run. I love you, E."

"Love you more, E2."

CHAPTER TWENTY-THREE

Sera

ATLANTIC OCEAN

Sera..." A whisper touched the air.

Still in a deep sleep, Sera began to ease through the layers of consciousness.

"Sera..."

Almost awake, she shifted her head, her crimson hair fanning out over the pillow.

"Hmm?" The last bits of sleep rolled away as she opened her eyes, squinting as her sight adjusted to the early rays of morning light illuminating the room through gaps in the drapes. Yawning, she glanced at the bedside clock. Six-fifteen.

"Ugh." Rubbing her eyes, she turned on her other side to try and fall back asleep.

"Sera."

Her eyes flew open, darting around the room as she sat up. There was nothing. *I fell back asleep. How weird.*

She scooted back down beneath the covers as the tingling of fright in her feet eased away.

"Sera."

Sera bolted straight up in her bed, blood rushing. "Who's there, damn it!"

No one was in the bedroom. She jumped up and ran into the sitting room. The door was still locked, and no one else was there either.

That's it, I'm going crazy.

She sank into the couch, squeezing her eyes shut. The same sudden falling of silence surrounded her as it had the night before.

"Open your eyes, Sera."

The heat of breath tickled her ear. The briefest touch, a warm caress, ran down the side of her cheek.

"Mom?" Slowly, Sera opened her eyes.

"Sera, it won't stop without you."

She wanted to reach out, touch her mother, hold her, and tell her how much she missed her.

But it wasn't real. *She* wasn't real. She couldn't be. Sera was only dreaming—a really weird awake-dream—just like when she was little. Calm fell over her. She was no longer afraid, only disbelieving. She started to count her fingertips again, as she had learned to do as a child.

One. Two. Three. Four. Five.

"I don't have much time. I don't think I'll be able to come again."

Five. Four. Three. Two. One.

Sera inhaled deeply and opened her eyes. Her mother was still there, smiling sweetly at her.

"Is it really you?" Sera whispered as she reached out.

"You are stronger than you think. Only you will be able to finish this."

"Mom, how is this poss..."

"They're getting closer now. I can't stop it. Please, Sera, believe in yourself. No one else will understand. No one else will know." Ella's face froze, rigid with fear, as she looked behind Sera toward some distant place. Sera looked behind her but saw nothing.

"Know what? I don't understand. What does that even mean?" Sera looked behind her again—still nothing.

"I love you, Baby Girl, to the moon and back and all around the sun and stars."

Sera whipped her head back, but her mother was already gone.

"Wait. Mom?" Sera's voice shook as she quickly looked around the room.

A scream tore through the pause of sound, bringing it crashing back all at once.

Sera jumped straight up on the couch, cold sweat dripping down the side of her face.

It took several deep breaths to slow her pounding heart before she trusted herself to stand. She stood in the tiny shower, letting the streams of extra hot water ease her tight muscles.

She'd never seen her mother or talked to her. She had never spoken to anyone, nor had she ever been herself while in the awake-dreams. There was no denying it, the awake-dreams were back and so different from before.

On the main deck, Sera slowed as the gathering crowd came into view ahead of her. Earlier, she'd thought it would be a good idea to get out of her cabin more, maybe even meet a few people. The ship held a variety of activities that seemed promising. It would be an easy way to turn over that new leaf, start getting herself out there more often, start living a little. Maybe it would also help take her mind off of the strange dreams.

But now she wasn't so sure she was ready for this much socializing all at once. She turned away from the group and started back toward the stairs when Adam caught up with her.

"Boy, am I happy to see you. I was thinking to myself that this was a bad idea. Too many happy-pappy vacationing people. At least now I have a dark and dreary partner to sulk with." Adam hooked her arm in his own and walked them toward the mostly silvered-haired, chatting bunch.

"Why don't we just escape before we're sucked in and never let out?" Sera suggested, exaggerating a smile.

"As tempting as that seems, you and I need some socialization. It's therapy, of sorts, supposed to help the grieving process and all that stuff. You should know that, you have a shrink for a stepdad...uncle? Besides, Ava suckered me into bringing her out here. I guess she and Victoria did something like this yesterday, and now she's addicted to anyone over the age of seventy."

As they joined the crowd, Sera saw a tall woman holding the child she had met the day before. The woman saw her, too, and gave Sera a long, stern look.

"Really, Adam. I don't think I'm up to this. Besides, you already have a partner who doesn't look too happy that you found me."

"Don't mind her. That's just her face. Apparently, it really can get stuck that way." He winked at her.

His smile flowed into a void she didn't realize she had. She hadn't known how much she needed a friend. A real friend, not just an acquaintance but someone she could talk to, someone who listened and understood without judgment or pity.

Sera laughed. "What a thing to say about your own mother."

"I dare correct you. She is my mother-in-law. Don't forget the *in-law*. It's vital to my mental well-being." Instead of just taking her arm again, he offered it to her this time, and she accepted willingly to go with him.

"Victoria, meet my new confidant, Sera. Sera, my mother-*in-law*," Adam emphasized.

The woman's stern look softened slightly. She put her hand on Sera's shoulder and spoke sincerely, "I am very sorry for your loss."

The unexpected words lumped a wave of emotion in Sera's throat. She placed her hand over Victoria's.

"Thank you. And I'm so sorry for yours as well."

Victoria nodded, tears welling in her eyes. She looked away quickly, taking her hand from Sera's shoulder, embracing Ava again.

"Sariee!" Ava squealed.

Such a wonderful sound.

Sera beamed back at her as she touched her cheek the way she had the day before, sending Ava into a fit of giggles.

The day was filled with unexpected entertainment. They had lost their other partner not long after Sera joined them. Between deck games and walks around the ship, Sera was mesmerized by Ava. How her little mind worked, how she had her own explanations for things in her broken language, and when she didn't, she listened intently as Sera explained something to her.

A deep sadness set in for Ava's lost mother as Sera watched Ava observing something microscopic on the deck floor. The mother who would never again see how the sun made Ava's hair look blonde instead of chestnut, who wouldn't see her grow into a young woman or meet her first boyfriend, who wouldn't be able to comfort her through her first heartbreak or watch her little girl get married.

"You've been quiet for a while. What's going on in there?" Adam gently nudged her with his shoulder.

"Oh, you know, this and that," she said, smiling timidly, then changed the subject. "Hey, I just realized I don't have the dish on you."

"Dish...? Like, how the birds and the bees created me? Or how I grew into such an interesting and fantastic man?" When Sera laughed and nodded, Adam shrugged.

"Me? Well, nothing too dramatic or anything. I'm a city boy, born and raised in New York. My father's, father's, father—and all that—built what turned out to be a prosperous architectural firm from the ground up. My parents worked together. They married and, several years later, thought it was time to do their due diligence and produce an heir to their kingdom. I was groomed to take over the family legacy since I could talk, yada, yada. When I was seventeen, my mother was diagnosed with cancer and died a couple of years later. My father continued on with business as usual as if he had lost a business partner instead of a wife. I first felt real, true love when I met Alex," Adam paused to smile. "The month before Ava was born, my father had a stroke. It was time to put all the grooming to work. Now, here I am, running one of New York's oldest and most successful architectural firms, a widower and single father to a two-year-old at the ripe old age of twenty-eight."

"I'm so sorry. You've had so much loss in your life. I feel horrible going on about myself when you've experienced so much."

"No, don't even think of it that way. No one should have to go through what you or I have. It's just life being shitty, I guess. My father is still alive, by the way.

He is living it up at a schmoozy assisted living place upstate, which he quite enjoys. He is the one who had to step in and force me into a mandatory leave of absence. A much-needed intervention, it turns out. Being on leave and not having work to drown myself in has forced me to face all of this," he said, gesturing to himself, "take this trip, find my way back to my daughter. I was a mess, I admit. Still have my moments." Adam got quiet again. He took Sera's hand in his and squeezed. "It's not a competition, you know. Don't ever think you can't tell me something. Ever. I'm not judgy. At least, I try not to be. I may have terrible timing with my comical relief, but hey, that's just who I am."

She laughed, looking into those blue eyes of his. Could she tell him what was happening to her, a virtual stranger? Though it felt as if they'd been friends for decades already. Could she tell anyone, really? Of course, Erinne and John knew, but they might be the only people who would ever understand.

"Not judgy, huh?"

"I promise."

"Okay. I think I might be going crazy," the words burst out before she talked herself into silence.

"Interesting. What's going on?" Adam let go of her hand to brush her hair away from her face, smoothing it down her back, a fatherly gesture she'd seen him do to Ava.

"I know it sounds insane, but I think I'm seeing people that aren't there, hearing voices I know are impossible to hear. I don't know. Maybe I'm schizophrenic, or maybe I have what my mom had. But *she* never had scary ghost people talking to her. Not that my mother is scary. I don't know what's happening to me." At first, she was embarrassed for blurting it out, but then as all her words tumbled out, her breath started coming quicker, shallow, her thoughts scattering as she tried to make sense of something there was no sense to be made of. The panic began to cave in, a collision of symptoms she was all too familiar with.

Another one of those dreadful moments was happening now in front of Adam and anyone who was within watching distance. Her shirt dampened with sweat as her uncontrolled breathing increased, her body beginning to tremble.

"Talking? How so?" Adam took Sera's hand, leading her to a nearby chair.

"I thought I was in a dream, a night terror. I used to have them as a kid. But I really can't be sure. There was such a horrible scream, like something was tearing her apart. My mom was there, but then she wasn't. It *had* to have been a dream. She couldn't be real. It's just not possible." Sera's breathing intensified, becoming more labored, her words slurring together.

"Slow down that breathing. Slow breaths, *shhh*. Someone call a medic!" Adam caught Sera in his arms as she lost consciousness.

"My Sariee." Arms extended, Ava ran up to Sera when she walked out of the infirmary room.

"Ava, let her be. Sera doesn't feel too good right now." Adam stood, ready to intervene. "They've had you back there for—" Adam looked at his watch, "well, twenty minutes. But it seemed like hours." He put his hand on her shoulder. "You scared me back there."

"I'm alright, really. Just a panic attack. I used to have them all the time. Especially when I first went back to San Francisco and started my pre-med courses at Stanford. Too many people, too many unknown dangers, too much helplessness." She bent down, eagerly picking Ava up. "But this makes everything better," Sera said, snuggling her close. "I just got myself all upset over nothing."

"Huh. That was *some* nothing. Your face drained faster than I ever thought possible. Then you just lost it and hit the floor. *Something* scared you."

"You let me hit the floor? Did you even try to catch me?" Sera teased.

Adam rolled his eyes with a smirk. "You don't have to play it down with me. You can talk to me. I'm here, for what it's worth. I know it's odd. We barely know each other, but you are part of the club now. Our club." He nodded toward Ava, who was staring adoringly at Sera.

"Thank you. I appreciate it, truly. I'll take you up on that. First, I think I need to do a lot of work with John when I get home. I think I'm finally ready. It only took me fifteen years."

"Hey, cut yourself some slack. Some people never get to this point. You're already miles ahead."

"Thanks for the note of confidence," Sera said with a snort. "This after-feeling of a panic attack is the worst part." She tried to shrug off the discomfort and embarrassment. "Shall we fix it with ice cream?" She set Ava down, took her hand, and walked back out into the light.

If she was going to fix this, be worthy of her life, stop being afraid of everything, and rid herself of these horrid panic attacks and night terrors, then she was going to have to do the work and face all the things she'd been hiding from, what she thought she'd been keeping herself safe from. And she would start as soon as she got home to Ireland.

But right now, she had the company of this beautiful little girl, who had also lost her mother so young, and her kind father, a man who had opened Sera's heart to possibilities she'd never let herself think of before. Never had she ever felt such strong emotion, let alone for people she didn't know. Yet with these two, she knew she had found family.

CHAPTER TWENTY-FOUR

Ella

STANFORD

All the way to bio-chem, Ella's mind was consumed with thoughts of Chris. His smile, the way he constantly made her laugh, the beautiful body that accompanied that gorgeous face, and the equally exquisite ways he was able to move that body. Ella and Chris had been enjoying each other's company, both in public and eagerly so in private.

He was easy to be with, fun to venture off with. His love for a well-lived life matched hers, which was a first. No one had ever been able to keep up with her before. He was special, indeed.

They had the family thing in common as well. Like her, Chris came from a family who valued reputation above all else. The fact that Stanford recruited Chris to play baseball added to his family's social standing. But, like Ella, he never let that hinder how he chose to live, never let his parents' constant disappointment hamper his outlook. In fact, it motivated him to make sure he experienced the fun in each day.

Chris had a reputation for being a hummingbird, flitting from girl to girl, always keeping things uncomplicated, which served Ella just fine. Though she totally and completely enjoyed each person she dated, she never promised them anything long-term. That would be unkind to these men, and she tried to be anything but unkind.

It had been light and fun for months. When they both had the time, they would venture off together, exploring their surroundings, and most often ended up exploring each other in those surroundings.

Her favorite adventure so far had been a surprise drive down the coast. No matter how much she begged, Chris wouldn't tell her where he was taking her. He wouldn't even give her a hint. They drove for a couple of hours south along the scenic Pacific Coast Highway when a giant field of daisies filling the entire hillside came into view.

"Oh my god, Chris, look!" Pointing, Ella couldn't help the girlish squeal that escaped her.

He just gave her that smile and kissed her hand. "You said your favorite flowers were daisies."

"They are. The happiest of all the flowers."

"Ta-da," he said, gesturing as he pulled the car into a scenic turnout. He opened the car door for her, led her over by the hand, then helped her climb over the fence and into the fields.

"Are we allowed to go in this way?" Ella asked.

Chris shrugged his shoulders. "Probably not."

Ella couldn't stop giggling as they walked hand in hand through acres of whites and yellows and purples. She ran her fingers delicately over the petals. Chris watched her, a pleased look on his face.

The man left her breathless. He never stopped surprising her, and that was a feat in itself. Just his presence constantly teased her, igniting an ever-present heat through her.

Surrounded by nothing but daisies, she turned to him, pulling him into her so she could get her lips on his and her hands on his body, which led to the two of them making love on a bed of daisies in the middle of that field.

More often than not, Ella was thinking about Chris. During classes when she should be totally focused on what the professors were saying, during labs, while she studied. He occupied space in her brain that was seriously distracting and dangerously tempting.

She caught herself wanting to spend more and more time with him, missing him when they were apart. Ella couldn't *actually* fall for someone. It was best for the other person that she didn't. That ticking of the countdown clock only got louder as time went on.

So, she tried backing off. But that didn't work, either. She couldn't help herself. She was an addict, and Chris was her drug.

That is, until the second line on the pregnancy test appeared, a deep, dark pink.

Chapter Twenty-Five

Her hair was blonde, almost white, and those eyes were the palest blue. She was just like *her*. The bitch who was the beginning of the end for us. If it weren't for this whore, all hell wouldn't have broken loose, and we wouldn't have had to move away from a half-decent life.

I'd been on my way to work, the way I usually go, minding my own business, when I noticed her walking through the park. I turned down the radio and rolled my window down. I'm not sure why. She was too far from the traffic light where I was stopped, so it wasn't like I would hear anything from her. And yet, I needed all of my senses focused on this woman—who was so much like *her*.

The person behind me honked, making me jump on the accelerator. I kept glancing in the rearview mirror, watching her for as long as possible.

Part of me wanted to pull over and wait for her, follow her. But I couldn't miss work again. I had to use up all of my sick time the last time I'd been put on another 72-hour hold at the hospital. Another time the darkness had been too inviting. But it hadn't worked. Again.

Now, here was this person who made my breath quicken and my heart race. Not because I was attracted to her, but because it had all started with *her*, all because *she* couldn't keep her legs closed.

"Why *me*?" The woman's delicate features betrayed the strength she was trying to portray, a strength I could tell she didn't actually possess. A flush spread up to her fair hairline, making her white-blonde hair look pink.

She was sassy. I'll give her that. Of course, she would be. How else would a homewrecker be?

"Why do you think?" I looked at her angry little scrunched-up face through the rearview mirror. This ought to be interesting. These self-righteous people always thought they were better than the rest of us. "Maybe because you're a homewrecker who takes whatever she wants, no matter the consequence."

"I'm not a homewrecker. I told you I have no idea what you're talking about," the woman whined, acting like a child instead of the middle-aged woman she was. Pathetic. She even rolled her eyes as she looked away from me like some broody teenager.

She was also trying to hide her desperate hope for anyone to drive up next to us, for someone to save her pitiful self. But of course, no one was around, no passing cars. We were already out of the city, heading toward nowhere, away from everyone and everything, so that we could have the conversation that had been burning inside of me for weeks now. Really, for years.

I had tried so hard to fight it, the thoughts never stopping. Day after day, I watched her walk through the park before I went to work. I'd followed her a few times to see what kind of life she got to have after ruining mine.

The more I watched her, the more infuriated I became. It wasn't fair that her life was so blissfully normal. You can't devastate something so completely and then get to walk away unscathed.

Wasn't that what was beaten into me my whole life, that those who sin need punishment, a cleansing, or else they would continue to do it over and over again? Never did some mythical all-powerful entity deliver that salvation. As I followed her, watching her live her happy little life, I knew that I needed to do it.

Now I had in my possession the first person who had stolen a piece of my life from me and it was time for her to pay the price for it.

"I just want to go home," the woman whispered and started to cry.

When I looked at her through the rearview mirror, her face looked different, almost as though it had changed. She was just a kid, a scared, willful teenager. I closed my eyes to clear my vision. When I looked back at her again, it was indeed the woman who led my father astray.

I couldn't speak, I couldn't think. The moment unnerved me and then began to infuriate me. My body started to quake with rage. I had to get off this road and out of this car.

It was a trick, of course. This bullshit she was spewing, acting like some kid, was some frantic attempt to get me to let her go without punishing her for what she did. But there was no way I'd let her trick her way out of it.

She slid from side to side in the backseat as I drove off the highway onto a dirt trail, dodging this tree and that one, at times fishtailing around an enormous redwood, even skimming the side of the car against one of them. That shut her up. The shakes calmed, and my confidence was restored.

I skid the car to a stop, sending up a cloud of dirt. I got out, slammed my door shut, and yanked open the back door that I'd engaged the child locks on. I reached in, grabbed her by the neck, dragged her out of the car, and threw her down onto the dirt, delivering a swift kick to the face as payment for spooking me.

"Get up and walk." I kicked her again in the ribs, hard. It felt good, inflicting pain upon someone who had inflicted pain on me felt right. Justified.

She stumbled, righting herself as best she could. I'm sure she had a broken nose and maybe a few broken ribs at this point.

There was so much more to come.

We walked until I was satisfied that we were far enough from the trail. I grabbed her by the back of her head and shoved it into the nearest tree.

Her body crumpled to the ground. A trickle of blood oozed down the side of her face, down her neck. I want her to hurt, hurt more than I hurt. I want her to suffer, suffer more than I had. Though that would be impossible. Mine was a lifetime of hurt and suffering.

"How could you do it?"

"Do...do what? I haven't done anything," she cried, sniveling like the coward I knew she was.

"Typical. Never admitting fault. You go through life destroying those around you, not giving a shit, never being punished for the transgressions you've committed."

"But, I...I don't know what you're talking about. I swear. I don't know what I did. Please, please don't hurt me anymore. I'm sorry," she stammered, cowering on her hands and knees against the tree.

"You're sorry? You just said you didn't know what you did, so how can you be sorry?" I kicked her again. "Stop lying!" Another kick. She coughed, spat out blood. "I had a nice enough life before you." I felt the control start to slip. Staying focused was necessary, but the rage was stronger in me, the injustice of my whole life creeping in, trying to take over. I pulled her up off her knees, slapped her hard, sending her body crumbling down again. Listening to the wind escape her body, her coughs and sputtering wheezes invigorated this rage monster, this beast.

"We had to move here after you wrecked our family. We were never happy again. *I* was never happy again." Another kick. "But you. Nothing happened to you, did it?" One more kick into the softness of her gut.

"...I'm...not...who you...think." Blood dripped from her mouth and ran from her nose.

"You are exactly what I know you are."

"It wasn't me," she whispered, her breath wet, wheezing.

"Then *who* was it? Your twin sister?"

"I don't...I don't have sisters. It's just me and my mom."

"Your *mom*? Aren't you a little too *old* to play that card?"

I couldn't listen to her any longer. I took her face in both of my hands, angled her head just right, and with a quick twist, I snapped her neck.

I have been vindicated.

CHAPTER TWENTY-SIX

Sera

ATLANTIC OCEAN

C lose your eyes and hold your ears, Baby Girl. Hold them tight and hum your songs." The words came from her but in Mommy's voice.

Flesh through flesh. Popping layers of skin through her fingers. Blood. The smell of it subtle, but distinct. She could taste it, coppery and thick, felt the warmth of it as it sprayed over her face, sticky and blinding. It burned her eyes, but still she kept jabbing, the feel of the screwdriver held tightly in her hand. Frantic, she was frantic.

This was their only chance. Get her baby out.

She glanced behind her. Her six-year-old self, curled up tight, rocking back and forth, eyes tightly shut, hands pressed to her ears, humming their favorite song. Rocking. Rocking.

She was ferocious and wild as she stuck her weapon through the thickness of skin and muscle with feral rage, again and again, in and out of his body, even after he finally crumpled to the ground. But her strength was drifting away. She couldn't hold on any longer. She was falling...

Then running. Sera's own child legs under her. Hobbling as fast as she could. Rocks, sticks, thorns stabbing the bottoms of her feet, dragging her

shattered leg behind her. Her body was so sore, it hurt everywhere. It was
hard to pick up her feet, make them move, her leg dragging, dragging.

Get away. Fast. She promised.

She was lost. There was nothing. Trees, only black trees, slapping at her
face, scraping her legs as the rocks tore the flesh off the soles of her feet.
The branch she was using as a crutch cutting into her armpit.

It was so dark.

Then a boy. Sweet. Angelic face. "Come on, you okay now."

A woman, kind, helping. "That is very sweet of you Davey."

Sera startled awake. Her heart thudded in her chest, her pulse roaring in her ears. Sweat clung her hair to her face.

It was never going to get easier, reliving it piece by piece, both as her mother experienced it and as she had. Sera pushed her hair back and took a few deep breaths.

Early morning light peeked through the gaps in the drawn curtains. The time on the clock showed that there was still a while before she was to meet Adam and Ava for breakfast in the dining room.

Might as well get started, Sera thought as she sat up and draped her legs over the side of the bed.

Sound stopped.

The darkness faded the room's surroundings. The floor became dirt, and the walls became tall trees.

There was a young girl, fifteen maybe. She was an aura of a dream, blurred colors, no real hues, just transparent hints. Her hair was a light shade, white-blonde. Her phantom eyes showed only black pupils centered in pale-tinted irises staring up at her.

And she was crying.

Sera couldn't hear her cries, she couldn't hear anything.

A leg struck out and kicked the girl in the face.

Her leg. But it *wasn't* hers. She had no control.

The leg kicked the girl again.

The young girl was spitting blood onto the dirt, crying, pleading.

Two gloved hands, *her* hands that *weren't* hers, reached out, taking the girl's face in them.

They twisted the girl's head in a quick, sudden motion.

The hands dropped the girl's body.

As it lay crumpled and broken at the base of a tree, Sera could only watch as the girl's life slipped away.

Finally, the forest disappeared, and her room's surroundings returned.

The banging on the door wouldn't stop. Sera tried to ignore it, but he wouldn't go away so easily. Sera was so weak that she almost couldn't drag herself up to open the door.

After everything came crashing back, she vomited until she lay in a heap on the cool bathroom floor, where she stayed until the insistent knocking on her cabin door.

"Our last day, and you stand us up, huh? What kind of—Sera? What's wrong? What happened?" Adam's smile fell as he rushed to her side.

"I can't tell if I'm awake or dreaming anymore, Adam. One minute I'm fine, and the next, I'm seeing ghosts. The night terrors, they're back, worse than ever before. I don't know what's happening to me. Am I crazy? Crazy people don't ask if they *are* crazy, right?" She started pacing, her hands manically flitting about.

Adam stepped toward her, stopping her pacing by embracing her against him.

"No. You are not crazy." Putting his arm around her shoulder, he led her to her bedroom. "I googled night terrors. Those things are no joke. I can tell you what is *not* helping. You aren't sleeping well, and you eat like an anorexic bird. So, get into that bed and take a nice long nap. I can get you one of Victoria's handy sleeping pills if need be. I will read one of these trusty magazines and scare off any nightmare goblins. When you wake up, I will feed you." He sat her on her bed.

"You're not old enough to be this paternal," she said, smirking as he tucked her in like a child. He did, after all, have a lot of practice.

"Um, thank you?" Adam said, snickering.

"I have books if you'd like, and I also have—"

Adam put a finger to her lips, signaling for silence. "Just. Sleep."

CHAPTER TWENTY-SEVEN

Sera

ATLANTIC OCEAN

Adam's long legs hung over the side of the couch, his head bent in an awkward, uncomfortable position. A magazine lay open across his chest, rising and falling rhythmically with each soft snore.

"Adam, that looks extremely uncomfortable." Sera knelt next to the couch, chuckling as she lightly nudged him.

"Hmm?" He moved a bit before opening his eyes. "You sure are pretty," he mumbled, closing his eyes again. His eyes popped open a fraction of a second later as he sat up quickly. "I'm sorry. I didn't mean—"

"Thank you. I take that as a compliment to my mom."

"Your mom? How so?" Adam looked away, quickly busying himself, brushing his rumpled shirt and pants.

Sera couldn't help but smile at the flush that rushed to Adam's face. She got up, went into the bedroom, and returned with the album.

"Apparently, I am a twin to my mom." Sera sat on the floor next to the couch, opened the album, and handed it to Adam. "That's Mom, that little scrawny thing is me, and that dashing young man is Dad."

"You really do look so much alike." Adam flipped through the pictures, admiring the young, happy family. He turned another page and found a letter inserted instead of more pictures.

"What's this?"

"Mom and Aunt Erinne wrote letters to each other for years. I got to know who my mother was in her own words because of those letters. I put a couple of my favorite ones in this album to read whenever I want to hear her voice."

He put his hand on her shoulder. "We'll both get through this. I know this might seem strange to say, seeing as we've known each other for such a short time, but for the first time since Alex's death, I feel connected to someone I can trust and rely on." His voice broke as emotion crept in. Quickly clearing his throat, he pointed to another picture. "What's happening here?"

Sara continued telling him the stories that went along with each picture as he flipped through the pages, and for once, it didn't hurt to look back.

"That is everything, right? Phone numbers, addresses, emails, and anything else." Adam entered all of his information into Sera's cell phone before they left the ship.

They docked in Southampton that morning and were being called off by order of deck floors. That last day, Ava and Sera had been inseparable. She'd taken the child to breakfast and played with her in the pool. She told Adam it was so that he and Victoria had a chance to pack without distraction. But it was more for herself than anyone else.

She'd felt such a connection with Ava. She was pulled to her, to the joy in her laughter, the pure innocence of the little girl. She couldn't wait to see Erinne and John and be home in the beauty of Ireland that she missed so much, but she wished she could take Ava with her to watch the little girl's excitement as she saw new sights, play princess in real castles, and watch her find precious pebbles as they walked the stony beaches. Instead, she'd spend as much time as she could with her before having to say goodbye.

"Of course. I've made an irreplaceable friend, my first friend, really. You two are now part of the family. There's no way I'm going to let go of you that easily. Besides, I'd never go back on my word to Ava." She picked up the little girl and held her close, the child scent and hints of baby shampoo had Sera missing her already.

"What did this little one talk you into?" Adam asked with a tickle to Ava's side. Ava let out a hearty giggle.

"I'm going to be the cool Auntie. You know, like, if she calls me and tells me that she is just dying to have something, I'll send it to her. Whenever she needs advice on boys, including dads, she'll call me. If she wants to visit California, I'll send her a ticket. Just regular girl stuff." She handed his phone back. "My email, cell number, and Lantern Light's front desk number. My dorm changes, so I'll let you know when I get my new assignment. You should be able to reach me anywhere I am." She kissed Ava's temple and handed her over to Adam when she saw Victoria heading toward them.

"I was thinking," Adam put Ava down, guiding her toward Victoria. "I love the idea of old-fashioned letter writing, like your mom and aunt did. It immortalizes moments in life. What do you say? Pen pals, some cool stationary, gel pens, and hand cramps?"

"Great idea." She hugged Adam, taking in all that had become familiar in such a short time. That feeling of not being alone anymore had been an unexpected pleasure. She had made a close friend, one who understood the pain and uncertainty of grief.

She already missed him as well.

"I guess this is it. Don't let those goblins get to you anymore, okay?"

"I won't forget you. Ever." When he started to pull away, she held on to him just a few seconds longer.

"You better not or I'll hunt you down and lecture you."

"Great, Dad lectures. Just what everyone wants."

"You make me sound ancient. I'm only, like, five or six years older than you are."

"But you're a much older soul."

"Gee. Thanks." He knuckled her head.

Sera picked up his bag and handed it to him. "They're going to leave you behind. You better hurry."

Victoria was already showing passes to disembark. He looked from his family to Sera and back again. "Write, text, call me. I want to hear about Ireland and your boring study habits, about all of the people you'll meet, the slave-driving professors, college parties, all of it. I mean it." He put the strap over his shoulder, kissed Sera's forehead, and walked away.

She watched as he gave the steward his pass and stepped off the ship. He looked back at her before he rounded the corner and called out, "It's been wild, hasn't it?"

That broad smile of his would stay etched in Sera's mind as he stepped past the wall and out of her sight. She stood there for several minutes staring at the wall he had vanished behind.

Knowing someone else going through similar feelings provided a sense of belonging. However, she could only imagine what Adam might think of her. He had to think she was a little wacky, talking about outrageous things, ghosts, phantom screams, and horrible night terrors. The funny thing was that he had listened to every word and never even blinked at the oddities she described.

Even though she knew that she could talk to him every day if she wanted, she felt painfully alone when she closed the door behind her in her room. Something she used to crave was now daunting.

But there was new purpose in her time alone now. She would use it to do the work she was finally ready for. While Adam spent time with his family, continuing his healing journey in London, she would begin her own in Ireland.

She needed to figure out why the night terrors were back and, hopefully, how to stop them. It was also past time for her to figure out who she was, how to move on, and how to heal. If that meant facing the worst moments of her life, then that's what she would do.

She was done living her life as a frightened blob hiding away, done letting Jeffrey Mason win. Her mother gave up everything for her, and she'd be damned to let *Him* take that from them as well.

When she stepped off the ship, her fear of visions and night terrors had been forgotten. The chaos of disembarking, finding taxis, and checking luggage had kept her occupied for more than two hours, diminishing the three-hour layover she was supposed to have had into a fifteen-minute sprint to find her gate and board the plane she was to take from Southampton to Shannon.

When the plane was on its way, Sera sat back in her seat and peeked out the small oval window, staring out into the endless blue of the sky. Though it had only been a year since she'd last seen them, she missed her family, Erinne, John, and the rest of her clan.

Lantern Light was the closest thing to a home she'd had. It was also the only time she felt connected to her parents. The moment she stepped on the property, she could feel them there. In the rooms and walking along the cliffs, their laughter echoing through the hallways. This was where Sera's mother came to give birth to her, where her father came to win her mother back, and where they became a family.

Sera pulled out the class lists for Stanford from her backpack. She should have picked her classes before leaving, but she kept putting it off. As she read through class descriptions, that wanting that had been nudging at her, that she'd kept pushing away, came back, prodding, taking hold again, that sense of what she wanted—no, *needed*—to do.

This was it, the time to decide. In her heart, she knew her path was in medicine, but as a nurse, not a doctor. Her life had been touched so many years before by a nurse. It was a nurse who held her hand, made her feel safe, and stayed by her side so she wouldn't go through the worst of it alone until Erinne could get to her.

That was what Sera wanted to be for someone else. An advocate for the scared child, the hand holder to the worried, the voice of assurance and hope. Though the guilt was still there, asserting that she was supposed to become the doctor her mother was supposed to have been, she also heard her mother's voice urging her on.

Do it.

Soon, the soft hum and gentle drifts of the plane lulled Sera to a light sleep, where she dreamt of the enchantment and romance that was Ireland, not of the visions and terrors that had begun to haunt her again.

Pulling her luggage behind her, Sera scanned faces as she walked out of the restricted area. Erinne's face came into view. It was obvious that she had seen Sera first as tears were already running down her cheeks, her arms outstretched. Sera dropped everything and fell into them. Warmth and the faint smell of freshly baked goods had Sera instantly home.

Erinne kissed Sera's cheeks, forehead, then cheeks again. She held Sera's face in her hands and stared at her.

"Only you can make me a crying fool like this. I still can't believe you're a woman now," Erinne sniffled as she looked at Sera.

"You say that every year."

"And it's even more true this year than it was last year."

Sera took Erinne's hands from her face, holding them in her own. "I've missed you so much," she said, hugging her again.

"Knowing me, I can stand here and bawl all day long. Let's get going." Erinne led Sera down to the baggage claim, never stopping the conversation.

"John had a few appointments today, but he is taking the rest of the week off to spend time at home with you."

"Good thing. I need his shrinky expertise."

"Like how? Are you okay?"

"It's a long story. I'd rather wait to have both of you together, so I don't have to tell it twice. Let's just say I'm being haunted by ghosts."

"Well now, remember, you are in a land famous for ghosts and phantoms roaming about. Nothing to be spooked about. It's just the way it is here." Laughter and joy beamed from Erinne as she looked at Sera. "I'm so happy you're home." She gave her another big squeeze, crushing the breath out of Sera's lungs.

"Me too. You were right. Those ten days on the ship were exactly what I needed," Sera said. She thought of Adam going to London to get away—not to forget, but to remember in a way that would help him move forward and go on living. Sera needed to do just that, to remember and figure out how to finally go on.

"So, Erinne, I saw Lantern Light featured in Travel Magazine. Best digs in town." She hooked an arm through hers as they walked out to Erinne's car, if you could call it that. It was the smallest vehicle ever. "When are you going to get rid of this thing and get a grown-up car?" Sera asked as Erinne opened the tiny hatchback for her luggage.

Ignoring Sera, Erinne reached for one of the bags, putting it in the perfectly functional car. "Not to be prideful or anything, but it happens to be true. In this part of the country, at least. There is a small bit of competition out east, near Dublin," she winked. "You'll see all the changes and additions we've made this year soon enough. It is almost there, almost done."

Chapter Twenty-Eight

I should have felt great. I should have felt such vast relief handing out the justice that was years overdue to a woman who had broken our family apart. She almost had me believing she was someone else, not the woman who had destroyed us. Almost. It *was* her, and she was trying to spook me into giving her a merciful death.

Well, she got it.

But I didn't like losing control. Control was the one thing I needed to possess at all times. Without control, I am no better than my crackhead brother, who willingly gave up his control to the chemical bliss that numbed him. No better than my weak-minded sister, who let the religious freaks control her.

Without control, what is real and what is not gets too convoluted, the whispers in my head conflicting. Without control, I can't trust myself to know the difference. I won't lose that control again.

An eerie feeling has followed me since that night, like someone was watching me, a breath on the back of my neck. Everything around me felt as though it lay witness, not just to my physical being but into the soul of who I am.

Maybe it had been that woman's eyes, in all of their iridescence.

It wasn't fear but anger that made me overly anxious to kill her. I had a precise plan to follow, but I got spooked. Now I almost feel, cursed.

For days after, I was torn. Am I a monster now? Have I always been this the whole time? I've been caged for so long, has the real me been let out? Would it tear me apart? Would it take my heart, my soul?

Over the years, I tried, in so many ways, to rid myself of it all. With razors, with handfuls of pills.

Nothing had worked, and I won't let them lock me up again in a place where they supervise as you defecate, where you have to earn points for the simple privilege of being a human, like going to an outside area surrounded by four concrete walls to feel a bit of sun on your face. I've been imprisoned enough in this life.

I should hate that I have become this.

Maybe the whole time this beast *was* my heart, it *is* my soul. Letting it free would be embracing who I have always been afraid to be. They tried to beat it out of me, but there is no denying what is inevitable.

It felt good, right, to have done it.

I must confess, it feels damn good to finally be me.

CHAPTER TWENTY-NINE

Sera

IRELAND

Soon after they cleared the city, there was nothing but open space as far as could be seen. Mile after mile, vibrant emerald mounds rolled past, the valleys organized in tidy squares, abundant with sheep dotting the landscape. Daffodils stretched along the roadsides while mist clung to the air like a walk through a cloud.

Erinne made the few uphill turns through a wooded area and onto a loose gravel road. Finally, they drove through the tall iron gate that stood open under a massive stone arch. Past the gate, rolling green grass swayed in the wind leading up to Lantern Light Inn. Beyond the grass valley, dense forest lined two sides of the property, the third side held cliffs that framed the ocean beyond.

After years of planning, building, and expanding, Erinne's visions had come to life. The main building was a combination of a medieval castle and southern plantation. Stone walls rose three stories high, white shutters flanked the paned windows. A wide staircase welcomed guests to a set of double red doors. Above the peaked rooftop were several chimney stacks, which, even though it was technically summer, all had puffs of white smoke wafting from them, assuring that inside was cozy and warm.

"Erinne, this is incredible. You did so much this past year. I never imagined it would be this big, this wonderful. Is it always this busy?" Others obviously shared Sera's attraction, as cars were parked in every available spot.

"It has been, yes. Kind of crazy, isn't it? Your mom always believed in Lantern Light, that it could be this."

"Mom always believed in *you*. I'm so proud of you, too. It is so beautiful. You did it." Sera hugged Erinne tight, throat burning from tears that stayed buried.

"The kid telling the adult they're proud. Why does that hit right here?" Through her tears, Erinne held her hand over her heart. "Now, I hope you haven't forgotten that summer here is far from California weather. You did bring sweaters?"

"You ask that every year, Aunt E."

They pried Sera's luggage out of the tiny car and went in through a back door that entered into a busy, modern, stainless-steel kitchen, which smelled as wonderful as it looked.

Nan dropped a ball of dough she'd been working and rushed to Sera, taking her in her arms. "My goodness, Love, you've grown up all the way now, haven't you?" Nan kissed Sera's cheeks, looked at her, and hugged her close.

"You guys always act like I've been gone for decades." But Sera adored every second of her family's love. This is what Adam was asking about, knowing it was the people in their lives that got them through. She was lucky enough to have it here, always waiting for her to come back to.

"Might as well have been. I've missed you so," Nan said, kissing her cheeks again. "Go, get settled, and then come have a glass with me and tell me all about your year." Nan shooed them out of the kitchen.

Another familiar voice called out when Erinne and Sera entered the main lobby.

"Sera!" Shelly, Uncle Brian's wife, made her way around the front desk and embraced Sera. Two adolescent boys came running through the lobby and out the front door.

"They got huge." Sera watched the two tornados wrestle around the front porch before dashing off.

"Nine and seven now. I'm made to be surrounded by boys," Shelly said, shaking her head.

"Not going for a third try?" Sera teased.

"Ach. Now, why in heaven's name would I do such a thing? Test the fates and you'll be sure to be payin' for doin' such a thing." Shelly handed Sera a room key. "All ready for you."

"Before I forget, has Brian finished the estimate for the new stable build?" Erinne asked.

"No, he's still waiting for the last contractor bid to come in. But Erick called and said that he and Rich were coming in to spend some time with our girl here." Shelly winked at Sera.

"You all sure know how to make a girl feel special."

"You are special." Erinne kissed Sera's cheek and led her to a set of stairs with *East Wing* engraved on a silver placard.

"East wing? Wow, you got fancy."

"Oh, stop." Erinne playfully nudged Sera. "About the rooms, I left your room as it has always been. I'll never have the heart to change it. Its history is too precious, no matter how much time passes. Oh, and we just finished the new Alaura suite."

"You did? Did it turn out as hauntingly romantic as you hoped?" Sera asked, knowing the room was supposed to be based on Lantern Lights' famous origin story.

"Even better. I have a confession. I made two suites. I just loved it so much. John said, "Make two then," so we renovated our suite to match. My man unabashedly spoils me." Erinne was beaming.

"Good job, John. You deserve it, Erinne." The heat of happy, unspilled tears burned behind Sera's eyes. "Now that I am an adult, you can tell me, how genuine is the story? I mean, it's romantic and all, but how *true* is it?" She looked at Erinne with exaggerated, suspicious eyes.

"I assure you every word is true. And I'd not be stretching the truth if I told you it has been said by some that sometimes, in the early morning mist, the nobleman can be seen riding along the edge of the cliffs. You don't have to believe in ghosts, but that doesn't mean that there isn't something else out there, more than what we can see and touch." She tousled Sera's hair.

"Now, let's get you to your room so you can relax, soak in a bath, and take a nap to head off the jet lag a bit."

"You moms really *do* know everything, don't you?" Sera smiled at Erinne.

"We really do."

After Erinne had left her to settle into her room, Sera closed the door, already feeling them there. If she closed her eyes, she could smell the body spray her dad wore, hear her mother's sweet singing voice, her laughter.

She looked around her room—their room—took a deep breath in and let it out slowly. The violin she'd insisted on learning to play when she was young stood gleaming on its stand in the corner. Smiling, Sera went over to it and plucked at the strings.

She unpacked, carefully putting her newly acquired stationary set on the old desk under the window that overlooked the cliffs and the sea beyond. Along with the stationary, she had bought an antique-looking pen at a gift store in the airport because it made her chuckle. An old-fashioned letter by an old-fashioned pen.

She wondered about him, if he and Ava were well and settled in London. Then decided that it was the perfect time to write her very first letter to them. She wrote of Lantern Light Inn, what her aunt had done to it since she'd last been there, and the story that went along with it. About the land and how green it was, the beauty of the country and its people, and how much she wished he and Ava could be there to show it all to. She sealed the envelope, addressed it, and set it on the desk to take down for mailing.

With the enticing idea of a bath still lingering in her mind, she set into the bathroom to explore the many different bath salts and scented soaps that Erinne had stocked for her. She set the water on hot and added her choice of fragrances and salts. After she lit some candles, she slowly eased herself into the water. It was magic.

Erinne had been right, as she usually was. After a long hot bath and a four-hour, nightmare-free nap later, she felt new. She also realized how hungry she was as aromas of something delicious wafted through the halls. By the time Sera made her way down, everyone was already at the table in a nook in the kitchen, a place made just for the family.

Erick and Rich got up, greeting Sera with hugs and kisses. Shelly was serving the boys, scolding them at the same time to stop messing with each other, Nan and Pops were pouring wine into glasses, John and Erinne were sweetly kissing hello since he had just walked in as well, to which Brian was teasing them to get a room.

Her loud, crazy, wonderful family, all together, celebrating another day accomplished. Which was all this family needed to get together. The table was abundant with food, and Sera couldn't help but grab a taste of some of it before getting to her seat.

"Hungry, are we?" Nan teased as Sera walked around the table, looking at the food and grazing on this or that.

"You could say I'm slightly starving," Sera said after popping a grape in her mouth. She tore some meat off a drumstick with her fingers and ate that as well.

"That's your piece now. Sit down, we'll eat." Erinne piled some of everything onto Sera's plate and handed it to her before she fixed her own. Sera was well into her food before Erinne sat back down.

"You act as if you eat but once a year," Brian joked with Sera.

"I can't help it. I feel as if I haven't eaten in decades. I haven't felt real hunger in I can't remember how long," Sera said with her mouth half-full, then stuck in another bite.

"Good Lord, slow down," John teased as he started to eat.

The conversation held out even longer than all of the food had. The laughter was loud, and the voices animated. Catching up on the past year was always a special treat in an Irish household, as there were no better storytellers anywhere else.

Sera told them about school and her classes, not that there was much to tell. She had no stories of her own, at least not that she wanted to share with the entire family. She was leaving that story for Erinne and John after family time was over.

"What you need is to make some friends. Good ones. Ones that will get you both into and out of trouble. Just ask my sister." Brian threw a small potato at Erinne.

"Ella and I were no trouble at all." Erinne threw it back at him.

"Ha! Those two always running around, getting into my stuff."

"Who could find anything in that room? It was always a mess," Erick teased.

"Don't make me tell everyone some of the stuff we did find," Erinne threatened.

"Ach."

But everyone was laughing, even Brian, with his reddened face.

"Why the blush, Bri? You feelin' guilty 'bout something?" Nan asked, chuckling.

"Speaking of friends, I met a person on the ship. I'm pretty sure I've made a good friend in him."

"*Him*?" Erinne and Shelly asked in unison, looking at Sera, searching, hoping for more in her eyes that she might not be saying.

"Yes, *his* name is Adam. He lost his wife last year. It is the one-year anniversary, actually. He has an adorable little girl, Ava. She is two years old, and I have just fallen in love with her. It was nice to have someone to talk to. Adam, that is." Her smile came quickly, remembering little Ava and the conversations she and Adam had.

"Heartbreaking for those poor dears. But I'm glad you both found a person in each other. It is so important to have a person. Your mother, she was mine." Erinne reached out and took Sera's hand in hers.

CHAPTER THIRTY

Chris Owens

Life kept him on his toes, which was always welcome in Chris's world. He was game for whatever came his way. If his parents hadn't been the uppity snobs they were, he probably would have leaned more on the level, cautious side. However, watching them do everything in such a meticulously planned way proved how boring living that way was. He made sure to be 100% opposite.

He met his football idol, Steve Young, just because he and a group of friends decided at the last minute to follow the player bus after a game. Was it a good idea? Hell no. They probably should have been arrested. But after a morning of tailgating at Candlestick and then celebrating a dominant victory, it seemed like a great idea.

If he hadn't ditched his cousin's debutante ball—he was supposed to be her dutiful escort—to sub-in last minute for a varsity baseball game as a JV player, then he wouldn't have been persuaded to join the varsity team, which his buddy promised would be a blast and filled with all the hot cheerleaders a guy could want. Which then turned into being drafted by Stanford, which led him to this moment, sitting alone in his room, contemplating his next move.

The phone stared at him, daring him to use it so that he could finally hear her voice, hear her tell him the reason why she disappeared on him.

Usually, Chris was quickly distracted and would lose interest in a girl after a few weeks, at most. Not that he was ever cruel when he broke up with someone. He made sure to never get close enough or do things that would give the wrong impression to the lady he was dating. When things were called off, usually by him, they would part ways, mutually satisfied with the result. For the most part.

But Ella couldn't be so easily cast aside.

Ella was this mythological creature. She was beautiful, smart as hell, and funny, with a far superior wit—even to his own, and he prided himself on his comical genius. Ella had this zest for life that most were too afraid to harness, living each moment to its fullest potential. She had big dreams and even bigger goals, and she never expected anything of him. She'd never promised herself to him, nor did she ask him to pledge himself to her, which was new for him.

More often than not, Chris thought about Ella, craved her. He'd had several months with her, and his infatuation only grew. So, when she suddenly stopped returning his calls, he didn't let it go as he usually would. He went looking for an explanation.

He had waited outside her classes, but she never came out of any of them. He went to the apartment she and a couple of other students rented together just off campus. Matt, one of her roommates, informed him that she had moved out a couple of weeks before.

Usually, he would have given up at that moment. Obviously, she was blowing him off. He'd been given the boot. But for some reason, this time, he needed to know *why*.

Knowing she was done with him only made him think about her more. His gut was twisted up, and his mind was distracted. None of which was like him at all. And he didn't like it.

Then Chris got angry. How dare she walk away without giving him a reason. He would never do that to anyone, even in the worst relationship. So he kept looking for an answer.

When he was able to find the address of Ella's parent's home, he drove straight over, hoping to find Ella there.

He stood in front of the massive oak door for he didn't know how long, trying to muster up enough courage to face Ella. It was absurd. But then, he'd always been on the receiving end of this conversation.

The woman who answered the door looked at Chris as though he were an enemy worthy of starting a nuclear war.

"Um, hello..."

"Young man, you are not welcome here. Now or ever. Leave this property before I have you arrested."

Then, the woman slammed the door in his face.

Chris stood there, stunned. He couldn't move his feet from that doorstep, and he couldn't move his eyes away from the wood of the door that was inches from his face.

He had no idea who the woman was, though he had a pretty good idea he had just encountered Ella's mother, he had no clue what he had possibly done to offend her so righteously, and he still had no idea where Ella had disappeared to or why.

Yet, Chris still couldn't let it go. Couldn't let *her* go.

It really started to piss him off when he realized he couldn't function in his life without Ella—talking to her, seeing her, being with her, tasting her lips. A couple of months had passed since she ditched him, yet he was still losing sleep thinking of her.

It got to the point that he became unfocused during practice. So much so that the coach took him aside and gave him a Come-to-Jesus talk—get it together, or get out.

No one had ever had this kind of hold on him before. He should be fine by now, not wondering where she was, what she was doing, or if she was with someone else. He shouldn't still want her so badly.

And then Chris realized it was because he had never been in love with anyone before, and he was deeply, totally, and completely in love with Ella.

Then he'd run into Ruby after one of his games. They'd made the typical small talk, a quick catch-up. But as they parted ways, she'd said, "By the way, congratulations."

It all clicked.

He spent days tracking down people who might know how to get a hold of Ella's best friend, Erinne, in Ireland. He could have kicked himself for not trying to get a hold of Erinne sooner and kicked himself harder for not realizing what had made Ella flee.

Now he was staring at the phone, about to make the call that would change the rest of his life as soon as he dialed. Crazy thing was, he was all for it.

Which was wild.

CHAPTER THIRTY-ONE

Erinne

IRELAND

There was a knock on her suite door. Erinne put the book she was reading down and got up to answer it. When she opened the door, she could have fainted from the shock that rippled through her.

Ella was standing in her doorway.

She didn't have that vibrant smile that lit the room, wasn't standing with her usual tall confidence. Never had Erinne seen Ella look the way she did at that moment. Usually, there was an ever-present radiance that all but glowed from Ella at all times. However, in her doorway, Ella looked dark and broken.

"What's wrong? What happened?" Erinne took Ella into her arms. She should have been elated at the surprise, but it scared her to see Ella like this.

"I'm pregnant."

Erinne stood back, looked at Ella. "Okay."

The word sounded way more confident than she felt. But it would be *okay*. She led Ella into her room and closed the door.

"What do you need? A shower, a bath, a nap?" Erinne needed something to keep her busy while she considered what to say and do.

Ella just stood there, and then she started crying. It was the worst sound in the world, Ella weeping. So instead of doing anything, Erinne held Ella for as long as the sobs wracked her body, even as she hiccupped after the tears ran out. She held her until Ella was the one to pull away.

"I'd say I needed some of that beautiful Irish whiskey, but..." Then Ella laughed. Not the kind of pity laugh one would have at a bad joke, but a full, joyous laugh, which made Erinne join in right along with her.

"A baby?" Erinne's eyes misted.

"A baby." Ella shrugged, but in her eyes was a happiness that she couldn't help. "Crazy, right?"

"Boy or girl?"

"I'm barely pregnant."

"You *Know*."

"Yeah, I do. She's a girl." Ella's smile spread wide.

"Oh my god, a baby, Ella," Erinne said, smiling. They hugged again and cried again. "Okay, we need snacks, lots of snacks, and hot cocoa. Unless you want tea?"

"No way, hot cocoa."

"I'll be right back."

"So, where *is* Mr. Special? What did he say? Do we hate him? I'm completely prepared to be all solidarity-sister." The fireplace was restoked and fully ablaze behind Erinne. The snacks they devoured spread across the rug like litter along a highway.

"I let Chris off the hook." Ella shrugged, popping another grape in her mouth.

Erinne looked at Ella, waiting for her to go on. Ella only looked back at Erinne, not saying a word more.

"Okay. We'll come back to that. What about your parents, what did *they* do?"

"My parents," Ella scoffed. "They said exactly what you'd think they'd say. How disappointed they were, how their reputation would suffer, and the kicker, how they didn't want me in their lives anymore because it was too much for *them* to handle. So, I stole the family album—Mom never gave a shit about family anyway—and left." Ella fingered the amethyst locket her mother had passed down to her on her twentieth birthday a couple of weeks before, the family heirloom Ella had actually looked forward to finally getting.

"Fuck them. They've never been there for you. You'll stay here with us, your real family. We'll take care of you. Wait, what about school?"

"I'm taking a break for now."

"Then you're staying here. You'll have an Irish baby in Ireland. It'll be grand," Erinne said with an exaggerated accent that she didn't actually possess. She'd always wanted one, like her parents had, but she was raised in San Francisco and sounded very Californian, much to her dismay.

"I don't know what I'd do without you, without all of you."

"Then it's a good thing we will never have to find out."

As expected, Erinne's family took Ella in with open arms, giving her all their love and support, as well as the adjoining room to Erinne's.

Finally, after all the years they'd wished for it, Erinne and Ella became the sisters they'd always dreamed of being. A little late in the game, but still a cherished time.

There were mornings, afternoons, and sometimes evenings when Erinne would hear Ella retching in her bathroom. She'd wet some washcloths with cool water, hold Ella's hair back, and hand her the washcloths.

It took a few weeks for the morning sickness to curb. After it did, Ella took on that glow they said pregnant women got. She was more radiant than ever, and the excitement was starting to build as her little tummy started to poke out ever so slightly.

"You should tell him, E." Erinne scrutinized her best friend with watchful eyes as the two of them manned the front desk, Ella staring off again with that distant look on her face.

Ella had become strangely quiet, not at all like her. Though Ella would never admit it, Erinne knew she was heartbroken over leaving Chris. Ella got scared and ran.

So not like her.

"Tell who what?" Ella's attention snapped back as she wiped down the desk.

"It's been a couple of months. You won't talk about him, not even with me. Do you think I can't tell that you're heartbroken? This is part of my Best-Friend-Sister-Soulmate job, you know." Erinne put her hand on Ella's to stop its wiping, wiping, wiping.

Finally, Ella looked up at Erinne, all that hurt in those green eyes of hers that mirrored her entire soul.

"I don't want to burden him, change his life. It's not fair to him. I should have realized who he was. I always knew I'd have a daughter, but I forgot about the guy who would give me the daughter. That's *my* mistake."

"Ella, that makes no sense. Hold on," Erinne quieted when guests walked in. She quickly checked them in, gave them a key to their room, and then called Brian over to cover the desk so they could walk outside and talk uninterrupted.

Walking along the cliffs that overlooked the sea had become their safe haven, a place for their more serious life talks, which they had a lot more of these days.

"Don't get me wrong. I am ecstatic to finally have you here with me, being roomies and all. When you showed up at our door, I thought it was my dream coming true. But not like this. You're having a baby. Which is wonderful. You think it's wonderful, I think it's wonderful. My parents are over the moon. Your parents—well, forget them. But you're sad, and it's not because of your parents being jerks. It's because of Chris. Besides, what *is* fair to him is to know. He has the right, honey."

"How could I do that to him? He has this great life, unattached, free to frolic wherever, whenever, and with whoever he pleases. He has this amazing, adventurous spirit. I don't want to be the one to kill that in him. What, do I call him and say, hey, no more adventures for you, sir? By the way, I'll be outta here soon, soooo, you'll be doing this alone?"

"But it's totally fine for *you* to do this alone? And stop saying you're going to die. That is not okay."

Ella took Erinne's hand in hers. "I'm sorry. I know it hurts you when I tell you that. Besides, I won't be doing this alone. I have you." They walked silently for a while. But silence never lasted too long with Ella.

"You know, this little girl is going to love it here. This land will be a part of her very soul. But please push her out of her comfort zone when it's time. She'll get too comfortable and forget how to live life." Ella put a hand to her tiny belly.

"A child of yours, not live a crazy adventurous life? Impossible." Erinne and Ella laughed, talking about the baby and everything they both hoped and dreamed for her.

Their talks along the cliffs always ground them both, bringing calm and clarity. When they returned to Lantern Light, Brian rushed out the front door, frustrated, waving them in.

"Will you get back to the desk so that I can finish the projects I am *supposed* to be doing. Shit, Erinne, I'm not a damn secretary. Speaking of which, there is a call for you, Ella. He said he'd wait on hold as long as it took." Without further explanation, Brian stalked off toward the stable.

"Oh shit." Ella's face turned a shade Erinne had never seen on her. Ella didn't get scared, rarely got mad, and certainly didn't let a conversation intimidate her. "It's Chris."

"Okay, okay. This is a good thing. It's time, Ella. You can do this." Erinne led her up the porch stairs and into her parent's office, where she could take the call in private. "You got this. I'll be at the desk if you need me." Erinne closed the door softly behind her.

CHAPTER THIRTY-TWO

Sera

IRELAND

After the dinner dishes were washed and put away, and either everyone left, or retired to their rooms, Sera asked Erinne and John if they were ready for the conversation.

Erinne led the way to their own newly renovated suite. After a quick look around, Sera knew this one was an exact replica of the Alaura Suite.

"Wow. You said you made a copy of the room, but even the furniture?" Most of the furnishings and rugs were the same. Even the windows and curtains were replicated in every detail.

"It's great, isn't it?"

"That it is," Sera said as she looked around the room, then sighed, knowing that she was about to ruin this homecoming so soon after getting there. "There are a few things I wanted to talk to you two about—"

"Wait. I'm sorry. I need to get this out before we get any further. I, too, need to have a conversation with you. Something that I've been putting off for too long. Maybe I've been too lenient or a coward. Either way," Erinne paused before continuing, "your mother would be heartbroken seeing her daughter so afraid. You don't have any friends, you never go out to have fun, you've never lived the true college experience, or any experience for that matter. Even though John assures me that you just need time, I can't help but worry sick every single day that you're throwing your life away."

"You're always worried about me," Sera huffed.

"Damn it, Sera, why don't you ever take me seriously? Don't you think that I have the right to be worried? Maybe if I had been a little *more* worried about Ella's constant foreshadowing of her own death, she might still be alive. But I wasn't, and now she's gone. My best friend trusted me to take care of you, to make sure you were happy. But you're wasting yourself."

"Wasting myself? My mother sacrificed her life for me. You don't think that puts a little pressure on me? What am I supposed to do with that?"

"She was your mother. Of course she sacrificed her life for yours. That's what moms do."

"Exactly. I'm supposed to honor that by doing what *she* was supposed to do. If I don't, I've failed her."

"No. You honor that by doing what *you* are supposed to do," Erinne said, exasperated, putting a hand to her forehead. "Fine. Let's play a game since you're so keen on punishing yourself in your mother's name. Pretend you have a child. A sweet, beautiful baby that you made with the wonderful man you adore. You've raised this child together, loving her, watching her first steps, hearing her first words, teaching her how to read and ride a bike. This child brings light and joy to your lives beyond anything you've ever known. As her mother, you want everything for this child. Success, love, happiness. Now pretend you're given a choice. Your life or hers. Of course, you are more than willing to choose her life over your own, she is your *child*. She has her whole life ahead of her. She hasn't even had a chance to live. Now pretend you're watching from beyond how her life turns out, the life you ended your own for, and she does *nothing* with it!"

"Erinne, Sera. Why don't we take a minute to breathe a little? Everyone is pretty upset right now." Always the peacekeeper, John walked over to Erinne, putting his hand on her shoulder.

"No. Let me finish." Erinne shrugged him off. "This child is alive, yes, but scared and sad all the time. She is not living. She is just existing. If it were your child, Sera, how would you want her to live her life?" Her anger turned to anguish. The tears she'd held back in fury escaped. "If you think *you* have failed *her*, then I have failed you *and* my best friend."

Sera closed her eyes and lowered her head.

"I just told you at dinner that I *have* made a friend. Not to mention that I just took this massive trip across the Atlantic Ocean by myself. Doesn't that count for anything?"

"Yes, of course it does. And I'm so glad—" Erinne started before Sera cut her off.

"I *do* want my life back. I do. I don't *want* to be scared of everything. Don't you think that I *want* to be able to let people in? To make friends without thinking they'll be taken from me? I want to be able to go out sometimes and have fun without thinking there is a monster lurking, waiting to destroy me again. I don't want to let that bastard win anymore, which is exactly what I've been letting *Him* do. I have forgotten my own mother and instead let *Him* win by stealing away my life for the last fifteen years. I *want* my damn life back!"

"Oh, sweetie." Erinne crossed the room and took Sera into her arms. "You're not forgetting her. You've just been lost. It's too easy to get comfortable in that safe feeling. But then it becomes really tough to break the habit. You have to find a new way, a new routine, one that is totally you. Not me, not John, not your mom, just wonderful *you*. After a while, that will become a habit, too. Ella loved you so much. She just wanted you to be happy above all else. So do I." Erinne pulled Sera away from her to look at her. "You set impossible standards for yourself, and why? What does it prove?"

"Geez, you're starting to sound like John," Sera said as she chuckled and reached out to hold John's hand.

"Thanks. I'll take that as a compliment. He's usually right."

"Yeah, I know." Sera smiled at John, took a breath, and let the rest pour out. "Have a seat, you two. There is a lot that's been going on."

Moisture started accumulating on Sera's palms as the weight of what she was about to ask of them, of John, set in. She wasn't just afraid to open the door she'd purposefully kept shut for all these years—she was terrified. Terrified that remembering things might break her again like they had as a child, the one who didn't speak for almost a year, the one who had night terrors.

She'd learned to control that fear, and it was by locking it up and forgetting about it. But where had that led her? An empty life with no experiences, friends—or *any* type of relationship—no emotion for much of anything. Nothing to love, nothing to hate. Nothing but a hollow shell of existence.

"After all that, and judging by the look on your face, I say the rest of this conversation needs a few fingers." John walked over to the small bar cart set up in the far corner of the room.

"I won't say no to that." Sera made herself comfortable on an ottoman next to the fireplace as John poured whiskey into glasses for each of them.

"Slainte." They raised their glasses and sipped. The warmth slid down Sera's throat, spreading through her chest.

"Okay," John said, sitting next to Erinne, "lay it on us."

"First, I think I have decided on something. It's probably crazy. I know you guys will tell me if I'm being unreasonable, won't you?" Sera sat at the edge of the ottoman, her back straight, a shield ready for whatever they might think.

"Of course. Didn't I just prove that?" Erinne winked at her, then rested her hand on Sera's, waiting patiently until Sera found her voice.

"I don't know if it'll work or if I'm reaching. I mean, I'd be basically starting all over," when Sera finally did speak, the words hurried out. "I called earlier today, and San Francisco State happens to have an open spot. I guess someone dropped at the last minute, and since I'd be a second-year transfer—which means I'll have to transfer my credits from Stanford, the ones that qualify, anyway—there is room for me. But it *is* possible. I think it's what I need to do, what I was meant to do," she paused to take a quick breath, then continued, "I want to study nursing instead of medicine. Well, it's still medicine, but, you know, a different route. A more personal one."

"Why, in God's sweet name, would we want to dishearten those dreams of yours? It sounds like a wonderful idea."

"You don't think it would be, I don't know, like betraying Mom? She was supposed to be this wonderful doctor. I was going to be the doctor *she* never got to be."

"No. It's far from betraying your mom. Finding *your* passion in life is honoring her. It is okay to want something different. It is more than okay to have your own goals, hopes, and dreams. You sound like your mother did when she knew she wanted to be a doctor. You'll be a fantastic nurse." Erinne caressed both of her palms against Sera's cheeks.

"I was really hoping you'd say something like that." Sera let out the breath she'd been holding. "I didn't realize just how much I wanted this until now. I was afraid you'd try and talk me out of it." She took Erinne's hands, squeezing them.

"Okay, now about the other part..."

"Good Lord, there's more?" Erinne stood to refill her glass, then refilled everyone else's. "We'll be smashed by the end of the evening at this rate."

Sera took another sip before starting.

"The awake-dreams and night terrors are back."

Sera told them of the experiences she'd had, from the first vision of her mother to the night terror of what looked like the vicious murder of a young girl with pale blonde hair.

"It's been so long. You're sure, then?" Erinne asked as she sipped her whiskey, her brows furrowed in thought.

"They're not easily mistaken for something else."

"No, of course not. But maybe they're memories of someone you've somehow connected with. When you were little, you didn't just have the awake-dreams, you'd pick up on memories or feelings from a room or a space. You don't remember that?"

"No. I really don't." Sera sipped the rest of the whiskey in her glass. "How do you know it wasn't something I was making up? I had a crazy imagination, I do remember that. I remember having an imaginary friend, Bee."

"Because you would know things you shouldn't have known." They told her about times she had displayed such abilities. John told her about when she talked about his grandfather, who had long passed before Sera was even born. Erinne told her of the Christmas story about Chris's funny gifts.

"Well, I don't need you to explain what the sock is for anymore. I got that one." Sera felt the heat of the whiskey loosen her nerves. "Why is it that this is so easy for you two to believe, but I can't believe it myself?"

"I should've done more to let you explore your abilities. Maybe I should have explained it better, or at all, for that matter. I never meant to keep anything from you. After you were finally able to control your night terrors, you seemed so happy, and you never really said anything about them again. I guess I just let it go," Erinne's voice faded softly, her eyes misting before she continued. "It's easier for me to believe because I've watched this kind of magic most of my life with your mom. And John, here, is the science nerd who looked it all up, so he's got proof of his own."

"I could show you the studies if you want. Got me big points with my girl," John said, trying to lighten the moment with a wiggle of his eyebrows at Erinne, who shook her head and rolled her eyes but smiled back at John. "Your mother seemed to have had abilities of premonition. You, on the other hand, have exhibited abilities as more of an empath, highly sensitive to others' emotions and their memories, absorbing them into yourself, which could be why you get overwhelmed in crowds or unfamiliar spaces. It could be the explanation as to how you're experiencing these troubling visions through another person. In theory, anyway. I could get all shrinky on you and tell you I think it's not a matter of you believing *it*, but you believing in *yourself*. Look at me, I mean it." When Sera looked away from them, John took Sera's chin in his palm and looked her in the eye. "This is what we are here for, to talk it all out with, no matter what you say or how long it takes."

"I don't remember any of it though. Why do you think I can't see or feel those abilities anymore? Is that what these night terrors are? Those abilities trying to push their way back?" It still didn't make sense. If she could do all that as a kid, why can't she do any of it now, on purpose, at least? She'd closed herself off to a lot, but having an extra sense of things didn't seem like it would be a part of anything else she'd locked away.

"Maybe you grew out of it? Or maybe it is a don't-use-it-lose-it type of thing?" Erinne offered.

"Okay then, why now? They've been gone for so long, what purpose could they possibly serve coming back after all these years?"

"You seem to have blocked out some of the events that happened to you, either by choice or necessity. In doing so, you've never actually let yourself deal with the trauma you went through. Sometimes, to heal, you have to allow yourself to feel the emotions so that you can deal with them properly. Then, you can choose what to let go of. Maybe in doing so, you'll regain control of your night terrors," John said.

"You see Doctor John, that's exactly what I needed to hear. I think I'm there now, ready to go back so that I can move forward. Maybe if I open myself to all of it, it will help me deal with everything else. I'd also like to look at the police reports and anything about what happened to us during those six days. Especially since everyone will know more than I do when they air that documentary about the whole thing this summer."

"They've tried calling us several times. To give that monster any infamy, can you imagine? Disgusting, if you ask me. And then to re-open someone's personal hell to the world. I hope it won't become a frenzy like last time. What they're doing should be illegal. They don't even have our permission." Anger crept into Erinne's voice.

"Unfortunately, they don't need it. It's public record," John replied.

"Nevertheless," Sera interrupted, bringing their attention back before she lost her nerve. "John, I was hoping you'd work with me on the hard stuff. I never let you in as a kid, not all the way. I want to do that now."

"Sera, sweetheart, I can't be the one to help you. We are family now. It blurs ethical boundaries."

"That didn't stop you from marrying your patient's family member."

"Touché."

"Seriously, though. How could I possibly begin to explain my mother's abilities and whatever it is that I am experiencing? I need *you*, John."

"It won't be easy. It will be messy and painful."

"I understand that. Why do you think I've waited so long?"

John sighed, then took both of Sera's hands in his. "I also don't want you to be angry with me while we do this. It happens, sometimes. Patients get angry at the therapist who brings all the hard stuff up to the surface."

"There is no one I trust more."

John nodded. "Alright then. When do you want to begin?"

"Is tomorrow too soon? I only have you for the summer while I'm here." Time wasn't exactly on her side. When she started the nursing program in the fall, she was determined to be well on her way down her healing path.

"Evenings after dinner, then. Don't be late, or I'll charge you extra."

"Deal."

Erinne took Sera into an embrace. "I'm proud of you. All of the courage it takes to do this, to face this head-on. You're sure you want to do this?"

Sera waited a moment before answering, "I've never been more sure of anything my whole life."

"I just want you to be alright." Worry forever etched on Erinne's face.

"I will be." Sera pulled out of Erinne's arms. "Now that you have successfully fed me and boozed me up a bit, I think I'm going to soak up some evening Irish lore." She stood up, straightening her clothes.

"Would you like company?" Erinne walked with Sera to the door.

"No. Thank you. I just need some air." Sera embraced Erinne tightly, kissed John's cheek, and left the room without waiting for a response.

Sera increased her pace, faster and faster down the hallways until she was running through the back door, out past the clearing, and into the woods. She pulled the air into her lungs in fast, hard gasps and didn't stop running.

Wind and a light mist of rain hit her face, pulling her hair down into long crimson waves. With each stride, the pain inside of her pooled down through her feet and stomped out onto the moss-covered forest ground. Her lungs contracted into spasms until they felt like they'd burst. Instead of stopping, she ran faster.

At first, she was running to escape—to escape the fear that dwelled within the memories that lived in the dark corners of her mind and the hurt that inevitably followed. She ran harder and faster, pushing the internal hurt into something physical.

The summer sun was low in the sky, though it was already late in the evening. Strobes of setting sunlight flickered through the trees as she raced past them. Soon, she was lost in her breathing rhythm and the sound of her footfalls. Everything else in her mind disappeared. She found a way to forget about her pain and her grief, even if it was only for the duration of a run.

Lungs on fire, she slowed to a jog, then to a walk when she felt more at peace. The wildness of the forest wouldn't allow her to run much further, even if her body hadn't given in to exhaustion.

No longer in rows, the trees tumbled and tangled into each other, many fallen and lying across the ground, grown over with moss and grass that sometimes reached knee-high in patches. She was in a different place out here, a wild place as ancient as it was fantastic.

Sera walked out into a meadow and took in its breathtaking beauty. Closing her eyes, she breathed in the clean, damp air, listened to the cricks and songs of the wildlife around her, and let her mind finally rest.

Chapter Thirty-Three

Jeffrey Mason

ARKANSAS

Over the years, Ingrid grew more and more rigid. With each pregnancy, she went further back to her holier-than-thou religious bullshit. Her cult ways were ridiculous, obnoxious, even.

To Ingrid, sex became an abomination, the worst of sins. Sex was only meant for reproductive purposes, never for pleasure. As time went on, she stopped letting Jeffrey touch her unless it was explicitly to make children, and he had never gotten her pregnant on purpose.

He took her if he wanted, willing or not. She was his wife, after all. As he would tell her afterward, it was part of her wifely duties. Wasn't *that* in the bible, too? Let her ball herself up on the bed and cry herself to sleep. He didn't care. It usually amused him when she behaved that way.

He'd wondered so many times over the years why she stayed. For fun, he would push limits to see how far he could go before she'd finally have enough and leave him. Strangely, she never did.

Maybe it was because her mother surely would never allow her back into their home as a divorced woman, or perhaps Ingrid stayed because she had zero skills to support her and the kids. Ingrid had never loved him, just as she knew he never felt much of anything for her. So maybe she'd been just as stuck as he was.

Not only had Ingrid become more like her mother in her extremist religious views, but also in looks. Plain, unattractively skinny, her long stringy hair pulled tightly back, always quiet, as mousy as ever. It disgusted him that this was his wife.

No matter. He had tired of her almost entirely now that she was pregnant with their second child.

In all fairness, there *were* a few moments when he thought about really trying. He'd put in the effort and time at work and made his way up in the company, getting some of the credit and recognition he deserved.

Another rare moment was when his son was born. Jeffrey finally felt a connection to something other than himself. He looked at his wife with an inkling of gratitude. That gratitude drove him to at least try to keep his tastes private.

But that had only lasted so long. Ingrid being extremely pregnant with kid number two made Jeffrey antsy and uneasy. The urges started coming on stronger than before, maybe too strong for him to control much longer.

And there was this chick at work who was hot for him. She never came out and said as much, but the way she looked at him told him all he needed to know.

CHAPTER THIRTY-FOUR

Ella

IRELAND

Ella had never been so nervous in all of her life, never experienced the accompanying churn of the stomach, the hard thumping of the heart, or the tingles that traveled all the way down to the fingertips.

It was astonishing, really, that she hadn't felt this way when she missed her period. Nor was she scared when the second line on the stick turned pink. She wasn't afraid when she told her parents she was pregnant or when they cast her out of their lives, telling her that she was no longer their daughter. She didn't feel this way when she dropped her classes, moved out of her apartment, or packed everything important to her into a few boxes and left for Ireland.

All of those feelings hit her now, and it was just a phone call. A phone call that would confirm how broken her heart was, and worse, would break his heart. She cared for Chris too much to hurt him that way. Slowly, she reached for the phone, the red light blinking, blinking.

"Chris?"

"Why didn't you tell me, El?"

"I..."

Chris's face flashed before her. He had never been sad or angry, but right now, he was both, and it was because of her.

She closed her eyes and saw him so clearly—the smile, the laugh. He was holding their baby girl's hand, teaching her how to walk, how to ride a bike, how to make Mommy laugh insanely, and eating gobs of ice cream with her.

"It was shitty of me. I got scared. I'm so sorry."

"Well, it's a start." Chris blew out a shaky breath. "I get it. It's a big scary thing, and you went into survival mode. But you should have told me."

"Chris, I don't know what I was thinking."

"You can make it up to me later. I'm just so happy to hear your damn voice. Let me in, Ella. Let me be there for you, with you. I'll go to you if I need to. I know Erinne and her family are *your* family, and I know that's what you need right now. I won't get in the way of that. I just want to be a part of it."

"You'd come here?"

"Hell yeah, I will. I'll be on a plane tomorrow."

"What about...!"

"*Nothing* is as important. School is a joke. I'm not going to be playing baseball my whole life. I can find work there. My family, well, they're assholes, so who cares what they think. Tell me the word, and I'm there."

"Why, Chris? I'll hold you back and eventually break your heart. You should be having fun, going out with other people, going on all your crazy escapades."

"*Other* people? El, you've botched that up for me. I can't joke my way out of this. You and our child *are* the rest of my life. It is only you. You are my biggest adventure. And I'm not wasting any more time."

"Do you even have a passport?"

"Am I not the adventure king? Of course I have a passport."

CHAPTER THIRTY-FIVE

Sera

IRELAND

Falling back into old routines and weaving in new ones was quick and natural. Sera would get up early, go on a run, then help Nan with breads and breakfast service. Afterward, she helped Brian and Pops with the horses. Her beloved Gypsy had died years before, but the new horses were just as sweet. She'd spend her afternoons grooming, mucking stalls, or riding.

Evenings were spent in the kitchen at the family table, eating stews and bread, drinking wine or whiskey, and having lively family conversations.

Late evenings were the hardest part of her routine. Working with John was as difficult as he'd warned, but they were progressing. Most of what she remembered still came in pieces, a jigsaw slowly getting pieced together, remembering the darkest parts of the nightmare she'd forgotten she knew.

The records of the police investigations took forever to locate but were finally emailed to them the week before. Sera spent hours reading through police reports, witness statements, and medical reports of the injury that brought Jeffrey Mason into her mother's hospital and into their lives.

After a particularly tough session with John, Sera gave in and watched the Docu-Series out of spite. She'd gone back to her room more angry than sad, which had never happened to her before. Fear and sadness had always won in her daily life. So, in her newfound fury, she decided to watch the thing she'd been dreading for months now. Maybe even years.

The strangeness of seeing actors portray them all was unsettling at first, but that tapered off as she learned more about the man who had taken everything from her. A psychopath, sure, but just a human man, nonetheless.

He'd had a wife named Ingrid and three children—Jacob, Jordan, and Judith. There were no additional segments about the children, and Sera couldn't find out much about them online.

What had kept her awake wasn't the documentary, it was thinking about how it might've felt to be one of the Mason children, wondering what kind of life they'd had. How had he treated them? Had he beaten them, carried out his sadistic tendencies on them? Had they lived in hell on earth with that man for a father?

In the aftermath, Sera had been the lucky one. She had a wonderful family who took her in and cared for her as their own. She was working on the feeling of well-being part, but it *was* possible to regain it.

For the Mason children, though, they might never escape the shadow of that man or the damage he may have left in his wake. Sera hadn't been Jeffrey Mason's only surviving victim.

After weeks of sessions with John, after all the background research she'd done, with all that she'd seen and learned, it all came down to this night. This was the day she'd been afraid of most of all.

They had worked each evening carefully retrieving memories of what happened. Not what she remembered through night terrors where she relived moments as her mother, but pulling her own memories from her mind, piece by piece. Tonight, she would put them all together.

"This session might be especially difficult. May I suggest that Erinne join us as extra support for you? A hand to hold."

"I'd like that, yes." She and John were sitting in his and Erinne's suite, the fire crackling in the background, soothing the nerves she felt every time they began.

John began after Erinne was sitting next to Sera on the loveseat by the fire. He always started by asking her to tell good stories about her mother and father, slowly leading to more uncomfortable questions.

"Sera, you told me you remember going out with your dad that day. When you're ready, take me back to that. What do you remember?"

Sera drew in a long breath and closed her eyes. In her mind, she could see her dad's handsome face and hear his laughter.

"Dad had taken me for ice cream, even though it was cold outside. He loved ice cream just as much as I did," Sera started, grinning as she remembered. It had started out as such a good day, then turned into the worst nightmare of her life.

Daddy got up from the bench and wiped ice cream off of Sera's face and hands.

"Mommy is on her way home. Are you ready to go?" Daddy ruffled her hair, making her giggle as he took her by the hand and led her back toward the car.

"Hey, did you know that your nose is smarter than your brain? It has more scents."

"You're so silly, Daddy." Sera giggled, skipping over the cracks in the sidewalk. "Do you *have* to go to work tonight?"

"No. I can stay home, and you can do my hair and makeup. Make me look pretty for Mommy."

"Nooo. Makeup *is* for Mommy."

"Okay then, I can do your hair and makeup."

"Nooo. Last time you tried to do my hair, it took Mommy a really long time to fix it," Sera said and laughed.

"Oh man, then I guess I better go to work since I'm not good at doing girly things."

"You are good at doing things. You're really good at teaching me how to play baseball and how to ride bikes. I only fell two times. And then you were good at making my knee ouchie stop hurting right after. Your magic kisses are even better than Mommy's. And you tell the best stories. You do all the voices and everything. And you are a really good singer."

Daddy stopped short and put his hand over his heart. "Why, those are the sweetest things anybody has ever said to me. Makes me tear right up." He exaggerated wiping fake tears away from his eyes, but then he took her into his arms, gave her a really big hug, and kissed the top of her head. Sera laughed again as he opened the back door for her to jump in.

Daddy was helping her buckle the seatbelt—it was always tricky to get it to click—and then he had all this red paint on him, which spilled on her pants and hands. Then he fell into her lap and slid down to the floor. Daddy was really heavy, and it kind of hurt when he fell on her.

But then there was another man she had never seen before. A big, bad-man. He was standing right behind Daddy. The bad-man shoved Daddy the rest of the way into the back seat at her feet. It was then that she started screaming. The bad-man reached for her.

"Shush little one. Everything will be okay. I'm your daddy now. I'll take care of you."

He held her head and covered her mouth and nose with a cloth. It smelled weird, and she kicked and cried and tried to get away. He wasn't her daddy. Daddy wasn't moving on the floor of the backseat. She cried and kicked and then started to feel really sleepy. Her eyes fluttered and finally closed.

When she could open her eyes again, they burned, and her head ached like a swarm of angry wasps stinging her brain. Her throat was dry, and her lips stuck to her gums. When she tried to rub her eyes, she felt the ropes holding her wrists down. The room was dark, so dark she couldn't even see shadows.

Then she remembered.

Daddy wouldn't wake up.

She wanted her mommy. She wanted to go home.

"Sera, sweetie. Are you awake?" Mommy's voice whispered through the terrifying dark. "Sera, I need you to listen to my voice."

"Mama?" her voice cracked as she began to cry. "It's dark."

"I know, baby. I'm right here. I can't reach you, but I'm right here."

"The...The bad-man...He hurt Daddy, and Daddy wouldn't wake up." Sera started to cry harder.

"I'm so sorry, Baby," Mommy's voice started to shake as she began to cry as well, their quiet weeping filling the room as they mourned a father and a love. It was a long time before Mommy spoke again.

"Sera, are your hands tied?"

"Yes, the ropes are pinching my wrists."

"Can you move your arms at all?"

"A little bit." Sera started crying again.

"I need you to do something for me. Try to reach your ears. Can you do that?"

"I can reach them."

"Good. Now, I need you to promise me something really important."

"Okay."

"The bad-man is going to come back. When he does, you might hear bad things, scary things. I need you to promise me that you'll cover your ears nice and tight and hum a song as loud as you can so that you won't hear the bad things. Promise me, sweetie."

"What ba-bad things?" Sera started to cry again.

"Any time you get scared, you cover your ears and hum. Please. Promise me, Sera."

"I prom-promise," she hiccupped through her cries.

"I love you, Baby Girl. To the moon and back and all around the sun and stars. Always, always remember that."

"I love you too, Mama."

It could have been days, she wasn't sure anymore. It was long enough to have lost control of her bladder. Sera was hungry, thirsty, and soaked in her urine.

She could feel him there, too, hear him breathing, the figure in the corner of the room, no features, just a shadow.

"Are you just going to keep us chained in our own filth?" Mommy was getting less scared and more angry as the days went on.

"We could be happy. We could be a real family."

"Not like this, we can't." Mommy slammed one of her chains on the floor, startling Sera.

Heavy footsteps approached. Whimpering, Sera shrank as small as she could, anticipating his touch. But he didn't touch her. Instead, he grabbed hold of Mommy's face.

"I have never loved anything as I love you. I knew it the moment I first saw you in that hospital. The instant you took my hand to stitch it up, I felt our connection and knew you were meant to be mine. Then I saw your daughter, *our* daughter. I knew we were meant to be a family. We could be happy," the bad-man whispered, the alcohol on his breath stinking up the air.

When he tried to kiss her, Mommy bit into his lip and didn't let go. At first, he shouted and thrashed, and Mommy held tight. But his fists were stronger than Mommy's will.

Sometimes, Sera could feel what the bad-man was feeling, like she could feel what Mommy was feeling. It would scare her so badly that she would just cry. Especially when he thought about Sera growing up and being *his* and doing bad things to her.

On that last day, the bad-man was putting up more boards around the windows. He seemed happy, whistling. Mommy sent her a surge of love that only Sera could feel in their special way before Mommy started screaming at the bad-man.

"You sick Bastard. She is a CHILD! How could you even think of doing those things to her?"

The whistling and hammering stopped abruptly. "What the hell do you know about anything?"

He yanked Mommy up from the floor. Sera felt it as if it happened to herself when Mommy's wrist dislocated, the flesh tearing off of her hand, freeing it from the chain.

Mommy screamed out in agony. So did Sera.

Sera slammed her hands to her ears and started to hum louder and louder, breaking the link between them. No matter how loudly Sera hummed, she could hear the bad-man slamming Mommy into walls, crashing her into furniture, until something in Mommy's body cracked. Only then did he let Mommy drop to the floor, a pool of blood quickly spreading around her, her breath ragged, wet, muffled.

The bad-man continued to storm through the cabin, screaming obscenities, smashing things, throwing the table, tossing chairs. Each time he passed Mommy, he kicked her with his full strength.

Finally, after his fit past, the bad-man stood in the middle of the room, panting heavily as though he'd just run miles.

And then he was staring at her, all quiet and scary.

"My sweet Sera, stop crying now. Everything will be different this time. We will have a wonderful life, you and me. Sera, stop that crying now. You'll forget this. You'll only remember all of the good times we are going to have. STOP CRYING!"

But she couldn't stop. She was so scared. Mommy wasn't moving, and now the bad-man was getting mad again and coming toward her, making her cry even harder.

His big hands came at her, pulling at her, the ropes burning like fire as they cut into her wrists and ankles. One rope let go from the wall, dangling from her ankle. The others only pulled tighter. Frustrated, the bad-man yanked off the rest of them.

He was so strong, too strong. There was no way to fight him off. No give to try and wiggle free from the vice grip of his hands, except for the few seconds Sera was free from his grasp as he placed her on the bed. She slipped off the bed and ran toward Mommy, but she couldn't get far before he grabbed her and threw her back on the bed, cracking Sera's leg across the footboard.

The pain was so terrible it made her dizzy, and when her head hit the headboard really hard, she almost went to sleep. That was when the bad-man started ripping at her clothes.

Sera was so scared and so dizzy that she started to throw up. The bad-man had to jump out of the way to avoid the splash of her vomit.

But that didn't keep him away for long. He tore at her again, his fingers holding her arms down so tightly they left bruises, as her body began burning from the inside out.

Sera's mind drifted off, the pain and burn falling away. Sleep took her under, hiding her mind somewhere far, far away, a place where she could talk to Daddy and hold Mommy again.

Sera started to wake up when she heard the wolves howling outside. But as she remembered where she was, she realized it wasn't wolves, it was Mommy.

Mommy was beating the bad-man, stabbing him over and over with one of his tools. Then, Mommy fell on the floor again.

Sera scooted toward the edge of the bed to get to Mommy, her body sore and hurt all over. When her feet touched the ground, a devastating pain shot up, and she fell to the floor, her leg unable to support her.

"Mommy," Sera started crying again, so hard that she could barely see as she pulled herself across the floor to where Mommy was lying.

She shook Mommy really hard, but Mommy wasn't moving. She pulled Mommy's head onto her lap, brushing the hair away from her face. Mommy's face was really broken and bad, but she could hear her breathing shallow, wet breaths.

Mommy was able to open the one eye that wasn't swollen shut and smiled up at Sera.

"My life, my heart."

"Mommy, let's go now."

"Can't baby. So sorry."

"Please, let's go."

"Run. Go fast."

"I don't want to leave you."

"You have to, Baby Girl. Please. Promise me."

"Okay, Mommy."

"Don't. Stop."

Sera couldn't stop crying. She didn't want to go, she couldn't leave Mommy by herself. She laid her head on Mommy's chest where Mommy's thoughts, emotions, and happiest memories connected with Sera as the rhythm of her heart began to slow.

The time when Ella was holding her pregnant belly, talking so softly to her tummy, whispering all of her stories to her unborn daughter. Erinne, her beautiful best friend—her soul sister—standing off to the side, the ocean at her back, sneaking a picture of the moment.

Her baby girl, just born, swaddled in her arms, her infant scent as intoxicating as any drug, the pure, true love she felt the moment they looked into each other's eyes, their souls connecting.

Watching Sera learning to crawl through the thick grasses of Ireland, already growing so quickly, a head of red curls shining in the sunlight, her tiny body rocking back and forth, trying to get that momentum to move forward, baby giggles carrying through the wind.

Sera's first unsure steps, toddling in the yard with Chris. His beautiful face smiling into their daughter's, her joyous laughter bounding through the neighborhood as he twirled with her.

Sera's second birthday, running naked through the house, cake smashed all over her face, her giggles echoing through the rooms as Ella gave chase trying to get her into the bath.

Her fifth birthday, her eyes closed tight, making that special wish as she blew out the candles.

Mommy closed her eye, and her memories drifted away from Sera, her breathing slowing to a stop.

"No, Mama!" she cried, shaking her as hard as she could. "Mama, wake up. Please."

But Mommy didn't wake back up. Sera lay down, put her face to Mommy's, and wept, her whole body shuddering.

It took a long time for Sera's tears to stop. Finally, when they did, she tried to stand up again, but her leg was bent funny and it made her scream when she tried to stand on it. She fell back down. She tried crawling, which she could do. It hurt a lot, but she could move. She tried dragging what used to be Mommy with her, but she was so heavy.

Out of strength, Sera stopped trying to drag her. She laid down with her again.

"I'm sorry, I can't bring you." She kissed her cheek softly. "Good night, Mommy."

Sera crawled out of the cabin. It was almost as dark outside as it was inside. The giant trees were so dense that no moonlight could steal through. Still, she crawled on. Rocks and sticks cut deep into her knees. She found a broken tree branch not too far from the cabin. She tried standing again, supporting her weight on the stick. It hurt so bad she screamed when the pain shot up from her leg through her body. But she could stand. Slowly, she limped step after step. After a while, her leg went numb, and she dragged it along.

Sera didn't know how long she had been trudging through that forest. Hours, it seemed. But she never, ever stopped.

She had promised.

Sera opened her eyes. John was next to her, holding one hand, a tear running down his face. Erinne on the other side of her, covering her mouth, sobbing quietly.

Erinne folded Sera into her arms and wept.

CHAPTER THIRTY-SIX

Ella

IRELAND

The year went by like a flash of a picture taken. Chris had been welcomed without question. He and Ella shared the room that adjoined with Erinne's. As a joke, they'd come up with a funny knock instead of the age-old sock on the door, just in case.

Chris and Ella didn't waste another moment rediscovering one another, making up for the months lost. Ella's ever-changing form intrigued Chris even more than before, and they couldn't get enough of each other.

Erinne and Ella would spend slow afternoons watching Chris and Brian bond over construction projects, Brian Senior teaching them both how to do certain things and how to work specific tools. After a day of good, hard work, the two of them would hang out and have a beer.

Even after Brian met Shelly, he hung out with Chris most evenings, and Shelly became part of the ladies' crew, who watched the men, laughing and teasing them about their adoring bro-mance.

It was a peaceful time for Ella. She ignored the loud ticking of the countdown clock, pushing it away from her mind so that she could enjoy those small but ever-so-important moments of her life.

What had been plaguing her thoughts was what would happen after she was gone. Her baby girl would be her moon and stars, but when she was gone, as the everlasting ticking reminded her, what would happen to her child? Ella would never stop living each moment for what it could be, but that didn't keep her from knowing that her precious time was short and to plan accordingly.

The baby inside her had grown to what seemed to be its peak, stretching her skin as far as humanly possible. The alien feeling of a knee or an elbow moving across her abdomen was a magic compared to nothing else. She already loved her daughter more than she loved anything ever before.

Annabelle was always fussing over Ella, making sure she was eating enough, drinking enough, resting enough. It was sweet. Ella couldn't imagine her life without them.

Where would she have ended up? Would she still be in her cell of a bedroom in San Francisco, prisoner to her parent's bidding and disappointment? She was thankful she'd never know.

On a crisp mid-spring morning, Ella was down in the stable petting the gentle old horse, Gypsy—the black and white paint that belonged to the land of Lantern Light as much as any of its human occupants—when an odd cringe crept through her back and around her abdomen. The horse nestled Ella's hand, pushing more than usual, neighing nervously. A silent pop she felt rather than heard, wet between her legs. Gypsy moved her head again as if telling Ella to get back to the house, whinnying softly. She didn't need to be told twice by the horse.

On her way back up to Lantern Light, she was brought to a stop with a pain unlike any other she'd ever had in her life. It was like lightning striking, starting from her abdomen, gripping its electric claws around the rest of her body and squeezing it like a vice. She bent over, clutching her belly, taking sharp, shaky breaths as the pain crested. When it finally subsided, she started walking again.

Chris was suddenly at her side. Ella had no idea where he'd come from or how he'd gotten to her so quickly, but he was there, his strong arm around her, the other holding her hand, guiding her back.

The moment they walked in through the back door of the Inn, Annabelle was upon them, then Erinne, and then Brian. Everyone was running about, talking quickly, excited, and nervous. The hospital was a thirty-minute drive with good weather, but as it was in Ireland, the roads were wet, and the rain was coming down steadily.

Brian Senior pulled out the four-wheel-drive truck and packed Ella, Chris, and most of the Byrne crew in with them. The drive was uneventful, with the exception of a few pains that would have brought Ella to her knees had she been standing. Chris looked like he would cry or pass out each time she had one. Erinne sat on Ella's other side, holding her hand, softly talking her through each pain.

Not long after she was admitted to the hospital, Ella's pains came faster. Erinne never left her side, and Chris stayed on her other. Annabelle cheered her on, holding a leg back, counting excitedly when it was time. Both Brians stayed out in the hall.

The evening came in moments, moments that she would measure her life in. The peak of excitement as the time drew near—the encouragement, the nervousness, and the love in that room immeasurable. Ella pushed when she was told, bearing down with a strength she never imagined she possessed. Then, there was a moment of absolute silence when no one made a sound.

The sweetest cry pierced the room, and everyone exhaled with relief, then cried with happiness.

The nurses placed the baby on Ella's chest as they wiped her down, encouraging her to keep crying. Ella wrapped her arms around the slick little body of the most beautiful creature, her baby girl. Already green eyes were wailing angrily, whisps of red hair drying.

Finally, as they settled the baby under Ella's hospital gown, she quieted in her mother's arms.

The baby looked up. Their souls connected.

Ella fell into unconditional, immense, fierce love that instant. Her whole life was meant for this. To bring this child into the world, to love her, to protect her.

"Welcome to the world, little Sera," Ella whispered to her daughter.

Ella looked up at Chris, who had tears trickling down his face. She reached out, cradled his cheek with her hand, and brought her lips to his.

"She's perfect," Chris said, awestruck, putting his finger in Sera's little hand, her tiny fingers immediately grabbing hold. "Marry me, Ella. Let's be a family."

Ella smiled up at Chris. "We *are* a family," she said, kissing him softly.

Erinne stood back, giving them their first moments together. But Ella needed her there, too, because she was just as much a part of the family she'd created. She motioned for Erinne to come closer.

"Thank you. For all that you've done, for everything you are," she said, putting her forehead to Erinne's. There were no words that Ella could say that would explain how much she felt, the love in her heart was so profound.

But that was the beauty of their friendship. Erinne knew Ella better than any other person, maybe even better than Ella knew herself. Erinne knew exactly what she was trying to tell her.

Chapter Thirty-Seven

An oscillating fan swirled hot sticky air around the humid basement. Florescent light filtered through the heaviness as I watched yet another program boasting about *Sera Delaney*, the golden child, and her miraculous survival and recovery. How brave she was, with her pretty aunt and the shrink who raised her.

Who couldn't thrive with that kind of entourage at your beck and call all the time?

Lucky little bitch is what she was.

It is the fifteenth anniversary of the story that rocked the nation into hysteria when some woman and her pretty little perfect daughter were allegedly kidnapped by Jeffrey Mason. The media loved that kind of shit.

I've probably watched this series a half-dozen times since it first aired last week, as if the content would change somehow. As if the media would tell the whole story, the true story.

But it was always the same. Jeffrey Mason, the stalker, kidnapper, pedophile, rapist, killer.

The narrator described who Jeffrey Mason had been. A married man with two children, his wife pregnant at the time with their third. He'd been successful in his job, interviews with his coworkers gave him nothing but praise. They even promoted him by sending him and his family from Arkansas to San Francisco. A man who had never even had a mark on his record before his alleged *victim* murdered him.

Then they really dug in. First, they accused him of being a wife-beater and a cheater. The reason for the promotion? An affair at work that escalated into a sexual harassment lawsuit. Then they accused him of stalking some young, beautiful medical student after she had treated him, saying he'd watched her for weeks. Of course, for maximum dramatic effect, they tied up their pretty bow of accusations by tagging him a kidnapper turned killer, saying that he had killed the boyfriend before taking the chick and her kid.

She was never accused of anything, though. Even though that woman savagely murdered Jeffrey Mason with a damn screwdriver, of all things. Stabbed him something like fifteen times before keeling over herself. Who could do something as vicious as that?

They never asked the right questions with stories like these. It was automatically the man's fault. But what I want to know is what *she* did to make him leave his family? Did it ever occur to them that maybe it was something the woman did that seduced an otherwise good man to turn on his own family? Why didn't they ever investigate that?

They were all the same, pretty women. They lured men away from their families. Just like the white-haired bitch had done to mine. And apparently, they could get away with murder, no questions asked.

The segment then turned to pictures of the sweet little girl with red hair and sad eyes, her picture frozen on the screen for audience emotional response, really letting it set in.

"*...Fifteen years after surviving such an ordeal, Sera Delaney is now a Stanford undergraduate with plans to follow in her mother's footsteps staying in the medical field. She'll start San Francisco State's prestigious nursing program in the fall...*"

I reached for the remote and turned off the TV. Poor, sweet Sera Delaney. Tormented, brave, survivor. Fucking saint. I'm surprised they haven't made a damn Hallmark movie about her yet.

They say everyone is the result of their upbringing. Nature vs. Nurture and all that. In my case, this seems to have mostly been true.

But if I'd had the privilege of being raised by a nice lady, her doctor husband—not just a doctor, a fucking therapist—and had the support of a sane, normal family, I might have grown up labeled a survivor and revered too.

Instead, I got screwed and got the crazies for family. What does that raise? A drug-addicted brother and a weak-minded follower of a sister. Then there's me.

I've waited for karma to deal out justice. Nothing. I waited for a judicial system to step in and save us, then enact proper punishment on those who committed monstrous atrocities. It never happened. I have a long list of people who have done such wrongs. To others, to me. Yet they are still out there, never once brought to their knees to answer for all they've done.

Not the mother who had basically abandoned her own children. She may have been present physically, but she left us unloved and unprotected from harm all the same.

Not the grandmother who beat children for existing, who made every moment of every day dark and full of terror.

Not the pretty redhead who stole a father from a family who was not hers to take.

Not even that little girl—who may not have technically done anything, but just the same was given everything and left nothing for anyone else.

As long as she exists, I would get nothing.

Patiently waiting for all the wrongs to be righted has gotten me nowhere, nothing. The only reason the white-hair bitch got hers is because *I* had been the one to bring her to justice.

Well, maybe it was time. Time to stop waiting and start doing. Eye for an eye and all that bullshit.

I may have needed righteousness, but I'll settle for revenge.

When I embraced my calling, many things happened. First, joy for finding purpose in what has been a dismal life so far. Second, the need to plan. Carefully. Each tiny detail as important as the big ones.

Like chess, even pawns can have great power when utilized properly. And that's what she is, a strategic pawn. A way to get one step closer to capturing the king—or princess, if you will.

If I was going to pull this off, I had to watch her carefully, record her habits, learn her schedule, master every part of who she is. Thinking about what doing this will make me become isn't allowable. I can't go there. Not now. The path has been shown to me, the path that will make my life worthy of existence. And I need to do whatever it takes to get there.

But this feels different. This is not someone who purposefully brought pain into my life. She is merely the right piece to move on the board.

The longer I watch her, the worse my nerves fray. Every time I think of when I'll have to get rid of her, which needs to be soon, my palms sweat and nausea threatens.

The beast inside my mind is useless. It is sleeping, dormant when I need it most to come out and do my bidding for me.

Maybe it's a sign that this isn't the right way, or the right person, or the right time.

Maybe it is all wrong.

I pound my temples with both of my fists to stop the doubt. Doubt is what leads to ultimate destruction.

It's funny how they've tried to beat faith into me since I can remember. It almost makes me want to spit after just thinking the word. But now that I know what I am meant for, I have to lean back on having faith.

Not the kind Grandmother tried brainwashing me into. Not some blind faith for some fantasy deity, but a faith in the universe, for what it has presented to me, all wrapped up in a pretty bow.

For this one sacrifice, redemption could be sought after it is finished.

Then, I will make sure that *she* pays for everything.

CHAPTER THIRTY-EIGHT

Sera

IRELAND

*H*umming, rocking. Stabbing. The thickness of skin and muscle popping through her fingers.

Running, hobbling as fast as she could, dragging the shattered leg.

Get away. Fast. She promised.

So dark. Black trees, slapping at her face.

Then a boy. Angelic face. "Come on, you okay now."

A kind woman. "That is very sweet of you, Davey."

Sera woke with a start. After such a difficult session, she should have expected to have a night terror. Sera started to reach for the glass of water on her bedside table when all the sounds around her stopped.

What little light there was in the room faded to complete blackness. Tracers flew through her vision, the objects too blurry to see, the pulsing of her own blood echoing in her ears.

Gloved hands that weren't Sera's came into focus. They were dragging a young, unconscious woman, who looked to be in her early or mid-twenties, along the dirt ground, dense redwoods surrounding them.

The hands treated the person they possessed with care instead of the viciousness the hands had previously shown they were more than capable of.

This time, there was no violence—obviously, the woman had been taken against her will—but there was no beating, no cutting, Sera felt no rage within the figure. Instead of hate, it was a necessity that drove the figure.

The woman did not move, nor did she wake as the gloved hands dragged the sleeping woman to what looked like a shallow hole, freshly dug, just large enough for a body. Once they'd reached the hand-dug grave, the gloved hands carefully set the woman down and almost...hesitated.

Finally, the gloved hands reached down, angled the woman's head just so, and gave a quick twist, snapping her neck.

As the gloved hands began to carefully place the body into the hole, Sera was pulled back out.

All the sounds of night came crashing back. Sera's body shook uncontrollably, everything soaked through with sweat—clothes, sheets, hair. She panted as she looked around her room, in the same position on her bed.

Bile rose to her throat. She barely made it to the bathroom, where she heaved until she was dry. After brushing her teeth, she sat back on her bed, curled her knees into her chest, resting her head against them.

Unfortunately, watching a person be brutalized was nothing she hadn't seen firsthand. But it never got easier to watch a life fade out of someone. Whether or not it actually was happening or were just really awful night terrors, it took a piece of her every time. If she could cry, it would be hard to stop after seeing such cruelty, such torture, such maddening waste of life at the hands of some madman. And for what purpose?

Why?

Knowing that sleep would not come again, Sera got up, pulled the sheets from the bed, and took a cool shower, all before the sun rose. Since it was still too dark to run and it was way too early for breakfast, she took out the stationery and began writing a letter to Adam, then one just for Ava, sketching a picture of the three of them on the ship on the back of it.

Writing to them had a way of recentering her soul enough to get her out of her room to face the day. For all the evil that existed, there was still pure innocence and joy that prevailed, such as little Ava, which was to be cherished and fiercely protected at all cost.

She addressed the envelope and took it downstairs with her when she finally went down to help Nan with breakfast service. A good kneading session was just what Sera needed to work out some nerves.

"You're up especially early this morning," Nan said as she kissed Sera's cheek when she approached her at the kitchen island.

"I need to work out some aggression." Sera took a ball of dough, spread some flour over the counter, and began working the mixture.

"Ah, well, I welcome the help and the company. You got a letter yesterday. I put it over there for you." Nan pointed to an envelope on the other side of the kitchen.

A grin spread across Sera's face. Adam. Somehow, he knew that she needed him. And wasn't it funny that in such a short time she developed such a need for her very first true friend?

After breakfast service mellowed, with a steaming cup of coffee in hand, Sera took Adam's letter out to the terrace and sat at the small table to read it.

Too soon, summer was gone. Mornings were becoming cooler, and leaves started to tease new colors. It was her last day, her last run, of her self-discovery summer in Ireland.

Streaks of sunlight hit her face like beams of gold. The trees were sparkling with morning dew, the wind-whipped cliffs where she'd spent hours sitting were free of the ever-present mist, and the ocean looked as if it was filled with sparkling sapphires. Sera already missed the magic of this place.

For the first time in her life, Sera made a point to take in everything around her, especially during her new running routine. Each day adventuring farther, exploring wild forestry, castles, cliffs, and other ancient remains. She ran through fields of wildflowers excellent in colors and rich with fragrance, and along the coast down below the cliffs among the crashing waves.

Though she'd grown up there, she had never let herself experience her surroundings. She'd always been too wrapped up in her tragic past, living a dead life, lost in her own protective bubble. She'd been given a second chance—third really—to live, a privilege not given to most.

Swearing never to take it for granted again, she breathed it all in, absorbing into memory every bit of this enchanting place. She closed her eyes, feeling the wind play through her hair, breathing in the freshness of the vegetation and the salty sea air. All of it surrounded Sera, pulling her in and helping her let go of the chaos of her thoughts.

After showering off her run, Sera took her time dressing and packing her things, trying to extend the last bit of time in the room that always brought her close to her parents. After she ran out of reasons to stall any further, she made her way down to the kitchen.

"How was your run this morning?" Erinne asked, already in the kitchen helping Nan with breakfast.

"It's always so hard leaving. It's so peaceful here. A run in old San Fran just won't live up to this place."

"This will always be here, waiting for you, whenever your heartstrings pull. I hope you're hungry. Nan has gone completely bonkers this morning, making all of your favorites." Erinne gestured over to the vast array of breakfast foods that were piled on the island.

"It's what I do. I feed my people. Besides, you can't go back without one last Irish feast." Nan kissed Sera's cheek as she handed her a cup of coffee.

"I will definitely miss being spoiled," Sera said as she sat at the kitchen table, watching the kitchen staff shuffle the food out to guests.

"Good morning my lovely ladies," John sang as he walked in and headed straight to the coffee.

"We wanted to offer it to you, even though I'm pretty sure I already know the answer." Erinne joined hands with John. "Why don't you stay and live here full-time? There is a university not too far from here. They even have a nursing program. It's here for you if you want it."

"It's beautiful here. It's my second home, and I'll never stop visiting. But since I was a kid, it has always been just that, a second home. My home is in San Francisco. Someday, I hope to move back to my house on the island." She kissed Erinne's cheek. "I love you both so much. Thank you for everything you've done for me. For being my mother, my father, for being my everything."

"You've been ours. When you are happy, we are above and beyond. I have one last thing for you." Erinne reached behind her neck, unclasping the diamond lightning bolt she wore. She draped it around Sera's neck and adjusted it to lie next to Ella's amethyst locket, which Sera never took off. Erinne stood back to admire it on her.

"Ella gave this to me when she and Chris left to go back to California with baby you. She told me I'd never forget the trouble we caused together every time I looked at it. I've worn it ever since." Raw emotions choked Erinne's words as the flow of tears started to run.

"No. I can't take this. It was for you, from her." Sera looked at it sparkling next to the Amethyst locket.

"Yes, but I want it to remind *you* now. Every time you look at it, remember to cause some decent trouble for your mother to be proud of."

"Thank you, Erinne. For everything." Sera kissed her wet cheek again and hugged her.

"Well now, that's enough of this. Let's get out of here. John, get the girls' bags, would you?" Erinne draped her arm around Sera and headed out to the miniature car to begin the long drive ahead.

CHAPTER THIRTY-NINE

Ella

IRELAND

It was time, she hated to admit, to return to San Francisco to finish what she started. Ella had been afraid and had run from everything. But life had a way of coming full circle.

Ella's entire pregnancy along with the first year of Sera's life in Ireland had been such a blessing. The Byrne family had been everything to Ella. Her support, her heart, and her love. From them, she learned how to be a mom and a family. They were her role models to aspire to.

She'd never be able to repay them for everything they'd given to her. Especially Erinne, when Ella knew there would be so much more to ask of her. But she would keep that to herself until the time came.

Ella would be forever grateful for those peaceful, heart-fulfilling years and would treasure them until the end. But Ella's fate was to return to school and continue working toward her medical degree.

The Knowing had never stopped pulling at her, pacing like a caged tiger, back and forth, needing to be released, its usefulness wasting away in its cage.

Ella and Erinne walked along the cliffs as they had probably done a hundred times before. This time, they walked with heavy hearts as Chris was packing up the last of their things to leave this place and its people that had become their sanctuary.

"I get why you have to go back. Can't say that I'm excited for you to leave, though. I'm selfish like that."

"You're the least selfish person I know, Erinne. We've had some amazing times, you and I, and made some great stories along the way with all the trouble we've gotten into."

"And out of. No one can stay upset with you for long. Not even that cop in junior year." Erinne laughed, even though tears wet her eyes.

"Your dad always said we were thunder and lightning, so I got this to remind you. When you wear it, remember all the trouble we made and the great times we had making it. Don't forget any of it." Ella pulled out a box that contained a diamond lightning bolt necklace. She motioned for Erinne to turn so that she could put it on her.

"Did I ever tell you, you're my hero?" Ella sang to Erinne, mostly because she couldn't stand seeing her sad for a moment longer.

"Oh my god. Shut up, dork." Erinne playfully pushed Ella, then wiped the tears from her cheeks.

"You really are, though. You were always my best birthday present. Don't forget that either." Ella hugged Erinne as her own tears started to spill over. In the distance, Ella saw Chris waving to them.

"I guess it's that time again."

"On to the next chapter."

"You said it, sister."

Arm in arm, Ella and Erinne walked back toward the Inn, where life would pull them apart once again.

It was like high school all over again, standing on that street, weeping. This time was no different, maybe even worse.

The entire family had become so attached to Sera. They loved her like a grandchild, a niece, a child of their own, and Sera loved them all. Hearing her baby cry for them as she and Chris drove away tore her heart into two pieces.

"You okay over there?" Chris kept his eyes on the tiny winding road, but he knew her too well.

"No. I'm not," Ella huffed, wiping her nose with a tissue as she tried to soothe Sera's cries along with her own.

"It's only for a little while. Maybe we'll come back, and you could practice here," Chris said, taking Ella's hand.

"No. We'll never get to come back here." The moment, the pictures she saw in her head, hit her hard and fast. Flashes tore through her mind, each picture bringing actual physical pain.

Hands of a man—no face—just hands.

A dark cabin in the woods.

A screwdriver.

Blood dripping to the floor.

"This is wrong. We shouldn't leave. If we stay, you'll both be safe. We should go back. Go back!" Ella grabbed at the wheel to make Chris pull over.

"Whoa. Hold on." Chris pulled off the road as best he could without putting them in the ditch. "What's going on?"

"Something is wrong. This is wrong. We need to go back."

"Did something happen to Erinne or the family?" Chris looked at Ella, confused and worried.

He was trying so hard to understand the cryptic messages spewing from her. She was giving him nothing but gibberish, scaring both him and Sera. Sera's wails got louder the more frantic Ella's voice got.

She took a few breaths, trying to calm herself.

"No, everyone is fine. I'm sorry. I haven't had one of these in a while." In fact, she hadn't had any since coming to Ireland. None during her entire pregnancy, and none during the whole first year of Sera's life. But now that they left Lantern Light, Ella had been hit with one like a freight train. "It's like it is trying to warn me. But I don't know exactly what or why. This thing has always been annoyingly cryptic. Not to mention inconvenient."

"Well, who likes taking the easy way? There's no fun in that. At least after you're done with med school, you'll put your *Knowing* to use. How can that be a bad thing? And when have you ever run from a challenge?"

"I ran from you."

"Yeah, but not for long. Look at us now." Chris winked and kissed Ella's hand. "Besides, when we get back to San Francisco, we're going to get hitched."

"Not if you know what's best for you." She kissed his cheek, then settled back in, ignoring the loud ticking all the way back to the airport.

CHAPTER FORTY

Sera

SAN FRANCISCO

The last days of summer held on with a hot and humid claw making the students filing in and out of San Francisco State's administration building damp with perspiration and hot with temper. Makeshift fans waved swiftly, toes tapped impatiently, and the wind was as calm as an airtight room, making circumstances miserable.

Chaos was all that Sera thought as she waited to see the academic advisor about her transferred credits and classes. Luckily, some of her undergrad classes qualified for about a year's worth of nursing prerequisites. If she did well, she could be graduating and sitting for the state boards in three years' time instead of four. The irony that she would be twenty-six years old when she graduates, the same age her mother had been when she died, didn't escape Sera.

Half the day had passed before she was finally hauling her luggage into her assigned dorm in student housing. The shock of how tiny and cramped the rooms were still surprised her. Furnishings meant to conserve space packed the room. Two twin beds were shoved to opposite walls of the room, a single dresser between them. Two small desks were crammed up against each other under the window, and a tiny closet stood next to the door.

She glanced around the room again, wondering which bed to take. The beds were positioned so that neither had an advantage over the other. Placing her bags on one of them, she began unpacking.

After everything was put away in half of what little storage there was, for fun, she took out her phone and snapped a few pictures of the room and one of her stationary sitting on the desk and sent it to Adam with a text, *More coming soon to a mailbox near you*. Then, she wrote her first letter to Adam and one to Ava from her new home.

As she sealed the envelope, a girl rushed through the door in a whirlwind of energy, carrying three huge bags. The girl whipped around the room, rapidly talking on a cell phone crunched between her face and shoulder. Her words flew at such speed that Sera would be amazed if the person on the other end could keep up.

The girl stopped in the middle of the room, looked around, acknowledged Sera, and threw her bags on the remaining bed.

"Yeah, I'm here already. Look, I gotta go...Dad...Yes, I heard you the first ten times...I will...I have a ton of luggage. Dad, I gotta go...Yes...*YES*. Love you too." She pushed a button on the phone and threw it on the bed. "You'd think they haven't sent any of their kids off to college before—me included."

After she had rid herself of the phone, she peeled out of two jackets, showing a lean, muscular figure. She took off two hats sending waist-length jet-black hair tumbling down. She smiled at Sera after removing her sunglasses, revealing light blue eyes as she walked to her with her hand extended, elaborate tattoos of twisting vines and flowers entwined up around each forearm.

"Hi, I'm Peyton. Peyton Davis. Sorry about that. My parents have like, half a dozen kids and freak out when any of us leave the nest. Even though I have already flown the coop. Twice, actually. After I finished my first year of prereq's in nursing, Europe was calling me, so I followed my heart. Anyway, I guess it's nice, but sometimes, rrrrgghh, you know?"

Gravity cemented Sera in place. She didn't move toward Peyton, didn't take her offered hand. Instead, she was lost in those eyes, unable to move her limbs. "You have beautiful eyes. Haunting." Sera felt her cheeks heat with flush as she broke the hypnotic eye contact with Peyton. "I'm so sorry. I'm rusty on social skills, as in I don't have any. Weren't you burning up in all that?" Sera finally shook Peyton's hand, then gestured to the heap of clothing she'd shed.

"Don't apologize, I live for compliments. As for all that, I ran out of suitcases and didn't feel like carrying them all so I just piled them on. Besides, a little sweat is good for the waistline." Peyton turned to admire her abdominals, which were now shown off by the bright red crop top she was wearing. "You work out?"

"I run in the morning," Sera said with a shrug. "But that's kind of new for me."

"Great. I run too. We can be running buddies." She dropped next to Sera on the bed. "I guess I should find out your name, huh?" Peyton had a dazzling smile.

"Sera. My name is Sera Delaney."

"Yeah. I thought I knew who you were. Not to be intrusive or insensitive or anything, but my dad knew your mom, and he was just devastated by the news. I'm really sorry." Without skipping a beat, she gave Sera a quick hug.

"He knew my mother?" Sera let herself be hugged without taking notice, seeing as her mind stopped with Peyton's comment. "But that was so long ago."

"Not, like, personally. My dad got himself hurt at some work retreat thing and had to get himself sewn up. Nothing terrible. It was minor. A brilliant medical student—your mom—patched him up flawlessly and sent him back home to his family. My mom sent her a thank you card and pictures of all of us," Peyton said, her voice like a bird chattering, light and sing-song. "She does that type of thing. Super proud and all that. And then that documentary. Wow." She patted Sera's knee, her eyes full of concern.

"I don't watch TV anymore. Too depressing," Sera said, shrugging.

"Amen to that. Okay, when I first walked in, this guy invited me to some welcome party tonight in one of the rooms downstairs. He was cute. Lots of cuties around here. Though there was this one chickadee, now she was hot. I might try and talk to her tonight. Anyway, you in?" Peyton got up from the bed and began to go through her bags, tossing clothes wherever. "I think I'm going to wear my new dress. I've missed this part of the whole college thing." She pulled out a tiny piece of red fabric and held it against her body. "Perfect, huh?" She turned toward Sera.

"Um, where's the rest of it?"

"You're a funny one, aren't you? That's the whole point. Less is more, am I right?" She walked over to a mirror that was attached to one of the closet doors to admire herself. "We should be there at like ten, no ten-thirty. Make the grand entrance and all." Peyton reached into the closet and took out a hanger for the dress.

"I'm not much for parties, and I have a heavy load coming, a lot to catch up on. I'm a pre-med transfer. But thanks for inviting me." Sera got up from the bed to help Peyton unpack.

Peyton stopped and turned to Sera. "Intriguing, ex-premed. So, you're a smarty pants. Well, that's exactly why you should get out while you can. You seem to be the studious type, so you'll be knee-deep in books soon. And I have to find a job almost immediately cause academic scholarships only pay for so much—which reminds me to apply at the grocery store down the street tomorrow. Anyway, this might be our only chance. At least you'll meet some people you'll basically be living with for the year. C'mon, you have to go." She stuck out her bottom lip in a sexy pout, a look that Sera had no doubt probably worked on everybody.

"I don't know. If you recognized me, I'm sure someone else will as well."

"So what if they do? Makes you a celebrity of sorts." She smiled and nudged Sera with her shoulder.

"Not the good kind."

"Haven't you heard the saying, there's no such thing as bad publicity? C'mon, just once. Go with me this *one* time, and I'll never bug you again." She added a puppy dog whine to her perfected pout.

Get into some trouble that would make your mother proud.

Sera felt her will begin to bend. "Just once?"

"I promise. Cross my heart." Peyton made a large X across her chest.

"Okay. But just for a little while."

"Great. I have just the thing for you." Peyton rummaged through her luggage.

Sera shook her head, waving her hands. "Oh, no. I'm not dressing up or, um, un-dressing up or anything like that." That old fear started rising to the surface.

"You really are funny. I could tell the minute I saw you that you weren't the type. No, I have a great top that will match those emerald eyes of yours." Finding it, she spun around and leaped back to Sera, holding it against her. "Perfect."

Sera looked down at the top. It was actually a nice, regular sized top. And it *was* almost the exact shade of green of her eyes. Peyton was not to be so quickly underestimated.

"It's really cute. I think my jeans will go well." She stood up and searched through her drawers. Even if it was just a small moment, for the first time, Sera was young, the way she was supposed to be.

"Thanks for talking me into going. I actually had a lot of fun." Sera plopped down on her bed and lay back on the pillow, looking up at the ceiling. It was later than she had intended to stay, but she had been the one saying, "Let's stay a little longer," when Peyton gestured to leave.

"Hey, no sweat. Maybe you'll come out with me more than once after all since I plan on doing *that* a lot more." Peyton began to undress, leaving her clothes draped over the desk and chair.

"Doubtful. I really do need to focus on classes. It took a lot of convincing, favors, and a lot of luck to get into this program. I can't waste this chance. Besides, I'd like to try to get honors if possible. I think that would have made my mom proud." Sera handed Peyton her blouse back, then carefully folded the rest of her clothes, putting them back into her drawer.

"I'm sure she'd be proud no matter what. You're here, going for it. Childhood trauma is all the rage these days and takes the blame for people doing all sorts of crazy things. But not you. You're lucky enough to have a lot more than others. A precious life. Don't forget that," Peyton got quiet, but then that dazzling smile came back. "What's not to be proud of?" She smiled and gave Sera another one of her bear hugs, and this time, Sera hugged back.

"Bedtime. Big day tomorrow." Peyton jumped into her bed, threw the covers off, and pulled the sheet over herself.

"Do you mind if I keep the light on for a little bit? I have a short letter to write before I go to sleep."

"Letter? As in paper and pen? Who does that anymore?" Peyton turned toward Sera, laughing in disbelief.

"It's our thing, kind of an inside joke." Sera shrugged. "It is actually kind of therapeutic, writing everything out."

"Aw. Romantic."

"It is *not* a romantic thing. We're just friends." Sera wadded a piece of paper and tossed it at Peyton.

"Mhm. Well, take all the time you need. I can sleep with all the light and noise in the world. I have like twenty brothers and sisters, remember?"

Chapter Forty-One

The news brief said she was a *young* girl and showed a picture of her in her school uniform side-by-side with a recorded video of a white tarp draped over the body discovered in the forest.

It *was* her. It *had* to have been.

The reporter announced that police hadn't officially identified the body yet since it was badly decomposed from such a long time exposed to the elements. But it was suspected that the body belonged to a teenage girl who had gone missing months before, Marlene Jacobs. The story went on about how Marlene had been a bright child, followed by the usual memoriam.

But I wasn't listening to the rest of the news segment anymore since my blood was roaring so loudly in my ears.

She *wasn't* a schoolgirl. She'd been a grown woman, the woman who had fucked my father and, by relation, fucked the rest of us.

It was *her*.

Wasn't it?

I don't understand why the news reports had gotten it all wrong. So wrong.

Hadn't they?

It was an agenda of some sort. That had to be it. They had to twist the truth into something that would fit whatever propaganda the media was trying to spin to scare the public. After all, the press was invented for hiding and twisting the truth.

I can't let them trick me into doubting myself.

My head started pounding again. The whispers started up again, too, shouting instead of whispering, that raging beast in my head trying to claw its way out.

I can't let it out. Not now. I've worked so hard and done too much to get as close as I am now. And there is still so much to be done.

This is my one and only chance. I need time to learn and observe. I will wrestle my rage into silence, forcing the beast to remain patient with the promise of the ultimate prize that is waiting for us both at the finish line.

PART THREE

STRENGTH & WISDOM

"The world breaks everyone, and afterward, some are strong at the broken places."

-Ernest Hemingway

CHAPTER FORTY-TWO

Sera

SAN FRANCISCO

W ake-y, wake-y. Time to run those buns into rocks, girlie."

Sera opened one eye and squinted at the bedside clock. "How do you do it?" she groaned.

Peyton was already up and dressed for their run. After three years as roommates, she still beat Sera every morning.

"I haven't been staying up until two AM every night since forever, studying my fragile brain to death. When was the last time you slept a full night?"

"You are, too, up until two AM pretty much every night. You're always out doing whatever, or *who*-ever, and hold down a job at the grocery store. Yet you're *still* up before me." Sera sleepily swatted at Peyton as she got dressed. Studying wasn't the only reason she chose to sleep as little as possible, but that was something she'd, thankfully, never had to explain to Peyton.

Sharing a dorm with someone presented its own fear—like her roommate witnessing one of her night terrors. She had no idea how she'd explain them, and she really didn't want to. Luckily, in the past three years with Peyton, she never had to. The dreams had become dormant. Maybe all the work she and John had done had helped her deal with it all. Or sleep deprivation helped ward them off. Either way, she was grateful.

"Ah, don't be jealous. It's called sexual freedom, my friend. It's the best part of our liberating feminism." Peyton laughed in her musical way as she watched Sera hurry around the room. "Don't worry, sweet Sera, people naturally want to give you everything. Not to mention, you're stunning. All you have to do is bat those gorgeous eyes, and some rich guy will be begging for you to marry him. If nursing doesn't work out for you, that is. You already have *one* waiting patiently for you."

"Peyton, you're terrible. First of all, no, I don't. He's my best friend only. Second, is sex *always* on your mind? Even at six in the morning?" Sera quickly pulled her hair up in a ponytail and opened the door for Peyton.

"Always. Besides, you brought it up. Now, c'mon, slowpoke, try and keep up with me today." Peyton took off down the hall, giggling as she ran. Shaking her head, Sera sprinted to catch up.

As Sera walked to her first class of the day, her body felt how tired she actually was, which was more than she led on. Most nights, she'd stayed up late, her face crammed into her notes or a textbook, trying to keep everything fresh in her mind. That hard work and missed sleep had paid off. She was in the top five percent of her class. All she needed to do now was stay focused for just a while longer. Graduation was finally only six months away.

"Sera. Wait up," the dorm RA called out as he jogged up to her, waving something in the air.

"Hey, Thomas. What's up?"

"I found one of your letters in my mail this morning." His face shyly blushed when he stopped in front of her.

"Thanks. You didn't have to bring it out to me. You could've slid it under my door," Sera said. She suspected he came out for more than just her mail but hoped she was wrong.

"It's alright, I don't mind. I noticed it's from that friend of yours in New York. I know how much you look forward to those." He stood there looking at Sera with his hands shoved into his pockets.

Awkward silence clung in the air.

"Well, thanks again. I have to get to class." She started to move away before he finally spoke.

"I, uh, I just knew how much you, um, you like those letters," he stammered.

"I do."

"*Um*, Sera. Is he...Well, *um*, is he like...your boyfriend, that guy from New York?" His face burned bright red as he stared down at his sneakers.

"No, he's not. He's just a friend of mine." The nerves in Sera's gut knotted, the urge to run away almost too enticing. Her breathing started increasing, trapping pockets of air in her chest as her palms moistened. Her eyes darted around, looking for an escape. Silly, really. Why would a casual conversation lead to panic attack status? It was a ridiculous reason to have a panic attack, but here it was, creeping up on her.

"He's not?" Thomas's face lit up with a new, shining hope.

"I have to go, or I'll be late for class. I'll see you later." She turned and quickly started to walk away, trying her hardest not to break into a full, panicky run.

Unfortunately, so did Thomas. "I was going to ask you something. I know you're in a hurry. I'll make it brief," he said, staying quiet as he trotted behind Sera.

Sera could feel her skin burning and her stomach clutching. If only he'd trip over something so she could get away. But no luck. He kept up without a stumble.

"Could I take you out sometime? Dinner, maybe?"

"That is sweet of you. But I can't. I'm sorry. I have to keep all of my focus and energy on my studies. You know how that is. But thank you anyway," Sera sputtered, changing paths, darting away from him.

She didn't slow her speed until she was safe in the restroom. She hurried into a stall, put her head between her legs, and pulled in deep, slow breaths until the panic began to fade. Only then did her heart rate slow, though a tension headache started to ache at the base of her skull.

Sera groaned as she massaged her neck and glanced at her watch. Now she was going to be late, of course. Quickly, she splashed cool water on her face and made her way to class. If she had the time, she would have video-called Adam as a means of decompression.

Hearing his voice and seeing that handsome face of his would ease the tension in her. It always did. But now she'd have to wait until after class.

CHAPTER FORTY-THREE

Adam

NEW YORK

Hey there. I just got your letter this morning. *Summa Cum Laude*, that's fantastic. You've done everything you said you would." No matter how busy Adam got, immersed in the day-to-day proposals, blueprints, coworker drama—*Marcy Brodenburgh*—a video chat with Sera was always his top priority.

They'd usually schedule their video chats in the evenings when he was home, and Ava was still awake so they could both get in their Sera fix. Ava loved it, and so did he. Their friendship had developed into his lifeline over the past three years. When he felt himself starting to drown, she was there for him. Just looking at her face brought ease to whatever was on his mind at the time. Her presence, primarily by technology, had that effect on him.

"It's been tough, but yes, I am doing it," Sera paused. "I just needed to hear your voice and see your face. I have lots of your words, but not always you."

"Uh oh. What's up?"

Sera was having one of her nervous episodes. Adam could tell just by the pitch of her voice, if not the adorable way her brows knit together the way they did when she was worried about something. The girl would never be a great poker player. Every emotion she ever had was written on that pretty face.

He'd witnessed firsthand how hard Sera had worked to open herself up to allow all those feelings. Even if it had been little by little, fighting small but crucial battles when a situation would arise that required her to take a moment to let the emotion in, feel it, and process it instead of immediately shutting down.

Now, mostly, Sera would go full throttle into what she wanted, not only in her education but letting go of the fear that had gripped her for so long. His admiration of her knew no bounds.

Though she *could* let herself have a little more fun. She still didn't go out much, if at all. Occasionally, Adam wanted to urge her to get out more and enjoy a little bit of the college scene, but he'd always stop himself.

Remembering his own college experience, he'd had some wild nights. During one of which, he'd met Alex. For some reason, thinking about Sera doing those types of things made him uncomfortable.

What if Sera did let loose, maybe even find another friend to replace him? A male one. Which was ridiculous. Theirs was a friendship that nothing could break apart.

It wasn't like she didn't have other friends. Sera and her roommate Peyton had become close. Peyton insisted on staying by Sera's side since their first year. At first, there was something about Peyton's clinginess that unnerved Adam. He couldn't figure out why it bothered him. Most likely, it was because he was slightly jealous that Peyton was there in San Francisco and he wasn't. So, he'd let the weird jealousy go, for the most part.

Sometimes though, her bouts of anxiety would resurface, such as whatever was happening now.

"Probably just overthinking once again. Maybe I *am* working too hard, not getting enough sleep, or both. I don't know."

"What happened?" Adam coaxed.

"Nothing big, it's okay. I just wanted to say hello. I know you're busy."

"Oh no you don't. There are very few perks about being the boss, one of which is that the entire office comes to a halt when you call. They don't want to risk the long lines of the unemployment office if they bother me while I'm talking to you."

He got her to laugh. When he could make Sera smile, it made everything worthwhile.

"Are you having nightmares again?"

"Nope. Still nightmare free, thankfully. Actually, you're probably going to laugh at me."

"I promise I will only laugh *with* you, not *at* you."

"Yeah, sure. Well, my dilemma of the day started when Thomas, our dorm RA, asked me out. Nothing crazy, just out to dinner."

Adam couldn't respond. The words fell out of his brain.

"Hello? No snarky comment, or did you freeze on me?" Sera was looking at her phone as if their video chat had frozen.

He had to clear his throat before responding to keep his voice even. "Did you accept?"

Adam wasn't sure what he'd been expecting her to say, but it wasn't this.

Not only did hearing those words surprise him, it made his breath skip and his pulse speed up. She'd been his best friend for so many years that he forgot to think of her as the woman she was. A beautiful one at that.

Okay so he never *forgot*, he just made a point to try not think of her that way. Of course men were going to want to be with her. So why had it shocked him when she told him about one of them?

"No. But that wasn't the issue. The problem is that I had a panic attack because of the whole exchange. It was mostly embarrassing, honestly. I knew that he was trying to ask me out, and I freaked out, like I was terrified. I wanted to run as fast as I could to get away from him. I couldn't even catch my breath until I locked myself in a bathroom stall. What is *wrong* with me?"

"Why didn't you accept?" Nothing was wrong with her, but what was wrong with *him*? At this point he'd usually be joking, poking fun. She was probably expecting that from him. Something to lighten the situation and make her feel better. But his brain went flat. It wasn't funny to him at all.

"What? Well, I'm not interested in the guy, for one. Or dating, for that matter. Why? Do you think there *is* something wrong with me? I mean, that is what you're supposed to do, right? Date? But then the minute someone asks me to dinner, I go into panic mode." The nervous hitch in her voice rose a notch.

Adam was not helping his friend like he should be. In truth, he was being absolutely absurd. He shook it off, then forced a smile. "There is nothing wrong with you. I just wanted to make sure you're okay. With everything that's happened, I just wondered if it wasn't because of all that other stuff, you know?" Adam massaged his temples as he sat at his desk, on the other side of the country from her. What was he saying? Now was he babbling? And why had it made him nervous that Sera might have accepted? It had been a long day. That had to be why.

"See, that's why I needed to talk to you. You make me feel sane no matter what. Even if I feel like an idiot when I tell you what's bothering me. You never let me down, though. You always make me feel like I'm totally rational and talk me through it."

"That's what I'm here for," he said, gazing out the window of his office. If only she were closer to him.

"Hey. Is everything okay? You seem a little...distant?" Sera was studying him through 3,000 miles of technology. He forgot that she knew him just as well as he knew her. He would never be a good poker player against her, either. Adam grinned back at her.

"Sorry. Just a busy day here at the job."

"I'm telling you, you need to take a vacation once in a while. It's been three years since you took time off."

"That wasn't exactly time off."

"See? You haven't had a proper vacation in forever. Which is why you should come visit. I want to show you and Ava around San Francisco. I could show you the island too. I haven't been back there in so long. We could go together. I know you're busy and can never get away, but I can't resist hoping that, miraculously, you'll be able to one day."

"I will when you will," he said, quickly searching his calendar on the computer to see if he had anything open.

"That's not fair. I would come to see you if I could, but I can't get away. Unless it was winter break, which is way too soon." She chuckled.

"Winter break, that's in what, two or three weeks? That might work. Come out here and I'll show you around the Big Apple. Take my two girls to a Broadway show and all that. And we will plan my trip out to your neck of the woods. What do you say?" His calendar was completely full for months. He began deleting entire days, which most likely would have Alice, his assistant, storming into his office any second.

"I have so much to read, Adam. It would be really hard to..."

"Books are travel-size. Better, you could download them. That eReader I got you for your birthday last year was just for that purpose."

"And what about the papers I have to write?"

"Flash drives are tiny. Fits right in your pocket."

"Or drop them in Dropbox." Sera's face smirked at him through the screen.

"Drop what?"

"It's basically an online version of flash drives."

"See, smarty pants? Even better."

"In other words, you're not going to let me say no, are you?"

"Now you're on to something." Adam looked up and smiled sheepishly at his exasperated assistant as she burst into his office, tablet in hand, his calendar showing. He was caught.

"You're slick." Excitement replaced the earlier anxiety in her voice.

"That's what all the ladies say. Ava is going to be thrilled. I can't wait to tell her," Adam said as Alice cast a formidable glare at him, shaking the tablet.

He gave her his sweetest smile and mouthed, 'Sorry. Love ya.' To which she mouthed back, 'Show me' and rubbed her fingers together, the universal gesture for money. He laughed aloud and shooed her out of the office.

"Tell her I can't wait to see her. Give her raspberries for me too."

"I will. I can't wait to see you."

"And next time you come here. Deal?"

"Hands down. I'm not missing your graduation. Now get to those studies, smart girl. I'll see you in three weeks."

After Adam ended the call, he sat reflecting on his strange, emotional behavior, the way his gut felt like it had been sucker punched and twisted. Yes, she was a woman, but she was his friend first and foremost. And he missed her. He had a lot of work to double up on so that he would be free to enjoy every minute of her visit in three short weeks.

CHAPTER FORTY-FOUR

Sera

SAN FRANCISCO

Three weeks flew by for Sera. Midterms kept her mind off the growing nervousness that would sneak in about seeing Adam again. It was absurd to feel that way. It was *Adam*, her best friend, the person she talked about anything and everything with. Nevertheless, it had her stomach fluttering.

She sat on her bed with coffee on one side, a sandwich on the other, and her books spread from edge to edge as she typed away on her laptop, trying to finish the last term paper she needed to turn in before she left the next day.

"Look at you. You are the vision that every professor dreams of when he thinks of all of his seemingly hopeless students," Peyton said as she breezed into the room, her knockout body wearing nothing but her hardly-there bikini, sarong, and flip-flops.

"You make me sick. You should look exactly like me right now. Not Malibu Barbie. Do you realize how torturous you are? You get to lounge by the indoor pool while I fry my brain with loads and loads of information." Sera didn't stop typing once, nor did she waste a second by glancing up. "And how is it you didn't freeze to death coming back in only that thing?"

"Malibu Barbie? Ew." Peyton flipped her hair and struck a pose. "At least give me something with substance and attitude, like a Bratz Doll. Besides, since when have you known me to stop swimming? Got to get in my laps as much as our morning run. And, sweetie, the reason I'm not doing exactly what you are right now is because I'm happy with being one of the average. Less pressure. You're going for spectacular, I'm going for graduate, that's it." She threw her towel on the chair and began dressing.

"Would you *please* stop throwing your dirty clothes just anywhere?" As soon as Sera said it, she regretted it.

"Hmm, snappy, aren't we? Someone is a little tense," Peyton sang.

"What I am tense about is this damn paper. It's due in..." Sera looked at her watch and gasped. "Thirty minutes! I'm never going to finish this. I knew I should have skipped the extra hour of sleep."

"Whoa, relax." Peyton pulled on her jeans and a sweater. "You have thirty good minutes."

Sera took a breath and sighed. "Thanks. Sorry I snapped at you. Maybe I am a little tense. I've been a bit nervous about seeing Adam and Ava after all this time. What if she doesn't remember me? What if he's changed, somehow?"

"What do you mean, *seeing Adam*?"

"I leave tomorrow for New York. Remember? I'm spending Christmas with Adam and Ava."

Peyton stood in the doorway, staring at Sera. Her face twisted into a combination of confusion and... anger? Sera waited a few seconds. "I told you a couple of weeks ago. Are you okay?"

"Oh. Yeah. I totally forgot. Anyways, I am kind of bummed we won't be able to spend Christmas together. I was looking forward to it. I'm going to grab us some pizza. I'll put a scarf on the door on my way out so you won't be bothered." Before Sera could respond, Peyton spun out the door.

Sera knew Peyton could be a little needy, and she really couldn't blame her. Peyton wasn't the type who liked to be alone, and she had a whole family that she never got to see. Still, her reaction to Sera leaving threw her off a bit, though she had been surprised by Peyton's sometimes unusual behavior in the past.

During their first summer break, when Sera told Peyton she was going home to Ireland to spend time with her family, as she usually did, Peyton was quiet with Sera, even surly—not at all like her usual outgoing, bouncy self. After a few days, Peyton finally warmed up, acting like nothing had happened.

Which reminded Sera to make sure Erinne had everyone booked for graduation since her whole clan was coming out in May to watch her get the degree she'd been stressing over for the last three years. And she missed her boisterous family. It had been the longest she'd ever gone without seeing them. Sera hadn't been able to go home the last two summers with the extra classes she took and the preceptorship she had to complete this past summer.

Which, she wouldn't get to graduate at all if she didn't finish this paper in...twenty-five minutes.

Sera pushed the Peyton situation and the Adam situation out of her mind to focus on the paper that would make or break her grade.

Exactly twenty-three minutes later, Sera hit submit on her laptop, and her term paper was sent. She was finished, and tomorrow she would be on her way to New York. She'd seen a glimpse of it on the drive from the airport to the ship. Now, she would get to see the rest of it with Adam, and she couldn't wait.

Chapter Forty-Five

Walking at night through this part of town wasn't something most people did. To me, it was peaceful at this hour, calming. It helped clear my head, taking the shouts down to whispers and keeping the headaches at an irritable hum instead of thundering pounds. It was a ritual that kept the confusion away and reality clear. Which is exactly what I need, especially right now.

The beast had been calm for so long that I thought maybe I was rid of it. Something happened that I never expected to have—a feeling of belonging. Or so I thought.

I was so wrong.

But the beast has shown that it will always protect me when I need it most. All it needed was a little push, and out it came. And that is exactly what happened. Just the right button had been pushed.

As if it wasn't already a day from hell, along my solo broody walk, I saw him, my brother.

I haven't seen him in years, not since we were kids. Not since the drugs took over what was once my big brother and left a skinny pod of a stranger. Not that he'd had much of a chance in that house. None of us did. But I still remember him the way he used to be when we were young and free and happy.

My brother mostly ignored me when his friends were around, but when it was just us, we'd play board games or go outside to find interesting trees to climb or innocent enough trouble to get into. He was the one who taught me how to ride a bike, and we would ride those things up and down the street, in and out of neighborhoods, waiting for our father to get home. He taught me how to hit a baseball, though the bat was almost as big as I was at the time.

But that all changed when Father left us, and we had to move back to live with Grandmother.

All these years later, I finally see what my brother has become. Homeless, dirty, rotting in the street. His body cocooned halfway in a sleeping bag on the floor of this random back alley behind a dumpster, the stench of aging garbage and decaying meat assaulting the air. He was lying in his own bodily fluids, his clothes were torn, disgustingly filthy, one arm draped out, a needle still protruding from one of the many needle tracks that scabbed his arms.

I nudged his shoulder with the toe of my boot, trying to wake him. Really, I was checking to see if he was alive. If he hadn't overdosed this time, it looked like it wouldn't be long before he did. He mumbled, shifting his weight onto his side and slipped back into his chemically induced stupor.

He was alive. For now.

My heart sank, knowing that this was what had become of my brother, who once had so much promise. He'd been a good-looking guy who had attracted many friends and girls until he found his own way to escape the everyday pain that was our lives.

I had to help him, take care of him, and there was only one way to do that. To give him mercy. He needed to be free of this burden. This was no life. And it was all because of *them*.

I jostled my brother until he woke.

"Whaaa the fuck man. Why do you keep bothering me?"

"Take it." I handed him the box of leftovers from my dinner. The drugs had so diminished his mind that he didn't even recognize me. So be it. It would be easier this way.

My brother took the food, scarfed it down, pieces of it dropping from his mouth, sticking to his beard as he noisily sucked the juice from his blackened fingertips. I waited for him to finish.

"I'm so sorry this happened to you, brother." I looked at him one last time, the grief of what I had to do heavy on me. I stepped behind him.

I quickly took out the dagger I kept in my boot and sliced fast and deep through his throat, from jugular to jugular.

As I stood staring down at what was left of my brother, a muffled scream sounded far, far away, as if from a dream.

I looked around to find the source of the sound, but there was no one around. Dead stillness remained between my brother's body and me. A few dogs barked in the distance, but other than that, nothingness. Too much nothingness.

I felt eyes watching me, but I couldn't figure out from where. I couldn't chance staying any longer. I pulled the box that I had given to him out of his hands. Blood spattered the white of the box, the sight of it made my gut turn.

Look what *they* have done to you. Look what *they* have made you do.

As I left his body, that raging beast came back to me full force.

I had gotten too comfortable. I let myself be seduced into a world that wasn't mine, pretending all the while that I belonged there.

It had been nice, fitting in for once. But it wasn't real, and I had forgotten.

But I swear, big brother, I will get us the justice we deserve. I will not stop until each and every one of them has paid for what they have stolen from us, what they have made our lives become.

CHAPTER FORTY-SIX

Sera

SAN FRANCISCO

*B**lood, the smell of it, the taste of it, sticky, burning, blinding.*

Running. Rocks, sticks, thorns, dragging her shattered leg.
Lost. Black trees, slapping at her face.
A sweet boy.
"Come on, you okay now."
"That is very sweet of you, Davey."

Sweat beaded on Sera's forehead and dripped down the sides of her face as her body jumped awake. The murderous feeling was overwhelming as she turned face down on the edge of the mattress, waiting for her breathing to slow back to normal.

When she trusted herself not to faint, she managed to sit upright, the fog of sleep lifting, the sense of reality coming back to her. She was in her dorm, safe in her bed.

She looked over at Peyton's bed. It was empty. Nothing unusual. She was probably out with one of her romantic interests, as she often was. Which meant Sera wouldn't have to explain anything.

Desperately needing a drink of water, Sera pushed off the blankets and dropped her legs over the side of the bed when the vision hit her.

Sound stilled.

Her room faded away to somewhere else. A cinder block wall, a dumpster, and a pair of gloved hands that weren't hers came into focus. Trails of color followed their movements, movements she couldn't control.

The hands reached out to a homeless man, handing him a Styrofoam box.

The homeless man had said a few words, but Sera could hear none of them. She saw only his mouth move. Then the homeless man was eating, the gloved hands folded together, patiently waiting.

The longer Sera was in the night terror, the more she sensed this figure, the looming desolation, the presence of the rage, an essence of madness.

The hands then slowly brought out something metal from a boot. A knife. The gloved hand touched the head of the homeless man with what looked like remorse.

The knife flashed in the light, and the homeless man slumped, a river of blood pooling in front of him.

Sera screamed out in horror in her mind, though no one would hear her.

The figure stopped. The area spun.

It took a moment before Sera realized it was because the figure was looking around, sensing something as well.

Quickly, the hand pried the box from the homeless man's clutched fingers, shook the blood from it, and quickly walked away.

Sounds roared back. Sera trembled, soaked with sweat, her breath quick and frantic. She still sat in her dorm bed, in her exact position, before the vision tore through her.

It had been *three* years. Three years since she'd done the work, reliving the worst moments of her life, and yet, the awake-dreams were back. Again.

Sera bolted down the hall to the shared bathroom in barely enough time to make it to the toilet before vomiting. She wasn't sure how long she'd been curled against the cold ceramic, but it was long enough for the sweat to freeze her to what felt like a hypothermic temperature.

Shivering, she pulled herself away from the toilet and into one of the showers, where she set the temperature to the hottest setting and let the hot water run over her until she warmed up. Since she had nothing with her—no soap, shampoo, clean clothing, or even a towel—she dried and covered herself as best she could with the pajamas she'd been wearing. Since it was the middle of the night, no one was out roaming the halls.

As soon as Sera returned to the dorm, she pulled on her warmest pajamas, wrapped herself in her thick robe, and curled up on the corner of the couch with a blanket. Yet her body wouldn't stop trembling.

She didn't want to think of what it might mean, the awake-dreams being back. She especially didn't want to think of what happened in the night terror. The savageness. The death. The remorse.

"Sera?" Peyton whispered as she quietly walked in. "Why are you out here? You're shaking. What's wrong?" She quickly went to Sera, pulling her into a hug.

"Night terrors...I...I used to have night terrors. They're back again." Sera let herself be hugged, welcoming the heat of Peyton's body.

"Back? I've never seen you have bad dreams before."

"I wish they were just bad dreams. They're so much more. I think...I think they're really happening. It feels like they're real. I know they are. They *have* to be."

"Hon, I'm going to need full sentences."

Everything spilled out, from how the nightmares started with Jeffrey Mason, how she'd experienced it in her mother's body, to how she was thrown into visions of horrific murders. She told Peyton about tonight's night terror about the homeless man.

Peyton didn't say a word. She just listened to Sera, her face expressionless.

"You think I'm insane now, don't you?"

Peyton still said nothing. She got up from the couch and walked across the room, staring out at the night beyond their little dorm window. It was killing

Sera, staring at Peyton's back, not knowing what she was thinking or feeling. She probably thought Sera was a raving lunatic now. She'd ask to change dorms and would avoid her for the rest of the semester.

"Peyton, I'm sorry, I shouldn't have said anything. Please say something."

"No, I'm glad you told me." Peyton's voice was so low that Sera barely heard her speak. "I've never had friends before. You're my only friend, Sera."

"What are you talking about? You have a ton of friends. You're always out with them." Sera kept staring at Peyton's back, confused.

"Don't be stupid. Those aren't *friends,*" Peyton growled, her back straightened as she drew a deep breath and turned back to Sera. "*You* are my friend."

Sera went over to Payton and hugged her. "I thought I scared you away."

"You won't scare me away." Peyton hugged Sera closer. "You shouldn't go to New York right now. You're under too much stress as it is. Stay here with me. We will figure this out together."

Sera sighed. "No. I think getting away is exactly what I need right now."

"You're just running away. Don't be a coward," Peyton snipped.

Sera shook her head. "I'm not a coward. I was my whole life, but not anymore. At least, I don't want to be. I'm not running away. I'm keeping my plans and not letting fear make me stay. Not this time." What Peyton said stung, more than a little.

Sera walked back into the bedroom and started stripping off her sheets since there was no point in trying to get any more sleep. Peyton followed her in.

"That didn't come out right. I don't think you're a coward. Not at all. Knowing all that I know about you. I've come to admire your strength, actually. I thought it would make me hate you, but it makes you surprisingly likable."

"You thought you'd *hate* me?" Sera couldn't help the open-mouthed stare she knew she looked at Peyton with.

"I'm just saying everything wrong, aren't I? I mean, competitively. You know, we women are always trying to compare ourselves to each other. But your resilience is incomparable. You're inspirational, really." Peyton shook her head and grinned. "Let me help you with those sheets." The old Peyton, with her dazzling smile, was back.

Sera couldn't blame her for being shocked when she told her about the night terrors. When your roommate says that she sees visions and murders in someone else's body and then tells her that she thinks they're real, of course, Peyton had the right to be more than a little freaked out. The fact that she stayed in the room with Sera after that spoke volumes.

So why was she still disturbed by the way Peyton's voice had changed, the way her expression made her face look so... different? Even if only for a few minutes.

CHAPTER FORTY-SEVEN

Sera

NEW YORK

The plane touched down easily and was quickly taxied from the runway. The day was bright and warm for December. The snow was unseasonably low and was not in the forecast for the rest of the week. But Sera's stomach was creating its own storms, fluttering wildly as the plane got closer to the terminal.

Adam was actually there with Ava, which made Sera a wreck. They had been writing, texting, and video-calling each other pretty much daily over the years. They knew more about each other now than they ever had.

But somehow, it was different. Maybe it was because they hadn't seen each other physically that made her fidgety. Ava was older now. What if she didn't remember Sera in the same way? Sure, Ava loved the letters, pictures, and video calls, but maybe she would feel differently in person. If Ava was shy or scared of her, it would break her heart.

Then it was Sera's turn to leave the plane, but her legs were stuck in place. When she finally made it out onto the ramp, her stomach started to ease and her legs found new energy, they were almost running. She went from nervous to thrilled and couldn't get to the baggage claim fast enough.

Finally, Adam was there, standing in front of her. He was still the solid six-foot-something guy with his easy smile, dark wavy hair, and kind blue eyes, her best friend in the world. Sera dropped her carry-on and threw herself into him, knocking him back a few steps.

"How have you been? Oh my gosh. How is it that you look *younger?* You look so good." She held him away from her to get a good look, then brought him back in for another hug.

"Yeah, it's funny what a little time will do, huh? I mean, look at you. I couldn't tell that you were such a hottie before with all that doom and gloom around you." He let out a playful whistle.

"Hottie? Okay, I said you look younger, but don't push it." She draped her arm around his waist as they walked toward the baggage carousel.

"Are you saying that I'm old, Miss Sera?" He playfully pinched her side, making her laugh.

"You just turned...fifty, right?"

"Ouch. Thirty-one is far away from fifty."

"That's okay, you're just perfect. For me, anyway." She laughed as she said it but gave herself a mental slap at her chosen words.

"Great. Then consider yourself taken." He kissed her forehead and took her suitcase from the conveyor belt.

"I have a bit of a surprise for you," he said as they walked out to a waiting SUV, a smiling driver opening the door for her.

"You didn't have to do this. Really, it's too much." Sera looked from the door to Adam and back to the door again. She didn't know whether to be excited, pleased, or embarrassed and since she had never been one to mask her feelings well, Adam picked up on it right away.

"Get used to it. I am officially spoiling you for the next five days. No arguments. You can either fight it, and ruin everyone's time by the way, or you can sit back, relax, and enjoy yourself. You've been working hard, and you deserve a little princess treatment. Besides, I wanted to hang out with my best friend. Let someone else do the driving."

"Thank you, Adam. Really." She leaned over and kissed his cheek before getting into the SUV. "Speaking of princesses, where's the fairest one of all?" Sera sat back in the seat, taking in everything around her, the sounds of the busy streets, the people, and the lights of the New York City skyline in the distance.

"It would have been too late for her by the time we got back. She should be going to sleep about now if she hasn't sweet-talked the sitter into a little more screen time. But in the morning, well, don't be afraid if a little monster crawls into bed with you," he said as he slid into the seat next to her.

Sera almost responded with something suggestive and had to bite her cheek to keep herself in check. What was wrong with her? She'd never been so blatant, especially with Adam. She looked up into those blue eyes that she remembered so well. They hadn't missed a beat at all. He was as familiar as if it was only yesterday that they were on the ship together. But would she be so fortunate with Ava?

"Will she remember me? I'm afraid she'll be shy with me. I know we've been video chatting, but three years is a long time for a little one."

"She remembers. Amazingly so."

"Good. That's been one of my biggest fears coming here." She looked away, trying to hide the weird anxiety she'd had about seeing Adam in person again.

"*One* of? Are you okay with being here?"

Ironically, Sera never felt safer than she did at that moment.

"I'm great with being here. It was a rough night last night. I'll tell you about that later. Right now, I think I was just afraid that you might have changed somehow. But you are exactly the way you've always been. I couldn't bear losing you and Ava." Remembering the strangeness in how Peyton reacted last night compared to how Adam had never reacted to anything Sera shared with him over the years made her appreciate him that much more. She set her head on his shoulder and gave an exaggerated sigh. "Alright, enough with the doom and gloom depression session."

"You seemed to have picked up quite the sense of humor somewhere. Whose fault is that?" he asked as he shed the coat and took off the tie he was still wearing from the office.

"Have I? Well, it must be all Peyton's fault. That's what happens when you've been roomies for as long as we have. She's been great. *Almost* as good as you." She nudged him playfully with her shoulder.

"No one is as good as I. You'll come to find this out in the years to come."

"Will I? I guess we're in this for the long haul then." She squeezed his hand and smiled, then continued to chat as she looked out the window, commenting on the lights, buildings, and sites of the city.

CHAPTER FORTY-EIGHT

Adam

New York

As Adam watched Sera's face fill with the wonders of the city, he thought in his most private of thoughts,

Yes, the long run with you would suit me just fine.

Adam laughed with her, easing back into her company. Though they spoke almost daily, he hadn't realized how much he missed her.

He'd been a mess the past three weeks since they'd planned her visit. Even that morning, he had been snapping at his coworkers, trying to get as much work finished as possible so that he wouldn't have to go back in for the five days Sera would be there. He beat himself up trying to rationalize why he was being so crazy about seeing her.

If he was being totally honest with himself, the whole someone-asking-her-out conversation had really gotten to him. He had no idea why it bothered him so much. Acting like an ass only made him angrier at himself.

Then, as time got closer to her arrival, he'd been more than a little afraid that the two of them would be strangers getting to know each other again. But the moment he saw her enter the baggage claim area, all that neurotic energy was gone, warmth and comfort settling those strange nerves.

This was Sera, the same gal he befriended on the ship more than three years before, his buddy in grief and life. Then, she'd looked like a lost and frightened girl, filled with fear and grief. She looked dramatically different now.

Physically seeing her, he saw that she'd grown into someone who had come into her own, comfortable in her own skin. The wisdom of it all still haunted those green jewels that looked at him now with hard-fought joy, framed by all that wild red hair.

What he hadn't expected was the heat that had surged through his body, filling him with a sudden, forgotten ache when she kissed his cheek. He insisted on putting her bags into the trunk to allow himself time to ease that sudden and infuriating burn.

He knew this friendship was about to become a little complicated.

Since Sera claimed she was starving, they picked up a pizza before arriving at Adam's house. He lit a fire where they sat as they ate themselves sick, laughing and talking. The firelight flickered through the room, illuminating the box of half-eaten pizza, glasses of wine, chocolate wrappers, cheese plate, and grapes that were littered along the coffee table.

"How have the nightmares been?"

"Always Mr. Serious," Sera sighed as she shook her head, smiling. "I wanted to wait a day before getting all Weird Girl."

"Weird Girl?" Adam asked, chuckling.

"Yeah, you know, I see dead people and such."

"It makes you far more interesting than other women."

"*Other* women?" Sera cocked an eyebrow at Adam.

"Now, don't get jealous on me." Adam threw a grape at Sera.

"I will always be jealous of *other women* stealing *my* Adam's attention," Sera said as she popped the grape he tossed at her in her mouth.

"I promise you that will never happen." No one could or would ever replace Sera. But he didn't say that part out loud.

"What? Don't sell yourself short. I'm surprised it hasn't happened yet."

"Nah. Besides, I still have some difficult days." The joking dissipated as he toyed with the wedding ring he still wore, remembering his wife sitting in 'her spot' on the sofa across the room.

Sera took his hand in hers. "Alex was your wife. You still live in the same house the two of you shared together, in a life you built together. That has to be really hard."

"It was for a while. I would think that I heard her voice. Or I would picture her walking through here like she used to. It has gotten better. It's become more of a comfort now. She's been gone now longer than we were married."

They sat in silence for a while, watching the flames.

"I think I'm going to be sick. I ate too much. I'm going to have to run ten miles for the next month just to work it all off." She held her stomach, laying her head on Adam's leg.

Adam watched her lie there with her eyes closed, serene. The glow of the flames lit her hair into a fiery halo. She was now a woman, and a magnificent one, Adam thought, one who was finding her true self.

"You look really good, Sera. Like you've found your peace."

Sera opened her eyes, beaming up at him. "I feel really good. I have some difficult days as well, but there are more good days than bad now. Except last night. I didn't want to bring us down so soon. But I might as well get the bad out now so we can get it out of the way." Sera propped herself up on an elbow and told him about the night terror, about Peyton, and how she reacted when she told her about everything.

"I don't think you should trust Peyton with too much."

"I tell you these horrible visions where seemingly random people are getting slaughtered right in front of my eyes, and you come back with, *'don't trust Peyton'*?"

"Sorry, just my opinion about that girl. Ever since you told me how weird she acted when you went back home to Ireland, I've thought that something was just a little...off."

"I think she is just really lonely. You'd feel differently if you met her."

"The stories you tell me about her extracurricular activities don't sound like she's alone much."

"Such a man thing to say," Sera snorted.

"Anyways, do you have a theory about the night terrors coming back? Before, you thought maybe it was because you needed to deal with all your trauma. The night terrors stopped for, what, three years? It seemed like you were right."

"I'm not sure. Doing all that therapy work with John, researching Jeffrey Mason and his family, reading all the police reports, all the witness statements—what few there were—and really learning about my mother's abilities put all the pieces together. This time it's different. Maybe because I'm more open to accepting it for what it might really be. I hope you don't think I'm totally crazy... but... I think it's all real. I think these murders are actually happening. I have no idea who the victims are, who is doing it, or why I am seeing this. But I do, I think it's real. I just have no idea how to prove it."

"Have you looked into it? Who those people are—or were?"

"Not yet. It's been," Sera looked at her watch, "nineteen hours. Besides, where would I even start?"

"Well, you never watch the news."

"God no. Too depressing."

Adam looked at her.

"Okay. I get it. How else would I know what's happening out there?"

"Exactly. And social media. Amazingly, it *can* sometimes be helpful."

"Talk about depressing."

"Smart ass. I'm not talking about trying to become an influencer or anything. I'm just saying that everything is out there these days. If you plug in the right words or descriptions, you just might find something."

"How would I ever live without you?"

"It's a good thing we will never have to find out." Adam brought their joined hands up to his lips and kissed the back of Sera's hand. "I'm stupid proud of you, by the way. All that you've done. You're a rockstar. Not many people can pull themselves out of that."

"Stop. I'm no rock star. If anyone is the rock star, it's you. Ava is one lucky little girl to have a father who has willed himself to go on just for her, to be there for her, to love her, and to protect her. Some of us don't get that luxury."

"Then, as the father in the house, I say it's time for bed. It's already past midnight, and Ava will be up at the crack of dawn, waking us both," he said as he stood, holding his hand out to Sera.

"Let me just sleep here. I can't move or I'll burst," she groaned.

"It's not every day that you have an escort to bed. C'mon, up." He pulled her up to her feet and nudged her toward the stairs.

"Meanie," Sera grumbled as she climbed each stair.

"Quit your moaning and groaning. People might get the wrong impression." Adam ducked as Sera playfully swatted at him, then clutched her stomach and doubled over when she missed.

"You're so mean. How come I never saw that on the ship? Which way am I going?" She stopped in the hallway at the top of the stairs.

"That way. Your room is the last one on the left. Sleep tight." He swatted her behind as she shuffled away.

"Tease," Sera mumbled as she made her way to her room.

"Tease? Me? I guess you don't know everything about me after all," he played right back.

"Yeah, sure. I'd bet that you still haven't even thought about dating yet." She turned to him, crossing her arms, daring him to prove her wrong.

"Look who's talking, Miss *Someone-Asked-Me-Out*. Why didn't you go out with him? Since we're so concerned about dating habits all of a sudden." Finally, he was able to mention the thing that had irked him for weeks without having to pry to get it.

"Hey. No fair. That really freaked me out. Like panic status." Sera half laughed, half whined. "Besides, if you saw him, you'd know why."

"So if he had been, I don't know, even half as handsome as I, you would have accepted?"

"Half? No, a quarter."

"Ah, so you're saying I have a chance?" His heart rate sputtered, and his mouth went dry as the words came out. What was he saying? What was he playing at? Sure, he was half joking, but *only* half. It was way too dangerous. But something held him there, waiting for her answer.

"Of course," Sera paused, "but you'd have to step up your dancing game," she stated with a teasing giggle.

"Hmph. Well, *that's* good to know."

"What is?" she asked.

"That you have extremely low standards. 'Night." He ducked the sock Sera threw at him before going into her room.

He quietly closed his bedroom door. Besides being perilously close to disrespecting his best friend, he suddenly felt like an adulterer.

Chapter Forty-Nine

Sera

New York

S er-ra." Soft, little fingers tousled her hair.

Sera heard the little voice and grinned before she opened her eyes.

"Seraaaa. Wake up." The little voice got a bit louder with an added gentle nudge.

She popped open one eye and looked into those magical blue eyes she remembered vividly—the same eyes of her father.

"Hey, who are you, and what are you doing in my room?" Sera joked before she grabbed the little girl and pulled her under the covers, covering her in tickles. Ava offered no resistance, bursting into giggles, and then cuddled up next to Sera.

"Wow, you smell good. I've missed you so much." Sera breathed in the delighting scents of fruity shampoo and child-like soap as she playfully kissed the top of Ava's head.

"Can you read my letters?" Giggling, Ava pushed a bundle of papers at Sera.

"Haven't you read them?" Sera asked as she sat up, bringing Ava into her chest.

"Daddy reads them to me all the time. But can you read them in your voice?" Ava put the letters closer to Sera's face until Sera laughed and gave in.

She sorted through them by date and read each one. With each letter, she lost herself deeper into the little girl curled up in her arms.

Neither one of them heard Adam standing at the door or saw the quiet tear he brushed off his cheek as he turned and quietly left.

Adam

NEW YORK

"Well, it's about time the two of you came down for breakfast." Adam set his phone down on the table when Ava and Sera came giggling down the stairs and into the kitchen.

"We were spending quality time getting reacquainted."

Sera grabbed a bagel from the platter on the counter as Ava jumped into her father's lap and started picking food from his plate.

"Hey, get your paws out of my food and get your own."

Ava squealed when Adam tickled her. He got up, fixed a plate of food for her, and set it by his.

"By Sera, by Sera!"

Adam threw his hands up in submission. "Please excuse me, Princess Ava. I shall set your plate next to Queen Sera, as you request."

"Queen. I like the sound of that," Sera said, smiling at Ava, making her giggle.

"How did you sleep?" Adam asked in his nonchalant voice, picking his phone back up, not really looking at anything in particular.

"So good that I forgot where I was when I woke up." She sat at her designated place next to Ava. "I can't remember the last time I've slept that well, or that long, for that matter."

"I guess that means you were comfortable enough, not too hot, not too cold."

"It was perfect. I find myself strangely famished after our junk-fest last night. Why am I this hungry?"

Adam chuckled. "Did you get your run in yet?"

"I was thinking, am I on vacation or what? I'll pick up my running when I get back." She slathered her bagel with more cream cheese and took another bite.

"Good for you. Everyone needs a rest now and then. Especially you."

"Yeah, tell my conscience that," she said, guiltily scraping the extra cream cheese back off.

"So, are you ready for today?" he asked, a sly grin widening across his face.

"You've made plans? I told you not to go to any trouble. I'm just here for a little rest and good company," Sera protested.

"And I told *you* that you were in for a good spoiling and not to argue about it. What kind of man would I be if I didn't spoil my girls?" He rose from his seat, putting his breakfast dishes in the sink.

"Your *girls*?" Sera laughed.

"*Mm*. And it's your first time in this great city. It would be a waste not to take advantage of it. Do you like to shop?"

Sera told Adam that she had never been much of a shopper, but standing in front of the real and true Bloomingdales, Sera stared, awestruck. Ava had been nothing but celebratory the entire day, never letting go of Sera's hand.

Adam quietly followed the two of them with what felt like a goofy smile that wouldn't go away. He followed them as they tried on fun and crazy outfits together and played in the toy department. The energy the two of them had together exhausted Adam just watching. They walked around Times Square, ate hot dogs from street stands, and then stuffed themselves with cookie dough ice cream until they could barely move.

Adam ached for his daughter. Since she didn't have a woman's presence in her life, Ava was absorbing every minute with Sera. Only now, he was afraid of how Ava will react when Sera had to leave.

"Why don't you ever go out? Shopping, clubbing, bars, whatever else you college people do these days." He figured he already knew the answer. She'd come a long way, but still, fear has a way of holding on.

Sera shrugged. "Mostly, I never have the time. It's not really my thing anyway." She looked down at Ava, who was rubbing her eyes and yawning at the same time. "Little one here is getting sleepy." Sera reached down and scooped her up. Ava set her head down on her shoulder, nuzzling her hair.

"I'm not sleepy," Ava quietly protested, rubbing her eyes.

Adam felt his heart tug and wished, just for a moment, as he watched his daughter fall asleep in Sera's arms, that Sera never had to go back to San Francisco. Adam ushered *his girls* into the SUV, settled into the driver's seat, and drove them home.

Sera watched from the doorway as Adam tucked a sleeping Ava into bed.

"She is precious, Adam. Such a sweet girl."

"She is my soul. I don't know what I would've done without her." Standing by her bed, he stroked Ava's hair. It was longer now but still fell in ringlets. He loved the feel of it twirled around his fingers. It was already starting to lose its baby fineness. She was growing up right in front of him and way too quickly.

"When do you think you'll find someone, or at least start looking?" Sera wasn't looking at Adam but at Ava when she asked, her voice a whisper.

"Still not funny." Instead of laughing, it reminded him of Marcy Brodenburgh, a woman at the office who had been hounding him, asking that same question repeatedly, hoping *she* would be that someone. He'd brushed her off more times than he wanted to count.

"I didn't mean it as a joke or to be hurtful. You are an amazing father, but as un-feminist as this is going to sound, I think she needs a woman around, a role model, someone to watch as she grows up. I know she's too young to really understand, but I hate to think she won't have it, that she'll miss out on having that female relationship. I didn't get to have that with my mother, I was so young when I lost her. But I did have Erinne, and I would hate it if Ava didn't have what I had with her growing up." She didn't take her eyes off Ava.

When Adam saw Sera's expression, the annoyance evaporated. Sera wanted everything for Ava just as he did, unselfishly. He watched her fight her emotions, her face caught between love and sadness. He also noticed that she didn't cry, as most did. He'd shed plenty, more than his fair share. But thinking back, he couldn't remember one time when he'd seen a single tear come from her.

He walked over to Sera at the door, kissed her forehead, and took her in his arms. "Do you ever cry, Sera?"

Her shock apparent, he found himself stumbling on his words, embarrassed that he had spoken his thoughts aloud.

"I mean, don't get me wrong, you are the strongest and bravest person I have ever met. But I noticed that you don't allow yourself to show the big feelings. Not really. You have this smile that lightens the whole room and a laugh that is contagious. But when it comes to the hard stuff, you close off. I guess I don't have you all figured out yet, either, do I?" He felt heat rush into his face as he fumbled through his unsure words.

"Answer mine, and I'll answer yours."

"Fair enough. How about some wine to ease these loaded questions?" They walked away from Ava's room and headed back downstairs.

With a glass of wine in hand, sitting in front of the fire, Adam took a sip and a deep breath and began.

"I know she needs someone to look up to. I want so much for her to have that. But if there is going to be a *someone*, I also need that person to be someone I love and care for deeply. Finding a woman just for my daughter seems noble, but it would only end up hurting her more. I need to be true to myself as well. Casual dating is beyond me at this point. I don't know if I'll ever be ready for that. But if it is meant to be, well, she will have to be exceptionally special."

Someone like you.

He almost spoke it aloud, the thought soaring into his mind. Before he said the wrong thing, he filled the pause, "Something that is quite challenging." Marcy's face flashed in his mind. He shuddered.

"What was that?" She bit her lip, stifling a chuckle.

"There is this woman at work who keeps asking me if she could be that someone special. Makes a man want to gouge his own eyes out."

"How terrible. She can't be that bad," Sera chuckled.

"She isn't ugly, but she's cold and mean. As mean as a horde of wasps. Oh, wait, that's my mother-in-law."

Sera hadn't stopped snickering and now started laughing openly. He couldn't help himself, joining in, their laughter growing from amusement to roaring hysterics, unable to stop themselves.

"Ow. My stomach." Sera doubled over as she tried to catch her breath. "This is the second time my stomach has felt like this for two very different reasons, both of them to do with you."

"You're welcome then." He put his arm around her and brought her in for a quick kiss on her forehead, but he paused for a fraction of a second too long near her lips. He rushed a quick peck on her forehead, jumped up, and headed toward the kitchen. "Want some ice cream?"

"You keep feeding me ice cream like this, I'll have to get a second seat on the plane." She got up and followed after him.

"You still didn't answer mine."

"Hm? Your what?" She licked off the last of the chocolate sauce from the spoon.

"My question. I answered yours. The deal was you'd answer mine." He took her dish and his own to the sink to rinse them.

"Right, the crying thing. To be honest, I don't think I can anymore. I'm all dried up inside. Blocked, maybe? I've never cried as hard as I did the last time I saw my mother's face in my arms."

"You haven't cried since you were a child?" His hands stilled under the running water as he looked at her, eyes wide.

She shook her head and shrugged. Her voice fell silent as she sat unmoving, staring down at the table. She might have acted as though it didn't bother her, but he noticed her eyes became haunted and hurt.

He shouldn't have asked, bringing up memories of that time. He turned off the faucet, then slid into the seat beside her, taking her face into his hands. "Good, because I can't stand crybabies."

Her eyes refocused on him, and after a moment, she started to laugh.

"You are such a punk." She shoved him away playfully, then got up from her seat and headed up the stairs. "It was a big day today. I'm going up to dream of Tiffany's and Bloomingdale's."

"Tomorrow, even bigger," he called up to her.

"I don't think that's possible," she sang back.

CHAPTER FIFTY-ONE

Ella

SAN FRANCISCO

Ella's status at Stanford was reinstated with a few additional requirements she would have to complete along with a short academic probation. All of which she passed with no problem. Chris had found a job with a construction crew that he enjoyed, enabling him to use the skills Brian Senior had taught him at Lantern Light.

Classes were going well, life was going well, and when she looked at her daughter, who was already almost two years old, there was nothing but pure joy and love.

It often made her think of her own mother. Her mother must have felt this way when Ella was a baby. Right? That feeling might have gotten lost as she grew older and became more challenging, but when she was a baby? Didn't every mother feel this way?

It surprised Ella that she actually missed her parents. Or maybe what she was missing was what could have been, that relationship they were never able to build.

She wanted to think that her parents might want to meet their first and only grandchild. Sera would undoubtedly enjoy having grandparents, seeing how much she adored Erinne's parents. Maybe Sera would bring them the happiness they never found in Ella.

Chris's parents had shut out all possibilities of any sort of relationship. They'd told Chris they would never accept Sera, that they didn't need that kind of talk among their peers. Ella's parents might be the same. But maybe, just maybe, they would surprise her this once.

One night, after Chris was at work and her assignments were finished, Ella mustered up just enough courage to bundle Sera and make the short drive to her parents' house.

Ella sat in the car way longer than she should have, staring at the house from the street.

She'd grown up here, yet it was as cold and unfamiliar as any other house on the street. Sitting there, looking at the house that could have been anyone's, ignited a determination in Ella to make theirs a warm and inviting home for Sera to grow up in. It might not be big or fancy, but it would be full of love and laughter.

Ella blew out a long breath, got out of the car, and unbuckled Sera from the car seat. Then she stood next to the car, unmoving, until she saw a neighbor's curtain conspicuously open and shut again.

Great, the cops would be called on her if she didn't make a move. Either back in the car or move her ass up the walkway.

Finally, she was at the door. Now, to just ring the bell. Her fingers didn't move. Sera squirmed in her arms. Minutes crawled by before she finally pushed the bell, her stomach dropping with the sound.

After what seemed like an eternity, her mother opened the door.

She just stood there, staring—first at Ella, then at Sera. For one fleeting moment, Ella thought, this is it, she is going to fall in love with her granddaughter. But her face was stone, and nothing was in her eyes but disappointment.

Leaving the door slightly ajar, her mother walked away from her. Not one word, not one expression, not one motion. She just walked away.

Ella wasn't sure how long she stood there in shock. She didn't expect much from her parents, but she expected *something*.

A few seconds later, Ella's father appeared at the door. He barely looked up, and he didn't bother looking at Sera. He pulled out his checkbook, scribbled something on one of them, then handed it to Ella.

"This is a one-time payoff. I don't need Fiona upset like this again. It's just better if you don't come back." He closed the door.

Fiona. Not even 'your mother'.

That was it. Ella no longer had parents. Sera would never have grandparents.

"Mama, can we be hungry now?" Sera started happily talking, bringing Ella back to where they were still standing. As she hurried back to the car, Ella vowed to never return to this house again.

Once they were in the car, all buckled in, Ella looked at the check amount. Apparently, her father wore a heavy conscience after all, or maybe felt guilty for what had become of their situation, or for their lack of parental love and support, or for just not giving a shit.

The check amount was enough to pay for the rest of Stanford, enough for a little house for them to plant roots in, and even enough to start a savings account for Sera's college fund.

Plans started forming as she drove back home. There were only a couple of weeks remaining in the semester. As soon as it ended, they could start looking at houses.

And then Ella remembered Alameda Island, a cute little town tucked in between two giant cities.

Erinne's parents had taken them there on a day trip back in junior high. The drive to and from the hospital and school might be a bit far, but that would only be temporary. She would find her dream hospital closer to home after she graduated.

Ella *Knew* Alameda Island would be the perfect place, with a perfect house waiting just for them.

CHAPTER FIFTY-TWO

Sera

NEW YORK

Magic. That was what this city was, pure Christmas magic. A tree taller than most buildings was decorated with thousands of lights, trumpeting angels guiding the way to it. An ice rink stood in the middle of this majestic city where wobbly would-be ice skaters glided alongside professionals. There wasn't much snow, but the glow cast from all of the white lights adorning the city gave it the magical aura of the holidays.

The two days leading up to Christmas day were filled with New York City sites and activities, including Ava's favorite, the Russian Ballet's *Nutcracker Suite*.

On Christmas morning, Ava woke them early excited to open gifts. Sera and Adam watched as Ava tore through miles of wrapping paper, squealing in joy with each present. Whether it was the bicycle her father gave her, the pink socks her grandmother had sent to her, or the violin Sera gave to her, Ava was equally pleased with each gift. When she opened the box that held the violin Erinne had passed to Sera, that she was now passing to Ava, she was so excited that she insisted on Sera giving her a lesson right then.

They had stuffed themselves with turkey and all the traditional trimmings before going on a long walk so Ava could break in her new bike. As the long and joyous day was coming to a close, Ava was dreaming happily in her bed as Sera and Adam were unwinding out on his veranda that overlooked the pond, wrapped in a shared blanket under an outdoor heater.

"I thought New York was all city. But this is some of the most beautiful land I have ever seen. In the States, at least."

"Most people don't realize that just a couple hours away from the city is some of the country's most wooded and green areas. I love it here, Ava loves it here. It's hard to imagine living anywhere else." He gazed over at the pond.

Sera didn't know why, but knowing that Adam would never leave New York unexpectedly hurt. "Someday, I'll show you my little island of Alameda. The people are genuine, and it has a small-town feel to it, even though it's in the middle of two giant cities. I miss it. Some days I miss it so much that I want to leave everything and go back. But then I remember that I have no one there to go back to. My house has been empty ever since Erinne took me back to Ireland when I was six. I've been a gypsy living in whatever dorm I'm assigned at school or in Ireland during the summers. I miss the feeling of having a home to go back to." She stopped, breathing through the tightness in her chest, that old pain resurfacing.

"Maybe someday you'll go back and live there again. Maybe you'll even work in the same hospital your mother did. It wouldn't be all that bad to go back." He reached for her, laid his hand on the back of her neck, and rubbed gently.

"I don't know if I have the courage to go back there to stay," she paused. "I'll show it to you someday. You'll see why nothing else could compare. It is a pretty house with shutters. There are pink cherry blossom trees in the front yard. There used to be flowers everywhere and hundreds of daisies, Mom's favorite. She said they were the happiest of all the flowers. My dad built this beautiful swing on the porch and the white fence surrounding the entire property. It has this harmonious air to it. There aren't any bad memories there. Nothing can change that. Ever."

They sat face to face, only inches from each other. He leaned in and kissed her gently on the lips, soft and swift.

"We'll find that courage for you one day, Sera. I'll make sure of it." He gave her neck a gentle squeeze, stood, and went back into the house.

Sera sat in the quiet, her mouth warm and tingling from the kiss. She brought a finger to her lips, touching them softly, a sudden need coursing through her, a feeling she'd never experienced before.

And she wanted more.

She forced the thought from her mind. Adam meant it as a comfort to his *friend*, that was all. If it were meant as more, he wouldn't have pulled away so quickly.

Needing time to cool off, she stood and headed down for a sobering walk around the pond. After which, she intended to lock herself away in her room so that she wouldn't be tempted to make the mistake of overstepping something she was sure she only imagined.

CHAPTER FIFTY-THREE

Adam

New York

Adam needed time to calm down. He stomped his way into the kitchen, threw open the refrigerator, and grabbed a cold beer from the shelf. He guzzled down the cold liquid and grabbed another before slamming the door shut. He took the second beer with him into the bathroom to splash cold water on his face.

He almost blew it, nearly made a huge mistake. All that emotion filled her eyes when she spoke of her home, the emptiness came over her as if a part of her soul was missing. He yearned to give it back to her, knowing it would give her happiness. He was going to kiss her forehead, as he did often, but lost control being so close to her lips. It took every ounce of will to pull himself away.

He respected her, he loved her as his closest friend. Still, he wanted more of her. To stymy these strange emotions, he locked himself in his study where he could throw himself into hours of good hard work.

CHAPTER FIFTY-FOUR

The beast was awake now, refusing to go back to sleep. If *it* stays, *I* will have to leave all I have worked for and the life I never thought possible.

But life, *my* life, was funny that way. When I yearned for it and prayed for it every day, I was given nothing. When I made peace with not ever having it, that's when it was given to me.

That is the way *my* cookie crumbles.

If I embrace the beast and let it stay, everything else will be taken away.

I tried to push it back again.

Until I saw the woman who brought us into this world, the woman who had never loved us, never wanted us, and never cared enough to protect us, come into the grocery store.

She looked old and frail, beaten down by the hand she was dealt, which had included us. Her already thin, dull brown hair had thinned to almost baldness and was now almost completely gray. Those miserable eyes were always cast down for fear of looking anyone in the eye. That precious little cross still hung around her neck.

Why my father had ever chosen this woman, I'll never understand.

I had to follow her and see what she did with her life after she left us vulnerable and defenseless with Grandmother. Not that she ever did anything to protect us from her when she was still around.

She never noticed me. Of course, she wouldn't. She never even looked up, the coward. She got on the bus. I got in behind her, sitting a few rows back so that I could stare at the back of her balding head.

Many times, I let myself fantasize about her. What if this woman, our mother, had stood up for us? What if she had fought back to Grandmother? What if she had loved us? What would my life have become? Father would have never left us. Maybe we would have been happy. But fantasies are only painful reminders of what never was and never would be.

When she got off the bus through the front doors, I left through the back. I followed her a few blocks to a rundown apartment building where half the neighborhood was mostly boarded up and forgotten. A suitable setting for a poor excuse of a woman such as my mother.

I ventured around her building, past her window, curious as to what her life was like. She looked to be alone, just as she'd always wanted.

I left there filled with renewed purpose. I'd be back in the dark when I could be one with the shadows.

Night came, quiet, swift, cloaking my car as I drove by once, twice. No one seemed to brave the darkness beyond the perceived safety of the walls of their homes.

I knocked on her door.

"Yes?" She just looked at me through her cracked open door. No reaction.

"Merry Christmas, Mother."

"What? I'm sorry, you must have the wrong..."

"You don't recognize me, Mother?" I pushed through the door, knocking her back inside, tased her with the handy tool I'd picked up for the occasion, then turned off the lights to make sure no one would see me escort this old woman out to my car. It was such a beautifully dark night that not even the moon came out to play.

"You have always been so weak. Weak-minded, weak in stature, just pathetically weak. You disgust me."

"I don't know who you think..."

I slapped her hard. She needed to shut up and listen to the reasoning as to why she was being brought to justice.

"You never tried to protect us. You never even stood up for yourself. You just let her beat us with that damn book. Let her destroy us. The only thing precious to you was your fucking religion. You were never a mother. You are just another pathetic excuse for a victim."

I slapped her again, sending her back into the dirt. It felt good to be the one delivering the pain for once instead of being the one to brunt it. I pulled her head back up by her hair, ripped the cross off of her neck, crushing the damn thing under my boot. Fire would have been better, but I can accommodate when I have to.

"Please, please don't hurt me anymore."

I shoved her back down to reach into my pack, which held the bible I brought with me just for her.

"Remember this?"

The bitch just cowered in the dirt, whimpering, her hand over her face as if that could help her.

"Look at me!" I kicked her in the gut, sent her tumbling a few feet. When her bobbing head looked up enough to see what I was holding, I brought the heavy book down on her face hard enough to hear a crack. The satisfying gush of blood from her nose encouraged me to hit her with the damn thing over and over.

"How does it feel, Mother? How do you like it? This is what you never protected us from. It's your turn to take it. Your turn to suffer."

You sick bastard!

I jumped and almost dropped the bloodied bible. The voice was that close, right behind me. The hairs on my neck stood. I looked back. No one was there. We were miles away from anything.

But then, I remembered, and I had to smile.

I refocused. I needed to slow myself down to regain control. I closed my eyes, took a few breaths. I couldn't lose control, or I would be no better than them.

"You always said we had to be cleansed of all of our sins. Well, I am here to wash you of yours."

It was time, eye for an eye—quite literally.

"What happens when you look away, Mother? When you turn a blind eye and let your own children suffer and bleed? I won't let you look away again."

I reached inside my boot and drew out the dagger I kept there. Mother started squirming and screaming again. Always the pathetic groveler. Some things never change.

I pushed her up against the tree, held her there by her forehead, and used my dagger to cut the lids from her eyes. She would never again be blind to the costs of her sins.

Her screams filled me with such ecstasy of victory. As I watched her bleed, my anger turned to rage, and my rage melded with my own agony.

"Why didn't you want us?" All I ever wanted was for her to want me, hold me. Without thinking, I raised the blade and cast it down on her with the force of all my pain.

"Why didn't you protect us?" For all those years, I had waited for this woman to help me, wondering why I was never worth saving. But she never saw anyone else's pain. My blade found her again, in and out of her flesh.

"Why couldn't you just love us?" It was so easy for other people. They just loved their children without effort, without thought. But this woman was so cold, so detached. She never cared, not even when her children were being beaten every single day for nothing. She hated us that much.

"If you had just cared a little bit." I've lost count of how many times I've stabbed my mother. The pain so raw, I'd lost complete control.

"We might have had a chance."

Finally, I carved deep into the skin of her neck, feeling the flesh tear through my fingers as I pulled the dagger slowly along from one side to the other. Mothers' screams had dulled from bubbling groans to nothing.

She had left me long ago, before tonight. I should have felt nothing as I watched the rest of her blood ooze from her. But all the pain and hurt resurfaced as if it had been yesterday. I dropped to my knees next to the heap that had been my mother.

Why did everyone leave me?

I had been teased with what a normal life felt like. Given just a small taste. But that didn't last either. It never will for me. I'll only ever be alone.

The aching took over, wracking my body into a curled-up ball of uselessness.

Until the beast came back out, promising sweet absolution, promising to give out proper judgment to those who condemned us, giving us the righteousness that my brother, me, my sister, even our father more than deserved. Though they have already destroyed us, they would no longer be triumphant.

Then I remembered something strange.

A memory of Mother, completely bald, her skeleton all but visible through the thin skin of her cancerous disease.

That couldn't be right because she was here, next to me, her blood soaking my knees.

Maybe I had been wrong.

She didn't die in that back room that day. She hadn't died at all, only escaped.

But she hadn't escaped me in the end.

CHAPTER FIFTY-FIVE

Sera

NEW YORK

F*lesh through flesh. Popping layers of skin.*

Blood, the smell of it, the taste of it, sticky, burning, blinding. Running. Lost. Black trees, slapping at her face.

"Dark! It's too dark!" Sera screamed out to no one.

"Sera?" Adam rushed into the bedroom, turned the light on, and hurried to Sera's side. "Sera, wake up. You're okay. You're home." He crawled onto the bed with Sera and rocked her in his arms.

The night air was cold. No, she wasn't outside. Sera could smell Adam's scent, feel his strong arms around her.

Home.

He was her home.

The web of sleep was diminishing as she opened her eyes and saw Adam, those dark blue eyes concerned, his arms holding her so sweetly.

"Are you alright?" Adam held Sera at arm's length to study her. He searched her eyes, making sure she was awake and aware. "That is so much worse than I imagined from what you've told me about these things."

"I woke you. I'm sorry." Embarrassed, Sera tried to pull away.

Adam held fast. "Don't do that. You don't have to pretend with me," he said, brushing the sweat-drenched hair from her face.

"I know. Really, I do." She shivered, the sweat cooling her body.

"Want some water?" Adam asked as he stood and headed toward the door.

"No, go back to sleep. I'm sorry I woke you." She straightened out the tangled blankets, pulling them up to her chin.

"I was awake doing some work. You're still shivering. I'll make us some tea. No arguments. I'll be right back."

Without waiting for an answer, Adam was out the door. She laid back pulling the blankets tight around her, trying to warm up.

That's when sound muted around her.

Shapes came into focus, blurred around the edges. She was looking into dark eyes of an older woman, which were transfixed with terror. Her face wet with tears, masked with pale-white desperation. Thin hair framed her face, slicked over her forehead. She was sobbing.

A gloved hand that should have been Sera's but wasn't slapped the woman hard across the face, pulled her back up by her thin hair, yanked off the cross necklace the woman wore, threw it down, stomped on it with a booted foot. The gloved hands shoved the woman back to the dirt, brought out a book, no, a bible, and started beating the woman with it.

You sick bastard! Sera shouted in her mind.

The figure shot a glance backward, then quickly scanned the area, waiting a few moments.

Going back to the woman, the figure loomed over her as she cowered in the dirt, her face bloodied, her eyes clenched shut, her hands covering her head, an attempt of protection from whatever violence might come to her next.

Sera could feel the rage, the primal need to hurt this woman, the vengeance seething from the figure. Also, sadness, a deep internal hurt.

Suddenly, the gloved hand pulled a knife from the boot and started to cut away at the woman's eyes.

Sera started screaming in her own mind, screaming not to see any more of the horror as the dagger kept stabbing, stabbing, stabbing until the woman's face was an unrecognizable pile of flesh.

Finally, the gloved hands slit the woman's throat, her life fading out in front of Sera's eyes.

Tones, vibrations, and echoes collided, throwing Sera out of terror and back into Adam's guest bedroom. Her body transitioned from chilled to frozen, her body and clothes soaked through. Her entire body shook, her teeth chattered.

That's how Adam found her when he returned.

"What happened?" The tea mugs forgotten at the door, Adam rushed over, yanking an extra blanket from the closet, wrapping Sera in it. He sat with her, trying to rub warmth back into her.

"They're getting worse. So much worse. It was so brutal."

"I'm so sorry." Adam held Sera in his arms, rocking with her. "What can I do?"

"You're doing it," she said, her body trembling with cold, with fright.

Adam held her close, keeping her head against his chest. Listening to the steady beat of his heart slowed her own.

They stayed like that for a long time before Adam bent down and kissed her forehead. "You're still frozen. Do you want me to start a hot bath for you?"

"That sounds good. But not yet." Sera clung to Adam as if he were her life preserver. "Would it be weird to ask if you'd stay with me while I was in the bath? Not in a sexy way. I just...I don't want to be alone."

"I'd stay either way," Adam grinned at Sera and winked. "There she is," he said when she chuckled and nudged him.

"There is something I'm not getting. Something familiar that I'm not remembering."

"What could possibly be familiar?" Adam said to the closed shower curtain.

"That's just it, there shouldn't be..." Sera stopped midsentence, almost remembering, but it was gone as quickly as it had come. "I have no idea."

"What I'm wondering is how we get these to stop. That was pretty scary, seeing what happens to you. I can't imagine seeing what you see, feeling what you feel. We have to stop this."

Sera smiled behind the curtain. Something about the way he'd kept saying, 'we'. She pulled the curtain open enough to see his face.

"*We*?"

"Well, yes. I don't want this happening to you. I'll do what I can to help stop it."

"You are the best person ever."

"I try," he shrugged, "but I'm no saint. Close that curtain before I pull it all the way open."

"Ha. Ha." Sera closed the curtain. "Seriously, though. How would I stop..." Her thoughts cut off her words. She jumped up from the bath and yanked open the curtain—just a little too far.

"That's it! That's what has been bugging me."

"Geez." Adam looked away after a second—or two. "Towel." He handed her a towel without looking back again.

Sera wrapped herself in it and kissed his cheek. "You asked how *we* could stop this."

"Yes."

"But *we* can't."

"So, why are you looking happy about this?"

"Because *I* can."

Sera took Adam's hand and led him back into her room. Adam insisted on facing the wall as Sera dressed in fresh pajamas, her words quickly tumbling from her.

"When we met on the ship, I had those first visions of my mother. I thought they were just the awake-dreams like I used to have as a kid. She told me that *only*

I would be able to stop this, only I would understand." Sera paced the room. "It's the connection. I am connected to this...person. Somehow."

"Okay. How do we find out who this serial killing monster is that you're connected to? And hearing what I just said, do we *want* to?"

Sera stopped and stared at Adam. "I have no idea." She plopped down on the bed, the momentary jubilation dying into the disappointment of reality. "I don't know if I can continue watching this—killing. It's too much. And this one was so terrible. I can't do anything about it, I can't stop it. I can't even look away or close my eyes when it's happening. I'm forced to just watch." She looked at him again. "You have never once doubted any crazy thing I've ever told you."

"I've never *not* believed in this kind of thing. I've never seen it firsthand, either, until tonight. But, Sera, I do believe in you. I know this is something that is happening to you. I'm afraid for you too." Adam sat next to Sera on the bed. "Until we figure this out, I don't like the idea of you going back to San Francisco alone. Why don't you stay here? We can get you transferred to NYU. They have a fantastic nursing program at its extension campus, one of the best in the country. I've researched it. There's plenty of room in the house, and Ava would be beyond happy to have you here."

Sera caressed Adam's face. "You researched NYU's nursing program?"

"Sure. I was curious."

"It's only five months until graduation."

"Then, I can go back with you. People work remotely all the time now."

"And Ava? I wouldn't want her to be around all of this."

"Ava can stay with..."

"No, sweet man. I love you so much for wanting to help me. But I will not take Ava from her father. I'll be okay."

"You don't know that." Adam put his forehead to hers.

"We have no idea if I'm right about any of this. Maybe it's not real at all and I'm just pulling you into my delusions."

"Nice try," Adam said, then jumped to the other side of the bed. "Then I'm not leaving your side until I put you on a plane. I'll hire bodyguards to follow you around if I have to." He got under the covers and patted the space next to him. "Come on."

"Sly way to get into bed with me."

"Beautiful Sera. When I get you into bed, there will be no mistaking it for anything else. Now get over here and get some sleep. We'll think more about this tomorrow."

As soon as Sera was wrapped in Adam's protective arms, she finally fell into a dreamless sleep.

CHAPTER FIFTY-SIX

Sera

SAN FRANCISCO

Now, gals and guys, time for your final assignment, the dreaded senior thesis." The professor turned on the projector and started the slide presentation. "Since this is an Ethics class, I will at least attempt to teach you something concerning the ethical conduct of humans in this world that you will be thrust into shortly. As an example, I have a little story for you. There once was a doctor who practiced in Chicago. Now, this doctor was well known for his extracurricular pharmaceutical vending. That is, he took cash for his signature on prescriptions, whether or not he physically examined and/or diagnosed any of those people. A big *no-no*, as you all will probably agree. The news is full of these juicy tidbits, and what you will do is find them. Not one, but five articles showing me obvious ethical dilemmas in our wonderful society. Your paper will include a theory and a solution connecting each one of your five pieces. No less than ten pages and not more than fifteen." He handed packets out to each row of students to be passed down.

"One last thing," the professor grinned as a muffled groan passed throughout the class, "I need your articles picked out by Wednesday, six days from today. Have a nice day."

Sera felt a headache begin to spread from the base of her neck. She looked at her watch. There was a bit of time before her next class. She might as well get started on some research for this colossal assignment.

She made herself comfortable in a shady spot near her next class and pulled out her laptop. An hour later, she had researched through a few local and state-wide news sites. She saved a few possible articles and then clicked on a local story that caught her eye. As the picture loaded, she started to read the text. Her breath caught in her throat. Pixel by pixel, the image loaded.

A familiar face stared at Sera, the woman she'd seen murdered in her night terror a few weeks before when she was in New York with Adam. In the picture, the woman wore a gold cross necklace, the same one she'd seen ripped from her neck.

Sera's hand trembled as she clicked on the picture and article to save them on her laptop. She searched it for dates. The woman had been reported missing the day after Christmas, the 26th. Sera's night terror had been on Christmas night.

Struggling to catch her breath, she shut her laptop, grabbed her notebooks, and stuffed them all into her bag. Once she was back in the dorm, she started researching further. It was a little fuzzy, but she could piece a timeline together. She researched details she recalled from the night terrors. The homeless man was the next article she found. His murder had been categorized as a hate crime. Another article had labeled it a drug deal gone wrong. Even though there were no pictures, Sera knew it was the man who'd had his throat slashed behind a dumpster in an alley.

She'd kept searching. It took a while, but then she found *her*. The first of them, the girl with almost white eyes and white-blonde hair. Her face large on the screen, staring back at her. Her name had been Marlene Jacobs.

It was real. She wasn't crazy.

She should have believed the way Erinne believed, the way John never questioned, the way her mother accepted, even embraced *The Knowing*. Even Adam believed without hesitation. Why had it been so difficult for her to believe in herself?

It is real.

Sera stood and backed slowly away from the desk, her hand covering her mouth. Her breath caught in her chest as panic began to envelop her. The immediate need to get out of this room impeded her.

Sera ran.

Mile after mile, she ran. Away from the dorms, away from the school, past the golf course and lake until the sand ran into the ocean. Her lungs burned, her legs began to ache, but she couldn't stop, afraid that if she did, everything would come crashing down on her.

How did her mother do it? How was she able to handle these awful feelings?

Sera was tired of it all. Tired of everyone always telling her that she was brave, strong. Tired of how broken she still was, even after all these years, never finding a way to mend that brokenness. She wanted to yell, to scream out.

She just wanted to be normal.

But she'd *never* be normal. This is her life now, a life filled with sick, twisted virtual reality. She had worked so hard to deal with everything that had happened to her, being raped as a child, having her parents murdered in front of her, dealing with crippling fear that kept her from trusting the outside world. And for what? To be gifted this slaughter-vision?

This was no gift. Her mother couldn't have done this to her.

As her body began to tire, she found a tree to drop down under. She leaned against it, tilting her head back, pulling air into her body.

Retreat was tempting. It would be easy to hide from the world, pretend it didn't exist until it all went away, to let herself drown in the hopelessness she was treading on.

There was only one time in her college career that Sera missed class. She'd had a high fever and couldn't even keep water down. This would be the second time she missed class.

Pulling out her cell, she called Adam. There was no answer on his cell. So, she called his office number.

Adam

New York

Just before Marcy Brodenburgh intruded on him, Adam told Alice to hold all of his calls for the rest of the afternoon. He had a meeting the next day with an important potential client and wanted to nail the presentation. He'd spent most of the night perfecting the virtual model and the proposal bid.

"Marcy, I don't have time for this right now." Adam could feel his skin crawl. He had always thought it was some dramatic narrative used in books and movies, but he felt his skin actually trying to shrivel up and escape. The woman never gave up.

Sure, she was attractive, but she also had the personality of a praying mantis, and Adam didn't feel like being eaten alive, at least not today, and not by her. She was standing over him, playfully pulling at his tie.

"So later then? I'm just inviting you out for some fun. No commitment required. You'll give in one of these days. You are a man, and sooner or later all men have needs, even virtuous ones such as yourself. When that happens, I'll be right here."

God bless the phone, for it saved him that day.

"Mr. Wallace, phone call from California."

And God bless Alice for knowing he'd be upset for turning a call from Sera into a message slip.

Marcy smirked slyly and gave him a suggestive wink as she sauntered out of his office. When his door closed, he blew out the billow of air he'd been holding in, then picked up the receiver.

"Well, hello beautiful, to what do I owe the pleasure this afternoon?" He sat back in his chair, smiling into the phone.

"Adam."

The tone in her one word made him bolt straight up in his chair. "What's wrong? Are you okay?"

"Adam, she's dead. It was her. She's dead. She disappeared the day I had the night terror. They found her body. It's real, Adam. It was always real," her words tumbled together in frenzied chaos.

"What? Who's dead? Peyton? Is she okay? Are you hurt? Sera, what's going on?" He jumped out of his chair, grabbed his cell phone, and started frantically looking for flights to San Francisco. He could catch the next flight and be by Sera's side in hours.

"No. No, Peyton's fine. I'm okay. I'm sorry." She took a breath and started again. "Remember in my night terrors, I told you about the girl with the white blonde hair, the homeless man, and then the night terror I had while I was there about the woman and the bible?"

"Yes, of course I remember. Not going to forget any of that, probably ever." He eased back in his chair, hoping the ramming in his chest would settle before actually bursting through. Only she could drive him instantly insane with worry.

"It's in a news article from a town not far from here. She was real, not just a night terror. So were the others. I'm *not* crazy."

"Of course you're not crazy. Nobody ever thought you were. What were you able to find out?"

"The bible woman is, or was, Julie. Julie Gorgio. And the girl from the ship, her name was Marlene Jacobs. There was another article about a homeless man who was murdered, exactly how I saw in the night terror, the exact night I had it.

There was only one I couldn't find anything about, the girl that was buried in the woods. Maybe they haven't found her body yet. But they're not just nightmares. These are happening in real-time. Their bodies were found in the same types of areas that I saw. She was happy in the picture they put in the paper, but it *is* her. No doubt about it," Sera's voice was quick, breathless, shaky.

"Where are you right now? You sound like you're starting to hyperventilate. Is Peyton with you?" She was losing it, he could hear it. And he hated that he was so far away. What could he do? He could call her local police, the school, Peyton. Anyone to get to her so she wouldn't be left to have a panic attack alone, wherever she was.

"Peyton? I haven't seen her," Sera's voice wheezed.

"I need you to take some deep breaths, okay? One at a time. Slow down with me." Adam guided Sera's breathing until he could hear her breaths even out.

He needed to be with Sera, couldn't stand her being alone in this. It would be difficult leaving his daughter behind, though Victoria would never pass up the chance to spend time with her granddaughter.

"Adam, I don't know if I can do this anymore. I'm all out of fight. I don't know what to do."

"You know, you don't have to do anything. Selfishly, I'd rather you didn't. I don't want you to put yourself in any kind of dangerous situation."

He looked at Sera holding Ava in the picture he had taken during Christmas, which now lived on his desk. He reached out and traced his finger along Sera's hair. He didn't know what he would do without her.

"I should be there. I can be there as early as this evening. I just have to get Victoria to watch Ava, and then I can..."

"No. Don't come. I don't want you to see me like this."

"That's what I am here for. Not just for the fun, good, non-complicated times. Sera, I am here for you, good and bad."

"How can you believe in me? I'm so—broken."

"You're scared, and I am too. That doesn't mean you're broken. Sera?" He couldn't hear anything on the other line. He looked down at the phone base. The light was off. She'd hung up.

Adam walked out to Alice's desk. "How terrible would it be to move my schedule back a few days?"

Alice looked up from her computer screen. "Well, without even looking at the calendar, I can tell you that you have the presentation with the big wig from San Francisco tomorrow. How could you forget that one? After that meeting, at best, I can push your other appointments to the day after tomorrow, two days tops."

"Shit." The war between heart and head tore Adam in two halves. There was work, a detrimental time in the next phase for the company, and his own life. But he couldn't just leave Sera alone when she was going through something that scared him down to his core. He took out his cell and dialed Sera. No answer. *Shit*.

"Can you do me a favor and try to get Sera on the line? If you get her, forward the call to me immediately."

"Sure. Everything okay, boss?" Alice asked as she picked up the phone on her desk, looking up Sera's number from the contacts on her computer.

"I don't know. I hope so," Adam said as he walked back into his office, where he tried calling Peyton. If he couldn't reach Peyton, he would call Erinne if he had to. He couldn't help the shiver from the ice that ran down his spine.

CHAPTER FIFTY-EIGHT

Sera

SAN FRANCISCO

The world was dark again, not only because Sera kept all of the drapes closed in the dorm so that she wouldn't have to see the world go on outside of the room but also because there was no place she felt safe anymore. When she was younger, she could hide away in her room and feel protected, away from what might be lurking. But not even that was a possibility now.

She couldn't escape in sleep, either, for fear that she would be forced to watch another human being torn apart. It had been days since she'd slept more than a couple of hours at a time. She couldn't leave the room, terrified whoever was doing the tearing apart would find her and finish her off.

Maybe that would be a relief. She would be finally rid of this paralyzing fear that kept everything and everyone far from her. With the return of the familiar grip of fear came a rage Sera had never felt in her life. And that rage was toward her mother.

Why?

Why had she done this to her? Not only giving her this godforsaken *gift*, but why hadn't she just let her die with her in that cabin? Why couldn't she have let her die alongside her, that way she wouldn't have wasted years in this pathetic excuse for a life where she was scared of everything and everyone, constantly in the state of panic, never able to be there for anything or anyone else. She was that constant burden, always in need of rescuing. If only her mother had let Sera go with her that night, she could have been with her mom and her dad, safe and warm with them, wherever they were now.

What was the point? Why had she been spared just to do nothing, to live like this? Sera had thought about it, ending this suffering on her own. But she was also too scared to do that either. Pathetic.

Sera scooted off the couch, made her way to the freezer, empty glass in her hand, and took out a bottle of vodka. She was supposed to be at clinicals at the hospital today, but she'd given up caring about that. Instead, she fixed herself a cocktail that numbed her mind and took her away from her reality.

Adam had called and called. But she couldn't let him see her like this. Worse, if Ava was with him, she would see just how much of a coward Sera was.

Peyton had been her enabler the past couple of days. She'd told the professors that Sera had been ill, though Sera told her not to. She didn't care if she got kicked out of the program. Not anymore. Peyton also came back to the dorm every night instead of trolloping out and about like she usually did. She'd been attentive to Sera, telling her to take the time she needed, keeping the room dark, keeping the door locked, keeping her glass filled.

It was Peyton's suggestion of a Girl's-Night-In that showed Sera her way out. The alcohol drowned out the thoughts, the dreams, the constant fears. So, Sera made sure to keep her mind marinating in just enough alcohol so that she didn't have to feel anything.

A knock on the door almost sent her glass to the floor. Her body began to shake, panic quickly taking over. Though no one could see through the door, she hid in the corner of the room, willing whoever it was to go away.

Another knock.

"Sera?" Adam's voice, soft, concerned, was on the other side of the door.

Sera started to shake more. He'd come all the way across the country. She couldn't let him see her like this. She put her drink on the coffee table and slowly walked over to the door, placing her forehead against it.

"Adam. Go home."

"I can't. I need to know you're okay. Please open the door."

"No."

CHAPTER FIFTY-NINE

Adam

SAN FRANCISCO

It's just me. I'm alone out here. I have to know you're okay. Don't think I won't cause a scene. I'll get someone to open this door or break it down myself if I have to." He waited for what seemed like forever before he heard the soft slide of the lock.

Adam tested the knob. The door opened. The room was so dark that he had to wait for his vision to adjust. Only a thin beam of light escaped between the curtains. He closed the door behind him and walked further into the room. She was there, he could feel her, hear her. But he couldn't see her.

"I told you not to come," she murmured.

He turned and saw the outline of her. "That's not possible. You should know that."

"I don't need saving. There is nothing left to save."

"Don't talk like that." Adam went to Sera, reached out to her. But she recoiled, which broke his heart more than her words.

"What did you think you could do? Say some funny things, get me to laugh and everything would be okay again? That everything would go away? That no one would be hacked up anymore? It's too much. And there is nothing I can do about it, nothing *you* can do about it. So just go home. Leave me alone."

It hurt to be dismissed like that. Even though he knew she was trying to push him away by hurting him, and though what she said crushed him, there was also an inkling of anger igniting for how little she thought of herself and of him.

"I can't do that." He reached for her again, taking her in his arms. Her body went rigid, ungiving. He held her against him anyway until he felt her start to soften.

Then she was clinging to him, reaching for him, running her fingers through his hair with desperation. She brought her mouth up, crushed her lips to his, pulling at him, frantic.

He wanted to kiss her back, to hold her, let her take him. But it wasn't right, not like this, and he could taste the alcohol on her lips.

He pulled away. "Have you been drinking?" He stepped away from her, went to the window and pulled open the drapes. There were several empty bottles of various types of alcohol on the counter. Empty glasses littered the room, and one full one was on the coffee table. "What is happening to you, Sera?"

"You kissed me in New York, but now, nothing. I knew it, that I just imagined it. You don't want me. I'm nothing to you, just this pitiful basket case that Saint Adam has to save, right?" Sera turned from him, stomping into the small bedroom.

"That's not true. At all. I'm here because I care deeply about you. I'm here for you, for all of it."

"But not really. You just shot down a big part of *All* of it."

"I know you're hurting. It's not the right time for that. You're not in your right mind right now..."

"I'm not in my right mind? You do think I'm crazy! I knew it." She threw an empty glass against the wall. "You don't want me, fine. I should have known. I mean, you can't even take off that damn ring. Go home, Adam, where you can stay hung up on your dead wife."

"Jesus Sera. That's enough. I never know what version of you I'm going to get—the optimistic, strong, sweet version or this pathetic woe-is-me version." Adam regretted it the minute he'd said it, but she had hit him where it hurt worst.

Sera glared at Adam, her fists clenched at her sides. "I should have never trusted you. Get out. Get out of my life," she said, her voice low and vibrating with rage.

"Call me when you've sobered up." Adam left her, standing in the middle of the room, looking as though she hated him, his eyes burning as he walked down the hall and out of the building.

He hadn't wanted to leave her alone when she needed someone most, but he couldn't be her punching bag, either. If he stayed, they might have said worse things to each other that would have damaged their relationship.

If they hadn't been already.

CHAPTER SIXTY

Sera

SAN FRANCISCO

When Sera opened her eyes the next morning, the pain instantly throbbed in her head and then in her heart as she remembered what she'd said to Adam, what he had said to her.

She had gotten what she wanted. She'd pushed him away, alright. And it broke her in two. But there was no other way. She wouldn't drag him down with her. She was unsavable, and Adam would never give up trying. It was just who he was.

She glanced at her cell phone. No missed calls. It was the first time in days he hadn't tried calling her. The burn of tears threatened but never came.

She'd wanted to let him go, but she hadn't meant to be so cruel. Even though this is what she wanted, for him, for Ava, she couldn't let that be the last thing she ever said to him.

She picked up her cell, called Adam. When it went to voice mail, which she figured it would, she left one last message for him.

"This is for the best. You'll realize it one day. You have always been the best friend anyone could ever hope for. You deserve to move on with your life out there in New York. The best way is to do it without me in it. I don't want to mess up your life, and I can't be the one to mess up Ava's."

Then she ended the call, turned back over, and went back to sleep, wishing she could cry as her heart shattered.

CHAPTER SIXTY-ONE

Adam

New York

Adam saw the call come in, her face lighting up the screen. But he couldn't bear to answer it, couldn't hear her voice just yet. When the icon flashed for a new voicemail, he didn't listen to it. It wasn't until he was back at the office the next day trying to catch up on the work he'd dropped to go to Sera that he finally did.

She'd said he'd been her best friend. But that wasn't enough for her. She wouldn't let him in, wouldn't let him help. And he'd left her, when she needed him most. She had hurt him, said things that made his heart fall to the floor, and then stomped on it while it lay there bleeding. It hurt as badly as she'd meant it to. Maybe more. So much so that his internal organs still felt as if they were being squeezed in a vice.

He listened to the voicemail again, sitting at his desk in his office, the door closed, the blinds shut, his head in his hands. She sounded so distant that he could actually feel her soul disconnecting from his.

She was gone. She didn't want him there. And he had left her alone.

He took the picture of them that sat on his desk and threw it across the room, watching it shatter against the wall like his heart.

"Alice, cancel my afternoon. I have to leave," Adam barked out as he stormed past Alice's desk.

"Sure. Everything okay?"

He couldn't answer. He just waved a hand as he left. He didn't know where he was going, only that he had to escape everything.

Sera's words kept echoing.

Go home where you can stay hung up on your dead wife.

He marched through the city, dodging taxis and weaving around rushing people, ultimately finding a lively pub around the corner.

Just in time to catch Marcy Brodenburgh having lunch.

Chapter Sixty-Two

The evening was mild, already warming with the coming turn of the season. It should be a pleasant night, but the beast is trying to trick me.

I saw my mother die once, when she was sick, riddled with disease. But then, she wasn't dead. She still roamed the earth, alone but alive, free to live without any burden of responsibility. She could not go unpunished for all that she had done—worse, for what she didn't do.

I should feel vindicated knowing that I have rid the world of one more of the weak-minded sheep. But I only feel lost, more than ever before.

I killed my own mother. The woman who should have played with me, talked to me, the mother who should have laughed, smiled, and taught me things. The mother who should have protected me to her last breath, the mother who should have loved me.

Of course she needed to die. The world needs protectors, not weaklings who let their children bleed, starve, and be beaten. I am not the sacrifice. She is. Judgment and justice had needed to find her. If I was the one who brought it to her, then it was fate.

It was late when I unlocked the door to the room that had been home. I looked into the mirror at the face that belonged to me. Nothing had changed. I didn't look like a murderer, but I didn't look like some righteous vigilante, either. I was still just pathetic, unloved, unwanted, damaged me.

I can still feel the darkness edging in, tempting me with that sweet, blissful peace.

But then *she* needed *me*.

And it quieted the beast. For a moment.

Until the real person behind the mask began to show through. She wasn't strong, she wasn't resilient. There was nothing to admire after all. She was a coward, like the rest of them.

Worse, she was a fake. She'd fooled everyone, all those who bowed to her, loved her, worshiped her, and gave everything to her. I knew because I had slipped and had become one of them. I had loved her, too.

But she was never any of that. Now that I know who she really is, I can't love her anymore, and I hate her even more for it.

Maybe the beast knew better than I did. It has always known what needed to be done. It knows that any kindness I may have found is easily taken away. Instead of waiting for others to give me some meager validation, I'll keep seeking justice because there isn't much else left without it.

I've already taken far too long to finish it.

CHAPTER SIXTY-THREE

Adam

NEW YORK

I want to video call Sera! We haven't talked to her in forever. Why won't you let me call her?" The last time Adam had seen his daughter this mad was when a boy in her class pulled her hair and called her a melon-head in front of everyone. Other than that, he had been blessed with a usually calm child.

This was different. Ava was on the verge of tears under all that rage. He knew why, but it couldn't be helped. Sera was family, and he was acting as if she had never existed. Worse, he was mad that Ava kept asking. He was angry all the time these days, at work, at home. Not that he had been home much.

Work had been his band-aid, at least for a little while. The minute he returned from San Francisco, he dove into work as though his life depended on it. Eventually, he'd asked Victoria to come so that Ava wouldn't be stuck with sitters day in and day out.

Ava usually loved having her grandmother around. This time though, he never heard the end of it.

"Grandma is no fun. She never lets me have more screen time. She always makes me eat too many vegetables. She doesn't let me eat any of the good snacks. She is boring. She kind of smells weird." And on and on Ava complained.

He had even yelled at her. Adam had never yelled at Ava before.

Ava had run down the stairs when she heard him come home, trying to show him something funny Snickers, her guinea pig named after her favorite candy bar, did. And Adam had actually yelled at her for it. That was the low point for him. Failing his daughter was not an option, but he had no idea how to get himself out of this slump.

Ava's wrath peaked when she heard him talking to Marcy with his phone on speaker. He knew what it sounded like, the way Marcy kept laughing and talking in that flirtatious way of hers. When he ended the call, Ava was staring him down, her arms crossed, her foot stomping, her little face flushed with anger.

"That woman was *not* Sera."

That argument continued until Ava stomped off to her room, slamming her door. He was sure that wouldn't be the last door slam he'd get from his daughter.

"We are not calling Sera right now. I know you're only six years old and can't understand complicated adult things. But no is no, and that is the end of it." Adam didn't know why he was doing this. He'd never wanted to deny his daughter a relationship with Sera. No matter what was happening or not happening between the two of them, Ava and Sera's relationship was important for Ava.

He just couldn't let go of the resentment, the hurt. And because he couldn't let it go, it had festered and boiled.

"Don't you like Sera anymore?" Ava glared at him.

"Of course I like her. She's my friend." Was he *lying* now? It couldn't get worse. He wanted to shrink away and disappear.

"No, Daddy. I mean, don't you *love* her anymore?" Ava flopped down on the couch in a frustrated huff, crossing her arms over her chest, the heartbreak etched across her face.

There it was.

He'd been holding it back. Ava certainly wasn't fooled, and he couldn't fool himself any longer, either. Adam had fallen deeply in love with Sera.

His wife had been young love. When everything was irrational, passionate, and all-encompassing. When Alex died, his world had turned inside out. Every day felt as though he'd die from the hurt of losing her. Surely, he would never be able to love again.

Then he met Sera. The circumstances of their meeting and the resulting devotion to each other were entirely opposite to that of his and Alex's crazy, youthful days. Falling in love with Sera had been different than it had been with Alex. It wasn't the same, but it was just as right.

Sera had worked herself into his mind and soul, as well as his daughters. He needed Sera and hoped she needed him back.

He prayed he hadn't lost her.

"You're supposed to be six. Not twenty-six." He sat next to Ava, pulling her onto his lap.

"I love Sera. You love her, too. And it's okay, Daddy." She snuggled into his chest.

Adam rocked with her.

The light reflected off the ring he still hadn't taken off, and for the first time, he knew in his heart that it was time.

CHAPTER SIXTY-FOUR

Sera

SAN FRANCISCO

Sera's phone rang somewhere in the dorm. She stumbled to where the sound was coming from—under a blanket, between the couch cushions. The administration office was calling her. Again.

She already knew, she was missing too much, they would kick her out if she missed any more, yada, yada. She ignored the call and then saw she'd missed three other calls from them, as well as a video chat from Ava. Her heart stopped.

Ava.

Sera slumped down on the couch, her gut twisting with guilt and sadness. Her whole body physically ached for the child, to hear her little voice and see her joyous smile. She longed to hold her again, to snuggle with her as she read to her, to watch that bundle of light laugh and take her hand. Along with everything else, she'd lost the little girl who lit up her soul.

If her heart hadn't been broken before, whatever was left shattered into dust.

Sera yanked a pillow from the couch, pushed her face into it, and from deep within, a primal howl emptied itself from her until the last of her breath left her lungs.

Sera let go.

Heat filled her chest, flushed her face, and burned her eyes—a long forgotten wetness seeped into them and spilled over as sobs shook her entire body.

Sera cried for all of the pain, the hurt, the violation, for the parents who had been stolen from her, for the weight of the burden of all that she'd lost. She cried for the little girl who had been terrified into silence, too scared to fight back, the little girl who could only cower, never letting anyone else in, so afraid to ever be hurt again.

Sera cried for all of the people who she'd watched lose their lives so viciously. She cried for those who she had loved and loved still. She cried for all of it, for all of them. And most all for Ava, the little girl she'd fallen in love with, the child who lost her mother before she ever got to know her.

The fire of all the evil Sera had seen in the world had burned her, had taken some of her humanity from her, leaving her a broken, shattered loner who could barely breathe instead of becoming the warrior she needed to be. For herself, for Ava.

She was failing Ava with every minute wasted wrapped up in her selfish cocoon of self-pity, withering away in a drunken numbness, wallowing because she was too scared to do anything. Sera had forgotten what was important—it was, and always would be, Ava.

Ava had to come first. She deserved to live in a world that was even just a little bit safer, which was something Sera *could* do.

My Gift. And *this* is why. I *can* do this.

This coming from the person who had been scared of people, of places, of everything most of her life. But she couldn't let it paralyze her any longer. She would stand up and brush herself off. She refused to be the broken one any longer.

No one would make her run and hide again. Sera was her mother's daughter, after all. She *was* brave and strong, and now she would be determined.

Sera picked herself up off the couch, opened the drapes, took a water from the fridge, and swallowed some Tylenol. She dumped out the remnants of several bottles, threw them into a trash bag, washed the glasses, put them away, picked up her laundry, made her bed, and then took a shower to wash off the stench of stale booze.

An hour later, she returned the administration office calls apologizing profusely, telling them she was feeling much better. She had some makeup work to do, clinical hours to make up, and she'd lost the Suma Cum Laud ranking, but they would allow her to continue, to graduate.

Finally, she watched Ava's video message. The video was shaky, but the context was clear enough. Adam was never home and refused to let Ava call Sera. He was also talking to a woman from his office, and Ava didn't like her.

A fist slugged her in the heart.

Adam hadn't called, texted, emailed, or written to her since she'd told him to get out of her life. He'd done exactly what she told him to do and moved on without her. It was her own fault that her heart was breaking.

She'd really lost him.

It shattered Sera to think of him touching, holding, and kissing someone. Kissing some woman the way he'd kissed her. But Sera was only Adam's friend, maybe not even that.

She had to put that away, not let it distract her. Stopping whoever was ripping innocent people apart had to be the only thing that occupied her mind. For Ava.

Maybe she could talk to the police? Their motto was to serve and protect, wasn't it? If she gave them details of her night terrors, both past and as they came, they'd know she wasn't making all of it up. Right? She was grasping, she knew.

But she had to try.

"Wow. You look...better?" Peyton walked in from the shower after washing away the day of clinicals at the hospital bundled up in a fluffy robe, a beauty mask adorning her face, just eye and mouth holes visible, her signature long black hair wrapped up in a towel. Her gaze fixed on Sera, who hadn't stopped pacing angrily.

"I am SO mad right now. I want to scream or throw something. Damn it, they all but laughed me out of there. What's worse is that I knew they would." Sera stormed about the dorm, trying not to throw everything she touched. Even though she'd been pacing for the last hour, she was still fuming.

Peyton smiled. "Sera, I've never seen such pure rage emanating from you before. I have to say, I like it. But, do you want to let me in on what you're talking about? *Who* laughed at you, and *why?*"

Sera started laughing manically. "I've officially lost it."

When the wildly inappropriate laughter abated, Sera took a couple of breaths and told Peyton what had happened that afternoon. She described her break-down, her realization, and her sudden urge to go to the police for help, which turned out to be a complete waste of time.

"Why would you get the police involved? It's not like they'll ever believe you." Sera may not have been able to see the expression through Peyton's white mask, but for the briefest moment, Sera heard the anger in Peyton's voice and saw it flash in her eyes. Then Peyton quickly got up. "I'm making us margaritas."

"No thanks. I'm good. I've had enough to last me a while."

"Suit yourself." As Peyton got the blender out of the cabinet, she asked, "They wouldn't listen to you at all?"

"Nope. They worse than laughed at me. The cop looked annoyed and bored as if he heard that sort of thing all the time. I knew it would be tough to get through to someone, but the little weasel was so cocky and arrogant that I just blew up. I threw my papers at him and stormed out as any dignified, respectable southern woman would do."

"Honey, you're not from the south," Peyton snorted as she mixed herself a drink.

"I know it, but I believe that all women are allowed to humor themselves once in a while," Sera said, faking a heavy southern drawl. "Bless that little turd's heart."

A sudden heavy pounding on the door made them both jump.

Peyton opened the door, still in her robe, hair wrapped in the towel, mask still plastered to her face, a fresh margarita in hand. Standing on the other side was a young, tall, good-looking black man with a wide bright smile, dressed in a suit, his hand holding out a badge for them to see.

"Sera Delaney?" His voice was deep and smooth, the slightest hint of a Louisianna drawl came through.

"I'm Sera."

"My name is Detective Drake Pardou. I am heading a murder investigation in the area. I have to apologize for the officer on duty's behavior. You should've been sent up to see me."

Peyton stood unmoving at the door, a barrier between the man and Sera.

"It's okay, Peyton. He can come in if he'd like," Sera said skeptically while looking the detective over.

Peyton shrugged and opened the door wider for the man to pass. "Margarita?" Peyton offered as she walked back to the small kitchenette.

"No thanks. Working," Detective Pardou answered as he entered the room, looking around their small dorm apartment.

Sera didn't bother trying to disguise the bite in her tone. "What can I help you with?"

"May I?" Detective Pardou asked, making his way to a chair at the small dining table without waiting for a response.

"Your officer made it quite clear that the police want nothing to do with anything I might be able to help with." She sat on the opposite chair, meeting Detective Pardou's gaze, eye to eye.

"Don't worry, I gave him hell for it. Next time, you'll be treated with a great deal more respect."

Sera scoffed. "Next time? There is no next time. Once was enough for me. Do you think I don't know what it sounds like? I barely believe it myself. That doesn't mean I want to be treated like a freak." She stood and walked to the door. "I'm sorry you've wasted your time."

"Actually, I haven't come to ask you to assist me. I have some questions I need you to clarify. I'd like to know how you know about some of these details because from where I'm standing, there is no other way to know other than by being involved somehow," he paused.

"*Involved?* How dare you. You need to leave. Now!" Sera screeched as she flung the door open. "You don't think that after all these years, after all of the horrendous visions of death and murder, seeing the desperation of those people, the fear and terror they went through, knowing that I might have been able to help them if I'd just believed in what I've been seeing hasn't already filled me with enough guilt? Now you come into *my* home and accuse me of being involved?"

"Now, wait a minute. What kind of detective would I be if I didn't check you out?" He took out a manila file folder and dropped it on the table, sending photographs of her mother's tattered dead body scattering.

Peyton came up behind the detective. She glanced down at the table, her eyes locking on the pictures, looking over each one as she slowly gathered them together.

"*You son-of-a-bitch*. I know what she looked like," Sera snarled, the crescendo of her voice building. "Take your shit and get the hell out!" Sera was screaming by then, drawing other students out of their rooms.

"I think you were told to leave." Peyton spoke firmly, moving toward him with her always prominent presence, the manila folder in her hand.

"Alright, this time I will. But consider this a warning. Don't leave town. No more of your trips to New York. We have much more to talk about."

"You don't have shit to talk about without a warrant." Protective fury edged in Peyton's voice, looking more like a monster than a woman in that white mask.

"I'll leave. I just thought we could have a heart-to-heart. Good day, ladies." He bowed his head and left the room, leaving his business card and the smell of his cologne behind.

Sera grabbed the folder from Peyton. "Don't forget this," she yelled as she threw it into the hallway at his back and slammed the door.

"Screw him. What a complete asshole." Peyton went to Sera's side, taking her by the shoulders. "Are you okay?"

"I can't believe he would come in here and do that, shove those things in my face. He had no right." Sera couldn't stop shaking, her hands, legs and mouth trembled uncontrollably.

Peyton wrapped her arms around Sera. "Don't worry about him. We will file a complaint at the station. I'd love to nail that miserable SOB. I hate it when they criminalize the victim. I've seen it too many times."

"He was testing me, checking if I was lying. I couldn't help but react, it was like I had no control. Let him think I was lying. I don't care." Sera gave in to Peyton's embrace, feeling her body melt in to her. "He had pictures of my mom."

"I know, I saw. Is that what she really looked like? Is that what he did to her?"

Something about the way Peyton asked had Sera pulling away to look up at her. Though Peyton's eyes were filled with concern, her tone suggested a darker interest.

"I wish you hadn't looked at those."

"I'm sorry. I just wanted to get them out of your sight. He just threw them all out. It was just plain mean. You really should file a complaint against him." Peyton's face lightened again.

"Well, I don't have time to worry about that jerk," Sera said, noticing the clock on the wall, "because I have to get to that makeup class. I can't miss a minute more. I'll deal with him somehow. I'll give it some thought, think of something really good." Sera got up to gather her books.

"Hey, at least the guy was hot." Peyton winked at her.

Sera rolled her eyes at Peyton as she rushed out the door.

CHAPTER SIXTY-FIVE

Sera

SAN FRANCISCO

Detective Drake Pardou walked up to Sera when she emerged from class and handed her a coffee and a small clear package containing some kind of pastry. A token, no doubt, of remorse for being so cruel.

Sera froze. "Wow. I...I have no words," she spat, her face growing hot, her muscles tensing. She turned and started walking away from him, the blood slamming through her body, keeping rhythm with the pounding of her feet. Sera might have decked the man when he took her arm, but he caught her hand before it made contact.

"Hey, I come in peace."

"Let go of me," Sera snarled, pulling her arm from his grip.

"I thought you could use this to feed all that knowledge simmering up there." He let go but didn't budge out of her path.

"You've done enough, so, no, thank you." She attempted to walk away, but he maneuvered himself to block her way.

"I know that, and I can't even begin to explain how stupid I was for losing my cool. I was awful, and I'm sorry. Take this as just the first of many ways I'm going to make it up to you." He offered the coffee and box out to her, his smile never wavering once.

It was a good smile, too. Peyton hadn't been wrong in her assessment of his attractiveness. However, it had been ruined by his unforgivable behavior.

To get him out of her way, Sera took his peace offering and started walking. He fell in step beside her.

"I messed up pretty bad, I know it, and I feel like shit about it. I tend to be one of those do-now-think-later kind of guys. I mean, I should carry around salt and pepper."

Annoyed, Sera couldn't help but ask, "Salt and pepper?"

"Yeah, for the foot that is constantly in my mouth."

"I don't have time for this," she said, shaking her head and quickening her step.

"Look, just hear me out for one minute, please," he pleaded with her, with his voice and his eyes. "I'm really not a bad guy. I promise you. But these cases have been getting to me. I've been taking them personally. Just the type of cop that I am, always have been. Now, I get a potential witness who shows up with information on not one, not two, but three of my unsolved cases. Cases that weren't connected before, and if you're right, a fourth that we don't even know about yet. Which means we got a problem. It also means there is a killer walking around free to do whatever it is that killers like to do. Which also means that this guy is a spook, a ghost. He's left nothing for us to nail him with. Help me figure out what's going on here." He led her to a nearby bench under a tree.

Sera sat apprehensively, though willingly, not sure whether or not to believe him, seeing as he had already tried to trick her once. She studied him, watching his face for any hint of deceit, feeling for dishonesty. But all she saw was genuine concern. Detective Drake Pardou might actually care about what was happening.

"What you did is unforgivable." Her eyes began to burn. After all the years of absence, tears found her again and wanted to take hold of her now.

"I am truly sorry, Miss Delaney. I thought that if you were involved or maybe knew who was, then maybe I could shock it out of you. It is a very old-school way, which actually works exceptionally well in a lot of cases. Again, doesn't excuse the behavior. I didn't even realize I was doing it until it was too late. A piss-poor decision on my part."

"Extremely risky, not to mention hurtful." Could she trust this man enough to tell him about everything? As she watched him, she realized that she didn't have to trust him, and he didn't have to trust her. She had nothing to hide. Let him investigate her. Maybe that would lead him to information that would help find out whoever was doing this.

"You've read my notes, then?" Sera asked him. When he nodded, she continued, "I'll start by telling you, I barely believe this is happening myself." She could see him in her peripheral. He was looking off unassumingly, patiently listening.

"I haven't had these night terrors since I was a kid. And then, out of nowhere, I started having them again as an adult. When I have the night terrors, I see these murders as if I am watching through the killer's eyes. It's like some virtual reality game. I can almost feel what this killer is feeling. I'm still myself, but I can feel the killer's rage and pain. It's impossible to explain." Embarrassment flushed her face. How foolish it all sounded. Worse, insane. There was no way he would believe her. Hell, *she* would never have believed her.

"What do you see, or more importantly, *when* do you have these nightmares?"

"I'm not completely sure, but when I read the articles on those victims, the dates they went missing seem to be the same dates that I had the night terrors. I think I am seeing it as it's happening. What I can see is blurry. I can't really tell where they are unless it is in direct line of sight, and I can't hear anything. Like it's all on mute. Which means, it doesn't let me help prevent anything. Some help, huh?" Shaking her head, she placed her face in her hands.

"Which means that if the dates these people go missing correlate with the dates they are murdered, then they aren't being held very long. That *is* something." Detective Pardou looked directly at her for the first time since they sat on the bench. "So, you have these visions as they are happening, and what you see is limited to the direct subject and what is in direct line of sight, and you can't hear anything that is being said. That does limit us quite a bit, doesn't it?"

"Us?" She eyed him skeptically.

"Of course. We have nothing on this guy. What we have been doing hasn't worked. I can quote Einstein, but I'm sure you already know that whole bit."

"Imagination or Insanity?" Sera asked.

"The insanity one. Look, if it's one guy doing this, and if we're going to stop him from devouring a buffet of people, then we have to try something different. There were plenty of respectable police departments using psychics for missing person cases. It certainly doesn't hurt, might as well give it a try. That's what I'm doing now, trying it out. I won't lie, it'll take the department some time to get a grip on you. But I have a feeling you can handle it." He held out his hand to Sera. "Partner?"

Suspicious, Sera looked at him, examining his face and body language. Was he ridiculing her, or did he actually believe her?

"*Partner?*"

"Well, not technically or officially, but close enough, for now at least," he said, giving her another bright smile. He stood and held out a hand to help her up. "Hungry?"

"Starving."

"What, does *everyone* fall for you?"

"What does that mean?" When Sera had returned from grabbing a sandwich with Detective Pardou, Peyton seemed to be in a rage, something Sera had never seen from her.

"You're just hanging out with that cop now? Does that mean *he* is going to be at your beck and call, too? Open a special case just for you?"

"All I did was tell him about the night terrors. That *was* the whole point of going to the police in the first place. What the hell is wrong with you, Peyton?"

"Nothing is wrong with *me*, sweet, special Sera. You're the one who has issues." Peyton grabbed her bag and slammed the door behind her as she stalked out.

Sera stared at the closed door, completely baffled at Peyton's reaction. Peyton could be a little jealous sometimes, but this was ridiculous. The way she had been behaving unnerved Sera to the point of sleeping somewhere else for the night, maybe longer. Peyton had been losing her cool a lot more often lately. And not in the normal tiff kind of way, but in a major, something-else-was-going-on way.

Because she felt the red flag go up in the strongest part of her intuition, Sera packed a bag along with what she needed for classes and left to stay at a hotel.

Chapter Sixty-Six

The need to escape blankets me. The wet air in this room drowns me. The drip, drip, drip of the faucet feels like bombs being set off in my brain with each plop into the metal sink. The constant hum of electricity sent my ears screaming with a nonstop ringing.

I could feel myself falling apart, breaking into pieces that would scatter into the wind. The itch to find a way out crawled beneath the surface of my skin.

I've had a taste of what normal felt like, what it felt like to be okay. That's all I want. I just want to feel okay again.

I fled the room and drove around town in circles with no place to go, using gas I shouldn't waste. The day was too clear, too nice, too perfect. If I crashed into one of these redwood trees, maybe the feeling of my skin slinking away, trying to escape me, would stop. It would stop me from feeling any of it, all of it. I would finally find a way out.

The only thing I could trust was that when I fell apart, the beast would come to me, lift me out of the darkness, and show me the way.

I ignored the alluring urge to crash my car into a giant redwood and instead took a hard left into a neighborhood I'd never been to before.

And that was when I saw my sweet, stupid sister.

She was leading a bunch of kids in a circle behind some church. A Sunday school teacher? Of course, she was. After a lifetime of being led by those who only sought to dominate others with the excuse of some man-made scripture, what else would Sister-Dearest have become?

I pulled over, hid under the shade of a tree, and watched Sister. She was still a little too small for her age, even though she was now an adult. She still looked beaten down, pale, depressed, distraught. When she took the kids back inside, I stayed staring at the building she disappeared into.

Time was sometimes irrelevant to me, hours passing in blocks that felt like minutes. Like now. When I looked down at the dash clock, two hours had passed when the crowd of people started filing out of the church, into their cars, heading back to their lives feeling better about themselves, having spent their weekly allotted time in that building.

As the last of the cars dispersed, Sister walked out with the wolf in sheep's clothing, the demon among humans. Sister never escaped her. How pitiful.

She walked Grandmother to the car, guiding her by the arm. It was worse than hell, Sister now had to care for Grandmother, a woman who never cared about anyone other than her putrid self.

Grandmother still held herself as stiff and rigid as ever, desperate to display her dominance over the rest of us heathens. She looked the same as the last time I set eyes on her shriveled face, her hair so white you could see through to her skull.

Control was important. Without it, there was only wrath. I needed to keep a firm hold on that control, even with my hate wide open, all of her crimes resurfacing. Control is what will allow me to bring rectitude and bestow judgment upon her, finally making her answer for all of the wreckage she caused.

They drove slowly through the streets. I followed, not even trying to be subtle. Sister was driving, and she was too stupid to notice. It wasn't far before they pulled into a driveway.

I watched them from across the street. I watched that old bat shuffle her way up to the door, wait at it until Sister got to it, carrying all of their belongings, unlock it, and open the door for Grandmother to waltz through—ever the royalty.

Time lapsed again, and it was dark. The lights glowed inside, a blue flickering dim, bright, and dim again. I got out and made my way around the house. The back fence was unlocked.

So unsafe.

The blinds were open just enough to peer inside the lit rooms. I don't know how long I watched them, Grandmother watching some moronic game show while Sister sweated over the stove in the kitchen. Typical. I watched Sister-Dearest make a plate of food and place it in front of Grandmother. I watched them clasp hands, I'm sure giving thanks to their deity. Then I watched Sister take Grandmother to her bedroom, tucking her in like an invalid child. After which, sweet, loyal, devoted Sister finished her duties by putting the food away, washing the dishes, and cleaning up the kitchen. Sister ended her night reading her bible like the good little girl she was brainwashed to be.

It was plain to see that rectification of this situation was way overdue. I left them to their devices for now. I would be back to free Sister and condemn Grandmother.

Sister-Dearest helped bring Grandmother to her sentencing. She had to have recognized me, even though she pretended not to know me when I approached her in her front yard. Dim-witted idiot that she was, all I had to do was ramble on about being interested in being saved by her Lord and Savior, and I was in. After that, getting them into their small half-finished basement room didn't take much effort.

The room was barely tall enough to stand upright, but it suited the situation just fine. There were no windows, which gave us the privacy we were going to need. Its brick build provided adequate soundproofing to implement proper sentencing. Pipes were concreted into the foundation, which provided a nice place to secure the two of them until their turn was upon them.

I looked at Sister. I can't remember ever feeling much of anything for her. My brother and I had bonded in our trauma, together in our pain and suffering. But this girl never had to go through any of it.

Dad was long gone by the time she was born, and her age made her ripe for the reaping, which is just what Grandmother did—twisting her mind into another hypocrite. Sadly, Sister may have had the worst outcome of all of us. She still serves this sadistic bitch as she rots with age.

"Did you ever even try?" I asked Sister, who whimpered in response, her chin quivering.

"...What?"

I couldn't stand her crying any longer. It was constant blubbering, prayers mixed with wails of pleads and begging. I slapped her. I almost felt bad for doing it. But she finally shut up. I took a breath and asked her again.

"Did you ever *try* to think for yourself? Want anything for yourself? Want to live your own goddamn life? Ever?"

She looked at me as if asking permission to speak. She was just too much, too pathetic to deal with any longer. Brother was shown mercy and given a way out of his misery. I would free Sister as well.

"Are you afraid? Yes, you're afraid of me. I can smell it on you, you poor, sweet thing. Dry your eyes now. I will give you mercy, free you from this traitorous world that has turned its back on us. I am truly sorry that we never got to be family."

Again, she looked at me with those big senseless eyes, like she had no idea what I was talking about. I couldn't stand it anymore, seeing what pitiful existence my baby sister had been forced to inhabit.

I took her head in my hands, angled it upward, and twisted, one quick snap.

Grandmother had the audacity to pretend to give a shit, her wails muffled through the gag.

"You. You've earned something special."

Control was key, I had to remind myself. I took a few deep breaths to even it out. Not too deep, not too fast. The beast has waited so very long for this moment. My whole life, *I* have waited for this moment.

I yanked Grandmother up from her crouched position on the basement floor and slid a piece of wood to her feet—the wood plank I had carefully crafted the day before, made especially for Grandmother.

"Kneel. Repent. Ask for forgiveness for the evil you brought upon us. Ask, beg, plead until your answer comes." I shoved the old bitch down on her knees to kneel on her altar of shattered glass.

"After hours kneeling on hard tile, it starts to feel like glass cutting into your knees, especially after they start bleeding. That's when it gets real fun."

Looking at her now, I wonder how she ever seemed scary. She was nothing, a sliver of a human. I pulled out a bible that I found in their living room. A nice-sized one, substantial enough to serve its purpose. I dropped it in front of her, a heavy thud sounding when it landed.

"Has this given you everything you ever hoped for? Did it make you as powerful as you ever wanted to be? Or did it just give you an excuse to reign your terror upon small, helpless kids? It's really all about power and control, isn't it? You wanted to control us. You lived just to break us."

I could feel the control slipping away. But I wasn't ready to let the beast loose just yet. I have so many things to say to this monster.

"I tried, you know. Really tried to make it through my life after I was finally free of you. I tried to reclaim it, tried to find some way to be normal. But you destroyed any chance of that ever happening. You were always in my way. All the lies you fed us, all this bullshit was just another way to break us down, bit by bit. Even after all these years.

"No matter how much I tried to be good and obey, it was never good enough. All I wanted was to feel, maybe not love, but the slightest bit of affection from you. But *I* was never good enough. Because of you, I never had anyone or anything. My life was empty of everything. Everything except misery. I wanted to shrink away and die, leave this earth.

"I never asked to be born. I didn't want Father to move us across the country just to dump us and go chase after some whore. I certainly never asked to be constantly terrified for the rest of my life, waiting for the next beating, the next vicious attack of words and fists. Your voice still fucks with my mind. I hear that squeaky pitch calling for me, searching for me so that you could put your hands on me again. You broke me into a million pieces. You've also taught me what true, pure hate is."

I put my knee on her back, my weight crushing her knees deeper into the glass of her beautiful altar. Her cries of torment filled me with sweet satisfaction. I picked up the bible, fanned the pages before bringing it up, and heaved it across her face. If the tethers hadn't kept her body secured to the pipe, she might have fallen off of her altar.

The blood trickled from her knees, dripping to the floor in lovely justice. Her face broken from just one blow of the book. I had withstood dozens of those hits. She wouldn't get out of it so easily.

"You killed my brother." I brought the book back across her face. "You took my sister's life from her." The book cracked down on her nose again. "And I let you steal too many years of my life." I took the heavy book into both hands and brought it across her head like a bat.

I brought the book back up and hesitated. The skin on the back of my neck prickled, the hairs stood.

I looked back at Sister, who was still crumpled on the floor, her head bent unnaturally, her wide, dead eyes staring at my back. I reached over and closed her eyes. But that wasn't who was watching.

She is here.

The precious princess who haunts me, watching my every move. I felt her there with my brother and I felt her even stronger again with my mother.

Let the bitch watch. Let her watch what will soon be coming to her.

I closed my eyes, willing the control to stop slipping and quiet the beast.

Grandmother hung limp, her hands tied to the pipe, kneeling bloody on her altar. She was still breathing, her gasps short, ragged.

"No matter how much you screamed at me, beat me, did all that you did, you haven't defeated me. And I'll never be broken again." I grabbed her face and forced her to look at me one last time. I removed the dagger from my boot and pressed it against her throat.

"I have one last question for you. Where the fuck is your God now?"

I sliced deep, one side to the other, and watched Grandmother fall away into darkness.

CHAPTER SIXTY-SEVEN

Sera

SAN FRANCISCO

Before Sera entered the hospital for a day of clinicals, she called Detective Pardou, leaving a message on the cell phone number he'd given her to call if any night terrors—or developments, as he called them—occurred. By her lunch break, he'd left a message to meet him at the police station when she was finished for the day.

When she arrived at the station, he'd escorted her to a private room in the back.

"Two women were killed this time. Maybe they were grandmother and grand-daughter? The older woman tried protecting the younger one. But the younger woman seemed to get a quick, almost merciful death, while the older woman was tortured viciously. The killer felt me, knew I was there. The killer stopped mid-hit and looked around just after I'd screamed in my mind. It seems like they are enjoying the idea of having a witness. I don't know. Nothing seems to make sense. Each of these people are so different from the other." Yet, Sera knew somewhere in her mind was the answer waiting for her to remember.

"You've had how many night terrors in the past week?" Detective Pardou asked, tablet in hand, typing down the details she gave him.

"Just the one. Something is changing. Everything was more aggressive, manic, like there is some new urgency to...do this."

"Kill, you mean," Detective Pardou said, then paused. "I didn't want to jump to any assumptions until after we met tonight. But we found two women earlier today who fit the descriptions of the two vics you gave, less than an hour from here."

"Nothing makes that better, knowing I was right." Sera didn't want to be right. She wanted to be very, very wrong. The weight of knowing more souls were lost pulled at her, especially since she'd been no help in stopping it.

The temptation of retreat started to prickle her mind. But she shut it down, pushed it out. She needed to do this for Ava, if nothing else. Sera closed her eyes and pinched the skin between her brows.

"You said that you have a few seconds, sometimes minutes, after your nightmare and before the vision. Have you tried taking anything into the dream?" Detective Pardou looked at her, doubt already imprinted on his face.

"Like on Nightmare on Elm Street?" Sera asked with a snort.

"Elm Street?" The detective looked confused.

"Yeah, you know, Freddy Krueger?"

"The Halloween costume guy?"

"Have you ever watched *any* classic horror movies?"

"Not really," the detective said, shrugging.

Sera shook her head in disbelief. "I'm so glad I had Erinne to teach me the way. Anyway, no, I haven't tried bringing anything with me. But like I said, I don't see myself. I don't think that would be possible."

"I know I'm grasping at straws here, but you never know until you try."

"I have tried. To do something, anything, to stop what is happening, to break through somehow. I have no control. I can't see myself or my body. I'm just *there*. It takes so much out of me to watch what's happening that, a lot of times, I vomit after. When I wake, I'm weak, sweaty, and exhausted." She took a long drink of the water bottle he gave her when they first sat down. "It always starts the same, a nightmare about my mom and Jeffrey Mason. Then, when I'm fully awake, the vision hits me. My nightmares of Jeffrey Mason are like a portal to the killer's mind," Sera muttered, staring at the detective, lost in thought, trying to capture that familiarity that eluded just out of reach.

"I need to reread the case files. I've read them before. The answer is there, something I should remember. I *know* it."

"That's way against protocol. There is a process to get records."

"I know the process. It took us weeks to get the records before. My Aunt has them now, in Ireland. I guess she could email them to me, but it's like three AM there. This would be faster."

He looked at her, contemplating. "They couldn't leave this building."

"I understand."

"You would have to read them here."

"Of course. You can babysit me while I read through them."

The detective sighed. "Give me a few minutes."

True to his word, minutes later, Detective Pardou came back into the room with a few manilla files and laid them out in front of Sera. "Part of the process of record copying is to redact names and pictures. Of course, doing this doesn't allow me to do that, so I have removed identifying pictures. And I want to warn you this time, yours is one of those files." He pointed to the last manilla folder.

"Thank you." Sera took a deep breath and once again stepped back into the mind of the monster who caused the worst moments of her life.

Twenty minutes later, after re-reading witness statements and Jeffrey Mason's background, she opened a file with a report she'd never seen before.

"What's this? Are these his..." Sera couldn't bring herself to say it aloud.

"Children. Yes. This is the county case file on Jeffrey Mason's children."

Sera read through the details of what had happened to the Mason children after their father had been killed by her mother. Sera had researched them before but hadn't been able to find much. All she knew was they had lived with a grandmother out of state. However, this report was full of terrible details that broke her heart.

There were three children. The county had visited the home several times on reports of alleged neglect and abuse. None that were ever fully pursued. The oldest son, Jacob, had ended up drug-addicted and homeless. He overdosed at the age of nineteen. The middle daughter, Jordan, had attempted suicide and was institutionalized after their mother, Ingrid Mason, died of cancer. The youngest daughter, Judith, remained with the abusive grandmother.

"Oh my god," Sera whispered.

"What is it?"

She held a hand up and kept reading, her eyes darting quickly through the text. "I need to see the files for the victims I described in my night terrors."

"Those are open investigations. I can't just let..."

"It's important." Her breathing rate increased, her heart began to race. For once, it wasn't because of fear or panic. She was on the brink of what it was this whole time that had been right there.

"Damn it." Detective Pardou stalked out, quickly returning with more manilla files. "I can get into serious trouble for doing this," he said, handing her the pile.

"Not if you can catch this killer, you won't." She opened file after file, looking back and forth between the current victims she had seen viciously attacked, Jeffrey Mason's background report, and the county file. Her hands began to tremble as everything began to fall into place.

"Is there a picture of this woman who filed the sexual harassment charges against Jeffrey Mason in Arkansas, the one that caused them to move to San Francisco?"

The detective nodded and started scrolling through the tablet he had with him. He set it in front of her. The face of a woman she'd never seen before stared up at her. Her heart stopped.

Sera jumped up, moving the tablet into position. She kept shuffling through reports, placing them strategically. A few minutes later, with her breath trapped in her chest, she stepped back from the table.

"Can I also see the pictures of these people?" she asked, pointing to the arrangement of papers.

"I can't, Sera. What I've shown you already is grounds for severe discipline. I have to keep their identities protected, at the very least."

"I promise you, they are the key to everything," she pleaded. All she needed was their pictures to prove it to the detective and to herself.

With another defeated sigh and shake of his head, Detective Pardou laid down pictures of the victims, along with three members of the Mason family, Ingrid, Jacob, and Judith Mason.

She pointed to the picture on the tablet, a woman with light blonde hair and light blue eyes. Next to it, she placed another picture, "Marlene Jacobs."

Words that weren't hers echoed through Sera's mind,

We had to move here after you tried to wreck our family. We were never happy again.

"The homeless man," Sera whispered as she placed the picture of Jacob Mason, the brother who had become a homeless drug addict, next to the victim report of the man whose throat was cut in an alley.

Look what they have done to you. Look what they have made you do.

"The woman with the cross." Sera placed Ingrid Mason's picture, a woman who looked hollow and soulless, next to the picture of the victim, Julie Gorgio.

Why couldn't you just love us?

"The two women who were killed last night." Sera placed the picture of Judith Mason next to the younger victim of the two women.

I will give you mercy, free you from this traitorous world that has turned its back on us.

And finally, Sera placed the grandmother's picture alongside the older victim of the two women. Sera looked at the cruel, cold expression of the grandmother's face.

No matter how much you screamed at me, beat me, you haven't defeated me.

All were different people, but their features were remarkably similar.

"It's Jordan Mason. The killer is Jeffrey Mason's middle daughter." She closed her eyes.

Sera remembered her clearly, their connection so strong since they were children. Jordan Mason was Bee, the one who had caught fireflies and hid in a tree. It was no imaginary friend, it had always been Jordan.

"In Jordan's mind, they were the same people. Her mother, her grandmother. She wanted them punished for what they had done to her. But she gave mercy to her siblings," Sera said, her eyes still closed. "There was one more victim. Another woman. She looked like she was in her early to mid-twenties. I saw her murder about three years ago, right before I started the nursing program at SFSU. She is buried in a shallow grave in the woods somewhere. I'm not sure how to connect her to the others, but I know she fits in somehow."

Sera opened her eyes. "Jordan's mind is fragmented. Some of these people died years ago. She is killing people who remind her of them, or maybe she thinks they *are* them, enacting her own punishments for all those who did her wrong. *Eye for an eye*." Sera's heart beat faster with a new realization.

"She'll be coming for me. It's *my* fault," Sera's words hurried out.

"How could it be?"

Sera felt moisture dampen her shirt. She tried to steady the shaking of her hands as she wiped her palms on her pants.

"He abandoned his family when he took me and my mother. In her mind, her father left *her* for *me*. This girl, who has been neglected and beaten her whole life, a girl who was never loved, thinks that my mother took her father away from her, that *I* took her life away from her." Tears spilled over in hot streaks down her cheeks.

"But that's not true."

"To her, it very much is. That's why we are connected. Not just because of her father but because of me. I am the one who will give her ultimate salvation." Sera gathered all of the pictures and reports together, shoving them back into their file folders. "What happened to her? Where did she go after the hospital?"

"There isn't much. A few odd jobs here and there, and then just drops off the grid. But if you're right, we know who is doing this." Detective Pardou placed an assuring hand on her shoulder. "We will find her."

CHAPTER SIXTY-EIGHT

Jeffrey Mason

SAN FRANCISCO

The children were somewhat entertaining at times, brief episodes of momentary delight. However, those moments were becoming fewer and farther between.

His daughter was especially appealing. Jordan was only five years old and already a beauty. Jeffrey found himself looking at her for longer periods of time, wondering what kind of woman she would grow into.

Lately, more often than not, he wondered what it would be like to feel her. Thinking about his little daughter, picturing those things was troubling, even to him.

Usually, he found other ways to get off. There was a particular porn shop he frequented that, for a handsome fee—for content as well as discretion—carried a secret room in the back that carried legal/illegal fetish pornography. But it did little to curb his lusts as they persisted in growing more ravenous.

Until he discovered specific places to go that, for the right price, would fulfill darker appetites and even more audacious fetishes. Jeffrey spent a lot of time there and more money than he should have. Even there, there was a limit to how far money went. He found that out when he was escorted out by a team of bouncers who easily outweighed him by fifty pounds, with a broken rib, a broken nose, and blacklisted from the establishment.

Then he'd made the mistake of fucking that woman from work. Bad move, as it had almost cost him his job.

That affair ended up being worse than sex with his wife. He learned too late that Marlene Jacobs only wanted vanilla, boring-as-hell sex. When Jeffrey tried to do somewhat unorthodox lascivious acts with Marlene, she all but called rape.

His team of good ol' boys got him out of that bind in a rare moment of luck. They assured him it had happened to all of them at one point or another. However, because a lawsuit had been filed against the company, they had to show that they 'took care' of the problem somehow.

They promoted him and sent him to run the start-up in San Francisco.

That was three years ago. It had only been a matter of time before the battle within started losing out to the hunger, making it harder to ignore than ever before.

It was Ingrid's fault, really. She left him blue-balled pretty much constantly, especially now that she was pregnant with their third child, a miracle in itself.

He hadn't touched her in years. But that night, he'd been on a drinking binge. Surprisingly, he not only got it up but apparently shot a goalie. He barely remembered it at all. He'd been frustrated with her, with the kids, with his life.

But then, he pictured himself smashing Ingrid's face with his fists, fantasizing about yanking her hair back, forcing himself into her mouth and wherever else he felt like, thrusting as hard as he wanted. Let her gag, let her writhe. Let her cry out and scream. And that is what got him rock hard.

He did exactly what he pictured, finally releasing some of what had been building inside. A few weeks later, she announces that she's pregnant. Again.

And baby makes three. Three godforsaken traps that drown him in this life he was stuck in. Jeffrey needed to find something to occupy his time, his mind, anything that might satiate the yearning—especially watching Ingrid's belly swell with yet another kid.

He started camping alone, as the kids would be the wrong type of distraction. Muir Woods became a place where he could lose himself. On one of his weekend hiking expeditions, Jeffrey found the cabin.

It was far from any other cabin and far enough off popular trails to be secluded and private, yet a mere forty-minute drive from the city.

The cabin would be the perfect place where he'd be able to let go and do whatever he needed to do to satisfy his urges in this pit of life he'd created for himself. A place that would allow him to store and expand his unique collection of photographs, movies, and magazines without fear of discovery. Sure, it needed a fair amount of repairs, but Jeffrey was handy enough.

He searched public records and found the current owners of the cabin, after which he contacted said owners and successfully negotiated the sale of one small cabin deep in Muir Woods.

More and more of his free time was spent carefully restoring his beloved cabin. He painstakingly considered each detail, from replacing old windows and removing old paneling from the walls, to laying new flooring.

Because there was no electricity at the cabin, he had to use his larger tools at home and then haul the materials from his house to the cabin. A small price to pay for a place that quickly became his sanctuary where he could be unabashedly himself.

It was because of the special attention to these details that led him to his destiny, to *her*.

Jeffrey was working on restoring the door frames that weekend when a piece of wood he was cutting kicked back on the table saw, sending the meat of his palm into the blade.

"Fuck!" Jeffrey screamed out, pulling his bloodied hand from the blade, holding fast to the flesh that hung free, bone visible through the gapping gash.

He grabbed a shop towel, wrapped his hand tightly, and drove to the closest hospital.

The dizziness pulled at his consciousness as he swerved into the parking lot. The loss of blood and the adrenaline wearing off had Jeffrey stumbling through the slider doors of the emergency department.

Security jumped up when they saw the blood dripping down his arm, his shirt soaked with it where he clutched his hand, immediately escorting him through the locked doors.

Nurses surrounded him, leading him to the closest available gurney, and began working immediately. He started to blink in and out of consciousness. He was undressed, leads were placed on his chest, a probe was placed on his finger, an IV line was started, and pain medications were given.

The angel appeared at his bedside only minutes later, the most exquisite vision in white he had ever seen. For a moment, he thought maybe he had died, and she was there to take him to the afterlife. But there was too much pain to be dead.

"Good afternoon, Mr. Mason. I am Dr. Wilson, and this is our student doctor, Ella Delaney. Are you up to answering some questions while Ms. Delaney and I assess your injuries?"

Jeffrey hadn't noticed the tall, older man standing with her. He had only seen *her*, the woman from his fantasies. He couldn't tear his eyes away from the green eyes that smiled back at him, her smile sweet and genuine, her long red braid cascading over her shoulder.

He wanted to touch that hair, pull it free from its binding and let it fall freely around that perfect face, run his fingers through it, and...

"Mr. Mason?" she spoke, her voice as sweet as the rest of her. "Are you okay? Can you hear us?"

"I'm sorry, I'm a little light-headed. They gave me something..."

"Yes, you were given a pretty strong pain medication. Just focus on my voice and answer what you can, alright?" She moved closer to him, watching the male doctor as he carefully unwound the now blood-soaked gauze from his mangled hand.

It was hard to keep his attention answering the questions, he was too focused on how her lips moved as she asked them. He told them what happened as best he could. She would smile after an answer here and there. How badly he wanted to keep that smile on her face.

"Delaney, come closer. Do you see how the blade's serrated teeth grated this muscle? It will make stitches a bit trickier. I'll show you how to do a maneuver that helps in these types of situations. I'll go put the orders in. While we wait for the supplies, if you'd irrigate and debride the wound." The male doctor stood to leave.

Jeffrey was alone with her.

"Don't worry, Mr. Mason, Dr. Wilson is one of our best here," Ella said, preparing the side table with supplies to clean his wound, then sat on the stool next to his gurney.

When she took his hand, two very different things happened simultaneously.

A flash of heat surged through Jeffrey Mason. An erotic heat that aroused him instantly. Careful to keep that hidden, he shifted his hip so that the sheet covered him inconspicuously.

This is what falling in love at first sight was like. He thought it was some bullshit fairytale morons told themselves to put hope in their pitiful mundane lives. But it was fucking real. He felt it, the jolt between them when she took his hand. Instant love. Lust. Both. It didn't matter.

As he walked to his car several hours and stitches later, he knew in his very being that this was the woman he was supposed to have as his partner in life. He knew it the moment he saw her, and she knew it, too.

When they joined hands, there was a connection. He saw it on her face, a recognition.

He had spent many years being patient. He tolerated the wife he was forced to take, tolerated the two-going-on-three children he'd made with that woman, tolerated the fuck-heads at work in order to be successful and not the pathetic trailer trash he'd come from. And now he was being presented with his gift for all of it.

He drove himself home to sleep off the grogginess of the drugs and dream of the new journey he was about to embark on. He was grateful for the maiming, for it led him to her.

Ella Delaney.

He was also glad it was his left hand, as he was right-handed. The doctor told him he might have damaged some of the nerves in that hand, and full feeling might never return completely. But he still had full capabilities of his right hand, which he had planned a lengthy use of when he got home and fantasized about *her*. The long red hair draped over her pale breasts, tickling his chest as she rode him. He could picture it so clearly.

Even when he pulled into his driveway, his son's bike strewn haphazardly in the driveway though he scolded him constantly to put the damn thing away or he'd trash it, and his boring wife blasting some awful back-woods gospel about some coming rapture, it didn't break his mood.

When he found Ingrid coming out of the bedroom, a pile of folded laundry in her arms resting above her pregnant belly, he had worked himself up so completely about the future doctor Ella Delaney that he shoved Ingrid back into the room, laundry scattering to the floor, slamming the door behind him with his foot.

"Jeffrey. Stop it. What are you doing? Don't. The baby. It is unclean. Stop it!" For once, Ingrid tried to fight him off, intensifying his arousal.

He reached out and grabbed the back of her head with his right hand, pulling her to him and crushing his face into hers. She pushed him away again, but this time, he slapped her across the face, hard, not once, but twice, sending her down to her knees.

Then he was on her, pushing her down on the floor, straddling her as he pinned both of her arms above her head to the floor. She tried to squirm free, but he held fast with his knees flanking her ribs.

"Stop it—the baby. Stop, Jeffrey!"

He let go of her hands and hit her closed-fisted until she lay there, whimpering. Jeffrey stood over her, looking down at her for a moment. He took a pillow from the bed.

When he put the pillow over Ingrid's face, she became Ella for him.

His body shuddered with lust, he wanted to devour her instantly, but also wanted to take his time. He took, pulled, bit into, tasted until he couldn't wait any longer. The sound of her screaming in such pleasurable pain made him climax quickly.

He took the pillow from her face. It was only Ingrid again.

Any trace of pleasure shriveled up along with the rest of him. When he got up, he noticed the blood. With any luck, she'd lose the kid after all.

With his mind still lingering on sweet, sweet Ella, he locked the door to the bathroom behind him to shower.

CHAPTER SIXTY-NINE

Jordan Mason

I stopped fighting, stopped trying to overanalyze. After I did that, everything became so easy, quick even. My mediocre, unimportant job only held me back from completing my purpose, so I quit to pursue what needed to be done.

It wasn't long before I was rewarded for my efforts. The pretty redhead, the second whore in my father's life, the one who made my father leave us once and for all because we weren't good enough for him to stay. *I* wasn't good enough for him.

The woman who took his life.

I watched her for a long time. I thought I would be enraged when I found her. But anger wasn't the first thing I felt this time. It was sadness.

Father had been the only good thing in our lives. Sure, he wasn't home often because he worked too much. He'd said he went camping or to his cabin because he needed to get away. From my mother, from us, from me. But when he was home, he was nice to me. He didn't hit us. He didn't look at us as though he hated us. He told me that he loved me. But then he found *her* and left Mother, us, me.

She was beautiful, indeed. Was that all that had mattered to him, something so temporary as beauty? Was it worth sacrificing his entire family for? Had she known he was married? Had she known about his family? Did she steal him away from us on purpose?

I couldn't stop watching her. I'd followed her to her job, to her home, out on errands. She should be the next one in this quest.

Instead, I only wanted to curl up in self-pity and cry myself to sleep when I thought about her. I should probably hate her more than any of the others. But I couldn't. All I could think of was how I had disappointed my father and hadn't been enough for him. And for the first time since I was a kid, I was angry at *him* for all of it.

That evening, when she left to go out with a bunch of her girlfriends, I followed them into the club they went to. I watched her from the bar while she danced and flirted with the men who approached her. She enjoyed the attention and left her friends time after time for this guy or that one.

She *had* known, and she hadn't cared. She was the homewrecking whore I always thought she'd been.

I gave her a lot of time, more than the others. She had many friends and was rarely alone. Of course, she was a social atrocity. That is how she attracted whoever she wanted. Be sweet to lure them in, use them for what she wanted, and then dump them—or kill them as she'd done to my father. She was a human praying mantis.

Finding the right time when people didn't flank her was tricky. The opportunity finally came after she had left a social gathering by herself late one night, stopping at a gas station. There were too many cameras to risk being seen approaching her there. I waited just far enough from the gas station to be out of camera range but close enough to watch her. I parked half off the road and activated my emergency flashers.

She pulled out of the station, turning my way. She slowed as she neared my out-of-commission car. I was standing just outside it, trying my best to look bewildered, distraught. She stopped, rolling down the window.

"You okay there? Need some help?" she asked with that overly nice smile of hers.

"Actually, yes, thank you so much. My cell is dead, forgot to charge it. Do you have one I can use really quick to call AAA?" I did my best to hide that burning rage that made my hands shake.

"Sure, no problem."

I approached the car. As she handed me her phone, I tased her neck, rendering her momentarily motionless. I got into her car, pushed her onto the passenger seat, moved her car off the road, and put the hazards on. She was a small woman, not hard to pull into my own car.

I drove for a long time, tasing her another time or two when she'd start coming to. I drove way out so no one would interrupt the game I had planned for her. The longer we drove, the brighter the fury became.

I took her to a special place. She should know it well.

CHAPTER SEVENTY

Sera

SAN FRANCISCO

Sera had startled awake cold and sweaty from another night terror about her mom. She was about to turn on the lamp when the vision hit her.

She hadn't slid into it as she usually did. Sounds weren't muted, the room didn't darken. She was thrust in mid-terror, every sound amplified, all colors vivid, clear, crashing in on her.

Headlights shined bright. A figure—a woman from what Sera could tell—ran away from the headlights. Sera could hear the footsteps as they pounded through the fallen leaves and broken sticks.

Trees. Nothing but trees everywhere. It was dark, so dark that there was nothing beyond.

Sera could feel potent emotions that weren't hers more than ever before. Excitement, madness, anger, vengeance radiated.

The woman was being hunted, a wicked game of Hide-N-Seek, through woods that were so familiar.

The woman whimpered, not far.

Footsteps running.

"I can hear you," a voice sang out.

"Leave me alone," the woman cried, running again.

A tongue clicked. "That's not the way to play. Now I know where you are."

The woman was cowering behind a redwood, her long red hair falling over her already brightly bruised neck and arms.

"Well, hello there."

"Someone help me! Please!" the woman screamed, starting to run, but the gloved hand reached out and grabbed her by the hair before she got away.

"You lose. It is time to pay your penalty."

The woman kept screaming, wails of terror. The gloved hand hit the woman again, much harder than before.

"Shut up. You're giving me a headache." The hands dragged the woman back toward the headlights, shoving her against the car, grabbing hold of her neck, squeezing the life from her.

"Because of you, he left. For you and your little bastard spawn. You're no better than us. She's no better than I am." The hands squeezed tighter, blood vessels bursting in the woman's eyes, tiny rivers of blood streaking through the white.

STOP!

Sera screamed out in her mind.

The figure paused, looking around.

She'd been heard. Sera tried as hard as she could to hold the connection.

The door was opened.

Jordan. Stop.

Get out of my head.

The voice echoed, not spoken aloud, but boomed in Sera's mind, a voice Sera knew so well.

Why? How could you do this?

You already know why.

Doing what you're doing makes you just as bad, maybe worse. Leave her alone.

Sorry, can't do that. She has to be punished.

Please, don't do this anymore. You don't understand what you're doing.

Don't try to mind fuck me.

I'm trying to help you.

You can't help anyone. Go back to your hiding place and leave me alone. Though, I do have to admit that when I found out you were my witness, I knew that this was meant to be, that this was my purpose.

What purpose do you think you have in killing these innocent people?

Innocent? These people are nothing close to innocent.

That is not her, Jordan. That is not Ella. None of them are who you think they are.

GET OUT OF MY HEAD! You don't understand. You have been given everything and left nothing for me. Nothing! You would never understand why I have to do this.

Jordan squeezed harder still. The woman lost consciousness.

With everything she had, Sera screamed as loud as she could in her head, blasting a roar like a derailing train slamming through both of their minds.

"Bitch," Jordan hissed and snapped the woman's neck.

The connection slammed shut, tearing their minds from each other.

There was no air when she woke. Drenched, shivering, and struggling for breath, Sera kicked off blankets, hitting the night table and sending the lamp crashing to the floor, clutching her throat, her lips turning blue.

Sera frantically gasped. She was losing consciousness, her throat tightening with each second. With the last bit of strength she had, she grabbed her cell phone and connected a call to 911 before the room faded behind the dark-spotted curtain.

Like a hammer, wind slammed into her chest. Her eyes flew open, and she was gasping in fire. The air burned her throat, turning the black spots red in her vision as coughing spasms wracked her body.

Detective Drake Pardou was kneeling over her. "I thought you were gone. Keep breathing. That's it." He stayed with her until the paramedics burst through the door.

"You had me under surveillance?" Sera coughed out, her voice hoarse, throat raw. She was sitting in the back of the ambulance, trying to assure them that she didn't need to go to a hospital. Of course, she wouldn't explain to them exactly why.

"It's a good thing, or I might not have heard you and gotten to you in time. I had to give you rescue breaths, Sera."

"So, you never really believed me?"

"I'm a detective. I have to gather actual evidence. I had to make sure. But I heard it myself tonight. I heard..." his voice was full of skeptical wonder before he stopped mid-sentence when the paramedic returned to Sera.

Sera quickly signed paperwork refusing additional treatment or observation. When they were finally back inside her hotel room, she tried to explain what happened.

"It was completely different from the second I was thrown into the vision. I could hear sound. And we spoke to each other." Sera sipped water, gingerly coating the burn in her throat.

"Detective, before I tell you the rest, I have to see Jordan's picture. I have to be sure."

"I've already broken every rule. Why not one more?" The detective pulled out his tablet, signed into the station's system, and pulled up the case file. He then handed the tablet to her.

Sera stared at the picture of a young woman with long black hair and bright blue eyes. The face of her dormmate, her *friend*, looked back at her. The betrayal ran deep, twisting fire in her gut, the shock of it took Sera's breath away as hot tears ran down her cheeks.

"I thought...I thought I could trust her. I thought she was my friend."

"You know her? Jordan Mason?" Detective Pardou grabbed the tablet and looked from the picture to Sera.

"I guess I lied to you. I *do* know her. And so do you. It's Peyton Davis, my roommate. Maybe you don't recognize her without the mask on her face and her hair in a towel. Jordan Mason is Peyton. I've known her the whole time. Excuse me." Sera rushed to the bathroom, where the contents of her stomach disbursed between retches and sobs until she was empty. She placed her forehead on the coolness of the ceramic seat.

How could she not have known? How could she have lived with this person and not *felt* something? She'd trusted her, with her story, with her feelings, with her life.

She slept next to the enemy for three years and never once felt anything. Instead, she'd called her a friend. Maybe there were little things here and there, some strange behavior, but nothing that screamed murderous sociopath like it should have.

When Sera felt steady, she rinsed her mouth, wiped the tears from her eyes, and splashed cool water on her face. She glanced at her reflection, the blotchiness from crying spread down her neck to her chest.

The grief of losing another friend, one she had come to care deeply about, had her crying again into the towel she had been drying her face with. After a few minutes, the grief began to evolve into anger. Then rage.

She'd been deceived, played.

That time was now over. She was done being the fool, the coward. Sera took a few deep breaths before returning to a patiently waiting Detective Pardou.

"I think Jordan thought the woman she killed tonight was my mother." Sera gave a detailed description of the woman she saw murdered and as much of the surroundings as she could.

"I'll put out an APB for Peyton—or—Jordan. Which also means we have a couple more bodies to find and two more families to inform of lost loved ones."

"The girl in the grave...I'm so sorry. I should have known. I should have realized. Then all of these people wouldn't have...I could have saved them."

"Don't do that. It's a dangerous place to put yourself. Let's focus on now. We know who she is. We will find her. Until then, we have to get you into a safe house."

It had been weeks, yet there was still no sign of Jordan, and fortunately, no more killings. But the silence made Sera edgy. Detective Pardou had assigned a security team to stay with her at all times. They had followed her to classes and clinicals and stood by while she studied for hours at the safe house.

Now that classes were over, clinicals were complete, and finals were finished, there was a copious amount of time for worrying. About where Jordan was, who would be her next target, and about Sera's family coming out for graduation.

"It's been too quiet. Do you think she's done?" Sera asked Detective Pardou as she slumped down on the chair in the dining room of the safe house.

"They don't usually just stop. I don't think Jordan is going to either. She hasn't gone back to the dorm, her job at the grocery store, or any of her classes—well, Peyton's classes—but we *will* find her," he assured her.

"What if she disappears and becomes someone else like she did with Peyton? I mean, it wasn't hard for her to find someone who was in my program with a full scholarship and just slide into her place. No wonder she never wanted to get an apartment off campus. That should have been a red flag. Obviously, she didn't want her credit run or have to provide real identification—too many things that could get her caught. How did I not *know*?"

"We'll find her."

Sera sighed. "Have you told the real Peyton's family yet?"

"We have."

Sera went quiet again. Her thoughts kept circling back to the same thing. "How did I not know? Three years..."

"Well, with all of your abilities, apparently, being psychic isn't one of them." His onyx eyes glinted, his smirk dazzled.

"That's not even close to funny," Sera said, almost smiling.

"Too soon?"

Sera stared at him.

"So, I'm no comic. Don't kill me for trying."

She chuckled, shaking her head. She hadn't laughed in who knew how long. Most likely at something Adam had said.

Adam.

Thinking of him hurt as suddenly as a shot to the heart.

She'd lost him too.

Sera caught herself checking her phone again, hoping to see Adam's name on the screen. But Adam was talking to someone else now, and he'd barely spoken to her in months, she reminded herself.

No, he hadn't spoken to her at all since their argument, not even on her birthday. Though she deserved the silence after what she'd said and how she treated him.

Sera had lost her best friend. Her remaining friend turned out to be the daughter of Jeffrey Mason, who was on some kind of killing vendetta, who had also been posing as her roommate for the last three years. And graduation was in three days.

She might have been tempted to fall back into that black pit of self-pity if she hadn't already spiraled to rock bottom and fought her way back up by her fingernails. But she had crawled out of that darkness, and it was because of her love for Ava. Even if Adam hated her, was with someone else, or whatever may become of their relationship, Sera would never abandon Ava, much like her own mother had never abandoned her—not even in death.

"What about the graduation ceremony? Should I cancel my family coming out?"

"Jordan has only struck isolated people. If you stay in public or with a large group, along with your handy security team here, everyone should be safe."

"*Should* be?"

"I'm no psychic."

"You've really got to stop."

"Okay. I'm done. Seriously though, everything should be fine." Detective Pardou patted her hand and stood to leave.

Sera went to the door with him, nodded at the security team standing outside, and then closed the door, engaging both locks.

Alone again, all she could think of was Adam. His face, his slightly lopsided smile, the dimple in his cheek, the kindness of his eyes. Her heart had known all along what took too long to accept. It was Adam. It always had been. She wouldn't deny that any longer, even if it meant that she'd end up alone.

So, Adam was talking to some woman from his office. She'd find out more about that, too.

But right now, she needed to focus on tomorrow, picking up her honorary mother, father, and the rest of her crazy, loud, wonderful clan from the airport, who she'd missed dearly, keeping them safe, and getting through graduation.

Sera

SAN FRANCISCO

I wish your parents could be here today." Erinne's eyes got watery as she secured Sera's graduation cap and helped her zip up the graduation gown over the shimmering red material of Ella's dress that Sera was wearing.

Sera smiled at Erinne, her own eyes tearing up.

"My whole life, I have never lacked in love or family. I am so lucky to have you. You stepped in when I had no one, dropped everything to become a mother to me, helped me through trauma, pulled me out of my shell, and shaped me as a person. No matter what has been taken, I've also been blessed more than I could have ever hoped for. I will forever be grateful for you. Thank you for being the best mother a gal could have."

"Oh, sweetie." Erinne embraced Sera. "She's here, I think, watching over you. Both of them are. Your own guardian angels. Even if you can't see them, they're proud of everything you've accomplished, as I am." Tears trickled down Erinne's cheeks. "Sorry. I can never help my melodramatic emotions."

The dean started ushering the students together to begin the walk into the auditorium.

Erinne laughed and wiped her cheeks. "Okay, let's stop this. You are finally done." She gave Sera another quick hug before rushing back to her seat with the rest of the family. They were all there. John, Nan, Pops, Brian, Shelly, and the boys, Erick and Rich, were all ready to celebrate her.

Sera sat quietly with the rest of the graduating class, listening to all of the faculty and student speeches. When it was time to stand in line and wait for her name to be called, Sera felt a sense of pride wash over her, a pride that wasn't only her own. She knew her mom and dad were indeed there with her that day.

Then her name was called. She stepped onto the stage, shook the dean's hand, took her credentials, and turned to traditionally switch her tassel to the other side of her cap when she saw him sitting in the front row, Ava enthusiastically waving both arms beside him.

Astonishment, joy, peace, and overwhelming love saturated her as she stood frozen, her eyes locked with Adam's.

Another student came up behind her, tapped her shoulder, gesturing her off the stage.

He came. He's here. Breathe Sera.

She told herself, over and over. She had to catch her breath and slow her heart, or she would explode in anticipation.

Sera gave up trying to focus on the rest of the ceremony. When it was finally wrapping up, jitters started to eat away at her composure.

No big deal, just go to him. It's Adam.

She started to head his way, but then her family was upon her before she could make it out of the aisle. Congratulatory hugs, pats, and kisses were exchanged, during which she would steal glances over toward Adam.

Erinne followed Sera's gaze, a knowing smirk spreading across her face. She kept the conversation lively with the family, nudging Sera to sneak away.

Finally, the path cleared. He was standing there in front of her, neither of them moving any closer. They looked at each other, searching.

"Still friends?" Adam asked when the silence couldn't be withstood any longer. Sera said nothing.

She took the last few steps, closing the gap between them, falling into him, her arms pulling him into an embrace. As she held him close, she took in everything about him—his scent, the feeling of him. He was Adam. Time away from him had been like living without breathing.

"I missed you," he whispered in her ear.

"I missed you more," she answered, immersed in him, not wanting to let go. Again, her eyes welled up, and a tear escaped down her face.

"This is new." Adam stroked the tear away, running his finger down the side of her cheek.

"Yeah, a whole new me." She smiled into the eyes that were everything to her heart.

"We came to surprise you!" Ava jumped up and down, unable to hold out any longer.

"Well, you did, that's for sure." Sera pulled herself away from Adam to pick Ava up.

"I've missed you so much," Sera said softly, breathing Ava in, holding her close, nuzzling her face in Ava's hair, Ava's little arms wrapped tightly around Sera's neck. More tears fell.

Sera's heart was Ava's. Sera never knew how encompassing true, unconditional love one could have for another was until she fell in love with this little girl. There was nothing she wouldn't do for the child she held in her arms.

"Boy, you're getting big. You have to stop growing so I can always pick you up and cover you with raspberries." Sera covered Ava's face and neck with quick kisses.

"Raspberries? Like the fruit?" Ava knit her little eyebrows together.

"Nope. Raspberries like this." Sera blew into her neck, sending the girl into hysterical bouts of giggles.

"Why don't you introduce us," Erinne said as she approached Sera. "Mr. Adam Wallace, I presume?"

Sera put Ava down to drape an arm around Erinne. "Adam, this is my honorary mother, Erinne, the saint of a woman who raised me. Erinne, *this* is Adam and sweet Ava, of course." Sera beamed.

"It's about time I finally get to meet you face to face."

"Erinne, it is an honor to finally meet you. I've heard many amazing things about you." He took Erinne's hand in his and held it for a moment before letting go.

"I, too, have heard a lot about you. All good things." Erinne looked him over with an appreciative grin. "She did leave out how pretty you are, though."

"Where did everyone go?" Sera asked, quickly changing the subject, her face suddenly on fire.

"It took a bit of convincing, but I was able to talk everyone into meeting at the restaurant. Will you be joining our family for the celebration?" Erinne asked Adam.

Adam looked to Sera, who was already nodding and smiling. "Yes, thank you. I'd love to."

"Fantastic. I'll meet you both at the restaurant then." Erinne pulled Sera aside before heading out. She put both hands on Sera's cheeks, looked into her eyes, and said, "Love lights the shadows from your face." She kissed Sera's cheeks, squeezed her hands, and walked out of the auditorium.

Sera's joyous and celebratory family took up half of the restaurant. The conversations were never boring, never timid, and along with the champagne, never stopped flowing the entire evening.

Though the many conversations among everyone limited the opportunity for personal side chats, Sera and Adam kept stealing glances at each other, casting secret smiles, their arms always touching, their hands finding reasons to graze the others.

Her family adored Adam instantly, and Ava was immediately intertwined into the family. She and the boys took to each other, even with the age differences.

Finally, as Sera's herd gathered in the parking lot to head back to the hotel, Erinne made her way over to Sera before leaving. "We'll see you tomorrow, help you move the rest of your things out of the dorm and into the safe house. Unless the security team is going to do it?"

"Security team? Safe house?" Adam's confused and now alarmed look was a painful reminder that they hadn't spoken in too long.

"Yes, I have a lot to tell you a little later," Sera said, looking down at Ava, who was absorbing every word.

"On that note, just let me know. Congratulations again, sweetie. I'll see you tomorrow. It's nice to have met you, Adam and little Ava." Erinne kissed Sera goodbye and waved as she walked away.

"Want to go somewhere and catch up?" Sera linked her arm through Adams and led him back to where they parked his rental car.

"I'd love it," he said as he opened the door for Ava to get into the backseat.

CHAPTER SEVENTY-TWO

Ella

SAN FRANCISCO

It was rare that Ella had much time away from her books, away from rotations at the hospital, away from school in general. Chris's adventurous spirit hadn't dimmed over the years. He'd patiently wait until he could steal moments with Ella, take her and Sera away on some escapade—if only for a weekend or even a night—whenever he possibly could.

That night was one of those rare occasions. They even had a sitter, which was almost unheard of.

"You deserve a fancy evening. I'm talking the dress, the hair, the makeup. All of it." Chris slid up behind her while she was studying for the umpteenth hour at the dining table.

"Mmm. That sounds nice, but I have to..."

Chris put a finger on Ella's mouth, replaced it with his lips, and kissed her sweetly. When Ella opened her eyes, Chris was holding up two tickets. Her smile widened as she read San Francisco Symphony on the headline for that coming weekend.

"Chris." After all these years, he still found ways to take her breath away.

"Just say yes," he whispered, his lips touching hers again.

"Yes."

Shopping for the dress hadn't only been fun, it was quick. Ella and Sera—six already, how time flew by—went to the fanciest store she could find that was closest to them.

Sera was even more excited than Ella by all the flowing, shimmering fabrics. Sera picked some interesting dresses for Ella to try on, but she happily obliged, trying on each one. The first two made Sera giggle and shake her head. While Ella was trying on a third dress, Sera must have found something that caught her eye. When Ella opened the curtain, Sera wasn't there waiting.

"Sera?" Ella called out.

"Hold on, Mommy," Sera answered from the other side of the store. She ran back, holding what looked like miles of sparkling red fabric. "This is the one, Mama!" She thrust the dress at Ella.

"Okay, this is the last one, and then we have to get serious about finding a nice dress."

As Ella slipped the dress over her head, she knew before she even looked in the mirror. It fit as if it had been made just for her, and Chris would love it. When she opened the curtain, Sera gasped.

"Mama, you are so beautiful." Sera clapped her hands and rushed to hug her.

Her words were so sincere they made Ella's eyes tear. "Good choice, Baby Girl."

"It told me it was just for you."

"The dress told you that?" Ella looked at Sera, the most honest of faces nodded back at her enthusiastically.

Sera was like *her*, she would have her own special *Knowing*.

Her heart tugged. After years of hating it, Ella had found a way to live with the *Knowing*, even when it terrified her. That burden wasn't something she'd wanted to pass on, never wanting her daughter to feel that kind of affliction.

But Sera had something Ella never had, a mother who would explain what it was and what was happening to her. Ella would help her cope with such an ability and maybe even help her learn to cherish it.

Unlike her own parents, Ella would never act weird around Sera. Above all, she would never make Sera feel like something was wrong with her.

Ella kissed the top of Sera's head. "How about some ice cream on the way home?"

Ella followed the now cheering Sera to the front register.

Ella hadn't put on makeup or done her hair in so long that it took twice as long as it should have to get just right. But when she walked into the living room where Chris and Sera waited, the extra effort was worth their reactions alone.

Sera jumped up and down in her footsie pajamas. Chris looked at her—no, into her—making her heart pound a little harder, a little quicker. He had pure love in his eyes, and that love was for her.

It made her eyes mist over, which she fanned away immediately so that her painstakingly applied makeup didn't run.

"El. Wow." Chris lifted his hand to his heart. "Breathtaking."

There had been few times in Ella's life when she'd been shy, but this man and the way he was looking at her had the edges of shyness flushing her cheeks.

"Thank you. You're looking quite dapper yourself." Chris's suit fit him well, accentuating his muscular arms and the width of his chest, Ella's favorite part of his body. That smile of his bright as ever and still cunning, always looking as though he was up to something.

She might have convinced herself that she was protecting him all these years by not officially committing to him, but it was inevitable. She'd been completely his since they first locked eyes at that party. Maybe even before that.

The beauty of the instruments and the sounds of the symphony were nothing short of magical. The music touched Ella's soul. At one point, she even saw Chris wipe an eye, which he adamantly denied later.

After the concert, Chris and Ella walked hand in hand back to the car. They passed a street musician playing on the lawn in front of the City Hall building, his voice crooning a love song as he strummed his guitar.

Flashing that sly smile, Chris led Ella over to the grass. She quickly kicked off her heels, giggling like a girl as she followed him. He took her into his arms and began moving to the music with her, singing along softly in her ear. There weren't many things Ella didn't know about Chris after all their years together, but she'd had no idea that Chris had such a wonderful singing voice.

They swayed slowly, their eyes never leaving each other's. The night was clear, no fog or clouds in sight. The moon was mostly full, shining a glow down upon them, the man she loved more than anything serenading her as he held her in his strong arms. The night couldn't be more perfect—until Chris kissed her and kneeled on one knee.

Usually, when Chris proposed to Ella every few months or so, he would say it in passing, half joking, that smile daring her to accept. But not this time. Chris never looked more serious, his eyes wet with tears, as he reached into his pocket and pulled out a little black box, opening it to the most delicate, beautiful ring she'd ever seen.

"El, you are the strongest woman I have ever met. Your love for life is not only amazing, it's inspirational. I never thought I would be the type to fall in love. But then there was you, and I fell head over heels. I knew my life would never be the same again. You challenge me. You lift me up. Then you added the cherry on top by giving me the most perfect little girl. I don't know what I did to be the man who gets to hold your hand and kiss your lips. I don't deserve you or the beautiful life we've made. But I swear to you that I will work every single day to make you proud and to make sure you are loved completely. Ella, would you honor me and make me the happiest man alive by being my wife?" He kissed her hand, then whispered, "Just say yes."

Makeup forgotten, Ella let her tears flow freely down her cheeks.

"Yes."

There was no denying that she couldn't live without this man by her side. No matter what might come to her, she wouldn't let it hold them apart any longer.

"A thousand times, yes."

Chris slid the pretty ring onto her finger, kissed her hand again, and then stood, pulling her into a kiss that pulsed down to her toes.

Applause erupted around them. Ella laughed through her tears as she looked up. She'd forgotten that anyone else had existed.

"Finally," Chris whispered in her ear.

CHAPTER SEVENTY-THREE

Sera

SAN FRANCISCO

I know I suggested bodyguards, but I gotta say, it's a little eerie having them around all the time," Adam said as he watched an officer patrol outside past the front window of the safe house.

Shrugging, Sera got up and drew the curtains closed. "You get used to it. Kind of. Well, not really. But right now, with Ava here, I'm glad they are right outside. I'm sorry. I should have warned you. I didn't know you'd come." Though Ava was now peacefully slumbering on a makeshift bed of winter blankets in the empty bedroom that Adam had just tucked her into, the team of officers outside didn't feel like enough to protect something so precious.

"Hey, I was the one who surprised you." Adam crossed over to her and brought her into his arms. He kissed her forehead as he'd done a hundred times before and nudged her playfully. "Got any wine glasses around here?"

While Adam poured them two glasses of wine, Sera found a couple of candles and lit them. "It's not a fancy fireplace like yours, but still nice."

"We'll work on getting you bigger fire after your crazy murderess is locked away."

"Ha. Ha. I forgot how not-funny you were. I forgot entirely too many things in such a short time. I don't want that to happen again. Let's never, ever fight again. Ever." Her heart was still tender from his absence.

"Never is too soon," Adam said, handing Sera a wine glass as he sat in a chair across from her, touching his knees to hers.

"Agreed."

"So now that you've solved their case for them, what? They just protect you until they find her?"

"Yes? I hope so, anyway."

"How are you, knowing about Peyton, Jordan, everything?"

"Not great, but I'm dealing with it. A little healthier this time. I'm not going to spiral like that again if that's what you're asking."

Adam smiled. "Good to know. I do have to say, though. I told you so."

"Not funny."

"No. It's not at all. I'm sorry I wasn't here." Adam took Sera's hand in his, sadness in his eyes.

"Don't do that. It's not like I kept you in the loop while I was being a miserable, self-loathing coward. It was Ava who brought me out of it. She was the light in my darkness. Even if you hated me, I still needed to be there for her. I've missed too much these past couple of months. How is she? She seems to have grown a foot already."

"She hasn't, but she's good. A dream child. She's been doing well in school. I don't have to hound her about doing her homework, I barely have to check it. I just hope it lasts past the first grade."

There was something magical about candlelight. How it spilled through the room, softening every edge, romanticizing every surface. Sera hadn't been able to peel her gaze away from Adam, the way his eyes crinkled at the corners when he laughed, the way his lips came up slightly higher on one side when he smiled, that dimple in his cheek.

This was the man who knew her better than any one person on this earth. He had watched her grow from the afraid girl who never wanted to leave her room, to the woman she'd fought to become now. He knew about the strange phenomenon in her family's history and never judged her or thought less of her for it. He was kind to a fault, slow to anger, quick to laughter, and the most dedicated of fathers. And she loved him with every fiber of her being. How could she not?

The thought of losing him again was more than she could handle. From that, she'd surely never recover. If that meant she'd have to keep her feelings in check in order to keep his friendship, so be it. Unrequited love was a price she was willing to pay.

Still, she *had* to know about this woman he'd been talking to.

Adam grinned, never taking his eyes from her face.

"Why are you looking at me like that?" Sera chuckled self-consciously. She'd been about to ask him about the woman, had a mind to just blurt it out and get it over with. But he had been looking at her—no *into* her—and smiling in such a way that had her melting inside, making her yearn for him to love her back. She pushed that want deep down where it would stay buried.

"I'm memorizing how you look at this moment."

Sera laughed. "Stop. It hasn't been *that* long," she said, nudging his knee with hers.

"Too long."

"Agreed." She couldn't look away from him, from those eyes.

"I know what's on your mind," he teased as he got up to refill their glasses.

Sera grinned. "I don't think you do."

"You want to ask me if I've been seeing anyone."

It took all of her control not to let her mouth drop open.

"I..." It was no use, she couldn't manage to stammer out any excuses. He knew her too well to fall for any of them anyway.

"You want the honest truth?"

"I wouldn't expect the truth to be anything else." Or did she? Sera needed to know, though she wasn't quite sure she was ready for the truth after all.

"I was hurt after our fight. I threw myself into work, but that didn't help for long. Marcy, that woman I work with, must have smelled the blood in the water because it didn't take her long to pounce on easy prey," he paused, still watching her closely. "Nothing happened."

"Oh. Well, if it did...I mean, it's none of my...Really?" Defeated, she gave in, letting him see her true feelings for the first time. It was dangerous. A risk that might prove too costly. But when Sera did have emotions, she was never one to hide them well, especially from Adam.

"Yes, really. She called a couple of times. And boy, Ava sure didn't like her calling me," he said, smirking. Then he looked at her with a question in his eyes. "I'm not sure if I want to know."

"Know what?"

"About the detective." Adam looked away, setting his wine glass down.

"There's nothing to know about Detective Pardou. Why would you think that?"

"I'm not blind. He's young, not bad to look at, and he was very *friendly* with you when he checked in after we got here."

The curve of a smile played at Sera's lips as she watched Adam fidget. If she didn't know better, he seemed almost jealous. "Well, we have locked lips."

Adam scoffed and stood.

"No...don't. I'm kidding. Kind of." Sera told him about the night the detective had to breathe life back into her. When she told him what had happened, his expression darkened.

"You almost died while I was being stubborn and stupid and far away from you." He stepped away from her, shaking his head angrily.

"But I didn't." Sera stayed quiet for a moment, wrestling with her next words. "Even if the detective *had* shown any interest, besides me not dying, it wouldn't have mattered, because of you, Adam."

At that, he looked back up at her. With how his eyes bore into hers, she had to turn away from him, but it still didn't stop everything from rushing out.

"When I visited you in New York, you kissed me. I know that it was only a small, friendly kiss. But it ruined everything and everyone else for me. I felt this desire I've never had before. The want was for you. But I knew, I *know*, that is not something I can have. You're not ready—which is fine—I'm so sorry for *ever* saying otherwise. And you and I are just friends." She turned to him, desperate, her eyes pleading with him. "This *can't* ruin everything. I couldn't stand losing you and Ava. These last months have almost killed me not talking to you both. Please promise you won't hate me or bail out on me. Just give me time. I'll work through it on my own. I don't know what I would do if we weren't friends, if I couldn't be close with Ava."

He closed the gap between them, took her hand in one of his, and cradled her face with the other.

"Don't ever think that, Sera. Ever." He stepped in closer. "I have a confession to make. It *wasn't* just a friendly kiss. I had to tear myself away from you to get control of myself. I don't know if I should say this, I don't know what the consequences will be, but I do know that I won't be able to live with myself if I don't. I've been battling my feelings and my ghosts. I've tried logic—you live here in San Francisco and I live completely across the country in New York. When that didn't work, I tried ignorance. But I've stopped trying to fool myself. I've been so in love with you for some time now."

An overwhelming rush of emotions swept through her. For so many years, she'd hidden herself away from anything real so that she'd be safe from the pain and sorrow that came with loss. She had felt it once, the gut-twisting grief, the emptiness, the fear of being alone in the world. But being safe had held her life in purgatory for too long, held her back from true happiness.

All of the feelings she'd never wanted, along with those she'd always yearned for, swelled to the surface. Tears veiled her eyes, spilling down her cheek.

"Really?" she whispered.

"Yes, really." He took his hand from hers and embraced her face in both of them.

"It has always been *you*, Adam. I've loved you all along."

Adam gently wiped away the tear and kissed her wet cheek. He slipped his hands from her face into her hair, pulling her in closer to him. Their bodies curled into one another, the beat of his heart harmonizing with her own, beating together.

Lifting her chin, he kissed her lips so softly at first that she barely felt them there, just the wind of breath touching them. He slowly deepened the kiss, melting their lips together.

The sweet taste of wine intertwining with his unique male scent sent pulses of heat through her. There was no longer any doubt or hesitation, just a deep need. She traced the hard line of his jaw with her lips, running her fingers down, slowly unbuttoning his shirt. When the skin of his bare chest was exposed, she kissed his collarbone and let her hands drift over his skin.

Adam lifted her up in his arms, wrapping her legs around his waist as he took her into the unoccupied bedroom. Their eyes never parted from each other as he laid her down on the bed, lowering himself to her. Their hands never stopped touching, fingers interlacing, always feeling for the others.

They became one—body, mind, soul, and heart—locking into one another as their bodies joined together. Every breath shared, every movement matched, first slow, mounting to a heated rush, then slowing again.

Each moment they had together was cherished and treasured, never again taking their time together for granted.

CHAPTER SEVENTY-FOUR

Adam

SAN FRANCISCO

Feeling Sera's breath on his neck made it hard for him to concentrate on slow and steady. He'd been yearning to hold her and touch her for longer than he realized. He took her mouth with his, slowly discovering her with his hands, tracing the softness of her skin with his fingertips as his lips tasted the sweetness of her shoulders, the curve of her neck. He took his time with each caress, each sight, every sensation, savoring every second intimately learning every part of her.

His walls came crumbling down, all of his emotions churning, the feelings that had been muted for so long opening as his heart woke again.

Adam found his reason to start over.

He would never forget. He'd learned the hard way how painfully precious time was and knew too well that tomorrow was never promised.

Having her intertwined with him under a blanket, the warmth of her skin against his, hours filled with lovemaking, conversation, and sweet, long kisses, had been a nice compensation for sleep deprivation.

Sera looked up at him, her eyes searching his, looking for answers neither one of them had.

"I guess it's time for the talk, isn't it?" Adam stated, always the icebreaker.

"It's bound to come up at some point," she said, smiling up at him.

"I don't have all the answers yet. There are things we'll have to work out. But what I do know is that I never want to be away from you again." He stroked her hair, winding it in his fingers. "Right now, what's most important is that you're safe. *We* are great. Nothing will change that. We'll figure out the rest as it comes." He kissed her forehead, as he'd done so many times before, bringing her closer to him as the first pinks and golds of the day painted the sky. Finally, she drifted off to sleep, tangled up with him.

He couldn't stop looking at her, the way her hair fell across her forehead, the small nose and full mouth, the way her face looked so peaceful.

He'd almost lost her, not only waiting foolishly too long to claim his feelings, but physically as well because he wasn't there when she had needed him most. Never again would he leave her alone in this world. With her hand in his, they would walk through hell together if need be.

Ava wouldn't be anything but thrilled about the two of them, even though what had been keeping him awake was what had always been between them. Distance. They had been far away from each other for far too long. But he would worry about that another day.

This night had been a gift, a special moment in which the world had stopped for the two of them. Tonight, he would soak in the love they were swaddled in. He laid his head down next to hers, closed his eyes, and let himself fall asleep in her arms.

"No way. You've done enough. We have to get you far away from here. We'll go back to New York until they catch this asshole. Damn it, why *haven't* they found her?" Fear diminished into boiling fury.

Adam was folding the last of Sera's clothing from the dresser and roughly tossing it in a box.

"Don't take it out on my clothes. They didn't do anything wrong," Sera teased.

Adam sighed, looking at his haphazard packing job. He and Ava had gone with Sera and Erinne to pack the rest of her things at the dorm, accompanied by the security team, of course. But he couldn't help the paralyzing fear that kept creeping up.

Once they had woken, reality slapped at him. Sera started adamantly trying to talk Adam into leaving with Ava, as if he would go home and leave Sera to battle this alone. Hell, he didn't want her in the crosshairs at all. He'd left her once. He wouldn't do it again.

"I have to agree with Mr. Hunky. Better yet, I think the three of you should come back to Ireland with all of us until this is done. The farther, the better," Erinne pleaded with Sera, her eyes full of the same worry Adam felt to his core.

"I have to finish it. I can find her and stop this. I never understood all these years since the day on the ship. But it's clear now." Sera took Adam's hands in hers.

"I can't let anything happen to you." He'd only just found his way to her. There was no way he could let her go into this maniac's line of fire. Adam pulled her into his arms and held her tight.

"I have to be the one. There's no other way." She kissed him softly, holding her forehead to his.

"No. That's bullshit, of course there is. It's the reason we have the police. You're not going to be some kind of bait for them. Please, Sera. Let me take you away from this. I can't...I can't lose you, too." There was more than one type of terror in the world, and right now, both were colliding, made worse by knowing that he wouldn't be able to change her mind.

Sera pulled away from Adam to face Erinne. "Aunt E, I need you to take the family home. You should be leaving soon to catch your flight, anyway. Adam, take Ava home. You all will be safe away from here. I can't do this if I know that any of you would be in danger."

"That's definitely bullshit. I'm not leaving you. I'll call Victoria and have her come get Ava. She'll be safe with her. But don't ever tell me to leave you again because I won't." He kissed her hard before he pulled out his cell phone.

"I can't just leave you either. If anything..." Erinne pulled Sera into a hug.

"Please trust me. This is something I am meant to do. What is there to worry about? I have Mom on my side. But I won't be able to do it if I am distracted by worrying about you. Please," Sera pleaded, tears wetting her eyes.

"Damn it, girl."

"I won't leave her side. I promise you that," Adam said as he returned to the conversation after calling Victoria, giving her the details of what she needed to do to come get Ava.

Erinne took Adam's arm and held it tight. "Promise me, swear to me, if this girl is in even the slightest possibility of danger, you do whatever you have to, drug her, knock her out, whatever it takes to drag her out of here."

"I swear with my own life." Adam put his hand on Erinne's and looked her in the eye as he swore. He never meant anything more. No matter the consequence, he would protect Sera with everything he had.

CHAPTER SEVENTY-FIVE

Ella

SAN FRANCISCO

D on't worry, Mr. Mason. Dr. Wilson is one of our best here," Ella said, preparing the side table with supplies to clean her patient's wound and then sat on the stool next to his gurney.

When she took his hand, two very different things happened simultaneously.

A flash of heat surged through Ella, followed by ice-cold dread. Never had *The Knowing* hit her so drastically, never had such complete darkness engulfed her. She had to fight the immediate urge to drop his mangled hand.

She gulped down the overwhelming fear that wanted her to run, far and fast, and forced herself to continue as if the blanket of evil wasn't suffocating her.

She focused on cleaning the wound, careful not to look him in the eye. Not only would she not be able to hide her emotions, she might run screaming from this bay in the emergency room if he made eye contact with her. She could already feel his cold stare—the dark yearning in it.

She'd felt the oppressive air weigh down on her the second she and Dr. Wilson entered the bay where this man waited. At first glance, he looked like any other unassuming, aging male in his late thirties. But this was no regular man. Malevolence all but radiated off of him. It took every ounce of will to keep her facial expression devoid of the emotional turmoil brewing within. Every passing moment that she had to maintain physical contact with him increased the bile that burned as it rose to her throat.

By the time Dr. Wilson returned, her hands were shaking with trepidation.

"Dr. Wilson, I'd like to ask the nurses to show me where the supplies are kept for this procedure. Half the battle is knowing where things are in emergencies."

"Absolutely. I'll get him numbed up while you find the rest of the supplies."

She almost ran. She used every bit of self-control not to run from the hospital, get into her car, and leave without ever coming back—which was totally absurd.

A supply closet substituted instead. Ella rushed in, putting her back against the closed door as she tried to catch her breath.

She couldn't ruin this chance at fulfilling her dream. What would she say when they asked why she had left so drastically?

Oh, that guy gave me the heebie-jeebies, so I ran home to hide?

Ella had been way off her game lately. Not long after their engagement, Ella's usual go-with-the-flow attitude vanished, replaced by way more anxiety than she'd ever had in her lifetime. She was unable to shake the strange and constant uneasiness. The smallest things had Ella overthinking and overanalyzing.

So not like her.

She was in her third year of medical school, which was finally hospital rotations. The ER was far from her favorite specialty, but she was already learning so much. Yet, darkness loomed, tainting what should be the most exciting days of her life.

It wouldn't be the last time a dark personality came through. It was why she was meant to be a doctor, *The Knowing* allowing her to sense someone, what was making them sick, how to make it better, and how to fix them. It was also why she preferred to work in pediatrics, where the soul was still pure and undamaged.

But everyone had to do their rotations in each discipline. It made for a well-rounded doctor. Or so they said.

She could do this. All she had to do was make it through. She could get through anything for her daughter.

Ella took breath after shaky breath, focusing her mind on her beautiful daughter until she was steadier and her trembling hands calmed.

Inhaling one last time, she straightened her posture and, holding her head high, opened the door and went back to finish her job like the professional she was.

Later, as Ella changed out of her scrubs and back into her street clothes in the doctor's lounge, she thought about the encounter she'd had earlier in the day.

The person she encountered was bad enough, but the resulting panic attack was one of the worst feelings she had ever experienced.

What was that?

She'd never in her life had a panic attack. It was more than annoying finding herself immersed in these weird episodes. Maybe it was overexposure, too many personalities all at once, all in pain, or in need of something from her.

That had to be it.

Ella really needed to find a way to calm *The Knowing* down to a tolerable level at work. She had failed so many times trying to control it over her lifetime, but there had to be some way to at least mellow it.

Finally, her mind drifted to other, happier thoughts. She was on her way home to her fiancé and her daughter, and it was spaghetti night, Sera's favorite.

It had been a long day, and she missed her little girl and her little girl's daddy. Thinking of the life they had built and the family they'd made had Ella smiling the rest of the way home.

CHAPTER SEVENTY-SIX

Jordan

SAN FRANCISCO

Sera had no idea just how close I had been to her for three years. It's kind of pathetic. The first few months, adrenaline pumped through me, wondering if she'd feel me so close to her. But she never even had a clue. Some ability she supposedly had.

Just as she had no idea how close I was still. Technology is a wonderful thing when you want to keep tabs on someone. The best inventions of my generation are those doorbell cameras. They're small enough to be strategically hidden, and they notify you of any movement through a handy app on your phone.

I could keep close to Sera almost constantly while she was in the dorm if I wanted. And by divine coincidence, it was Sera who had been with me the whole time. I couldn't have planned it closer to perfection if I tried. It was the ultimate sign. Everything had been going flawlessly.

Until something else switched on.

For the first time, I became *someone*. I had a life. Classes were easy enough. I was successful at something I put my mind to and worked hard for. I was someone that people went to, listened to. People trusted me, wanted to talk to me. I was no longer the pathetic daughter of so-and-so, the damaged one, the abused one, the strange one. I was normal. Something I never thought I would ever be, and I had a true friend. I had it all, for a little while.

Now the guy was back in her life with his kid, hoarding her, taking her attention. And she left me, just as everyone else had.

It had all been a lie. Sera had taken everything away from me. Again.

I am ready for what is to come. I am ready to do what I need to do.

She had an entourage with her all the time now. I would figure out a way around them, a way to get to her. Some way to get her to come willingly, even. All it took was patience.

And then the guy laid it all out for me. Made it so easy. Too easy.

The old woman was coming for the kid.

For the kid, Sera would give herself up without any trouble. And then, finally, it will all be over.

Finally, I will be at peace after all these years.

When a woman rushed out of the airport doors, staring at me and the sign I held, I knew everything was about to fall into place.

"I am Victoria Spencer."

"Great. I'm parked right here." The woman willingly followed me to my car, parked in the loading zone.

Step one. Success.

Twenty minutes later, I listened to her conversation with the guy, letting him know we were pulling up. That's when my nerves started getting jumpy. This part was crucial. I busied myself, trying to look as nonchalant as possible.

Adam walked out—I recognized him from the picture Sera kept on her lock screen—the little brat bouncing happily beside him. Victoria got out of the car to greet them.

"Are you ready to go on an adventure?" she asked as she took Ava's bag from Adam.

"Yes! Can we get ice cream, too?"

"What would an adventure be without ice cream?" Victoria got the kid into the car, fastened her seatbelt, then stayed outside to talk to Adam.

I could leave right now, so I don't have to worry about getting rid of the hag. I dared a glance in the rearview mirror at the child who was the golden ticket to my finale. Instead, I waited so as not to draw attention to myself any sooner than necessary and listened to the adults having their oh-so-important conversation.

Idiots.

I hadn't wanted it to come to this. I wasn't about hurting kids. But Sera didn't leave me a choice. Really, she had only herself to blame.

"Adam, what's going on? Are you okay? Should I be worried?"

"I'm fine. Everyone is fine. It's just not the best place for Ava to be right now. I promise I'll tell you everything after we take care of this situation. No need to worry you more than need be. I need to know Ava is safe with you."

"Alright. Yes, she'll be perfectly safe at home with me. Please check in with us so we know you're okay."

"I will. I'll call every evening." He walked Victoria to the other door and opened it for her.

"Bye, Sweet Pea. I'll call you tonight before bedtime, okay? And not too much ice cream, got it?" Adam kissed the kid.

"Okay, Daddy." Ava was already playing with some stuffed gerbil.

"Thank you, Victoria."

"No need to thank me. I'd do anything for my granddaughter."

But Adam wasn't looking at her anymore. He was looking at me. I kept my face down, inputting information into the GPS on my phone.

Over the years, I tried to be as careful as possible, never taking stupid selfies with Sera or letting him see me in the background during their video calls. But I couldn't be 100% positive he never saw me, either.

"Adam?"

"Oh. Yes. I know you would. I'll still thank you anyway." He closed the door. I could feel his eyes still looking at me.

If he made one move, I'd speed off. I had them in the car. I didn't have to wait. It would be mere minutes before he realized the mistake he just made anyway. But those few minutes might make or break the whole scene I had meticulously planned.

Instead, he just waved as I pulled away from the curb, nice and easy.

I let out the breath I didn't realize I'd been holding. "Do you mind if I play music?" I asked as we merged onto the interstate.

"Sure. Go ahead."

I turned up some jazzy blues music a little louder than necessary to give myself a moment to calm my nerves.

Step two. Complete.

"Is this another way to the airport?"

"Yeah, it looks like there is an accident up ahead. I'm just trying to get around it." I don't know how familiar this lady was with the area, but if she was, she would recognize that we were going in the opposite direction of the airport. She would know that we were headed toward the national park and into the woods.

"Excuse me, Miss? This is the wrong way. The airport is—"

The loud click that sounded when I engaged the child locks cut her off. She looked into the rearview mirror, her eyes meeting mine. She knew the sound and probably used the locks herself when the brat was in the car with her.

In her eyes, I could see that she knew something was wrong. *Very* wrong.

CHAPTER SEVENTY-SEVEN

Sera

SAN FRANCISCO

After many more promises and about a dozen goodbye hugs, Erinne finally left to meet the rest of the family at the airport. If this day hadn't been overshadowed by what lurked somewhere out there, spending the day with the people she loved most would have been one of those memories Sera would treasure forever.

This little girl was hers now to love and cherish. She loved this little girl's father with everything she had, but Sera had fallen in love with his child even before.

Ava's smile lit the dark parts of her soul. Her precious chattering on and on about guinea pigs and her friends in her class pushed away any thoughts of nightmares and the evil of the world. There was no doubt that Sera would do whatever it took to keep this little girl, who was now entrusted to her, safe.

As they were putting the last of Sera's boxes in Adam's rental car, Detective Drake Pardou walked up from the other side of the parking lot.

"Good, I caught you guys before you left." Detective Pardou extended his hand to Adam.

"Detective. You remember Adam and Ava."

Adam shook the detective's hand as his cell phone rang.

"Excuse me a second," Adam said, answering the phone as he walked a few steps away.

"Any updates?" Sera asked hopefully. Her heart sparked with hope when she saw the detective approach. Maybe they found Jordan and took her into custody. Then Sera could leave with Adam and Ava and celebrate that it was finally over. But the look on his face dashed the brief flash of hope.

"Unfortunately, I do not. I just wanted to check on everything here and see if you were still planning on staying at the safe house or if you were going to leave with your family."

Sera was torn. She wanted to leave with her family and go for a brief vacation with Adam and Ava before she had to start studying for her boards. Be free of this monster who has betrayed her, invaded her dreams, stalked her life, and now threatened all she held dear.

But she couldn't. She wouldn't be a coward anymore, couldn't live with herself if one more life was taken because she'd been too scared to stop it.

Besides, how could she begin her life with Ava and Adam if Jordan was still lurking in the shadows with some lifelong vendetta against her? Sera lived her life in fear once, she wouldn't do it again, and she wouldn't put Ava in danger for one second.

"I'll be staying until we find Jordan. If I have another night terror, if I could be any help at all..."

"Hey, Victoria is here. I'm going to walk Ava out," Adam interrupted.

"I need hugs and kisses first." Sera picked up Ava, blowing raspberries into her neck, sending the girl into a burst of laughter. "I love you, little Ava. Be good to your grandma, okay?"

Ava looked at Sera, her big blue eyes surprised. "I love you too." Then she hugged Sera tighter than she ever had, kissing Sera's cheek.

Sera put her back down, her eyes wet. She watched as Adam took Ava's hand and led her down the sidewalk. It killed Sera that Ava had to leave so soon. But she would never forgive herself if even one hair on that little girl's head was hurt.

Sera spoke with the detective, planning out what would happen for the next few days until Adam walked back in a few minutes later with a strange, confused look on his face.

"What's wrong?" Sera's heart thrashed in her chest. Something was off. Wrong.

"Nothing. I just...I got a weird feeling about the Uber driver. I'm probably just being paranoid, knowing a mad person is roaming about. It's getting to my head, I think." But Adam's look didn't soften. Instead, it etched deeper into the creases on his forehead.

His phone sounded. "It's from Uber." Adam's face blanched. "It's from the driver. He says that Victoria never showed up at the pickup area and that he can't wait any longer. The driver—this driver—was a woman." Adam's phone trembled in his hands, which he dropped as he ran back toward the street.

The detective pulled out his phone, calling into the station. "We've got a possible child abduction and kidnapping in progress. Six years old, long brown hair, blue eyes, approximately three feet eight inches tall. Standby for car description." Detective Pardou ran after Adam.

Sera sank to her knees, the scream that came from the depth of her soul echoed throughout the buildings.

An hour later, red and blue lights reflected throughout the street, bouncing off the walls of the dorm residence buildings. Adam described every detail he could, over and over: the color of the car, the woman, and long black hair. They showed Adam a picture of Jordan Mason, to which he confirmed that she was the driver who left with his daughter and mother-in-law.

Sera couldn't pick herself up off the grass where she'd crumbled. She couldn't move from that spot, couldn't think, couldn't focus on what any of the officers were saying. Her mind was stuck.

Jordan had Ava.

Sera knew what Jordan was capable of, knew that her mind was fragile, broken. Too much time had passed already. Too much time. Sera had to find Jordan. But how?

Think.

Sera roughly massaged her temples. She could find her, she knew it in her bones that there was a way to connect with Jordan. They'd been connected since they were children. There *had* to be a way.

As an adult, Sera only connected with Jordan when she was hurting someone, and Sera needed to connect with her before she came remotely close to hurting her little girl.

As children, she watched Jordan play with fireflies, play in the woods, and hide in trees when she was scared. Jordan had never hurt anyone when they connected then.

Think, damn it!

Sera closed her eyes, tuning out all the voices surrounding her. She thought of Ava, deep into every essence of the sweet little girl, her beautiful face, her boisterous giggle, her innocent soul.

The sound around her started to dim, fading away into a dull hum until it was gone altogether.

Sera concentrated on Jordan as a child, the fireflies, the tree with the hole. She reached out and felt for Jordan, all that she'd ever felt from her.

Light faded to black behind her eyelids.

She could feel her, the sadness, the rage, the broken madness that was Jordan. The faint glimmer started to intensify into a dull ache, then grew into sharp, searing pain until Sera was clenching her head, screaming.

All sounds magnified, each whisper roaring, each booming footstep trampling through her head.

Then she was somewhere else.

A quiet and steady heartbeat thudded in the background. Sera's vision cleared slightly, the edges fuzzy, her hands not her own. Sera found her way into Jordan's mind, feeling her and hearing her thoughts.

I can feel you.

Where is she?

I can hear you, listening to all those things in my head that are supposed to be my own. It is strange, isn't it, this little connection, you and me? Poetic really. Seeing as it was you who ruined my life. You and your sweet, pretty mommy. The universe has given me the chance to put it right, to fix its mistakes.

Where is she, Jordan?

Jordan turned so that Sera could see Victoria lying on the floor and sweet Ava next to her, looking as if she was just asleep. They were both alive, unconscious, but moving and breathing.

What have you done?

What have I done? I haven't done anything. At least, not yet.

Don't you dare hurt her. I'll kill you myself if you touch her.

My, my. Such threats from the little coward who is scared of her own shadow.

What do you want from me?

What do I want from the sweet, perfect Sera Delaney? Everything. I want everything you stole from me. My family, my father, my life.

Let them go. They have nothing to do with this, with us. She is just a child.

Then don't give me a reason to hurt her. I just want you. You are going to do exactly what I tell you to, or your friend's daughter here is going to get her pretty little face all sliced up. I swear I will do it.

Jordan took the dagger from her boot and let the gleam of light reflect off it.

Don't, please. What do you want me to do?

Good answer. Here are the rules. You'll come alone. Don't even tell them what you saw, or she's dead. I'm going to give you one quick look around. You have an hour to figure out where we are. If you're late, she's dead. If you're not alone, she's dead. If you don't show, she's dead, and so are

you. Get where this is going? Don't think I won't do it. You don't know me. You never did. Not really.

I do know who you are. You are the little girl who caught fireflies in jars and hid in trees. The little girl who was forced to kneel until her knees bled, the little girl who got beat with a bible. The little girl who deserved so much more. I've known you your whole life, Jordan.

Get out of my head.

I was there with you. I saw it, I saw you. I am sorry you had a shitty childhood, shitty parents. But you can choose not to be a product of their abuse. You will always have a choice not to do horrible things, not be like them.

How would you know? You've always had everything handed to you. A nice, wealthy family that took you in and gave you this nice little life.

Because I know you. You were my friend. I cared about you. I was there for you as you were there for me. I saw you, who you really are, under all the hurt, under the pain. That wasn't an act. I have known you intimately for three years. I see you, Jordan. You can't hurt a child, not like you were hurt. It is not who you are. Do not do to her what your family did to you.

You don't know shit! You have no idea what it's like. You never had to fear every minute of every day. Fear that if you were too loud, someone would come after you and hit you with a belt until you bled. Fear that if you even reminded them that you were alive, you'd get thrown around, forced to kneel for hours until the skin on your knees scraped away into bloody blobs of flesh. While you got a nice hot meal to fill your belly, I had to sneak food so I wouldn't be beaten for being a burden because I was hungry. While you got nice clothes to wear, I got a broken nose as punishment for losing a shoe. While your mother told you she loved you, mine told me that I ruined her life over and over again. You, you had everything, and my life was empty. And it was because of you that my father left us. He left me for you! Fuck you!

Jordan was in a rage. The area flashed by Sera quickly. She heard bird calls screeching above, saw trees, hundreds of giant redwoods, a broken dirt trail that seemed endless into the woods. And in the background, just a flash, was the place that lived in the worst of all of Sera's terrors.

Everything was gone. The sounds of the world surrounding her shrieked back into her ears again. Sera tried to scream as she came to in Adam's arms, with Detective Pardou hovering over her.

"Sera. What happened? Are you alright? Sera!"

Watching the scene, she couldn't answer, couldn't breathe. It was happening again, as it did in the hotel. She was struggling for breath, clutching at her throat, but nothing helped the blackness that started to overtake her again. Her eyes rolled back, fluttering shut.

Detective Pardou took her from Adam and pressed his mouth to hers, blowing his own breath into her. He had to do it several times before she responded.

She coughed and gasped for air that burned into her lungs. It took up precious minutes of what little time they had. Ignoring the wave of dizziness, she scrambled up. Adam tried to hold her, but she shook herself loose.

"It's getting worse," Detective Pardou said. "It took twice as long to get you back. What happened? Did you talk to her again?"

"Yes...I mean, I can't talk about it, I have an hour. No, *shit*, fifty minutes. I have to go." She started to run but stopped, not knowing where to go. She couldn't think, couldn't focus, her head still recovering from the shock to her body.

Focus.

"Sera," Adam pleaded, holding her by the shoulders, making her face him. "It's in your eyes. You saw Ava. Whatever you saw, I need to know. I can handle it."

"Please. I can't tell you. It has to be me. Only me. I have to go." She tried to pull away but was held by Adam's strong hands.

"This is my daughter, Sera. Nothing will keep me away."

If she didn't tell them, they would keep her from getting to Ava. If she did tell them, Jordan might hurt Ava. But Adam was right. The choice was not only hers to make.

"Muir Woods. Jordan is holding Ava at the cabin, *his* cabin."

"Let's go then," Adam stated with a determined nod.

"No," she cried, "you have to stay back. Please, trust me. I have to do this. I have to get there first. She has to think I'm alone. I'll give my life for hers if I have to. I promise you." She kissed Adam hard, then ran toward his rental car.

Another officer grabbed Adam's arm as Detective Pardou took off after Sera, jumping into the passenger seat as she started to drive away.

"Pardou is the cop. He has the weapon. We have to be smart about this. Come on, you'll ride with us."

CHAPTER SEVENTY-EIGHT

Jeffrey Mason

ALAMEDA ISLAND

With the children staying at the neighbor's house and his wife under antepartum observation at the hospital, Jeffrey was free, giving him extra time to do whatever he wanted. He showed up at his job, put in the hours, then went home to the cabin, where he continued all of the necessary renovations. Especially now that he had a new deadline looming.

Each day, he went to the hospital. Not the one where his wife was admitted, but the teaching hospital where he'd met the love of his life.

The day after his serendipitous accident, he took a bouquet of flowers to the emergency room, where he asked for the beautiful doctor, Ella Delaney. The nurse who had greeted him at the intake window was all smiles at the flowers, going on about how it was such a sweet gesture and whatnot. But she was sorry to say that the medical students wouldn't return until Tuesday. He gave the flowers to the nurse, telling her it was to thank all of them for taking such good care of him.

On Tuesday, he went back, parked, and waited for Ella's shift to end. He followed her home, parking a few houses down, far enough away to be hidden in the shadows, and watched. He watched her park in the driveway next to a blue sedan. He watched her get out of the car, white coat draped over one arm, book bag slung over the other. He watched as she made her way to the house. Before she reached the door, it was flung open.

The most perfect child, a little girl who was an almost identical copy of Ella, came out. The little girl ran up to Ella, hugging her fiercely, making Ella laugh and nearly drop all of her things.

Exhilaration jolted through Jeffrey. Destiny had brought them into his life. These two creatures had been made especially for him, the trophies for his hard work and dedication.

A young man followed the child out of the house. The guy put an arm around Ella's shoulders, kissing her temple, then led the two of them into the house.

Interesting.

A husband? Boyfriend? Brother? He'd need to find out.

For the next several hours, Jeffrey sat in his car and watched the house. Windows would light or darken as they moved through rooms, curtains were closed when dusk set in. He only left after the last light had been shut off, and the house remained dark for a long period of time. The blue car never left its spot on the driveway.

He did this daily for weeks, diagramming her every move until he knew every hour of her schedule. He even grew so bold as to look through Ella's trash. There are so many intimate things one could learn about a person just by looking at what they discard from their lives.

Nothing deterred him from watching Ella, learning her routine, learning everything he could about her. Even after his wife had been discharged to continue bedrest at home. Their son was more than capable of helping care for his mother, allowing Jeffrey to make excuses of working late and rarely went home.

His mind obsessed over Ella Delaney, consuming every thought. He even called off work a few times—which he'd never done before—to get to know his future wife and daughter all the better.

On the days Ella was at the hospital, the guy would stay with the child, taking her to and from school, playing in the front yard with her. Dangerous, if you asked Jeffrey. The guy should have a mind to keep such a child hidden from the world. There was true evil out there waiting to do horrible things to such beautiful things.

On the nights Ella was home, the guy left for some mediocre job. That would be Jeffrey's window when he would take possession of his new family. He'd have no problem slipping into the house after the guy left for one of his shifts.

It took a while, but finally, the cabin was ready for them. He was ready as well. The itch was getting more aggressive. But he calmed himself, as this couldn't be rushed. It needed to be perfect, each little detail. The beautifully intelligent medical student and her perfect daughter would soon be his, to own, to possess, to have whenever he chose. All of his research, patience, and dedication would be rewarded.

Jeffrey told Ingrid he would be gone for the entire week for a business convention in Las Vegas. Ingrid seemed relieved to be rid of him. It didn't bother him, as he felt the same way toward her. Her mother would be flying in to care for her and the children while he was away. He was free once again. For good this time.

He barely slept the night before and got up extra early, not bothering to say goodbye to his horrid wife. He gathered his bags quickly and quietly, only hesitating momentarily at the doors of his children's rooms.

There was an odd pang in his chest, a quick pull of regret and guilt, knowing he wouldn't be returning and would most likely never see them again, also knowing who he was leaving them to be raised by.

Maybe he would bring the kids as soon as he had Ella and the girl settled. Maybe.

The day dragged on slower than usual, it seemed, waiting to put his plan in motion. For some reason, as he sat hidden in the shadows, he realized he'd never planned out what he'd do with the guy. He would draw too much attention too quickly. That was going to be a bigger problem than he anticipated. Jeffrey would have to get rid of him.

He would wait until the lights went out in the house, make his way in, then, quick and quiet, slash the guy's throat. There was plenty of land around the cabin to get rid of a body. Or maybe he'd throw it out on the side of some obscure road. There were plenty of rough neighborhoods to choose from. It would look like a random act of violence. Either way, once he was rid of the guy, he could claim his family. It was an easy plan. Effortless.

The front door opened. The guy came out with the child far too early. Ella shouldn't be home for at least another hour. The girl clapped her hands and skipped to the blue sedan, happier than usual.

Jeffrey started his car, waiting to follow discreetly behind. He followed them through the streets of the small island community until they pulled into the parking lot of an ice cream parlor. He watched as the two of them went inside and came out a few minutes later with cones, the child eagerly licking the side as the guy led her to an outdoor bench.

He watched the two of them for a long time, the little girl giggling at whatever the guy said. The easy way between the two of them began to brew a jealous rage. His own kids wanted nothing to do with him and mostly kept to themselves.

Jeffrey's son had his face plastered in video games most of the time. His daughter, about the little girl's age, was too timid—like her stupid mother—to want to do much with him when he was home. She was too scared of Ingrid's harsh tongue, which found any reason to scold her.

Your dress is too small, temptation is sinful. No jumping, you'll show your sinful parts. Stop yelling, we only shout for the Lord.

It was easier to avoid the whole situation that was his home life.

With this new family, Ella and the child would be his world. He would be the one who made them laugh. He would be the one Ella would look at with that playful smile she had. This would be his second chance, the chance to do it right.

His envy grew to rage the longer he watched. Waiting patiently and not acting before it was time became difficult, until it became impossible. The minutes ticked by slower and slower.

This guy didn't deserve them. He was glorified childcare, that was all. Jeffrey could kill the bastard right then, take the child from him, and gleefully watch the life in his eyes fade away.

The guy flipped open his cell phone and began speaking. It had to be her. She must be on her way home.

It was a terrible idea to change the plan at the last minute. He should wait until they got back to the house and carry out the plan he had meticulously made. But the rage took over.

Jeffrey got out of his car and quickly strolled over.

It was now or never.

CHAPTER SEVENTY-NINE

Chris

ALAMEDA ISLAND

There were moments when Chris would sit and stare at his daughter. She was his miracle. He meant nothing more when he'd told Ella he didn't deserve her or this life that had been so generously handed to him.

In his previous life, he had fantasized about fortune and fame. Once he played professionally on a major league team, all of his dreams would finally come true.

He had been the most foolish of idiots.

None of that would have brought a fraction of the true happiness that conversing with his chatterbug daughter did on a daily basis.

Never once had he regretted giving up baseball. He never even missed it. He felt more joy teaching Sera how to use a mitt and catch with it than he ever had bringing his team to any victory. Teaching her the things he knew made him feel not only useful, but like he was contributing something to this world.

His family, the one he had made with Ella, had become everything to him. His job wasn't fancy, but it brought him more pride than anything else he'd ever done. If only because he'd learned a skill and worked hard using it. Working with like-minded people with similar values was also something he enjoyed—values his parents never had.

They had no idea what it was to earn something with their own two hands. Nor had his parents instilled in him what unconditional love felt like, as their approval had been solely based on his accomplishments and how those accomplishments would benefit them.

So when they turned their self-centered noses up at becoming grandparents in what was their idea of less-than-ideal circumstances, Chris couldn't say he was shocked or even surprised. It didn't bother him, though. They'd never really been significant enough in his life to give him pause.

Their loss.

Chris had found real, true love with Ella that he'd never before had in his life. A love that was not only unconditional but all-encompassing. He felt the heat for his soon-to-be wife in every fiber of his being, even after more than seven years together. Lust for each other had never waned, and his love grew stronger each day, along with admiration and respect for the woman who had his heart, the mother of his child.

His wife. His child.

Never in his wildest dreams would he have thought he'd find his purpose as a devoted family man, that nothing else would ever make him as happy as being Ella's man and Sera's father.

It was one of those chilly San Francisco afternoons on the island. The fog lingered throughout most of the day, and the temperature never really warmed up much. Yet as he built a fort with Sera in the dining room, he craved an ice cream outing—a love he knew Sera shared.

"Hey, kiddo. You know what I'm feeling right now?"

Sera popped her head up from behind a sheet she was tying to a chair. "Ice cream?" she squealed, jumping up.

"Yep. Let's do it. Mommy won't be home for another hour, plenty of time to hide the evidence. C'mon, off on another adventure," Chris announced, grabbing his keys and their jackets, a cheering Sera following close behind.

Sera continued chattering on the entire drive to the ice cream parlor, a quality she definitely inherited from her mother. Theirs was a home that was rarely quiet. Chris wouldn't have it any other way.

Once they had their cones in hand, he led Sera back outside, armed with a plethora of napkins. Sera had inherited Ella's clumsiness as well.

His cell phone rang.

"Hey, beautiful," he answered.

"Hey, beautiful yourself. What is my man up to?"

"Oh, you know, spoiling our perfect daughter, as usual."

"More ice cream, Chris? It's freezing outside."

"Builds character. Besides, she's got a jacket on. No worries, Mommy," he teased, listening to Ella's laughter on the other end. A sound he would never tire of. "I also made my famous spaghetti sauce."

"My heart. Have I mentioned how much I love that my man spoils me and my daughter so wonderfully?"

"'Yes, but don't let that stop you from telling him again."

"I adore you," Ella whispered and sighed.

"Good, because I'm obsessed with you. Now get your butt home. It's spaghetti night." This announcement had Sera cheering, then repeatedly chanting *'Spaghetti!'* in the background. "Maybe even a little dessert after our little one goes to sleep."

"But you've already had your ice cream."

"Say the word, and I'll bring some home to eat off of you. Better yet, you can eat it off me."

Ella laughed again. "Sounds like a plan. Love you. Forever and always."

"Love you back. See you soon."

Chris got up from the bench and wiped ice cream smudges off Sera's face and hands.

"Mommy is on her way home. Are you ready to go?" He ruffled her hair, making her giggle as he took her by the hand and led her back toward the car.

"Hey, did you know that your nose is smarter than your brain? It has more scents."

"You're so silly, Daddy," Sera laughed, skipping over the cracks in the sidewalk. "Do you *have* to go to work tonight?"

"No. I can stay home, and you can do my hair and makeup. Make me look pretty for Mommy."

"Nooo. Makeup *is* for Mommy."

"Okay then, I can do your hair and makeup."

"Nooo. Last time you tried to do my hair, it took Mommy a really long time to fix it," Sera said and laughed again.

"Oh man, I guess I better go to work since I'm not good at doing girly things."

"You are good at doing things! You're really good at teaching me how to play baseball and how to ride bikes. I only fell two times. And then you were good at making my knee ouchie stop hurting right after. Your magic kisses are even better than Mommy's. And you tell the best stories. You do all the voices and everything. And you are a really good singer."

Chris stopped short and put his hand over his heart. His daughter's compliments brought love, so intense, so pure, to the surface. Nothing Chris could have ever done, not even if he would have won the World Series, would have brought on the pride his heart felt at that moment.

If nothing else, he'd gotten this right.

"Why, those are the sweetest things anybody has ever said to me. Makes me tear right up," he exaggerated, wiping fake tears away, though real tears did arise.

He reached down and pulled her into a hug. When the threat of actual tears passed, he kissed the top of her head and let her go to open the car door.

He waited as his little girl crawled into the car and tried her hardest to independently buckle the seatbelt, which she didn't quite have enough strength to buckle yet, but insisted on trying to do herself every time. After a few seconds, Chris laughed and leaned in to help her.

CHAPTER EIGHTY

Jordan

MUIR WOODS

"Daddy?" the girl kept calling out, her giant blue eyes full of tears, full of fear. "Where is he?" her little voice quaked.

To keep her calm, I had promised her that her daddy would be waiting for us at the cabin. Of course, he wasn't, but I couldn't stand this little girl's screaming, crying, and quivering lips.

It was making the beast scratch and pull at me. I needed her calm and quiet. I needed the quiet to think, to hear my own thoughts.

"I told you he'll be meeting us here," I snapped at her. I couldn't help it, those pathetic, scared eyes were unnerving me.

The girl flinched and ran to the far corner of the single room, crouching down, making herself as small as possible, trying to get as far from me as she could, her eyes darting around, looking for an escape like a wild thing.

"You...you said he would already be here." More tears, and now hiccups between cries. "I want my...my daddy."

"You'll be back with him soon. Just stop that. I'm not going to hurt you." I knew she wasn't going to believe me since she had seen me point the small pistol I got just for today at her grandmother when she tried to refuse to give up her phone, then when I had to use the taser on her to knock her out. That old lady still had some fight left in her. "This won't be for long. You're a kid. Kids can endure anything for a little while. I withstood a lot more for a lot longer."

But the girl wouldn't calm down. She kept looking at me with that terror, a terror that shook me to my soul.

I knew that look. I knew that fear. At the same age, I lived it every single day of my life. I was her. But this time, it was *me* who was doing the terrifying.

I couldn't stand the child looking at me like that any longer.

"Okay. Okay, let's get you home. Come here." I forced my calmest, most friendly tone, even though my head was screaming, battling with my demons. I beckoned for her to come to me.

"I can go home now?" her little voice hiccupped, those eyes so full of hope. Finally, she stopped crying. She stood from her protective corner, slowly approaching me.

When she was within my reach, I pulled her in, and with the least amount of force possible, I held the rag I had soaked with chloroform against her mouth and nose. I'd found some hidden in this cabin ages ago. That stuff was so old I'm sure it had become toxic by now. But it gave me the idea to stock some—which was surprisingly easy to get my hands on—in case I ever needed it.

Her big blue eyes looked at me with such betrayal. She struggled against me, kicked, hit, screamed, cried. I wanted to cry with her. Her tears broke me. I didn't want her to remember. I didn't want her nightmares to be of me. It would be over for her soon enough.

"Don't do that. I'm not going to hurt you. Stop. JUST STOP FIGHTING ME!"

Finally, the girl went limp in my arms. I carefully laid her next to her grandmother.

A scream erupted from deep within.

I beat my fists to my head, trying to pound out the warping of her face into my own. This was not my purpose. I *was* the hurt child. I was supposed to be the protector that had never come for me. I would not do what had been done to me, or I would be no better than Grandmother. No better at all.

My mind wasn't where it should be. I knew that I needed this little girl sleeping in front of me to get to Sera. I only wanted Sera.

Sera was the one to blame for all of this. If she had just faced me, woman to woman, and not run and hid like she always did, I wouldn't have had to stoop this low, and I wouldn't have had to involve this child.

Sera would pay dearly for this, too.

It took too long to pull myself together when time was dangerously short.

Sera had been right about one thing, this place, this cabin, was just a reminder of my father's choices. I stood there for a moment, leering at the cabin around me. I've already planned to get rid of it. I had hoped it would be with Sera in it, but I want—no, *need*—to enact a much more extensive punishment for her.

She would finally pay the cost of getting everything.

I got out the gas cans I brought and soaked the outer walls. When the time comes, I will throw the old kerosene lantern that I'd also found in the cabin at the walls that shaped my fate. I will watch the fire eat away all of the misery this place gave to me. This was *his* place, the place he came to leave us behind.

I lit the kerosene lamp and placed it next to the cabin.

I heard running steps nearby. It was almost time.

CHAPTER EIGHTY-ONE

Sera

MUIR WOODS

Sera had been a runner for years but discovered she was no sprinter that day. Once they got to Muir Woods, fallen trees and water runoff had taken out most of the service road to the cabin, so they'd had to go by foot from a distance away.

Sera ducked under trees as she ran, branches slapping her face, trying not to trip or roll an ankle, the detective following close. Daylight was slipping away from them, darkening their surroundings, making the path harder to see, reminiscent of when she had run through this forest long ago.

The cabin loomed ahead in the distance, its dilapidated sides sagging with the horrors it held.

As they approached without a minute to spare, Detective Pardou gestured to Sera and then quietly ran off in the opposite direction. As soon as he left her side, fear started to overshadow adrenaline. She was back in these woods, back at *that* cabin.

She shook the fear away. If Ava wasn't there, somewhere, Sera might not have been able to fight the urge to shrink away, back into the black pit of horror. She might have turned and run far from here. Instead, she pressed on, death itself being the only thing that would stop her from getting to Ava.

The closer Sera got to the cabin, the stronger she felt Jordan, the madness and wrath lurking. Sera slowed, walking out of the trees and into the clearing at the mouth of the cabin door.

"I'm here! Get out here and face me!" Sera's voice shook, out of breath and full of rage.

"Nothing like waiting until the last second. Tick tock, Sera. You almost lost." There was no movement seen, no hovering shadow, just the sound of Jordan's voice echoing off of the trees.

"Where is she?" There was no answer. "Where is Ava, damn it!"

"No need to get crazy, now."

"This isn't one of your games, Jordan. This is a *child*. Take me to her, you sadistic bitch!"

"Now, now, language."

"I swear I will rip you apart with my bare hands."

"Who knew you had been holstering so much violence, sweet little scaredy-cat Sera."

"Please, take me. I'll stay. Let Ava go." There was no response. "She has nothing to do with any of this. Please! Please let her go before you do something you might actually regret. Where is she?" Sera was screaming. She couldn't help the waver in her voice. The tears she couldn't hold back sapped the power out of her words, desperation echoing through the otherwise deafeningly silent woods.

"You're right. Those two have nothing to do with my purpose. That's what you're here for. Ava is nice and safe inside. As much as you'd like to think, I'm not a monster."

"Ava!" Sera wouldn't waste any more time. It didn't matter where Jordan hid, she just had to get to Ava. She started running toward the cabin, the place where all of her nightmares began, her hands trembling, her mind wanting to retreat, hide from this place, the place where she'd dragged herself out of, the place that held the last moments of her mother's life. But she refused to let Ava succumb to the same fate.

She heard footsteps run up behind her.

Sera spun, saw Jordan running toward her, a metal object in her hand.

Sera lifted her arms in defense, hitting at Jordan in an attempt to deflect the object. The cold metal grazed her arm before it flew out of Jordan's hand. The shock zapped through Sera's body, freezing her limbs for a moment.

Still, she wrestled with Jordan as much as her body would allow. Sera wasn't about to go down without expending every ounce of fight she had. Sera kicked, scratched, and tore at the eyes of the woman she'd once trusted enough to call friend, anything she could do to get away and get to Ava.

"Ava!" Sera's tone betrayed her. It had lost its fierceness and instead wavered with emotion. She couldn't hold the tears back from her voice or from pouring down her face.

The bushes started to rustle nearby.

CHAPTER EIGHTY-TWO

Ella

ALAMEDA ISLAND

Spring rarely brought warm temperatures to the island. It was a chilly evening, but Chris had taken Sera out for ice cream. Ella couldn't help but laugh at the shared addiction between father and daughter. It could be snowing outside, and the two of them would still be guzzling down ice cream.

Her daughter also inherited Chris's sense of adventure and was always a willing participant in any of her father's antics. The two of them were always conspiring to whisk Ella away from her books and the hours of grueling studying she was always doing. Most of the time, it was a welcome distraction.

Always mindful of Ella's precious little time, Chris kept their adventures short and sweet. She hoped that Sera would keep that adventurous spirit.

If she allowed herself to fantasize, Ella could definitely imagine a long and happy life with Chris. God knew he'd asked enough over the years.

Ella wasn't ashamed to admit that she loved the look and feel of the pretty ring on her finger. She never wore it to the hospital, afraid to lose it. Even though it had only been a few weeks since she had said yes, she already felt the absence of the ring when she didn't wear it.

As she came to a stop at a light on her way home, an abrupt, cold fear surged through her. Her entire body began to tremble as absolute doom pressed down on her. The moment the light turned green, she accelerated, driving as fast as she dared.

She had to get to them. She needed to get to her daughter.

When she swung into the driveway, Chris's car was in its usual spot, and he was still sitting inside.

Bizarre.

The feeling wouldn't subside as she quickly pulled into the open garage, her fingers shaking so badly she almost dropped the keys from the ignition. She looked in the rearview mirror.

Chris didn't get out of the car, his 49er cap tucked low, looking downward. He was probably just on his cell phone.

Still, the dread didn't ease.

She prayed that her wobbly legs would support her as she got out of the car and walked over. When she got to the open driver's side window, she saw her daughter sprawled across the front seat, asleep, her head on the lap of a man who was *not* Chris, a knife to her baby girl's throat.

"Don't even think about screaming, or she's dead."

Ella's body stopped quivering.

This was the moment she'd dreaded her entire life. This was how it would end for her.

Whatever happened to her, whatever she did, she refused to let it include her daughter's life.

She quietly went to the passenger side, got in, and softly closed the door. Finally, Ella saw the face under Chris's ball cap.

"You."

"You remember me. Of course, you would. You felt it, too, our connection. I knew you did." Jeffrey Mason started the car and slowly backed out of the driveway to avoid drawing attention to them.

Once they were safely past the toll road cameras of I-580, he took the knife away from Sera's throat and threw the cap onto the floorboard, his slightly overgrown, thinning hair slick across his moist forehead.

Ella gathered her daughter up, clutching her closely, willing her arms to keep Sera safe, no matter the cost.

"What did you give her?" Ella's voice growled low and dangerous.

"That is what I have grown to love most about you. Mama Bear, first and foremost. The intelligence is a welcome bonus. Don't get me wrong, your beauty can't be compared, but anyone can be beautiful. Most of those with beauty let it lead their lives. But not you. Don't worry, Mama Bear, it is just the smallest amount of chloroform. She should be waking up soon." Jeffrey reached over to stroke Sera's knee.

Ella yanked Sera away from his touch. "You will not touch my daughter. I will kill you first."

"I'd be very careful if I were you. You're not exactly in any position to negotiate terms. If you want to continue such a blessed life and you want Sera to continue her happy existence, you will listen carefully. There are rules, and you will follow them precisely. Little Sera here has some of your fire, so getting her to understand these rules might take some work. I'm getting ahead of myself. We will get into all that later. For now, you're going to take that cloth there and take a few nice deep breaths. I don't want you to ruin the surprise. I've worked really hard to make it worthy of my new family."

"I'd rather stay awake."

With a disappointed sigh, Jeffrey yanked the steering wheel hard right to the side of the road and slammed the brakes, sending debris and dirt flying. In one fluid movement, he reached over, grabbed a handful of Sera's hair, yanked her out of Ella's arms, putting the knife back to Sera's throat.

He had been fast, too fast. Faster than Ella expected. She wouldn't make the mistake of underestimating him again.

"No!" Ella grabbed for Sera, trying to pull her back. A bead of blood appeared as the knife pierced Sera's delicate skin and slowly rolled down her throat.

"See what you made me do?"

Ella let go. "Don't hurt my baby. Please."

"What did I just get finished telling you?" The knife cut deeper, another bead of blood.

"I'll follow your rules. I will, I promise. Please stop. You're cutting her," she whimpered as tears began to fall. The complete terror of not being able to protect her child broke her will of defiance. Sera's well-being was more important than anything else. Ella would do whatever he wanted as long as it kept Sera safe.

"Consequences of breaking the rules will not be pleasant. Not for me, either. I don't want to hurt you or little Sera. I love you both. But I will punish you. Is that clear?"

"Crystal."

Jeffrey pushed Sera back into Ella's arms, watching her, waiting for her to comply.

Ella kissed Sera's forehead, took the cloth from Jeffrey, and placed it over her mouth and nose, breathing in deeply until she was light-headed and drifted away.

CHAPTER EIGHTY-THREE

Erinne

SAN FRANCISCO

I t was a rare sunny spring morning in Ireland, warm enough to open the windows and let fresh air circulate through the rooms as Erinne applied a fresh coat of paint in one of the suites, readying Lantern Light for the summer.

The birds sang their songs, the breeze whispered through the grass, and the ocean crashed in the distance.

Though it was still early spring, repairs needed to be made, orders filled, and rooms perfected before the tourist crowds started coming back.

Her cell phone rang.

Smiling, Erinne placed the roller in the tray to retrieve her phone from her back pocket, expecting it to finally be Ella calling with some wild story about where she had been the past couple of days.

They communicated, in some way, every day. A call, a letter, a Skype session on the computer. But too much time had passed, and Ella was still AWOL, which worried Erinne.

The only thing that stopped Erinne from calling Alameda Island's police department to do a wellness check was that once in a while, Chris could coax Ella away from her studies and take her and Sera on one of his adventures. Those trips were always short and sweet, as extra time was sparse, and Ella didn't have much time away from school or the hospital.

Ella would always tell Erinne when they'd be gone. Until this time, that is.

It had definitely been too long.

Erinne flipped open her cell phone and looked at the number calling. It was from the San Francisco area, but not a number she recognized. An ominous chill pierced her body as she answered.

Her worst nightmare had become real, something Erinne had never wanted to think about, even got angry at Ella every time she mentioned it over the decades. Though Ella had insisted this would eventually come, nothing could've prepared Erinne for the moment she received the worst news of her life.

Almost stumbling down the stairs, Erinne made her way into the kitchen, where her mother was prepping the next day's menus.

"They found Chris...Chris's body. He's, he's gone..." As soon as she saw her mother, Erinne couldn't hold back the sobs.

"What? What are you saying? Dear God." Annabelle caught Erinne in her arms, sinking with her to the cold kitchen floor, wrapping herself with her daughter, and wept with her.

When Brian walked into the kitchen and found them, he joined them, tears and all, when he heard the news of his friend's fate.

"We have a little room on the credit card to get you to San Francisco. I wish we could go with you," Annabelle said as she helped Erinne pack a suitcase so that she could catch her flight back to the States.

"You're doing enough. I'm sorry to leave you without help."

"Nonsense. God willing, those girls are okay. You go, be the beacon of light for our girls to find their way back home to."

"What if..." Erinne couldn't let herself finish the words that stuck in her throat. If she said them out loud, it might make it come true, and she didn't want to think about that possibility. Not yet.

"No. Don't think it. She is strong."

"Ella always said...Damn it." Erinne stopped folding, dropping to the bed, and crying again.

"Ella was wrong sometimes, too." Annabelle wiped the tears from her own face as she went to Erinne's side. She took her by the shoulders, forcing Erinne to look up at her. "Ella was wrong sometimes, too."

Erinne nodded, took a few deep breaths, and started packing again.

Ella *had* been wrong at times, but something in her heart told her that Ella wouldn't be so lucky to be wrong this time.

Erinne had been at Ella's house for two days, which meant the sun was now setting on the sixth day since Ella and Sera had gone missing. Police had conducted daily searches, complete with search dogs, but no one had found any trace of them.

The last hints of hope were fraying at the ends. However, she couldn't lose faith now. She had to hold on to any atom she could to get through. Erinne could still feel Ella, her best friend, her sister, soulmate. Ella couldn't be gone, she had to believe that.

Erinne wrapped herself in a blanket on the couch and turned on the news, hoping for any shred of information. As report after report drudged on with nothing new on Ella or Sera, Erinne turned the TV off. She couldn't stand all the evil in the world, and the news was full of it, one story after another, of the horrendous things people did to each other.

She'd make tea instead.

While waiting for the kettle to boil, a wave of cold grief blasted her.

"No. No. No. No."

Again, Erinne found herself on the kitchen floor. Her body trembled as she emptied a wail of the worst pain she had ever had in her life.

She cried for the little girl who had so easily befriended her, who she played Barbies with, laughed, and grew up with. For the teenager who she stumbled through boys, clothes, hair, and makeup with. For the woman who had been an inspiration, between conquering college and becoming a mother. For all of the laughter and tears they'd shed through a lifetime together. Erinne cried for the smile she would never see again.

Even after her tears stopped, Erinne stayed on the kitchen floor. She'd sat there so long that both legs were numb when she jumped up to get her phone when it rang.

She didn't want to answer it. It wouldn't be real if she didn't answer the call, it wouldn't be true. The phone stopped ringing. A few seconds later, the notification for a voicemail dinged. Then the phone started ringing again.

"Yes?" the single word croaked out.

"Erinne Byrne?" a deep official sounding voice asked.

"Yes."

"This is Officer Stan Walters. We found Sera. She's been taken to Merin General Hospital. You're her guardian, right? We'll need you to meet us there as soon as possible."

"Sera. She's...she's alive?" Erinne stuttered, the oddest sense of joy, relief, and utter grief twisting like a tornado in her gut, especially when she heard the word *"guardian."*

"She is. Can you be at the hospital within the hour?"

"Yes. Yes, I'll leave immediately."

She couldn't ask about Ella, Not yet. She had to focus on Sera and concentrate on doing the next thing, which was to get to her.

Sera was *alive*.

Erinne should call her mother to let her know, but she didn't want to delay getting to Sera for one second longer.

The parking lot was full of news vans and cop cars, red and blue lights swirling, illuminating the entire lot. Erinne's legs wouldn't move as fast as she wanted them to as she ran into the hospital emergency room entrance. Inside, several uniformed officers were waiting.

"I'm Erinne Byrne. I'm here for Sera Delaney."

One of the officers stepped forward, holding out his hand. "I'm Officer Walters. I spoke to you on the phone. Let's go over here to talk." He took her to the ER doors, stopping before going through. "We got a call from a family off Hwy 1. They found Sera in the road. She is scared, and she isn't talking."

Nodding, Erinne snipped, "Just take me to her." Erinne couldn't stop wringing her hands together. One over the other, again and again.

He led her through the ER doors and past several waiting would-be patients on chairs. The constant beeping, monitors alarming, an overhead operator announcing codes and other urgent-sounding events booming over the moans of dire-looking people on gurney after gurney put Erinne's nerves on overload. The odor of antiseptic mixed with god only knew what thickened the air with illness, the room's warmth dizzying.

Sera was back here, all alone, with all of these sick people. She had to get her out of there.

As they walked past a nurse's station, a nurse popped up from her seat to join them.

"I'm Julie. I'm the nurse who has been taking care of little Miss Sera. I'll take you to her. I want to update you before we go in. Our forensic nurse has just brought her back from the evidence extraction procedure. She wanted to stay with Sera until you were able to get here. I also want to warn you that it might be shocking when you see Sera. She's been through a lot. She is quite traumatized and won't talk to any of us," the nurse said, stopping in front of the closed curtain. "I'll let the doctor know you're here so she can update you on everything that is going on with Sera." Then she slowly opened the curtain.

Another nurse was sitting next to Sera, holding her hand. When she saw Erinne, she nodded, then got up to give them privacy.

All of the oxygen left Erinne's lungs. She had to restrain herself from gasping out loud.

Sera was in a hospital gown, finger-sized bruises all over her arms and legs, one leg twisted, swollen, and terribly purple. Abrasions branded her wrists and ankles, old blood caked around the ligature marks, new bruises blossomed over her little face, fading yellow-green ones marked the skin underneath.

"Oh, baby." Erinne rushed over and sat on her bed, pulling Sera into her arms, rocking with her, holding her as close as she could.

The tears came from Erinne's soul, anguish so deep, anger so fierce that Erinne now knew why people were acquitted by temporary insanity. If the person who did this walked in at that moment, she would not hesitate to murder the bastard with her bare hands in front of everyone here, including the policemen who were still standing around.

"Miss Byrne?" A woman wearing a white coat popped her head through the curtain. "I'm Dr. Moore. Can I have a minute?"

Erinne kissed Sera's cheeks and forehead. "I'll be right back, okay?" Sera didn't respond. She didn't look up. She hadn't even put her arms around Erinne when she held her. Sera just sat there.

"First, I wanted to extend my deepest sympathy." The doctor then began explaining the extent of Sera's injuries, telling her that a nurse specializing in forensics had been called in to gather evidence and assess Sera's internal injuries.

Internal injuries.

Erinne's worst fears were confirmed in those words.

The next several minutes were filled with a laundry list of all of Sera's other physical injuries, including results of X-rays, CT scans, lab results, and possible surgery on the broken leg, after which Doctor Moore finally said, "I strongly recommend that she also work with therapists for her emotional needs."

Erinne stood empty in a hallway full of other people. Her mind went numb. She couldn't think, couldn't speak. The child needed an immense amount of medical and psychiatric care, and she was now *her* responsibility. Scheduling all of the appointments, ensuring that Sera got the care she needed, making sure it all got done, making all of the decisions. The weight of it all now rested on Erinne's shoulders.

She looked over at Officer Walters, who was still standing at the nurses' station. She'd never be ready, but Erinne needed to hear it said out loud. She walked over to the officer, looked him in the eyes, and asked, "Have you found Ella, Sera's mother?"

The officer hesitated, looking away.

"Please. I have to know."

"I'm sorry, she didn't survive."

If he'd punched her in the stomach, it would have felt the same.

Erinne nodded, swallowing the sob that wanted to erupt from her. "When...when can I have her back?"

"Her body will be held until the investigation is complete. Then someone from the coroner's office will contact you and ask what your wishes are." The officer awkwardly put his hand on Erinne's shoulder. "I'm sorry for your loss."

Erinne nodded again because she had no idea what else to do. She couldn't lose it now, not with Sera so close by. She needed to be at her strongest to help Sera get through the hell she'd just been through.

Erinne would do that for Ella.

Erinne would do whatever it took, however long it took, to help Ella's daughter heal, to recover.

Once upon a time, Erinne had promised her best friend that she would take care of her most precious gift, the child Erinne watched come into this world.

It would be a long, hard road, but Erinne wouldn't rest if that's what it took to make sure she kept her promise to her sister, the best person she had ever known.

CHAPTER EIGHTY-FOUR

Jordan

MUIR WOODS

Running footsteps were closing in fast.

There he is, one of her brave knights.

I pulled Sera up against me to shield myself as I pulled the gun from my back pocket.

The detective charged out of the woods, his gun aimed at me.

Sera was still fighting, even though half of her body was unresponsive. She had just enough control to kick out and move my arm an inch, the recoil of the gun knocking me off balance. I had to step back to catch both of us, but not before I accidentally kicked the kerosene lamp, sending it flying into the side of the cabin.

Everything happened at once.

The sound of the shot exploded through the forest, the loud crack rung my ears, the sudden red splash of blood across the detective's chest, Sera screaming, the side of the cabin almost immediately catching, burning.

Fuck.

Sera was still screaming when I hit the back of her head with the pistol, sending her into blackness.

There wasn't much time. I had a choice to make.

I dropped the now unconscious Sera to the floor and ran back to the cabin. The only door was already engulfed in flames. I ran to the other side, toward a semi-boarded-up window, and looked inside. The little girl was still sound asleep. I dropped the gun to pull the boards away with my hands, then climbed into the fire-consumed cabin.

The smoke burned my eyes and constricted my lungs. Flames danced around and above us, quickly spreading to the window I'd just come through. I picked up the little girl, pushed her out of the window, and climbed out after her.

The old woman would have to be a sacrifice. I didn't mean for her to get hurt, but I didn't have enough time for both.

I placed the little girl in the tree line where she should be safe from the fire. Besides, I knew that her father couldn't be too far behind Sera and the detective. I'm actually surprised he wasn't with Sera to begin with.

I ran back over, coughing, my chest burning, and grabbed Sera, dragging her away to a spot where we would have the time and privacy that I needed to finish this once and for all.

I pulled Sera as far as the burning in my lungs allowed me to. That, and the creek stopped me from dragging her any further.

I watched her for a while. There was precious little time to do what I needed to do, but I couldn't help it. I had hated this person for as long as I could remember. But I had also loved her.

She'd become my friend, an actual friend. She hadn't known who I was, so she let me into her world. She had been kind, talked to me about personal things, things that I knew, myself, were hard to vocalize. We shared moments and time. We laughed together. Real laughter. I hadn't pretended any of that.

But when she found out who I was born as, she left me. All those years of friendship she threw away and took everything away from me. I was five years old again.

I knelt down, slapped her a couple of times, and then splashed her with cold water from the creek to rouse her.

Sera's eyes fluttered open.

"Why did he love you more than me?"

"What? Who? Where is Ava?"

I slapped Sera again harder. I couldn't help it. The anger was boiling over. The beast pacing, ready for its long-awaited reward.

Sera backed up against the tree, rubbing her head, trying to catch her breath. She was pathetic. I hate her more now than I ever had.

"All these years, I blamed myself. I wasn't good enough. I could have done this or that. But none of that was ever true. I wasn't to blame at all. You are."

"Then why didn't you just kill me that first day? Why wait? If it's all my fault and you hate me so much, why let me live? Isn't that what this is all about—me?"

"See, therein lies the problem. This is not about *you*. It is about *me*. For once in my life, *I* was normal. I had a friend, I even had lovers. In class I was respected for my brain, people talked to me, laughed with me. For the first time, I wasn't *that Mason girl*. I wasn't some pariah. Killing you meant killing that life. You were worth less than that. But you're right. Maybe I made the wrong decision. If I'd done away with you in those first weeks, hidden your body here, I might have been able to stay Peyton. I could have had a career, one that meant something. I could have had a real life. And now you've taken that from me again. Why? Why can't you just let me be? You never bother seeing anyone else around you, what you're doing to them, how everything you do affects the rest of us. *That* is what this is all about, making sure you pay for everything you've been given. *Why did he love you more than he loved me?*" I screamed, some of my spittle hitting her face.

"Jordan, your father didn't love me. He didn't love my mother. He was obsessed with her. Obsession isn't love."

"I don't give a shit what you try to call it."

"Why do you blame *me* for what your father did? I was a child. It wasn't my choice. It wasn't my fault. And it wasn't your fault either." Sera was yelling back at me now.

"Stop psycho-babbling me." Shaking my head, I lunged, grabbed her by the neck, pressing her against the tree.

"The truth is not psycho-babble. I was just a kid when your father kidnapped my mother and me. When your father killed *my* father, when he raped and killed my mother. Jordan, I was *six years old* when your father raped me. Do you think I *wanted* any of that? None of us had a choice. Just like you never had the choice in your father leaving, and it wasn't *your* choice to have a family who did terrible things to you. I am truly sorry you had that for your life. None of it was fair." Tears were now pouring down Sera's face.

"He didn't! He wouldn't have done that to a child....You're lying. Lying all the way to the end. Making up stories to tell the media to tarnish his name. What the fuck do *you* know about fair?" I sneered.

This was it, my vengeance due, my purpose would be fulfilled. It would all finally be over. I held her by the throat with one hand as I pulled the dagger from my boot with my other. I held it as high as I could to be able to bring it down with as much force as possible to match the fury that was consuming me.

"I'm not lying, Jordan, and you know it. This isn't who I met in the dorm. That girl was sweet, funny, bubbly, and so damn smart. Where did that girl go? Where are *you*?" Sera's tears kept coming.

She was looking at me in a way that started to prick at me. It was a different kind of hurt I saw in her eyes. Not the physical kind, but the kind of hurt I remember feeling when I would look at my mother and wonder why she hated me.

And then Sera's eyes started to brighten as she looked at me—no, she was looking into me—as she put her hand on my chest, over my heart.

Those memories of all that I had escaped came hurdling back. Those people, that hell house. A social worker at the hospital, holding my hand as I wept, my wrists bandaged and sore, as I told him of the terror we grew up in.

But I found my brother in that alley.

"That wasn't your brother. None of those people were them. They weren't the family who betrayed you. They were just people who looked like them. Can you remember Jordan? Your mother passed away from cancer when you were twenty-one. That's when you tried to take your own life. I was there with you when you tried to kill yourself. That hurt so raw, so desperate." Sera's eyes kept changing, the green of them so bright, they were practically glowing.

"I know that there is no way you could have known, but your brother overdosed when he was nineteen. He died that day. The man you saw in the alley wasn't your brother. He was just another lost man. Can you remember his face, the man in the alley? Can you see that it wasn't your brother?" Her eyes grew brighter still.

"Your grandmother died about five years ago, not long after you left that house. Your sister, Judith, is still alive. She lives back in Arkansas. She moved back there after your grandmother died. She wants to see you, Jordan. She wants to find you, get reacquainted."

"No. No. You're just trying to mind-fuck me. GET OUT OF MY HEAD!" I let go of her throat, pressing my fists to my temples, the dagger still gripped tight.

My brother's face morphed into the face of the stranger in the alley, then back to his. But that wasn't true. It couldn't be.

I saw myself slowly walking to the door at the end of the hallway. Behind it was my decaying mother, gasping, dying. The nurse smiling at me when I would go into that room that smelled of rot, of urine, of disease. My mother's gray face interchanged with the woman from the bus. So similar.

No. My mother had escaped. She hadn't died in that back room. I *saw* her. *Didn't I?*

"It wasn't your mother. It was a woman named Julie Gorgio. I have never lied to you, ever. We all have darkness in us. We all have those moments when those lies seem so real. They seem to overtake us, taking our will, taking our choice. But there is *always* a choice. Every day is a chance to start over. You don't want the rest of your life to be led by hate. I can help get you the help you need."

"Why would you want to do that? If all of this is true, why would you do that for me?"

"Why wouldn't I? You deserve a second chance. Hell, a first chance." Sera's eyes dimmed back to their normal hue as they refocused on my face.

I felt my own tears sting my eyes. "How did this happen?" I couldn't think. I couldn't see what was real.

She'd been in my head and taken me into hers. I'd seen what she'd seen, felt what she felt. She wasn't wrong, and if she wasn't wrong, then what had I done? My thoughts ran round and round in my head.

What is wrong with me? Why can't I just be okay? Why can't I just be normal?

"Get away from her!" Adam yelled, running out from the trees, heading straight for me.

CHAPTER EIGHTY-FIVE

Adam

MUIR WOODS

The black blanket of night made it almost impossible for Adam to see. Twigs and branches struck and scratched as he ran through the wild brush. Air pushed and squeezed through his lungs as he gasped in and out, the orange glow of the sky guiding him to his daughter, to Sera. He'd jumped from the still-moving police sedan when they'd come to a rough road that wouldn't let them get up to the speed Adam desperately needed to get to his family.

His body wanted to stop, his own weight making his legs protest. He cursed himself for spending more time behind a desk than at the gym. Pure determination pushed him on.

As Adam raced to the fire-engulfed cabin, a gleam in the dirt caught his eye, making him stop short. Sera's necklace. The diamond lightning bolt and amethyst locket Sera never took off was lying in the dirt next to drag marks. He snatched it up and put it in his pocket.

Then he heard a low moan.

He looked toward the noise and saw Detective Pardou lying in a pool of blood. "Detective."

"Where's that dirty shit?" he coughed.

"I don't know. Where did it hit?" Adam tried to pull away his shirt, but the blood was already drenched through. He pulled off his own button-up shirt, balled it up, and held it to where the blood seemed to be coming from.

"It's just my shoulder."

It wasn't just his shoulder. It was low and central to his collarbone. Adam was no doctor, but it wasn't the no-big-deal wound that the detective was trying to pass off.

"Did you see them? My daughter?"

"No. I didn't see Ava," Detective Pardou coughed again, blood spittle sprayed over his face.

This couldn't be happening. Adam's mind began to fog over with grief.

"Daddy?" The smallest, sweetest voice sounded from the tree line.

Adam jumped up and ran over. His little girl, his miracle, sat up, rubbing her eyes as if waking up from a nap.

"Are you okay? Are you hurt? Where does it hurt?" Adam picked Ava up, gathering her into his chest, sobbing with gratitude.

"I'm not hurt." Dirt and soot smudged her face, dried tear streaks stained her cheeks.

"I'm so sorry I left you. I'm so sorry." Relief, guilt, joy, and the worst fear he'd ever felt tightened his chest.

"She took Sera. That's the last thing I saw before the bitch shot me." Detective Pardou was trying to move, his face graying from the loss of blood.

Adam wasn't sure how much longer the detective would be conscious. Taking Ava with him, Adam reached down and replaced the shirt against the wound.

"Hold this," Adam said as he placed the detective's hand over the now blood-soaked shirt. Two officers ran into the clearing. Then another two ran in from the other direction, a fire crew following, a helicopter whomping above them. Paramedics were also already on scene. It seemed to have become a war zone in mere minutes.

"There is a woman inside," one of the firemen called out from the backside of the cabin. A group started to hack away at a wall. Moments later, they pulled Victoria from the blaze.

Still holding Ava, Adam ran over. "Is she alright? Victoria, can you hear me?"

Victoria's eyes fluttered in response. Before she could try to speak, an oxygen mask was placed over her mouth and nose.

"Sorry, sir, we have to get her out of here."

Adam nodded and watched as his mother-in-law was strapped to a stretcher and whisked away. His eyes darted between his daughter, the detective, his mother-in-law, and the drag marks along the forest floor. He heard K9 units approaching.

"The mean lady has Sera?" Ava's cries started again, new tears spilling over.

Adam nodded, then held his daughter close, stroking her hair down her back.

"Aren't you going to go get her, Daddy?"

"I'm staying here with you, sweetie. Keep you safe." He looked at his little girl, who was still trembling in his arms.

"Who's gonna keep Sera safe?" Ava hiccupped between sniffles. Adam looked back at the drag marks leading out into the woods.

"We have officers out there looking, sir. Not a good idea to run off all renegade again." Officer Abraham Matthews, the officer who had driven Adam into Muir Woods, walked up behind him as if he knew what he was contemplating.

"Yeah, but will you get to her in time?" Adam's last words fell away, his breath catching in his throat. It couldn't happen again. The universe couldn't be that cruel.

"Daddy?" Ava pulled at his t-shirt.

"Yeah, baby?"

"I *am* safe now. There are lots of police here. We can't let that mean lady hurt Sera."

Adam's mind and heart tore him into two halves.

"Sir?" Officer Matthews' voice took on a warning tone.

Adam put Ava down and kneeled down to look eye-to-eye with her. "Are you okay with staying with this officer?"

Ava nodded her little head, hugged him tight, then took Officer Matthews' hand as she wiped the tears from her cheeks, putting on her best brave face.

The fright on her face she tried so hard to hide boiled a rage in Adam that he'd never felt in his life. This monster took his daughter, a precious innocent, just because she could. And now she had the woman he loved.

"Sir, don't..."

"Keep her safe."

As Adam ran off toward the drag marks, he heard Officer Matthews call out on his radio for an available unit to follow him. He stopped listening, focusing instead on those drag marks that made his blood run ice cold. He wouldn't think about how his stomach was in his toes or how his heart seemed to stop beating.

He had to believe in Sera. At her core, she was a fighter and would fight to the very end.

Frantically trying to find his way through pitch-black darkness without falling or twisting an ankle, Adam heard K9 dogs not far from him. Hearing their unrelenting howls brought a newfound confidence. If Adam couldn't find Sera, those dogs would, and they were certainly faster than he was.

Finally, he heard raised voices, both female. Adam picked up his speed, following the sound of Sera's angry and very much alive voice.

When he found them in a small clearing by a creek, Adam saw Jordan straddled in front of Sera, a dagger in her hand.

His fury erased every rational thought from his mind as he screamed out and ran full force into Jordan. Something stung his side, setting his abdomen on fire as they both crashed to the ground.

Adam wrestled with Jordan, reaching to get a grip on her wrist, but she was quick and a lot stronger than he expected.

Jordan kicked Adam back, jumped on top of him, brought up the dagger she still had in her hand, and thrust it down.

Adam barely moved fast enough as the knife came down, missing the center of his chest, hitting the soft crevice under his left shoulder instead, rendering it useless. Jordan screamed out as she struck down again, this time grazing Adam's neck. Adam fought, pushing at her with his one arm, feeling his body start to weaken.

"Drop it! Drop your weapon," an officer's voice boomed from behind them. Ignoring the warning, Jordan took up the dagger again.

Adam heard the shot ring out. A hole in Jordan's shoulder exploded, blood splattered his face, the dagger dropped to the floor next to him. Jordan grabbed her arm and started to run.

The excited barks of the K9 dog suddenly stopped as the dog charged Jordan, taking her leg in its mouth and shaking it with violent efficiency.

Adam watched as Jordan crashed face-first into the dirt, the officer running up, cuffing her hands behind her.

Jordan was crying.

The K9 dog was barking in triumph.

The black spots in his vision took over, and Adam lost consciousness.

CHAPTER EIGHTY-SIX

Sera

MUIR WOODS

Sera could only watch as the scene unfolded in front of her. Everything was happening in slow motion: Adam tackling Jordan, the two of them falling to the floor, the gleam of metal vanishing into Adam, and then the vigilant barking of a dog.

Sera wanted to scream out, but something stole her voice. She tried to move, but cold fear kept her limbs cemented. Her stomach rolled, her vision started to splotch. She had to help Adam, had to get Jordan off of him, had to do *something*.

Then, there was a cop running out of the trees. She heard the shot, saw Jordan get up and run, saw a dog run by. Sera turned her attention back to Adam. She pushed herself, willed her deadened limbs to move.

This couldn't be happening. Not again.

As she dragged herself over to where Adam lay, his face had changed. It wasn't Adam anymore. It was her mother's beaten face.

"No, hold on. Don't go." She reached him, took his head into her lap. "I'm not going to let you die, not this time." Tears ran down her face as she rocked with him. "I'm sorry. I'm so sorry."

Adam's face came back to her, his breathing slow and shallow. Too shallow. Too slow.

CHAPTER EIGHTY-SEVEN

Jordan

MUIR WOODS

There were lightning bugs everywhere, little bursts of light creating the magical forest where I was safe. They were everywhere, surrounding me and landing on my hand.

Impossible. Lightning bugs didn't live in San Francisco. It was another lie.

All these lies had been my own, the beast in my mind tricking me into believing everything I knew in my heart was never true. And I had let it lead me. I was no better than any of the people I thought to vindicate myself from. I was worse, even.

Worse.

There were people everywhere. Paramedics, police, firefighters. All of them are here because of me. This is what I had done.

They'd strapped me to a board and carried me out to the main road, two police officers following closely. A medivac was flying off the highway, an ambulance driving away, sirens blaring. There was one more, and it was waiting for me.

It might as well have been a hearse.

I can't go back.

Every time they had taken me *there*, they'd only kept me for the minimum amount of time, pushing a prescription bottle in my hands and throwing me back out into the world, even more broken than before. I couldn't go back into that place where the truly insane screamed and moaned and cried, shouting out vulgarities all night long.

But then I realized, I *was* one of them. *They* had become *me*.

I hadn't felt my authentic self in so long I'd forgotten who that even was. My mind had robbed me. I'm not even sure for how long. While I am still me, I can think of only one thing to do. But time was against me. Even as the paramedics made it up to the road, I could feel the beast of my mind trying to claw its way back, trying to trick me back into letting it take over.

The minute the paramedic unfastened the belt to transfer me to a gurney—my hands still cuffed behind me, one leg useless from the mauled tissue of what was left of my calf muscle—I kicked her as hard as I possibly could with my good leg, sending her down the embankment.

This distracted one of the officers as he went to pull the paramedic back to safety long enough for me to slide off the gurney, my leg screaming in protest as I forced it to hold my weight.

The second officer was closing in fast. I was able to headbutt him, breaking his nose and delaying him from following me further.

My salvation was coming at me, fast.

Finally, I would no longer feel the void of the darkness. I would no longer be controlled by anything or anyone. Not by the beast inside my mind, not by any of the people who'd only hurt me. No longer would I have to feel the agony of loneliness.

I could hear them shouting behind me. But really, this was what was best for everybody, especially for me.

I stepped in front of the semi-truck, and the emptiness was finally over.

CHAPTER EIGHTY-EIGHT

Sera

SAN FRANCISCO

G ood morning," Officer Matthews said as he bound through the door, his arms full of flowers, books, and candy. "How is Ava and the mother-in-law?" the officer asked as he set the gifts on the side table.

Sera smiled up from Adam's hospital bed at the officer who had driven Adam to her that night, the one who then stayed with Ava, keeping her safe.

"Ava is doing well, bouncing around and chatting with all the nurses. She is keeping Victoria company at the moment. Victoria will be here for at least a few more days. They still have her on oxygen. Her lungs took on a bit of damage from the smoke inhalation..."

"But she is already getting back to her old self. She's griping about the food and missing her weekly bridge night at home, which tells me she's going to be fine," Adam interrupted and laughed, then clutched his abdomen.

"Careful there, Renegade. You'll pop a stitch. Looks like the surgery went well enough?"

Sera answered before Adam had the chance to brush it all off. "They stitched up his neck, and the shoulder wound should heal well enough, not likely to have caused any permanent damage. The doctor was worried about the abdominal wound for a little while, but the surgery did go well, no complications. They said he should get through just fine because he is young, healthy, and strong." Sera took his hand again. The terror she'd felt in the hours from the ambulance ride—to the same hospital she'd been taken to when she was found as a child did nothing to help ease her nerves—and the recovery room where she was finally reunited with Adam were the longest, most grueling hours of her life.

She'd stayed with Ava in the emergency room until they finished all their assessments and examinations, assuring Sera, several times, that Ava was completely fine. No smoke inhalation, no residual effects from the chloroform, no cuts, scrapes, or even bruises on her body. Only then did she go to the surgery wing to wait for updates on Adam's condition. Little Ava was fast asleep on Sera's lap when the surgeon came out and updated her. The relief that washed over Sera had her crying openly, hugging the surgeon, thanking him profusely.

Sera never left his side, her hand in his when he first woke. She would never leave his side again and made sure to tell him as much, over and over.

"Glad to hear it. I bring updates of my own as well. Detective Pardou is going to be pissed off when he finds out he'll be off of work for a while. He got hit pretty good and he's looking at quite a bit of rehab to get everything functioning up to par. But he's alive, mad as a hornet, but on this earth with the rest of us. They transferred him to that bigwig hospital for a couple more surgeries."

"I'm glad he's okay. He risked his life for us." Sera looked up at Adam, who had also endangered his life for her and also got scarred for it.

"The cabin is no more, just ashes. Cadaver dogs found the remains of Peyton Davis in a shallow grave behind the cabin. Her family has been notified. They can have the closure they deserve. I also have other news that I think you should know. Jordan Mason was finally successful at ending her life. That night, while Jordan was being transferred into the ambulance, she was able to get away, ran into oncoming traffic, and threw herself in front of a semi-truck. She died at the scene."

"Oh," Sera didn't know what else to say.

Like Sera, Jordan had lived through hell as a child. But Sera had been the lucky one. She'd had Erinne, a good woman who became her guardian, while Jordan was given an abusive one. Sera was given a loving and supportive family, a step-father who had taught her how to manage her fears. Jordan had no one and was never able to defeat her demons.

Sera had seen the potential in Jordan when she was Peyton, the person who had been a friend, the person she should have been able to become. But Jordan had never been able to find a way out of her trauma. Sera felt the heat rise in her face and the tears burn her eyes.

"It is so damn sad. If she'd only had a chance," Sera said as she wiped the tears from her cheek. "Maybe now Jordan has finally found her peace."

"It *is* sad. Too sad," Officer Matthews muttered, shaking his head. The three of them fell quiet in thought. "Hey, you guys should get some rest. You both look like you've been through a war or something," he said, breaking the silence.

"I'm considering taking a good, long vacation." Adam chuckled, clutching his abdomen again.

"You two deserve it." Officer Matthews shook Sera and Adam's hands and waved as he walked out the door.

"Vacation, huh? What did you have in mind?"

"How about Florida? We could take Ava to Disney World."

Sera shook her head. "Too many people. Besides, you won't be doing rides for a while."

"Okay. Then how about a relaxing vacation on a Hawaiian beach?"

"*Mmm*. That sounds great. What's the occasion, surviving?" She kissed his cheek and looked at him, alive and well and hers.

"I was thinking more along the lines of a honeymoon."

Sera laughed. "Honeymoon? Who's getting married?"

"I was thinking that we would. I don't have a ring yet, but I hope this can be a start." He took the amethyst locket and lightning bolt from under his pillow.

"You found this?" Her eyes misted over with the site of her mother's locket and Erinne's lightning bolt dangling between Adam's fingers. "I thought it was gone forever."

"You thought I was, too, but we're both still here and ready for the rest of our lives together. I'm considering the last few years a very long engagement. I love you, Sera. You are my best friend. After everything we've been through, I can't imagine waiting another minute or living another day without being by your side."

"I can't imagine it, either," she said, smiling through her tears, taking the locket and clasping it around her neck.

"So, is that a yes?"

"That's a forever and always yes." She kissed him softly, carefully crawling into his bed, laying her head on his chest.

"I was hoping you'd say that," he whispered, kissing the top of her head.

It had cost both of them dearly to meet, but in the end, Sera was exactly where she was supposed to be. A time not too long ago, Sera might have felt the guilt crush down on her for finding happiness after so much loss.

She had spent years hiding away from the world that had betrayed her, her wounds so deeply etched that she'd given up on ever having joy in her life. She wasn't sure how she had survived some of those days at all. But she found a way to crawl out of the darkness and fought each day to move forward out of the labyrinth of hurt.

Bad things would still happen, there was no way around that, but Sera figured out how to rise above the nagging urge to run and hide, even coexist with it.

Even though her internal wounds may bleed from time to time, she learned that letting people in, loving them against all odds, and leaning on them when things got hard didn't weaken you. It made you stronger.

Epilogue

The sun warmed the side of Sera's face as she swayed on the porch swing, looking down at the old family album. It had been hard at first, opening it after so long. Seeing her mother and father's smiling faces, picture after picture of the good times they'd had, as few as there were, with the turn of each page.

After the initial heartache, comfort and happiness flowed back in as they always had. She'd been given several years of memories shared with her parents, captured in pictures that would keep them alive forever.

Sera's first contribution to the album was of her first day as an RN in the pediatric unit of the hospital that had cared for her as a child and saved the love of her life. She'd been dressed in scrubs, holding her stethoscope, beaming proudly with Adam's arm draped around her waist, Ava laughing in front of them. It had been a good day.

She smiled as she pushed the picture securely in place next to the picture of her mother's first day as a student doctor.

Sera glanced up to check on Ava and the baby. Both were squealing as they chased each other around the garden. Ava hid behind a bush and then popped out in front of the baby with a quick shout of peek-a-boo before she ran off again. No matter how many times she did this, it never failed to send the toddling boy into peals of laughter.

The weather had finally warmed enough for the two of them to play outdoors. Cabin fever was interesting when one had a ten-year-old and a two-year-old occupying the same space.

Chuckling, Sera gave the album her attention once again, placing another printed photograph, one of her most cherished. Adam and Sera were looking into each other's eyes as they danced their first dance as husband and wife in the garden where their children were presently playing.

Since Adam had faced a long recovery after the stabbing, they never made it to that Hawaiian beach. Instead, they spent the year at a plethora of doctor appointments and PT sessions. Even then, before Adam was up and walking again, he began opening the second branch of his architecture firm on the West Coast. Not only were his clients' buildings going up, but Adam had called in a few favors to secretly have Sera's childhood home restored, the house her mother bought, the house that held her best memories.

He'd told her he had an engagement gift for her, blindfolded her, and driven her to the house. He'd placed a small box in her hand, the bow almost bigger than the white box, then took off her blindfold. Smiling, she looked down at the box and opened it, revealing the small brass key. She looked at him, curious as to what the key was for. He kissed her, turning her around.

The house stood welcoming and freshly painted. The white fence surrounded the small yard, which was bursting with wildflowers and hundreds of daisies, just as it had been a lifetime ago. The swing swayed in the breeze, still perfectly hung on the white porch. Everything was just as she remembered it.

"New locks for a new life." He kissed her tear-streaked cheeks and led her to the front door. The house had woken up again, its warmth renewed.

They married there, making the house even more of a treasure. Erinne helped Sera get ready in what was once her parents' room, which was now their own. The ceremony and reception held in its pretty yard, with all of their family and close friends sharing in their joy.

After the last guest had left that evening, after Erinne had taken Ava with her for the night, Sera and Adam sat on the porch swing, his tie off, dress shirt unbuttoned at the collar, sleeves rolled up, Sera still in her wedding gown and barefoot, taking in the day, taking in each other, her husband, his wife.

"You know, this was quite the engagement gift."

"I thought so." Adam smiled, leaned in, and kissed his wife.

"It makes an even better baby gift."

When he just stared at her, she laughed. Adam scooped her up and twirled her around the garden, laughing, asking her over and over if she was sure, Sera repeating yes, each time. That, too, had been a good day.

Sera gazed down at her wedding rings, the diamond band Adam put on her finger next to her mother's engagement ring, sparkling in the sunlight.

She carefully placed picture after picture of the wedding, her pregnancy, and of their son David Adam Wallace, Davey for short.

Ava had fallen desperately in love with her baby brother. Hundreds of pictures were taken of their two smiling faces. Sera printed some of her favorites to place in the album.

She *had* been given everything, and so much more.

After years of trying to overcome the all-consuming guilt of surviving and the feelings of unworthiness of the life her mother gave up for her, the day Ava became her daughter and Davey became her son finally showed her. Erinne had been right all along, as Sera now knew firsthand, that there was nothing a mother wouldn't do for her child.

Watching the two of them run around, she laughed at the irony. Sera had been her mother's twin, Ava was Adam's, but little Davey was a perfect combination of the two of them. His daddy's chestnut hair shone in the sun, and his mommy's green eyes sparkled.

Sera closed the album and went out to play with her children, chasing after Ava and tickling her son's tummy. Their laughter carried through the neighborhood, through the house, and into the depths of Adam's soul as he watched his family from an upstairs window.

He couldn't let them have all the fun without him.

He walked downstairs and out onto the grass, taking his wife into an embrace from behind.

She smiled and let the warmth of his touch encompass her. When she turned her face to look up at him, he kissed the tip of her nose. Their eyes held each other's for a moment, but the glance was broken by the attack of tickles he gripped into her sides.

Davey toddled over to his parents and tried to help Daddy make Mommy laugh. Ava raced in as well, jumping on her dad's back to defend her mom.

"Gammy! Gammy!" Davey squealed, pointing his chubby finger across the yard toward the bed of daisies. Then he started waving, giggling.

Sera looked back. She couldn't see her mother standing there, but she could feel her, happy and at peace.

Hey Mama.

Sera closed her eyes, letting her mother's presence fill her, then went back to deploy another tickle attack on Adam, who had Ava in a tickle hold. Davey clapped and laughed along.

If somebody had taken a picture from the sidelines watching the family play together, innocent and carefree, it would show that this day was the best of them all.

Afterword & Acknowledgements

It took twenty years to get this story where it needed to be, and I couldn't be happier where these characters have lead it to. Thank you for taking the journey with the characters I've fallen in love with.

Live each moment to its absolute fullest, because tomorrow is never promised.

Live like Ella.

Have Courage like Sera.

And have Heart like Erinne.

Writing means using up a lot of time and attention. Away from partners, kids (even grown ones), jobs, etc. All for a need, a dream, that may never come to fruition. But that need is so strong to tell the story trapped in your mind that you can't do anything else until it is told.

So I have to thank my husband, first and foremost, for giving me the freedom to do what I must do, and for listening to me yammer on and on about it.

I also want to thank the developmental editor for pointing out everything that needed improvement and encouraging the story's development into a stronger, tighter piece.

Of course, thank you to my friends and co-workers—my first readers—who let me force upon them these lumps of clay that were this story in the making, begging for honest opinions. I must say, nurses really are the most avid set of readers. In our line of work, a morbid sense of humor is a must and makes for the best kind of beta readers.

And thank you, Bonnie, most of all. For letting me bleed your ears, for all your unconditional support, for all your words and encouragement. Thank you for letting me be in your life and for being not only my best friend—but my sister, my soulmate.

About the Author

J. Elle Ross is a California native, still residing in Southern California with her husband, three dogs, 26 chickens (since last count), and two turkeys (until November, that is). The four children have become adults and are doing their own thing, these days.

She is a writer by day, NICU RN by night, and a wannabe homesteader in between.

When not working with the babies, writing the stories, or tending to the animals and garden, she is reading anything she can get her hands on, watching way too many movies, binging TV shows, finding joy in stories in each and every form.

Also by J. Elle Ross

- **Someone Who Knows (Book One)**

- **The One Who Knew (Book Two)**

- **Those Who Know (Cinematic Edition-Both Books in chronological order)**